GOTCHA!

WITHDRAWN
BY
WILLIAMSBURG REGIONAL LIBRARY

JANE FLAGELLO

ZIG ZAG PRESS LLC

ISBN-13: 978-0-9961237-2-3

Editing by Demon for Details
Cover design by WickedSmartDesigns.com
Interior formatting by Author E.M.S.

Zig Zag Press LLC
Williamsburg, VA
2015

Published in the United States of America

OTHER BOOKS BY JANE FLAGELLO

Fiction
Bamboozled

Non-Fiction
*The Change Intelligence Factor: Mastering the
Promise of Extra-Ordinary*

PROLOGUE

1982

She was young. She was pretty. She was dead—very, very dead.

The seven-year-old boy who found the body in a park in the middle of a cement city had been playing hide and seek with his cousins.

It had rained all week. Every night, when he had said his prayers, Thaddeus had prayed the sun would shine on Sunday. The entire family got together in the park every Sunday. Before lunch he played with his cousins, brother, and sister, while their parents started up the charcoal grills and laid out a spectacular picnic. After lunch all the dads, uncles, and cousins played stickball while their moms, sisters, aunts, and grandparents sat in the shade and cheered them on.

Sundays were totally special—and different. Different because his parents didn't fight. And he and his brother and sister weren't scared of being hit. That was only done behind closed doors away from prying eyes, and never on Sundays. On Sunday—God's day—everyone got along. In Thaddeus' mind, that was what family was supposed to be like. The moment he opened his eyes Sunday morning, he could see his prayers had been answered. It promised to be a beautiful summer day.

Now it was his turn to hide. Thaddeus set off running toward the woods with the rest of the kids. He could hear his cousin Ernie screaming the count.

"…six…seven…eight…nine…ten! Ready or not, here I come."

Thaddeus needed to find a place to hide quickly. Ernie was on his way. Slippery, rain-soaked ground slowed his progress. He jumped over a fallen tree trunk and lost his balance, landing hard on his hands and knees. He blinked. A face, empty eye sockets, strands of dirty, wet hair plastered against white, lifeless skin. His eyes bulged at the sight of the body. His stomach knotted and he retched. He couldn't even hear his own bloodcurdling screams as he threw himself backwards and crab-crawled away from the gruesome sight.

Newly promoted Detective Daniel Berger and his partner Steve Ambrose arrived at the scene about the time the ME ripped off his rubber gloves. A sheet covered the body, and rope barricades and police officers cordoned off the area to ensure no one contaminated the crime scene. Criminalists were already hard at work—taking pictures, making impression molds of footprints in the mud—collecting anything and everything they thought might be relevant to solving the who, what, when, where and why behind the young girl's death. The how was easy. The knotted red silk cord still dug into her neck.

Berger could see a young boy sitting on a fallen tree trunk, struggling to control his tears. Streaks of mud marked his reddened and puffy face, and also covered his jeans and sneakers. Looked like he fell into a mud pit. Apparently everyone was too busy to take note of the kid's tears. Where were his parents?

Berger lifted the corner of the sheet. Not his first dead body, and it wouldn't be his last. His eyes drifted back to the boy, sitting alone, trying hard to be brave.

"Who's the kid?" Berger asked one of the officers congregated around the body.

"That kid?" asked the patrolman, jerking his thumb over his shoulder toward the boy. "He found the body. Tripped right over it. Scared the shit out of him."

"That's a lot for a little boy to handle. Where are his parents?"

"Got me. An old woman was with him when I talked to him. Figured it was his grandmother. Don't see her now."

Berger stood staring at the shrouded body shaking his head. Dr. Gary Meyer, the Kings County ME, walked up to him, placing a fatherly hand on his shoulder.

"This is so wrong," said Meyer sadly.

"What do you mean?" asked Berger.

"Too young to wind up like this."

"I agree. And she's not the first. Over the past year, four young girls have been found dead at different locations in this park. Found by innocent people like that kid. Not good advertising for a day of fun in the park. Damn it."

"Young girls these days. Want to grow up fast. Too fast," said Stuart Chambrel, Meyer's assistant. He lowered the gurney next to the body.

"They dress up in sexy clothes that reveal way too much. Put on so much makeup, it's hard to see even a hint of their natural beauty. Go strutting off—and wind up here, in the kind of trouble they can't recover from," said Meyer.

"My wife and I spend a lot of time here. We love this park. We're always at the zoo or renting horses," said Chambrel.

"Parks in the middle of cities are priceless. You guys and city officials have done so much to make this one safe so families can come and spend the day. Too bad stuff like this has to ruin it," said Meyer.

"Looks to me," said Berger, "like someone didn't get the memo."

Meyer put on a fresh pair of gloves. "Okay, Stu, let's get her back to the lab."

Berger approached the boy slowly.

"Hi. I'm Daniel Berger. What's your name?"

"Thaddeus Jamison."

"That's a big name. An important name." Berger allowed a few moments to pass before continuing. "Mind if I sit with you for a sec?"

Daniel took the boy's shoulder shrug as a yes and sat down on the log next to him.

"Are you here with your family?"

"Yeah," mumbled the boy.

"I always loved coming here with my family on Sundays. Was that your grandmother with you before?"

"Yeah."

"I understand you had a rough morning." Daniel picked up a stone and tossed it away. "You know, sometimes it helps to talk about things like this, things a kid your age should never see." He picked up and tossed another stone. "What do you think? Do you want to talk about what you saw?"

Shoulders shrugged.

A tall man in khaki shorts and a Yankees T-shirt stormed down the path. Daniel watched as he spoke to his partner, pointing at the boy.

"That your dad?"

"Yeah."

"Thaddeus, food's ready," the father barked as he approached them. "They said you could go." The man's hands were on his hips, and his face telegraphed a level of annoyance that surprised Daniel.

"You better get going, then. Don't want to keep him waiting."

The boy stood up and brushed off his shorts.

"Hey, Thaddeus," Daniel said waiting till the boy turned and made eye contact with him. "I know it's hard sometimes, and you grew up a bit too fast this morning." Daniel held out his business card. "Here, take my phone number. If you want to talk, you call me. Okay?"

"'K."

Daniel watched the boy catch up to his father, who was already on his way back to the picnic area. The total lack of even the smallest fatherly hug or pat surprised him. After what the kid had experienced, you'd think his dad would show more compassion. He sighed and rejoined his partner, who was talking to the ME.

"Sure hope that kid finds someone to talk to about what he saw. His father looks to be an asshole," said Berger. "No hug or nothing for the kid."

"Yeah. Probably not going to happen," said Ambrose. "Guy seems like a real jerk."

Daniel stared down the path after them. In his heart, he knew the boy had experienced a life-changing event. What happened next could easily determine his path for the rest of his life.

CHAPTER 1

"It's an interesting theory, Mrs. Conrad. Mind if I make a copy of these?"

When she nodded, Detective Braden stood, pulled the photos Carolyn had laid out on the table together, tapped them into a neat pile and headed for the door.

"I'll be right back. Can I get you anything? Coffee?"

"No. I'm fine."

Some detective, she thought, twisting the cap off the full bottle of water in front of her and taking a sip. *How old is this guy, ten? Does he even shave yet? Okay, I'm being unfair. It's not easy to make detective. He had to work hard to earn his gold shield.*

Today's meeting was another useless stab at getting someone to listen to her, to help her find her daughter, Amelia, who had been missing for five years. People didn't just vanish. But that's exactly what had happened. Amelia had simply vanished off the face of the earth. Never found her car. No cell phone. When the police searched her apartment, they found nothing to indicate foul play. Like she'd been abducted by aliens to a galaxy far, far away. Carolyn knew Amelia was still alive—somewhere. A mother would know, would feel it, if her only child was dead, right?

She had not been able to tell the police exactly when Amelia went missing. They spoke once a week on Sunday mornings. More of a check-in than an actual conversation. It was a "Hi, I'm okay. You okay? Good-bye," affair. Carolyn had considered it a major achievement because for years they hadn't spoken at all.

Seven years ago this June, Amelia graduated from high school, packed her bag, and left the next day, exclaiming that freezing her ass off in Bangor, Maine was not what she planned for her life.

Carolyn had been frantic at first, not knowing where she had gone. The PI she finally hired found Amelia in Biloxi, Mississippi working as a waitress. He kept tabs on her, phoning in a weekly report. It took another three years for mother and daughter to reconnect on a regular basis. When Amelia finally did contact her mother, she was excited about her new job as a croupier at one of the big casinos. Carolyn listened while she gushed about her success during training, how she scored at the top of her class, and was the first one to land a full-time job. She was meeting all sorts of interesting people. She was on her way.

The casino didn't think anything of it when she failed to show up for her Tuesday shift. Figured she'd quit without giving notice. Young employees did it all the time. When Amelia missed their Sunday morning call, Carolyn got worried and began calling the casino, police, hospitals, and everywhere else she could think of.

That was five years ago today. It was now designated a cold case by the Biloxi detectives, but it didn't stop Carolyn's yearly trek here. And today's visit was a replay of last year's visit, and the year before that, and the year before that. The answer was always the same. If there was any new information, the case would be reopened, but until there was some new, solid lead to follow...blah...blah...blah.

She'd heard it all before. Could recite the lines. They were doing their job. And who could blame them? Biloxi was no different from many other cities. Watch the evening news. What was the cliché? If it bleeds, it leads. Every night presented the police with new murders and mayhem. Dealing with a five-year-old missing person case couldn't be a priority.

She had hoped today would be different because she had something new to offer: photographs. And someone new to listen to her: Detective Ronald Braden. She tried to connect the dots for him, told him what she believed the photos meant. At least this guy had the courtesy to listen.

"Here you go." Detective Braden handed the photos back to her and placed a set into the file. "I'll share our conversation with my lieutenant when he gets out of his meeting. He'll be sorry he missed you. I'm sure he'll follow up."

"Thank you for your time."

"I can appreciate how hard this must be for you."

"Can you? Really?" Her sarcastic tone and whip-like head snap forced him to step back. She stuffed the photographs in her tote. "One phone call and my life went to shit."

"I've had to make that call a few times. A missing child is the worst. Some parents become withdrawn and resigned. Mourn the loss while waiting for the fateful phone call that ends their not knowing."

"Did that. Every time the phone rang I braced myself for the news I didn't want to hear. Felt helpless. A mother's worst nightmare." She white-knuckled her water bottle, crushing the plastic.

"I can see from the file you keep in touch a lot. Weekly phone calls. And you come here every year."

"Helpless doesn't work for me. She's out there somewhere, possibly hurt and suffering, and acting powerless is not who I am. I can feel her in my arms, smell her sweetness, and I want to do more than imagine it. Wanting to hold her again drives me, gives me strength." Carolyn hoisted her tote over her shoulder. She looked Detective Braden squarely in the eyes, resolve fueling her words. "I can't stop. I won't stop. I want to hold her for real, and I'm determined to find her with or without your help."

"You have to understand," Braden said, tapping the file folder on the table, "there are so many cases, and we can only do so much with our resources. The city budget is spread pretty thin these days. Lieutenant Harrison will get a full report about our meeting."

"Lieutenant Harrison? Where's Carson?"

"He retired at the end of last year. Been on the job for a long time."

"Too long, if you ask me. Does explain why I never heard back from him. I left several messages on his voicemail. Sent him emails about the photos to make sure he knew I was coming today."

"The city has changed a lot since Hurricane Katrina. All the rebuilding. New casinos brought new problems. Let's just say his style wasn't in line with some of the newer policing methodologies." He stopped talking, looked away, and then changed the subject. "I've only been here five months. Came in with Harrison. He was my boss in Mobile and offered me a new opportunity here."

"Well then, congratulations on your new jobs, you and Lieutenant Harrison. I look forward to meeting him."

"Thanks. It's a big step. Born and raised in Mobile. Wife, too. All the family's there. We just had a baby girl. Named her Emily Sue after my mom. I don't know what I'd do if anything like this ever happened to her."

"Don't think about it. Do everything in your power to keep her safe."

"Yes, ma'am. That's the plan."

Carolyn walked out of the Biloxi police station into blistering sunshine and oppressive heat. She felt her skin prickle under the sun's assault. The tightness in her chest made it hard to breathe. The humidity didn't help much either. In less than a minute, she'd be drenched in sweat.

Tension knotted her brows tightly, and the blinding sunshine forced her to squint. Pulling out her sunglasses, she inhaled slowly—counted to three as she held her breath—then slowly exhaled, counting to five as she released a long, cleansing breath. Wrapping her arms around her chest, she secured her large black tote against her body and headed for the parking lot, oblivious to the passers-by, coffee cups clenched in their hands, going about their usual Friday morning business.

Forty-five minutes later she was back at Gulfport/Biloxi airport. Watching some people sadly saying their good-byes while others happily embraced with warm hellos did nothing to lighten her mood. Her Delta flight to Atlanta showed an on-time status. Hopefully, it would remain that way. She wanted to be in Orlando, her final destination, in time for dinner.

One way or another, the next few days could prove very interesting. Screw the police. She was taking matters into her own hands and following her new lead—meeting her new BFF at a mah jongg tournament. By hook or by crook, she planned to find out whether her theory about her daughter's disappearance had legs.

❖

Daniel's grumblings and restlessness woke her. Rachel reached over, soothing him with a gentle touch. He mumbled a thank you, patted her hand where it rested on his shoulder, muttered "sorry," which turned into a gusty sigh as he rolled onto his side. Moments later, his heavy breathing told her the episode had passed. In the morning she'd ask him about his dream, even though she knew full well he wouldn't remember the details.

Of course, she was now wide awake. The predawn hush stirred all kinds of thoughts for the sleepless. Hers turned to the man sharing her bed. How quickly things changed. Not too long ago she couldn't imagine having another man in her life. Then fate took over and brought her Daniel. Now she couldn't imagine life without him.

He wanted to be all things to her: protector, fixer, companion, and lover. Talk about worlds colliding. Different goals ruled each of these roles. She could see him struggle when a situation called for him to juggle more than one. Hard to shed one role to assume another when your recent experiences leave you clueless about how to manage it. He tended to overdo each one.

She knew he struggled with his looming retirement. People reacted so differently to the natural progression of life. It was harder to contemplate the rites of passage in later years than it was when you were young and looking forward to falling in love, careers, marriage, families. Retirement was a huge change. Some people couldn't wait. Others dreaded every minute. The latter usually didn't even want to talk about it because retirement was twisted together with the end times, with illness, with death.

What would become of them? Of their relationship? Some things she was sure about. Others inhabited the fuzzy world on the edges of dreams, desires, and reality.

One definite: Daniel needed to work. He needed to believe what he did still mattered—needed a reason to get out of bed in the morning. Too many of his police brothers and sisters died a slow inner death while sitting around waiting for the real thing to commandeer their bodies. They could swap war stories with buddies at the bar only so long before they started to rot from the inside out.

She also knew Daniel loved her. She sensed this scared the shit out of him...partly, she thought, because he hadn't been in a loving relationship for more than ten years. It had ended suddenly—tragically—on 9/11. Heartbreaking. His wife had been in the North Tower.

People dealt with grief and loss differently. Some enjoyed being in love so much they leaped right back in. Others tended to shy away, fearing another painful outcome. Some ping-ponged, unable or unwilling to make the necessary commitments to have a new love grow strong, but unwilling to give up on love completely. Daniel ping-ponged. At times he was all in. At other times, she could feel him pull back, disengage. The more she thought about it, the more she realized she ping-ponged, too.

Daniel's snorts broke her mental replay. The grandfather clock in her living room chimed six. He'd be getting up soon. They both had places to go, people to see. Daniel was off to D.C. for a meeting with an old Marine buddy, something about a new FBI task force. She was off to meet her BFF Sara at a two-day mah jongg tournament in Orlando—R&R girlfriend style.

Rachel loved the Newport News/Williamsburg International airport. Its name made it seem big, important, when in truth it was small, intimate, and largely empty, with only fourteen gates. The saying, "you can't get there from here" fit. No nonstop flights to Orlando. It was the only downside of no longer having a major airport like JFK, La Guardia, or Newark in her backyard.

"You sure you have everything?" Daniel asked as he put her carry-on bag on a bench near the entrance to security.

"Yes," she said, digging into her tote. She could practically feel steam hissing out of her ears. His question irritated her no end, not least because it had been asked and answered twice already. She knew he meant well, but it infuriated her nonetheless. His constant hovering drove her crazy—so different from her first husband, who had expected her to do everything perfectly without prompting. One day they'd have this conversation. Not today. She was already a nervous flyer, and the last thing she needed was an argument when they were both traveling.

"Everything's here. Besides, if I've forgotten anything, I can buy it there. It's not like I'm going to Outer Mongolia. Orlando has stores and I'll be with Sara, for whom shopping is an Olympic sport."

She saw Daniel wince at her sharp retort. Good, she thought. Let him stew a bit and wonder what he said to provoke me.

"You ladies have big plans?"

"Other than trying to win at the mah jongg tournament? The usual—shopping, eating, some spa time, more shopping, and lots and lots of girl talk."

"Will my ears be ringing?" asked Daniel with a chuckle. "I suspect I'll be one of the topics."

"Oooh. Ego showing. Don't flatter yourself," said Rachel as she lovingly wrapped her arms around his neck. She planted a soft kiss on his lips.

"We have lots to talk about besides you. Haven't seen each other for a few weeks."

"You two talk almost every day. Your friendship goes beyond words."

"We are very close. We know everything about each other. She loves me, warts and all, and I love her the same way. She knows my secrets, my weaknesses, my fears, and my dreams. We don't judge, don't have expectations. We're simply there for each other in good times and in bad. I can be totally myself, let it all hang out, be vulnerable."

She fussed with the collar of his golf shirt. "Of course, you *are* an interesting person to talk about. Lots of ammunition here." She smiled to let him know whatever had triggered her snappy retort a moment ago had passed. "When are you leaving for D.C.?"

"Slight change of plans. I'm heading back to New York first. My meeting in D.C. isn't until Monday. Cooper's swamped. Evans, the guy they're bringing in to replace me, had a personal issue pop up, something with his wife and medical tests. I didn't ask too many questions. He needs to take a few days off. Told Cooper I'd be there later today, stay the weekend to cover for Evans."

"Good. It will give you something to do. Can't sit around twiddling your thumbs. You know what they say, 'Idle hands are the Devil's workshop.'"

"Just what I need. A beautiful, Bible-quoting lover." Daniel gently tucked the hair falling across her eyes behind her right ear.

"You were going to bum around here. This will be better for you. Working keeps you from being bored and getting into trouble."

"What kind of trouble can I get into without you here? That's no fun."

"Good point. Hold that thought until I get back. We can make trouble together."

"I'm ready whenever you are."

There they stood, wrapped in each other's arms. Goodbyes were getting harder every time they parted.

"Travel safe," he whispered in her ear, sending goose bumps rippling down her back.

"B'ezrat Hashem. With God's help."

One final kiss—a deep, long one—before she headed through the rope corral to the first security checkpoint.

Rachel quickly slipped on the neon green sneaker socks she kept in her travel tote. Walking barefoot on the dirty floor grossed her out. All those germs. After placing her belongings into two dirty gray bins, she glanced over her shoulder to see Daniel standing like a sentinel at the glass, watching her progress. Stepping into the AIT machine, she raised her hands. She pitied the guy examining all these images. Ugh. Not pretty.

After proving she was not a threat to the civilized world, or at least the people on the plane, Rachel gathered her belongings and turned to see Daniel still at the glass. With one last wave, she headed down the concourse to her gate. She bought a bottle of water and a muffin at a food cart and settled in. Her American flight to Charlotte, NC was supposed to depart in forty-five minutes, change planes, and then on to Orlando. If everything ran on time—a big if in the world of airline travel—the entire trip would take a tad under four hours. But there was no plane at her gate. Never a good sign.

Competing thoughts bombarded her...playing well at the tournament...how much she hated flying...how to reach out to more wounded warriors so the Raphael Fund could help them...Daniel. What kind of future did she really want with him? The little voice inside her head had been working overtime lately, trying to answer that question. Her past might not be the best barometer. She'd spent years being quiet, the good wife and mother, second-guessing every word, wanting people to like her.

"Well, I'm done with that nonsense. That me is so totally gone." Realizing she'd said it out loud made her blush. Not to worry, she thought. Anyone hearing me will think I'm talking to someone on my cell.

David, may he rest in peace, was her past. A Ketubah, the Jewish marriage contract, signed and vows made in the presence of God. So many memories to cherish. The early times had been good times, when there was little money, when they considered mac and cheese and tuna noodle casserole gourmet meals. Jenny and Scott were the results of their love, not a hot and heavy affair, more like a union of responsibility and commitment.

Aunt Lil had given her a card with a quote from Joseph Campbell after David's funeral two years ago. "We must be willing to let go of the life we've planned so we can accept the life that is waiting for us." It seemed so appropriate right now. She was not afraid of being alone anymore. After all, alone didn't mean lonely. It was better to be alone than be with the wrong person.

She knew the problem with looking back was that a person's memory prism had a tendency toward poetic license, glorifying the good times and often minimizing the bad. The only thing she knew for sure was she wanted to feel real love...the kind that took her breath away and still allowed her to stand on her own two feet.

And she knew she was with the right person—Daniel— and they were talking about things serious, committed couples talked about. Exciting possibilities. She was in love with him. It was so different this time around. Romantic. Intimate. Tender. God had blessed her when He brought

Daniel into her life. She felt lucky. Happy. A new vision of the next twenty-plus years was taking shape. Would there be another Ketubah? Only time would tell.

Shit! Her head throbbed. All this thinking was giving her a headache. Pain shot up the nape of her neck. Pulling off the scrunchie holding her ponytail, she kneaded the back of her neck, hoping to relieve some tension. After gulping down two aspirins, she quickly ate the muffin to ward off an upset stomach.

Picking up her iPad, Rachel opened to Candy Crush. Tucking that same elusive strand of hair behind her ear, she immersed herself in the mindlessness of the game. Everything else could wait.

CHAPTER 2

Bella gaped at her reflection in the full-length mirror.

"Oh…My…God! I don't look like me. My own mother wouldn't recognize me."

"See? I told you I could do it. You look soooo hot," said her cousin Claire. "The guys won't be able to take their eyes off you."

"Love the hot pink extensions and how you got them to curl into my own hair. And the color matches this halter top you loaned me."

"Yep. You are lookin' good, cousin, lookin' good."

"Not sure I can dance in these heels."

"Sure you can. Stilettos make your legs look sexy, and my black leather skirt shows off your legs."

"Do you think we'll be able to fool them? Get past the bouncers?"

"I've got it covered. Now get over here so I can add a little more eye shadow and mascara. You want to show off those beautiful eyes, don't you?"

Bella sat while Claire finished her glamor look. She added liquid eyeliner to give Bella's almond-shaped brown eyes a seductive, cat-like appearance, and topped that with shimmery Magenta Magic eye shadow, saying the flecks of gold would catch the light at the dance club and make her eyes sparkle.

They stood next to each other, looking in the mirror.

"Your dress is awesome," said Bella. "I love how the silver sequins sparkle."

"And you've got to see this." Claire lifted her dress to reveal a tiny, fire-red thong. "Isn't it great? Sorry I don't have another one for you."

"Borrowing this top and skirt is more than enough. I don't have anything like this in my closet. And these shoes. Your stuff is to die for."

Bella was painfully aware of the envy in her voice. She had lived in Claire's shadow her entire life, all seventeen years of it. No matter what Bella accomplished, Claire went one better. When Bella was chosen to be a cheerleader, Claire tried out at her high school. Not only did she win a spot on the squad, she became its co-captain. Bella's debate team triumph was topped when Claire became president of the Junior Class. Bella's casting as a dancer in the school play was bettered by Claire landing the leading female role in her school's play. It went on and on. Compared to Claire, Bella was totally a plain Jane, pure vanilla. In every way, Claire was prettier, faster, smarter, more talented, and had a better body. At least, to Bella.

"Thanks for coming out with me tonight. Staying home is so lame on a Friday night. My stupid friends are going to miss a great time."

"No problem. I didn't want to study anyway. This will be way more fun."

"Metamorphosis is the hottest club. Wait till you tell your friends. They're gonna be so jealous."

"I don't think I'm going to tell them. I don't want my mother to find out I lied to her."

The lie tugged at Bella's heart. Although Claire hadn't

needed to do much convincing to get her to go to a dance club instead of studying, lying to her parents was a whole other matter.

Bella saw clubbing with Claire as her opportunity to break out and have some fun, if only for one night. She loved listening to Claire's stories about her adventures. She envied Claire's freedom, popularity, and especially her ease with boys. Her street-wise instincts were well developed. As were her boobs. Bella desperately wanted to be like Claire.

So she told her parents a lie. The big statewide achievement tests were the following week. She and Claire planned to study at the library. It was a little lie. What harm could it do? As usual, her parents tag-teamed her with the third degree. The only thing missing was the glaring klieg light aimed at her face. Who all was going? Which library? Who was driving? Were any boys going? And her curfew was set at eleven o'clock. She knew there would be a huge price to pay if she broke curfew.

Claire's situation was the opposite, no rules. With three younger brothers, there were too many kids at home, and no man around to help with anything. Claire always said her mother's only wish for her was that she not get pregnant. Finish high school. Go to community college. Get a good job. Find a good man who would take care of her. From conversations Bella overheard between her own parents, she knew Aunt Estella's plea was that of a disillusioned, brokenhearted woman whose dreams for a better life had crumbled to dust when she got pregnant at fifteen.

Carolyn reeled in her paper target. She smiled at the tight

grouping of bullet holes. Four right between the eyes and four to the heart. Hooking up a fresh target, she reloaded her Kimber 9 mm caliber pistol.

She'd come straight to the Orlando Gun Club range from the airport to relax and unwind a bit from a very stressful day. Some people drank to unwind. When possible, she found a gun club and expended lots of bullets. The pleasant surprise had been free entry, because Friday night was ladies' night. She still had half an hour to shoot before the club closed for the evening. Then she'd check into the hotel and get some food.

Two tours in Iraq and she never fired a shot. In spite of all her training, she always questioned the depth of her resolve. Could she really pull the trigger with a human being in her sights? Here, it was easy, almost mindless. A silhouette doesn't breathe, move away or shoot back. She convinced herself she could pull the trigger. Everyone told themselves they could. Circumstances had never tested her resolve, however.

The Kimber 9 mm she was trying out felt right in her hands. *Good weight, comfortable grip, controllable recoil. Might buy one. Always good to have more than one gun around.* Her Beretta Nano had been her constant companion for over ten years. She named it Harry. She had a concealed carry permit for it, but she couldn't take it on a plane, so she'd left it home this trip.

Carolyn pushed the button and the black silhouette rode the fifty foot wire back into place. Repositioning her eye and ear protection, she took a deep breath, squared her shoulders and firmed up her stance. Her left hand supported the weight of the gun in her right. She sighted the target for a head shot and squeezed the trigger.

After emptying the clip, Carolyn put the gun down and twisted the silver ring on her index finger. She flipped open the top and stared at the snowy white powder inside its secret compartment. Shooting someone was not her plan. Making someone sick was. Just a pinch, administered surreptitiously was all it would take to get her new BFF out of the picture for a short time. Then she'd access the woman's phone and laptop, plant a few bugs, and wait. Carolyn picked up the gun and sighted the target. Plans had a way of going to hell. Being prepared was always best.

Hours later Bella told her second lie.

"Mom, just calling to let you know Claire and I are back at her house. And I'm going to spend the night here. Aunt Estella said it was okay. So I hope it's okay with you. See you in the morning. Love you."

Bella disconnected the call blowing out a whoosh of air. Her shoulders drooped. Two lies on the same night. She'd surely go to hell now.

"See how easy that was? There's nothing to worry about. My mom's out, and my brothers won't even bother to answer the phone if your mom calls."

"It was easy because I got her voice mail. I don't know if I could have done it if she'd answered."

"Then it's a good thing she didn't," laughed Claire. "It's already ten thirty. With an eleven o'clock curfew, you'd have to leave now to get home, and we haven't even gotten into the club yet. Now we've got the whole night. Smile pretty for the guys at the door."

The IDs worked. The bouncers welcomed them both without inspecting their licenses closely at all. They were in. Bella couldn't believe the price Claire paid—one hundred dollars apiece. When she asked Claire where she got the money, she shrugged and said she earned it babysitting. And not to worry where the money came from. The evening would be worth it.

"Metamorphosis is soooo hot. YOLO. You only live once. Wait till my girlfriends hear about this. I'm going to tell them every little detail, maybe stretch some a bit to make them even more jealous. They'll be sorry they stayed home." With that Claire wiggled and jiggled her way down the narrow entrance hallway, the silver sequins on her dress twinkling in the dim light.

The lights flashed. The walls sparkled. The whole room vibrated. Unconsciously, Bella began to move her body to the bass thump of the music. The sequins on the hot pink halter top Claire lent her sparkled and reflected the flashing lights. She could barely hear herself think. Claire was right. Metamorphosis was the hottest club, thought Bella. Of course, it was her first time in a nightclub, so she had nothing to compare it to.

"What?" she asked Claire, whose words were drowned out by the music blasting from the huge black speakers.

"This is so cool," repeated Claire, screaming into Bella's ear. "I'm so glad we got past the bouncers. Didn't think it would be that easy."

"Me neither," said Bella, too late for Claire to hear. She was already on her way out to the dance floor. Hundreds of bodies, male and female, undulated and swayed. Arms up, fingers snapping, turning and swerving, with one partner and then another.

Bella didn't know anyone. She had no friends in this crowd to hang with. As she pushed through the crowd searching for Claire, a strong hand grabbed her arm and twirled her around. She came face to face with a very handsome guy. His hands went to her hips, pressing them against his, getting them to move in sync with his gyrations. And then he was gone, taking the hand of another girl, twirling her around and then bending her backwards over his right arm as he laid his chest over hers. His free hand caressed her breast as he lifted her to him. Their hips were locked, pulsing as one.

Bella felt her mouth hanging open. Quickly, she moved off the dance floor to a side wall to get her bearings. No matter how hard she tried, finding Claire in the mass of moving bodies proved impossible. She'd wait until the music stopped. Would it stop?

"Come. Dance with me." He was tall. He was good looking. He was holding out his hand, asking her to dance.

Before she could answer, he had his arm wrapped around her waist and was leading her out into the crowd. He turned to her and began to move. She followed. When he turned, she turned. When he held out his hand for hers, she offered it.

"You're very pretty," he yelled leaning into her right ear.

"Thank you. I'm Bella."

"Enrique. My friends call me Rick." He took her in his powerful arms when the music changed to a Latin Samba, and said, "Follow me."

And she did. For that dance. And the next. And the next.

"I'm out of breath. I need to stop for a bit," Bella begged.

"Sure. Let's get a drink. The bartender is a friend of mine. He'll fix us up."

"Looks like Rick's got himself a looker," said Matt, who was enjoying the nightly show in front of a bank of CCTV monitors. He had a complete view of the activities inside Metamorphosis. There were visible cameras and hidden cameras everywhere, each one strategically placed. No spot inside the club, or outside in the parking lot and driveway leading to Metamorphosis, had been overlooked. Even the bathrooms had cameras discreetly hidden behind the mirrors.

The individual stalls were the only places in the entire club not under surveillance—except for the boss, Julio's, office, and you had to go through the security room to get in there.

Carl swiveled in his seat to take a look. "Yeah." His tongue ran over his upper lip. "She is mighty pretty. She alone?"

"Can't tell," said Matt. "Run the backup feed of the front door. Let's see who she came with."

Carl turned back to his bank of monitors, pushed the rewind button on the DVD closest to him. Then hit play.

"Got it. There," said Carl, pointing at the screen. "Shit, man. The damn bouncer barely even looked at the ID's. Who is that? Fred? What the fuck do we pay him for?"

"We pay him to let in pretty young things like these two so our male customers are happy. That's what we pay him for."

"She came with that one. Silver dress."

Matt scanned his monitors to find the other girl.

"There she is," Matt said, leaning back in his chair. "Ah, she came with Claire."

"Know her?"

"Yeah. Party girl—gets around." A shit-eating grin spread across his face. "Go tell Javier to take extra special care of them."

Carl exited the security room, walked down the narrow hallway past the bathrooms, and out into the main club. The place was packed. He zigged and zagged through the crowd, copping quick feels wherever he could. By the time a girl turned around to protest getting her ass groped, he was gone. At the bar, he got Javier's attention and nodded in Bella's direction.

As Bella and Rick approached the bar, she prayed the fake ID Claire gave her would hold up as well under the scrutiny of a bartender as it had at the door.

"Javier, my friend," said Rick, "this is Bella. Isn't she beautiful?" He put his arm around Bella's shoulder and pulled her to him. "We're thirsty and need some refreshment. Right, Bella? What do you want?"

"I'll have a Margarita," said Bella, expecting the bartender to ask for her ID. She started moving her wrist clutch around to open it.

"That sounds good. Make it two." Rick noticed Carl standing at the end of the bar. Knowing looks passed between them.

Javier had already moved away to make the Margaritas. No ID required. Relieved, Bella felt the tension drain away. She turned to look at her new friend.

"Don't you love this place?" asked Rick. "My friend, Julio, is an owner. I come here all the time. How about you? I don't think I've seen you here before. I'm sure I would have noticed someone as beautiful as you."

"My first time. I'm with my cousin, Claire." Spotting her on the dance floor, she said, "There she is. The girl in the silver dress."

"I know her," said Rick. "So Claire is your cousin? How nice. Two of a kind. Two beautiful ladies."

Their drinks arrived just as Claire and her dance partner joined them.

"Hey cuz, I see you've met my friend, Rick. He's a great dancer, isn't he?" Claire stood on her toes to give Rick a kiss on the cheek. "And this is Pete," she said, introducing her companion to Bella.

"Javier, two more Margaritas please," said Rick. "And make them extra special good for my friends."

"You got it."

"Isn't she pretty, Rick? I told you she was pretty." Claire's voice rose above the music as she gushed over Bella.

When their drinks arrived, Rick held his glass high as he offered a toast.

"To my new beautiful love, Bella, and her equally beautiful cousin, Claire. May our night of fun never end." Glasses clinked and everyone took a sip.

The music shifted to an energizing Latin beat. Orange, red and yellow strobe lights flashed. Mirrored wall panels, angled down from the ceiling, amplified the colors. The dance floor glowed and writhed with the frenzied dancing.

"C'mon, Pete, dance with me," said Claire. She gulped down more of her Margarita, put her remaining drink on the bar and grabbed his hand. "Now you two get friendly. Have fun."

Taking Bella's drink out of her hand and placing it on the bar, Rick said, "Come. You can finish this later. Time for more dancing." Calling out to the bartender, he added, "Javier, take care of these drinks for us, will you?"

"Sure thing, Rick. I'll take special care of them." Javier took the four drinks and placed them on the counter behind the bar. He took note of which two glasses had slight lipstick smudges.

By the time Bella and Rick moved back to the dance floor, Claire and Pete were nowhere to be seen.

"Follow me," shouted Rick, twirling Bella around to face him. One arm went around Bella's waist, the other extended outward taking her hand in his. His movements were graceful, his arms strong. He led her through the twists and sultry turns of a salsa.

Bella felt her body come alive in ways she had never experienced before. The non-stop music unleashed her spirited heart, giving license to her emerging sexual fantasies. She gave in to the heat rising inside her. Undulating hips swayed and teased. Willingly, she aligned her pulsing hips with Rick's. Eyes sparkling, their bodies moved closer and closer together.

"Having fun?"

"Yes. This is great. I love to dance. The music is fantastic." Bella turned her back to Rick and pressed her hips into him. Just as she turned to face him again, the music transitioned to a tango. She found herself in his arms, her heaving chest pressing against his.

In the security room, Carl and Matt's eyes were glued to their monitors, watching the scene on the dance floor. Bella and Claire were not the only two girls in their crosshairs. There were so many nubile young things to watch. Fantasies exploded in their minds. Hard-ons pressed urgently against their zippers.

Time blurred while more Margaritas flowed. Bella glanced at her watch. It was twelve thirty a.m., way past her curfew. Between the loud, unending music, the drinks, and the lies she told her mother haunting her conscience, she wasn't feeling very good. Glancing over at her cousin, Bella could tell Claire was past feeling any pain. Her gyrations on the dance floor were beyond flirtatious. Bella thought them downright dirty. She could see Pete had his hands on Claire's hips underneath her dress.

Grabbing her arm, and pulling her away from Pete, Bella confronted her cousin. "I think we need to leave. It's really late."

"What are you worried about?" Claire's speech slurred a bit. "You're with me. Your mama thinks you're safe at my house. A few more dances. Then we'll go. Okay?"

"Okay. Two more. Then we have to go."

Backing away, Bella bumped into Rick. Turning to face him, she put one hand on his chest and rubbed her forehead with the other. "I don't feel so hot. I'm going to the bathroom."

Bella felt Rick's body heat close behind her. He hadn't

left her side since they first met hours earlier. He was the most exciting boy she had ever met. She was grateful he hadn't tried anything yet, but she knew it was only a matter of time. He held her tighter against him with every dance.

The bathroom was filthy. There were paper towels scattered all around, and only a few had actually made it into the garbage can. Only one stall still had toilet paper. She did her business, washed her hands, and took a deep breath. The room was spinning. She'd only had two Margaritas...had that much at family parties before and never felt this bad. She wet a paper towel and held it to her forehead.

Feeling this crappy must be God's way of paying me back for lying to my mother, she thought. She'd already decided she would tell her parents everything when she got home. She'd apologize, accept her punishment, and work hard to regain their trust.

Rick was waiting for her when she opened the bathroom door. He twirled her around—which made her head spin more—pushed her against the wall, pinned her arms above her head, and started to kiss her neck.

"Stop...Please...Rick...No...Don't."

"Come on Bella. It's just a little kissing. Can't hurt."

He let go, which meant his hands were free to roam her body. He cupped her face, his kisses getting harder, more demanding. She pushed her hands hard against his chest to no avail. Rick's hips were grinding into hers. The weight and strength of his body leaning into her made it impossible to free herself. His tongue assaulted hers, probing every crevice inside her mouth as he squeezed her breasts hard and pinched her nipples. Her squirming proved useless against his greater height, weight, and the force of his onslaught.

"Relax, Bella. Look at Claire," said Rick, breathing hard into her ear and nodding to his right, "She's enjoying herself."

Backed into the corner between the wall and the back door, Claire appeared to indeed be enjoying herself. On the dance floor Pete's hands had been slightly up her dress, resting on her hips, his thumbs hooked into the narrow side elastic of her red thong. Now his hands had gone much farther. Her dress was hiked up to her waist and he had pulled her red thong down around her thighs. One of his hands was rubbing hard and fast between her legs while the other pushed her bottom forward from behind. Bella could see nothing gentle about Pete's touch.

Eyes closed, Claire moved rhythmically, obviously responding to what Pete was doing, because her hips thrust upward in counterpoint to Pete's hand. Suddenly, the pressure of Claire's hips grinding against the crash bar opened the back door and she and Pete literally fell into the alley. The door slammed shut. No sirens sounded.

"Claire," screamed Bella.

She broke free from Rick and ran toward the back door to help her cousin, rushing through it with Rick on her heels.

Pete had regained his feet. He pulled Claire up and pushed her against the side of a black van parked outside the door. Claire seemed dazed, her red thong down around her ankles now. The van door slid open. Claire was hoisted inside.

When Bella reached out for her, an arm wrapped around her throat. She felt a sharp pinprick against her neck. An alarm bell sounded in her brain. Her arms flailed up and back toward where trouble's breath lurked. Then she felt herself slipping…sliding…drifting away…into the dark.

CHAPTER 3

Lying on the chaise lounge, wrapped in her favorite afghan to ward off the nighttime chill, Marissa had a front row seat to watch the stars twinkling and dancing over her head and across the ocean, as far as her eyes could see. Tonight proved to be another one of her infamous sleepless nights. She was alone in the darkness, the roar of crashing waves her only companion.

Marco's dinner party had been a smashing success. Rosa, Marissa's assistant, had helped with all the preparations. She worked with Jesse, Marco's private chef, and the catering company to prepare a lavish feast which included Beluga caviar, chateaubriand, Dom Pérignon, and imported French pastries. Rosa's husband, TJ, the head of Marco's security team, had remained in the background, ever vigilant.

Not that Marco's guests were a rowdy crowd. They were bankers, lawyers, and business owners, pillars of the local community. Marco wanted them to see him as an important and respected member of their community, hence the elaborate party. And they wanted Marco to invest in a new shopping and entertainment center they were planning to build. Quid pro quo at its finest.

Marissa had loved being Marco's hostess for the evening.

31

Dressed in a flowing midnight blue silk Dolce & Gabbana pants ensemble, she greeted everyone with air kisses when they arrived, and saw to their every comfort while they circulated and chatted, and again at dinner. Conversation ranged from the weather, to tourism, to sports. No topic ventured into territory that might be the least controversial.

The ever-flirtatious Desiree De Maurier stole the evening. She always did. One whiff of her heavy, sweet floral scent announced to all concerned that Desiree had arrived. From her grand entrance, to the stories that made the ladies laugh so hard tears smudged their carefully applied makeup, all eyes were on Desiree all the time. This evening she had been dressed to the nines in a green chiffon Versace dress, cut to her navel, revealing hints of breasts Marissa was sure couldn't be real. A five carat, brilliant cut emerald ring sat on her index finger, with assorted diamond rings on her remaining fingers.

Her signature piece of jewelry, an intricately carved dragon of translucent white jade with piercing emerald green eyes, rested dead center on her chest, suspended from a thin gold filigree necklace. Marissa admired the pendant, both for the skillful carving, and because jade was a highly prized gemstone in China, often considered more precious than diamonds and gold.

Mysterious Desiree, thought Marissa. No one quite knew her history. She had arrived in Sand Isle about a year ago and had taken the small community by storm. She claimed to be from New Orleans, but in Marissa's opinion, neither her French nor her Southern drawl sounded quite right. There was something off about her, reminding Marissa of some of the characters she had played in past cons.

A myriad of stories circulated about how Desiree had acquired her wealth. She never denied or confirmed any, preferring to remain secretive about her past. She did talk about her history with men. Marry them, milk them, and move on, she liked to say.

To Marissa, the mystery of Desiree was a total bore.

The evening, however, had been a total success for Marco. She heard him agree to think about the offer of an investment opportunity, promising to get back to the Mayor in a few days with his answer. The Mayor had even wangled a half-baked commitment of two million dollars from Desiree. Everyone left happy.

Sipping her wine under the star-rich sky, Marissa brushed away thoughts of the party. She had more exciting things to think about. She and Marco had finally made love in Paris. Repeatedly.

That's what you do when you're in Paris with the man you love, isn't it? You make love.

And what glorious love it had been. Better than she had imagined when she occasionally dared let her thoughts wander in that direction. His touch warmed her. His kisses were heavenly; some ever so gentle, while others revealed the power that was the essence of this man. No moment rushed. He knew how to take his time, pay attention to the details that intensified their union, making the most of every touch, every kiss. Locked together...pulsing...her pleasure deepening with every thrust. And then lingering in each other's arms as dawn's light tiptoed into their luxury suite at the George V.

She thought about how lucky she was—how lucky all of them, Marco, Sophia and Dom—were. Shitty childhoods were their common denominator. They had found one another on the streets of desperation. Their early life struggles united them, their common sufferings unspoken, but shared. They knew each other's ugly stories of survival intimately.

Unwanted and unloved, they made a pact many years

ago: they would live and work together, nothing would separate them, they would share both the good times and any bad times that came their way. They committed to becoming a family, together by choice, not by birth or marriage. And they found common challenge, refuge and delight in playing people for all they could steal.

A shudder ran down her spine as she thought about the complications that had plagued their most recent and final con.

It began when Marco stopped at a bar in Soho for a drink and overheard a big-mouthed punk named Jimmy brag about stealing some diamonds from an old lady. Marco had insinuated himself into the plan, offering Jimmy a better idea. After a few weeks, things got out of hand. The old lady died suddenly, and her niece became the new owner of the diamonds. Then a NYPD detective started snooping around, investigating the deaths of a bunch of old people. The con spiraled out of control. Too many people involved.

Marco decided to end the con, and they all walked away free and clear.

Why tempt fate? At the after-action debrief, they agreed it was time to mend their wayward ways and go straight. Besides, Marco's investment skills had paid off handsomely. He had taken what they earned from their cons and bought property, insisting the stock market was a fool's game, nothing more than legalized gambling. Real estate was the better bet. It was tangible, solid. You could walk on it, touch it, buy it—and sell it. He claimed it was all about timing, and, of course, location, location, location.

Years earlier, when the market took a dive, he made the best purchase ever. He bought this island. Each one of them had a home on this beautiful stretch of private beach along Florida's east coast. There were also homes for the people who worked for them and took care of their every need.

There was a school and a small, fully-equipped medical clinic run by Dom's wife, Karli. Plus there was more than enough money to support the lavish lifestyles the four of them had only dreamed about once upon a time.

Thinking about her time with Marco in Paris, she wondered how things might change for the family if she and Marco really became a couple. What would Dom and Sophia think?

Refilling her wine glass, she looked up in time to spot a shooting star flying across the sky. Closing her eyes, Marissa softly whispered to the star spirits.

My wish is to have our love grow. My wish is to be with this wonderful man. My wish is to spend what remains of my life wrapped in his loving embrace.

Big wish, thought Marissa. Could a shooting star even begin to deliver on such a big one?

Like a lullaby, Marissa allowed the hypnotic, rhythmic crashing of the waves to rule her senses. Her thoughts drifted in and out with the waves. Perhaps sleep would come soon.

She needed to sleep. She and Sophia were flying off in the family's private jet to a two-day mah jongg tournament in Orlando in a few hours. And she was out to win.

Rosa and TJ walked into their home after two a.m. Saturday morning. Measured by the laughter, the amount of food and wine consumed, and the guests' late departure, they agreed Marco's party had been a huge success.

"I'm glad that's over. I'm soooo tired," said Rosa as she kicked off her shoes by the kitchen door.

"Don't wake me until at least noon," said TJ as he pulled Rosa into his arms and kissed the top of her head. "I'm not on duty until the Sunday noon shift, so we have all of today to hang out. And with Miss Marissa away, you've got the rest of weekend to relax."

"I'll go back to Marco's later and finish putting things away and tidy up a bit more. Then I'm going to pour myself some wine and lose myself in a good book for the rest of the day."

"How about steaks and a salad for dinner tonight? We can open a bottle of wine and watch the sun go down."

"Sounds good to me. I'm going to check on the kids. Think I'll take a hot shower before I come to bed." Rosa walked down the hall to the bedrooms.

"I wasn't kidding about my noon wake-up call," TJ said as he headed in the other direction to lock up his gun in his office.

Moments later he looked up to find Rosa standing his office doorway, a worried look on her face and her phone in her hand.

"What's up, babe?"

"Eddie's sound asleep. But Bella. She's not home. I checked my phone. She left me a message about staying at Claire's tonight. Something about getting home late from the library and my sister saying it was okay."

"So? What's the problem? Estella said it was okay."

"TJ, you know Estella." Her worried look didn't waver. "Why didn't she call me too? To make sure it was okay with me."

"She knew you were doing Marco's party. You'd be busy. She's trying to be helpful, here. That's all, babe. Don't worry. What could happen?"

"You're kidding, right? Estella doesn't exactly run a tight ship. The kids do anything they want to do. For all we know, Estella's not even home. And it's too late to call and find out."

"Give Bella some credit. She's smart. We raised her

right. She and Claire will be up late talking like they usually do. Eat a lot of junk food we don't let her have here. Come home exhausted and sleep through Sunday."

"If you say so." Her voiced sounded resigned, but not convinced. "I wish Estella had called me first to ask if it was okay."

"Don't worry. Come on. It's been a long day. Let's go to bed."

Closing the gun safe, TJ came across the room and flipped off the light. Planting another kiss on top of her head, he wrapped his arm around her waist and led her down the hall to their bedroom.

CHAPTER 4

Saturday

"Holy shit!" Sara stood in the doorway of the grand ballroom at the Mystique, staring at a sea of card tables. "Look at all these tables." Her voice dropped an octave. "I'm not sure I can do this."

"Of course you can do this. Don't let the size psych you out. You're a much better mah jongg player than I am. If I can do this, and I can, you can do this."

"Makes the tournaments I've played in so far seem like child's play. How many friggin' players are there?"

"The table on the end over there has a one hundred and twenty-five number card taped to it. Four players at a table. Do the math. Five hundred players."

"Shit. My stomach is doing flip-flops."

"The first game is the hardest. My insides go crazy, and I burp the cheese egg muffin sandwich we ate for breakfast all morning. Then I settle down, especially once I win a game. You'll be fine."

"Keep talking. I need all the encouragement you have to offer. Where do we go?"

Rachel turned the manila envelope in Sara's hands around so she could see the label.

"You're at table twenty-four and your seat position is North. Looks like I'm right behind you—twenty-three North. Norths move up one table at the end of each session. Looks like my ass will be following your ass around the room."

"Nice mouth," laughed Sara. "How much time do we have before we start? I need more coffee and maybe another one of those cheesy pastries. Can't believe I let you talk me into this."

"Sara, what could be better than a just-us-girls weekend of mah jongg, food, wine and shopping in a town built around happiness?"

"Not feeling the happy yet. More like ready to barf."

"Relax, woman! You'll be fine. We've got thirty minutes before the first session starts. More coffee sounds good to me. And the bathroom is a definite must. Can't count on when you'll be able to go next, so watch your drinking," laughed Rachel.

"Good point. I'll get the coffee. You get the cheesy things. And a few strawberries. Ya gotta eat healthy, you know."

"Meet you at that table along the back wall," said Rachel, pointing to an empty one.

"Better to see our competition from there."

"Look at all these women," said Sara when they got settled. "Where do they all come from?"

"All over. Some are fierce players—real killer instincts. Others want to get away from home. A weekend mah jongg tournament screams freedom. No crying babies, no husbands demanding dinner, no nine-to-five crap. For two nirvana days, game after game after game. There's even a mini-tournament tonight. And women ready to play into the wee hours.

"Do any men come to these things?"

"I played with three in Vegas last year. Don't see any here so far."

The announcement that the newcomer session would start in fifteen minutes got everyone's attention. Like swimmers leaping off the platform when the start gun goes off, hordes of women stood. Human priorities trumped small talk and food: the bathrooms called. They even commandeered the men's room. "Hell, why not?" chirped some faceless voice in the crowd.

"Any last minute words of wisdom?" asked Sara when they left the bathroom and went to find their tables.

"Play your game. Keep your conversations low key. No true confessions about how long you've played, how many tournaments you've done. And since we're here to win, don't play helpful Hannah. I know how much you like helping people play better. Keep your opinions about how anyone is playing to yourself. You can share them with me later so you don't bust a gut."

"Gotcha."

Across the room, two other women were moving with the mob of women now heading for their tables.

"Oh…my…God!"

"What is it, Marissa?" Sophia touched Marissa's arm lightly. "You look like you've seen a ghost."

"Worse. I swear I saw that woman Rachel, the one we went after for those diamonds before Marco and I went to Paris."

"Where? Point her out to me."

"Over there. I don't see her now. Too many people in the way. Should I call Marco?"

"Why? You could have been mistaken. He took losing that one hard. No point getting him riled up for nothing.

Besides, what's he going to do, even if you did see her?"

"Yeah. You're right. Come on. Let's find our tables."

Marissa again felt Sophia's touch on her arm, more forcefully this time, slowing her down.

"What?"

"Don't walk too fast." Sophia pointed toward the elevators, where more women were flooding into the lobby. "Look who showed up."

"Is that Desiree? She plays mah jongg? Not possible."

"Must be possible because there she is."

"Just what we need, a weekend with Desiree. She didn't say anything about coming up here today." Marissa shook her head in disbelief. "Had more than enough of her at the party last night. Every time she got near Marco, I felt a mad urge to scratch her eyes out."

"Oh, really? Aren't we getting a tad possessive?"

"You know what I mean."

"Yeah. Agree totally. Let's go this way. Maybe she won't see us."

Rachel found her table. None of the other players were there yet. The red bag holding the mah jongg tiles and racks sat at the center of the table. Soon the rattle and clack of tiles mixed by ladies with perfectly manicured nails, knock-off designer handbags, and outfits bought at discount outlets would fill the room. These few minutes alone were precious.

She needed this girls' weekend badly. The tournament would force her to focus on something other than her life at the moment. Nothing serious. Nothing to prove. No big life and death decisions. Just fun. It was all good. She was retired. What the hell else did she have to do with her time?

"God, please help me not screw up. Let me hold my own, win a few games, and not do anything too stupid."

The last few months had been challenging. Her

inheritance from Aunt Lil gave her the financial resources to help her other best friend Beth's son, Adam, as he recovered from wounds received in Afghanistan. Lost his legs from an IED. Setting up the Raphael Fund for wounded service people was important, but managing the fund turned out to be more time-consuming than she'd realized.

A hollow squeal brought her attention to the front of the room. Brenda, the tournament director, fiddled with the microphone, vying for everyone's attention. Not an easy task, since hundreds of women were finding their seats, introducing themselves to the other players at their tables, and settling in for three hours of mah jongg.

"Testing 1, 2, 3. Can you all hear me?"

Those paying attention shouted the traditional "Yes!"

"Welcome, ladies and gentlemen. At least I think we have a few men in the room," she said with a laugh. "Welcome to the fifth annual Eastern Invitational Magical Mah Jongg Tournament. We are glad to see so many familiar faces. And so many new faces! Mah Jongg is definitely getting more popular."

More women came into the room.

"Find your seats, ladies. I want to take the next few minutes to go over some of the rules for our newcomers. There are more than one hundred first-time players here. And, yes, I know holding this tournament in May is more challenging. You've only had this year's official playing card for a few weeks. We'll get to find out together who the really good players are. You'll find a rules sheet in your packets, your official score cards, and your name tag. Be sure to wear your name tag to all meals. It's your meal ticket."

Looking around the room, Rachel could see most of the seats were filled. Brenda went over some of the newer rule changes the National Mah Jongg League had implemented for tournaments and answered questions.

As Rachel listened to Brenda's comments, she thought about the comfort of familiar routines. She'd been coming to this tournament and the one in Las Vegas for well over five years. She only missed Vegas this past year because the Dallas airport had an ice storm and all flights were cancelled.

Examining her own reactions to her current surroundings, she realized she was behaving true to form. She always started out at tournaments the same way. Her nerves began getting the better of her as soon as she walked into the room. Her stomach was doing flip-flops. She was nauseous. She swallowed two aspirins simply because she always swallowed two aspirins before the first game of the first round on the first day. Superstition ruled!

Brenda called for quiet so everyone could hear which hand had been chosen as the bonus hand for the first round. Rachel's heartbeat quickened. Brenda continued.

"The North seat position will deal for the first session. Fifty-five minutes on the clock. You can begin now. Good luck, everyone."

Rachel was in the North seat. Her heart pounded as she picked up the dice. Before she threw for the first deal, she completed her own little ritual by saying, "Good luck, ladies. Let's have fun."

Players started their games. One player's focus was not on the game. Marissa kept scanning the room, sitting bolt upright on the edge of her chair, straining to add height to her five foot six frame. Her violet blue eyes narrowed their focus, working to isolate and study each face they locked onto. One by one, each face examined. Her target was one specific face. Unseen under the table, her right leg bounced and jiggled.

She had briefly stood in the doorway, searching the throng of women moving as one into the ballroom, searching for one face—Rachel's—even as she tried to avoid being seen by Desiree. Now that she was seated, it was harder to distinguish individual faces.

She had not been hallucinating. She knew who she'd seen. Clear as day. Rachel was here. What are the odds, she thought, that both she and Rachel played in mah jongg tournaments? What if they wound up at the same table?

There was not a chance in hell Rachel would recognize her. Rachel's memory was of Millie Raconti, a dowdy-looking woman with a hundred extra pounds thanks to the body suit she wore during the con. Brown contact lenses had concealed her striking violet-blue eye color, and both nose and neck prostheses made her appear older and fatter. Marissa had ditched all vestiges of Millie Raconti in one of the ladies' rooms at JFK last October.

Tiles clicked and clattered. The room hummed like bees buzzing around their hive. The games moved fast—a blur of motion. Someone would cry mah jongg and then tiles would thunder onto the table, get shuffled and stacked for the next game.

"Wait," called the player to Rachel's right. "I want that." Picking up the three Bam from the table, she exposed two more to make a pong of three Bams.

Rachel scanned her card for hand possibilities. She found too many to worry about this early in the game. Around they went. Pick. Rack. Decide. Discard. Pick. Rack. Decide. Discard. Someone threw a one Bam.

"Mah Jongg!" cried the player across the table. "I thought I was dead when you put up those three Bams, but the joker spirits smiled on me. Picked three in a row. I know, easy hand. But points are points. Twenty-five points for me and minus ten for you. I didn't have any exposures, but you threw my mahj tile."

"Fast game. Think we could slow it down a bit?" asked the woman who had thrown the mahj tile and lost ten points. "We've got plenty of time left. We can always rush through the last game if we need to"

"God, I love this game," said the woman who won while they mixed the clacking tiles and built walls for the next game. "I'm a mahj slut. Anytime, anywhere. Tell me there's a game and I'm there."

"Me, too," said Rachel. "Though lately other things have gotten in the way."

And so it went, at Rachel's table, and all the other tables around the room. The morning session zoomed by. Lunch was a buffet affair. Deli, salads, an assortment of rolls, and sliced breads if someone wanted to make a sandwich. It always fascinated Rachel to watch people at buffets. And these ladies did not disappoint, plates piled high with enough food for three people.

She and Sara got their food and made a beeline for a table along the wall. There were far better opportunities for people-watching along the sides of the room than in the center. Two women approached their table.

"May we join you?" asked an elegantly dressed woman whose name tag read Sophia. A richly colored orange and yellow scarf hung loosely over her shoulders, nicely complementing her cream lace tank top and darker brown capris. A huge citrine pendant hung from a simple gold omega necklace.

Her friend's outfit matched in elegance. A royal blue, red, and purple flowered chiffon overblouse revealed hints of the red silk tank top underneath with matching red capris. The cameo necklace she wore was gorgeous.

"Of course," said Rachel. She couldn't take her eyes off the cameo. It was identical to her Aunt Lil's which she had gifted to a kindly neighbor after her aunt's death. "I'm

Rachel and this is Sara. I have to say that is one beautiful cameo necklace."

"Thank you. The cameo was a gift. It's a pin, really. I love how the gold, rubies and small pearls highlight the delicate face. You don't see cameos much anymore. I'm Marissa, and this is Sophia. Where are you ladies from?"

"I'm from New Jersey, and Rachel's from Virginia. And you?"

"We're Florida people," said Sophia. "Sand Isle. North of Ft. Lauderdale. You come to these often?"

"Yes," said Sara. "Rachel does tournaments more than I do. This is my first time here. Mostly I go to smaller tournaments in Jersey and New York. They don't hold a candle to this. How about you?"

"Whenever we can. These are great getaway weekends. And we're so close. Flew in this morning." Sophia poked at her full plate with her fork. "Lunch doesn't look half bad."

A server approached the table with a plate overflowing with warm chocolate chip, oatmeal, and snickerdoodle cookies.

"No one goes hungry, that's for sure," laughed Rachel as her eyes met those of Marissa, who was clearly staring at her.

"Do you need something? The salt?" she asked Marissa across the table.

"No, I'm sorry. I don't mean to stare. You look like someone I once knew. Yes, lunch does look good. But I think I'll follow my own inner urges and eat dessert first while these are warm."

Marissa snagged a chocolate chip cookie and began to break it into small pieces. Rachel couldn't help but notice that Marissa continued to glance at her surreptitiously, a mysteriously little smile on her face, like she had a secret only she knew.

CHAPTER 5

It was after noon when Rosa peeked in to check on TJ. He was still in la-la land, the crisp white sheet wrapped around his butt, accentuating his heavily tanned arms, back and legs. She knew he needed the sleep.

Rosa had been up since eight o'clock, had her coffee, and done a load of wash. Anything to keep her hands occupied and hold at bay the dark thoughts creeping around in the shadows of her mind.

Finally, she couldn't stand waiting another minute. She woke TJ by gently stroking his exposed arm. He opened one eye. Rolling over, he pulled her close. She knew her resistance surprised him because he sat up.

"What's wrong, babe?"

"Bella's still not home. There's no answer on her cell. It just rings and rings. Doesn't even go to voice mail. Nothing on Claire's, either. And no one is answering at Estella's house."

"Okay. Let me take a quick shower and get dressed. We'll head over there to see what's up."

His words said don't worry. How fast he showered and dressed screamed worry.

Thirty minutes later they were pulling up at Estella's

house. The car barely stopped when Rosa jumped from the passenger seat and ran up the walk, TJ close on her heels. The living room looked like a cyclone hit it. Empty food containers were everywhere. Two of her nephews, Ramon and Pedro, were watching soccer on TV. The third, Paulo, was totally engrossed with something on his iPad.

"Is Bella here?"

"Hey, Aunt Rosa. No. Haven't seen her," said Ramon. "What's rocking, Uncle TJ?"

"This is important. Have any of you seen Bella?" asked TJ. "She and your sister told us they were going to the library last night. And Bella was sleeping over."

"Claire left with one of her friends last night. Really pretty. Don't know who she was. Hadn't seen her before," said Pedro.

Putting down his iPad, Paulo said, "Come to think of it, I did see Bella yesterday. She stopped by and went into Claire's room. Never saw her leave. Then Claire and her friend left. I figured Bella left when I went to get something to eat."

TJ thought about what Paulo said. Turning to Pedro, he asked, "Could the friend you saw leave with Claire have been Bella? Think about it, Pedro. This is important."

"Didn't look like Bella." His attention remained glued to the TV and the soccer game.

"She was one hot chica, man," said Paulo, his thumbs moving furiously on the keypad.

TJ approached Paulo and pulled the tablet out of his hands.

"Hey. Give that back."

"In time. What do you remember about Claire's friend? What did she look like? What was she wearing?" persisted TJ, following a hunch.

"She was really pretty. Long brown hair, all loose and

falling round her shoulders. She had this streak of hot pink hair on the side, like. She was all dressed up, too. Hot pink top, black skirt, and really high heels. Claire said they were going clubbing and would be home late, if Mom asked."

TJ threw the tablet back into Paulo's lap. His mind raced ahead, and the direction his thoughts took frightened him. He feared he was right. *Damn Claire. Always acting like the big shot. Library, my ass.* Whatever she talked Bella into doing last night, he knew the possibility of a bad outcome was high. His little girl, his baby girl, had somehow gotten herself into something she probably wasn't ready to handle.

Rosa's heart sank. Bella had lied to her. Beyond the lie Bella had told her about where she and Claire were going, and what their plans were for the night, loomed the stark reality that Bella could be in serious trouble. She could read her husband's body language, his narrowed eyes and hands fisted at his sides. He asked the boys a few more questions and then stormed out the front door.

"Will one of you remember to tell your mom to call me when she gets home?"

The "yeah" she heard was not convincing. Rosa stared at her nephews, who were already fully immersed in their own worlds. A moment later, she followed TJ out the door.

"Marco, it's TJ." He white knuckled his cell as he backed out of the driveway. "Sorry to bother you. Bella's missing. I need your help. I'm on my way in. Can you gather the guys? I'll be there in ten. Fifteen tops."

Wheels were set in motion with one phone call. Marco made the next call. Within minutes, seven men were assembled at his home awaiting TJ's arrival. Three more currently working security patrol would be brought up to speed later. Dom also joined the group.

Marco saw the white SUV pull around his curved

driveway. TJ strode through the door Dom held open and joined all the men waiting in the large living room. Everyone stood when he walked in. Determination and testosterone filled the room.

"Thanks for coming." TJ made eye contact with each man in the room. Marco had recruited TJ to lead the security team protecting the compound, and TJ had turned to his buddies, comrades in arms, each one a former member of special forces, Marine Recon or SEALs.

"What's up?" asked Marco.

"Bella is missing. Her cousin Claire is missing too. Neither one came home last night. I dropped Rosa off at the house in case a call comes in on the house phone."

"What do you know?" asked Kyle. He'd been at TJ's side for more than two decades. Kyle and TJ met during SEAL training, bonded in combat. He'd been best man when TJ married Rosa. And was Bella's godfather. Anything TJ felt, Kyle felt.

"Not much. Just left Estella's. Claire's brothers said she left with a girlfriend to go to some club. Both girls were all dressed up. Paulo remembers Bella coming over earlier. No one remembers seeing her leave. I'm thinking the friend could have been Bella."

"Any action on their phones?" asked Casey, another one of TJ's security crew.

"She's not answering her cell. Nothing after she left the message on her mother's phone. No texts, Instagrams, nothing"

"Strange. Young girls live on their phones," said Brett. "What about Claire's phone? Anything there?"

"No answer when we call it. Don't know about texts."

"Where'd they go? Which club?" asked Casey.

"Not sure. Estella finally called Rosa back when we were on our way back here. Rosa filled her in. She had already started calling some of Claire's girlfriends to see if they knew anything. One of them, some girl named Natalie, told her she got a text from Claire last night. It said 'Having fun. You're missing a great party. Wish me luck. YOLO.'"

"Luck for what?" asked Kyle.

"Didn't say. And the girl didn't know. Don't know what good it will do." Every fiber of TJ's being wanted to leap into action, his nerves strung tighter than violin strings.

"Every little bit helps. You know that, man," said Brett.

"Neither of them is twenty-one, right?" asked Steve. "Did they go to one of those teen clubs, or try to get into the real thing with fake IDs?"

"Good questions, Steve. Don't have any answers."

Silence took over the room. Some of the men had families of their own. They worshiped their kids. Others had tried it and hadn't been successful in the relationship department, but they all could relate on some level.

Dom leaned against the sideboard, staring at nothing, then glanced at Marco. "I don't know what I'd do if my little Cassie went missing."

"Let's pray that never happens, because knowing you, it wouldn't be pretty," Marco replied.

"What did the police say?" asked Steve.

"Rosa and I are going there next. We don't have much to tell them, because we don't really know what she was up to. She told us she and Claire went to the library and we know that wasn't true. Which is why I came here first. I wanted to fill you all in. You're my first and last line of defense."

Marco placed a fatherly hand on TJ's shoulder and handed him a shot of Crown Royal over ice.

"Drink this."

"Can't. Don't want the police to smell alcohol on my breath. Save it for me until I get back."

"Good point. The rest of you, help yourselves. You know

where everything is. I'll get Jessie to bring in some food so we can plan our next steps."

❖

"I'm starved," said Sara when their dinner arrived.

"Me too." Rachel leaned forward fanning the scents to her nose. "I think after this dinner, our leftover lunch cookies will be trashed."

"You never know. Don't sell late night snacks short. One never knows when the urge for a chocolate chip cookie will strike."

Rachel's Chilean sea bass sat on a bed of risotto, surrounded by a delicate lobster cream sauce. Sara's veal piccata al limone was centered on angel hair pasta and enveloped in a light garlic and wine sauce.

"If what they say is true—that you eat with your eyes first—the chef has outdone himself. Or herself. This looks amazing." Rachel's fork hovered over her fish.

"So does this," said Sara, digging into the angel hair pasta, making eye contact and nodding a thank you to the sommelier who discreetly refilled their wine glasses.

"How did you find this place?"

"Marv found it on one of his business trips. He brought me here on vacation years ago. Too funny. It was our last vacation together. You know, the one where you try to make the marriage all better by getting away together to recreate the magic. What better place to create magic than in Orlando?"

"Didn't work, did it?" laughed Rachel.

"Not so much. But Christini's totally does. No trip to Orlando is complete without at least one dinner here."

"I love this place. Makes me feel rich."

"Rachel. You *are* rich."

"Oh, yeah. Good point."

"So, what's up with you and Daniel? How's it going?"

"Good, I guess."

"Your tone doesn't match your words. Spill."

"It's nothing. Did I tell you we're talking about building a house?"

"No. When did that get started?"

"A few weeks ago. We were driving Colonial Parkway and talking about how wonderful it would be to have a house with a view of the James River. I mentioned that the community where I live had opened up the last section for development, and it had lots along the James. Next thing I knew we were looking at lots. May have found one too."

"Nothing like building a house together to test your love! Jeez, talk about challenging a new relationship to its core. I think my first fight with my first husband was over hanging wallpaper. A lot of firsts there." Sara shook her head back and forth. "Young, dumb, and horny. We never tried it again."

"Yeah. Tell me about it. Thinking about building my own house...the way I want it...choosing tile and plumbing fixtures, and countertops. Exciting and overwhelming at the same time."

"Would be too much for me. Give me a no-maintenance townhouse any day."

"The whole thing is surreal. I feel like a fish out of water, flip-flopping on the sand. It's all happening so fast. Maybe too fast. I love it when we spend time together. I love waking up next to someone I love. I love how he treats me, looks out for me, and then when he leaves, I miss him. But I love my alone time. Am I crazy?"

"No. Not crazy at all. It's different when you get to be our age. You have a different take on life and what you want. Ready for my theory on the whole thing?"

"Oh, yeah. Always love hearing your theories," laughed Rachel before putting a forkful of fish in her mouth. "This is so good. We need more bread so I can dip it in this sauce." Looking around, she caught their server's eye and pointed to their empty breadbasket. "Sorry. What's your theory?"

"When you're young, you think about this huge future...the house, the kids, how you'll grow old together. Happily ever after. So much hope. So much expectation." Sara waved her fork in the air punctuating her words. "Then shit happens. If you are really lucky, you survive the shit and emerge scarred but victorious, ready to face your next challenge. But there comes a time—totally a mental abstraction and different for everyone—when your thoughts are more focused on the limited time left, and you start trying to fit it all in. You know, the whole bucket list thing. Stuff you never did way back then when you really could climb a mountain."

"Good theory. I like it." Breaking off a piece of fresh bread the server had brought, Rachel ran it through the sauce on her plate and popped it into her mouth.

"Daniel is nothing like David," she continued. "And I'm not the Rachel I was back then. There's a new me in here. I feel...sometimes I feel off balance when I'm with Daniel. There's like this huge battle raging inside me. Want him close. Don't want to feel trapped. Not that he suffocates me. He doesn't. Doesn't push. Doesn't pressure. Funny, maybe what I want is for him to put some pressure on. Too crazy."

"Rachel, he adores you. I can see it in his eyes, the way he looks at you."

"I know and I am totally in love with him. Sometimes I want to jump him. The sex is amazing. Who'da thunk it! I'm sixty and I want to jump Daniel every time I see him. I never thought about sex, about making love like this, when David was alive. Oh God, I don't believe I'm saying this. And you're right. If I'm going to have a relationship with a man, with Daniel, I want it to be on different terms. We're not young pups madly in love."

"But you are madly in love, true?"

"Yeah." A heavy sigh. "I do love him very much. But it's not the wild, ravaging, passionate, sex-crazed, rip-your-clothes-off thing like you see in the movies."

"Oh, now, see, that sounds like fun to me. I could go for a handsome man and wild, passionate, rip-your-clothes-off sex."

"You're impossible," laughed Rachel.

"Just divorced. Twice. Not dead."

"As I was saying, what Daniel and I are sharing is slower, softer, in some ways more intimate than what I had with David." Her marriage to David seemed so far in the past, even though he had only died two years ago. They had spent the better part of forty years together, and produced two children who were now in their own stress-filled marriages. In this moment, though, it seemed like an eternity ago.

"So, what's the problem?"

"The problem..." said Rachel, reflecting while she traced her index finger around the rim of her now empty wine glass. "The problem is... I can't think of anything to stop us from being together. And I've been thinking hard about it a lot lately. There is nothing in our way. Our children are all grown and settled with families and issues of their own. Previous spouses are dead, not divorced and hanging around to haunt and taunt us. We're free. We can set our own rules. Do our relationship our own way. Create it as we go."

"And how is this a problem?"

"I don't know...maybe because I'm used to rules and expectations, and I feel like I'm flying blind with this."

"Any mention of the 'M' word?"

"No, and I'm not convinced marrying is our next step.

Why marry? We're not going to have children. Isn't that why people marry, to start a family?"

"When you're young, yep, though lately having kids without the benefits of marriage seems more the norm. Men have become superfluous, glorified sperm donors."

"Do you think about it? Marrying again? Number three?"

"I've thought about it. I think about it. Considering the last two didn't turn out so well, I'm not sure I'm marriage material. Damaged goods, if you catch my drift."

"Sara, there is nothing damaged about you. You are smart, beautiful, talented, and my very best friend. Okay, you've had two shitty marriages. So what? I know people who are going on husband number four and even five. Doesn't stop them."

Reaching out, Rachel pulled the wine bottle from its silver chilling bucket next to the table and refilled both glasses.

"To us and our new adventures with men. Time to start making some new memories. I've found someone I love very much. Now we need to help you find your next love."

"From your lips to God's ears," said Sara as she raised her glass. "I'll drink to that." Their glasses clinked. Sara's eyes went wide. "Oh my God, here comes dessert!"

CHAPTER 6

Sunday

Scores were posted. Gaggles of women approached the score sheets, scanning for their player numbers, then searching for where they ranked.

"Look, Rachel. I think we may be contenders for money."

"Woo-hoo! I came in ninth in Vegas last year. This is so exciting. Hope I don't screw up today."

"Yeah. Scores can change in a heartbeat. May the mah jongg spirits be with both of us today."

"Yeah. And the joker spirits, too. Let's grab breakfast and find a table."

"Hope there are more of those yummy cheese-filled pastries."

"Those are always here. And don't hold your hopes out for a different breakfast. Same egg sandwiches as yesterday only on croissants instead of English muffins."

"Works for me," said Sara. "I'm actually hungry. Let's go."

Across the room, Marissa and Sophia sat nibbling on muffins and picking at their egg sandwiches.

"Do you see her yet?" asked Sophia, today a vision in royal blue and cream. Marissa was a statement in black and gold, with the cameo brooch firmly pinned below her right shoulder.

"Yes, she's over there," said Marissa, pointing to the far entrance door. "Let me see if I can accidentally bump into them and invite them to join us."

"Do you think that's smart? She might recognize you."

"Not possible," said Marissa standing up. "I told you yesterday. I was in costume when our paths crossed. She doesn't know me. She knows Millie Raconti, and trust me, Mille Raconti is never making a return appearance."

"She recognized the cameo." Sophia jerked her head toward the pin at Marissa's shoulder. "Her eyes got so big when she saw it. Kept looking at it while we were having lunch yesterday. I kept waiting for her to ask you where you got it or something."

"Sophia, don't be silly. There are hundreds of cameo pins. There is no way she can know the one I'm wearing was her aunt's."

"Marissa, trust me. She knows."

"You and your Middle Eastern mysticism. Anyway, this will be fun." Off Marissa went to ensnare her target.

Returning to the table a few minutes later, Marissa said, "Too late. They were already eating by the time I got near them. I'll try again at lunch. I want to spend some time with them...with her. Don't ask me why. Not like we could ever be friends. There's just something about her."

"You're playing with fire, girl."

"Marco felt something about her too. He changed after he met her. I want to understand why. And I can only do that if I get to know her. It's Kismet. Us both being here."

"Marco will not be happy."

"Maybe, maybe not. What he doesn't know he can't get

angry about. Right?" Marissa took a sip of coffee. "Any sign of Desiree?"

"Saw her get off the elevator, but don't see her now. Can't believe she'd eat at this buffet. She's more the serve me type. Bet she's having breakfast at the cafe downstairs."

"You're probably right. Didn't see where she was sitting, so I don't know if she'll wind up at either of our tables."

"Oh," sighed Sophia. "Not something I'm looking forward to. She's nice and all, but a little over the top for my taste."

The morning session passed quickly. Three hours and twelve games of mah jongg played in fifty-five minute increments whizzed by. A shout rang out when one of the players won the hardest hand on the card and immediately collected two hundred dollars.

At lunch Marissa positioned herself for action. When Rachel and Sara walked away from the buffet line, she purposely bumped into Sara.

"Sorry," said Marissa absently as she turned around. "Hey, nice to see you again."

"You, too," smiled Sara.

"Having fun? How are you doing?"

"Good. And you?"

"Okay. Not as well as I'd hoped. Come join us. We've got room at our table." Not waiting for a response, Marissa slipped her free hand through Sara's arm. Rachel followed behind. Careful not to drop their lunches, the threesome wove their way through the cramped ballroom to a table along the side wall.

"Look who I found, Sophia," Marissa said.

"How nice. Come sit. There's plenty of room."

Two servers stood to the side of the buffet tables idly

talking while the women filled their plates. Except for the fact that one had on his complete uniform and the other was missing his gold vest and name tag, they could have been twins—white-collared shirts, black pants, dark curly hair, brown eyes, about six feet tall.

"Young man. Young man!" called Desiree from the buffet line. Both servers turned their heads in her direction. "Could you be a dear and see if there is any horseradish in the kitchen that you could bring out? I know it's a lot to ask, and you're probably very busy, but it would make this roast beef taste ever so much better."

"Of course, ma'am," said the one in his full uniform. "It will take me a few minutes. Where are you sitting? I'll bring it right to you."

"My stars. We haven't chosen a table yet, and besides, you'll never find me in the ballroom. You put it out here on the buffet table, and I'll come back to get it in a few minutes."

The server without the vest watched Desiree walk away, noticing the direction she took through the sea of tables in the ballroom. Then he turned, caught up with the other server, and they headed down the service corridor back to the kitchen.

As Marissa, Rachel and Sara were getting settled at Sophia's table, a high-pitched voice called out above the crowd.

"Marissa! Sophia! Is it really you? I do declare, what a pleasant surprise."

"Desiree," said Marissa, flashing Sophia a quick sideways look. "We didn't realize you were coming to this tournament."

"Well, I never thought to say anything. Didn't know you two even played mah jongg. Isn't this the best time ever?"

"Yes, it is," said Marissa.

"May I join y'all? Have you got two seats?"

"Of course," said Sophia, turning on her own version of Southern charm. "Come sit down. Rachel, Sara, this is our dearest friend, Desiree."

"Nice to meet you," said Rachel.

"You, too. And this is Carolyn."

Marissa hadn't even noticed the blond woman standing next to Desiree; she'd somehow disappeared into the background. Her black slacks, simple blue V-neck sweater, and sparse makeup were a stark contrast to Desiree's stunning jewel-toned floral blouse worn over black leggings with glamour-shots-quality makeup. And Carolyn's lone silver ring couldn't compete with Desiree's jewelry. Marissa noticed Desiree was wearing the white jade dragon pendant again. After Marco's party, she had wondered about its symbolism, and had searched the internet for information about jade and dragons.

To her surprise, jade was considered a royal gem by the Chinese, embodying Confucian virtues like wisdom, compassion and modesty. It was also connected to female erotica. Strange, thought Marissa. How could a stone mean both modesty and female erotica? The combination made it even more curious that Desiree should wear such a stone. Then again, the pendant was beautiful. Marissa remembered feeling the dragon's brilliant emerald green eyes follow her every move at Marco's party Friday night.

Marissa also remembered jealousy's fire igniting inside her every time Desiree got near Marco. Jealousy was such an ugly emotion. She hated herself when it reared its ugly head. She never saw any indication that Marco was about to succumb to Desiree's rather obvious charms. He moved away whenever she got close. At one point, he signaled Marissa with a look that brought her zooming to his rescue when Desiree had him cornered on the patio.

"I was saying to Carolyn, you meet such wonderful people at these tournaments. Well, that's how we met. What's it been two...three years now?" said Desiree, her words leaving her mouth at the speed of a runaway train. "Well, no matter. It's always so nice to know Carolyn is going to be here. And we have such a good time, don't we? Where are you girls from?"

"Rachel is from Williamsburg, Virginia, and I'm from New Jersey."

"Williamsburg. Well, bless your heart. What a lovely little town. So quaint. Full of history and all."

Sophia and Marissa rolled their eyes in unison. Sara caught the look and nudged Rachel under the table. And Desiree? She kept talking and talking and talking, clearly a woman in love with the sound of her own voice. She was too busy holding court at the lunch table to even notice anyone's reaction.

"I love mah jongg don't y'all? I do declare," said Desiree in her best Scarlett O'Hara imitation. "It is the most fun game ever."

A server came out of the kitchen carrying two small dishes of horseradish. He placed one on the buffet table next to the roast beef wraps and carried the other into the ballroom, heading straight for Desiree's table.

"Excuse me, ma'am. Here's the horseradish you requested." He placed the second small dish of horseradish next to her plate.

As he turned to walk away, Desiree reached out and grabbed his arm.

"How kind of you to bring this right to me. My stars, I can hardly believe you were able to find me in this sea of women. Wait a moment." Desiree opened her purse and pulled out a five dollar bill. "Thank you so much."

"Thank you, ma'am. There's some on the buffet table if

you need more." Pocketing the tip, he turned and left the ballroom.

"Wasn't that sweet? He actually found me. I love horseradish. It gives roast beef the right little zing it needs to be great. Do any of you want some? There's more than enough to share here."

"Sure," said Sophia. "I'll take some." She reached out for the small dish, dipped her knife tip into it, and spread the creamy white sauce on her wrap. Taking a bite she waved her hand in front of her mouth. "Whoa. That'll open your sinuses."

At three thirty the first woman literally fell out of her chair. White as a sheet, she hit the floor, holding her stomach and moaning as she writhed from side to side. Her cream pants took on a yellowish tinge as bodily fluids seeped into the carpet around her. Within moments, two women who said they were nurses rushed to help her. Someone called 911.

By the time hotel security and the paramedics arrived, four other women were in similar conditions at different locations around the ballroom. By then chaos had erupted, and all play stopped. Women raced out of the ballroom, their hands over their mouths, heading to the bathrooms. Other women huddled together, concerned about the people getting sick, but unable to do much more than watch. And pray they wouldn't be next.

"You feeling okay?" asked Sara when she found Rachel in the crowd.

"Yeah. You?"

"So far so good." They watched as the paramedics arrived and attended to the woman lying closest to them. "What do you think? Something they ate?"

"Could be. What did they all eat that we didn't eat?"

"You had the tuna," said Sara, "and I had the turkey. Everyone probably ate the fruit. And the warm cookies were too good to pass up. We didn't eat the roast beef. You know what they say. Stay away from red meat."

"Not funny," chastised Rachel. "These women are really sick. The one at the table behind me totally lost it. She messed herself and the floor big time."

A stifled scream from the far side of the ballroom had everyone turning their heads.

"There goes another one. Down for the count."

"Sara!" Rachel's teeth dug into her lower lip. "There's nothing funny about getting sick."

"Wasn't that Desiree, the woman we had lunch with?" asked Sara.

"I think so. Let's get out of here," said Rachel. "I need some air. We'll be able to hear any announcement and watch what's going on. And I want to talk to you."

Following Rachel out of the ballroom, Sara noticed several more women looking really bad. The last thing she wanted was for either of them to get sick.

"What's up? Other than all the sick people."

"The women we ate lunch with—Marissa, Sophia, and Desiree. Did anything seem strange to you?"

"Not really. We ate with two of them yesterday. Love their clothes. Their jewelry more. Marissa saw us getting our food and invited us to join her."

"Desiree was a bit much," Rachel said. "All Botox and collagen. Didn't think she'd ever shut up."

"She must think her navel is the center of the universe. It looked like Marissa wanted to kill her at lunch...or kill herself. She didn't look happy when Desiree and her friend Carolyn sat down. Total opposites, those two. Carolyn hardly said a word. She kept twisting the ring on her finger. Barely ate her lunch. What's bothering you?"

"I don't know. Probably nothing." Rachel twisted her hair around her finger. "It's Marissa. The cameo she's wearing. It's the same pin my Aunt Lil had. The one I gave to the neighbor woman, Millie. Remember her?"

"Yeah. Never did find out where she disappeared to, did they?"

"No. Daniel said they found the guy's body in a dumpster on Staten Island. Knifed. Chalked it up to a gang initiation."

"Couldn't happen to a sleazier guy."

"True." Rachel's eyebrows twisted together.

"Talk about an odd couple. They weren't really mother and son were they?"

"No. They weren't." Rachel stared off into space.

"What?"

"Marissa has my aunt's pin. I mean, identical. Rubies and small pearls around the cameo."

"Rachel, there have to be hundreds of cameos out there in antique shops, consignment places. Hell, Millie could have sold it or pawned it."

"Don't think so. Her reaction—how excited she was when I gave it to her."

"Maybe so. But let's face it. This is an older crowd. Remember, when we were young, cameos were very popular. Do you know if your aunt had it made special for her?"

"I think she bought the cameo. Or Uncle Abe bought it for her. Guess I'm not over her death yet. I miss talking to her."

"She was a big part of your life. I'm so sorry she's gone. Dare I say you can still talk to her?"

"I know…and I do. But it's not the same. She's not answering me."

"Sure she is. Not with words. Listen with your heart. You'll hear her."

Rachel looked away. Taking a deep breath, she

swallowed the tickle in her throat, a telltale sign tears could soon be flowing freely. Not the place, not the time, she thought.

"Here come more paramedics. And speaking of Marissa and Sophia, there they are."

As if on cue, Sophia and Marissa walked out of the ballroom. Sophia's stooped posture broadcast trouble. Holding her stomach and leaning on Marissa for support, she stopped past the doorway, lines of pain etched across her pasty face. Bracing her back against the wall for support she slid down in a heap.

Rachel, Sara, and a newly arrived paramedic team rushed to her.

"I'm okay. Really," said Sophia, trying to get up. "There are people in the ballroom who need you more than I do."

"Just relax, ma'am. Let us do our job. We've got people taking care of them. You relax."

"Thank you," said Sophia, leaning back, too weak to fuss. The paramedics went to work.

Rachel peered into the ballroom, struggling to process what she saw. In a heartbeat, the room had transformed from women having fun to pure, unadulterated chaos. Chairs overturned. Tables abandoned with tiles left on the racks. Several women were very, very sick, and a few had not been fast enough to make it to the bathrooms. The ballroom reeked. It would take a cleaning crew hours, if not days, to make the place usable again.

"Look at all the tiles on the floor," said Sara. "Brenda is going to have one hell of a time sorting all these out."

"Yeah. There's no way we can continue. This will take hours to clean up."

"Lots of serious-looking people in suits showing up with interesting ID badges," said Sara. "FBI, DEA, and the one over there says DHS. Shit, the whole alphabet is here."

"Wonder why? What's really going on?"

"Don't know. But someone sure thinks it's serious. More serious than a few people getting sick after lunch. Here come the crime scene guys."

Crime scene technicians in navy blue overalls and white disposable shoe covers opened their cases and started taking pictures. Out in the lobby area, small groups of women clustered together for comfort, whispering and gawking at the action while waiting for their turn to be interviewed by detectives. Some stood alone, clutching their mah jongg cards, naked fear laid bare on their faces, worried about who would get sick next—praying it wouldn't be them.

Noting a commotion at the far end of the lobby, Sara said, "Wait here. I'll be right back."

Rachel watched her bob and weave her way through the crowded lobby space to the far end. She stopped, fidgeted with her purse, turned, and retraced her steps.

Within a few minutes Sara was back. "Let's get out of here." Nudging Rachel's arm, she pointed toward the exit.

"Good idea," said Rachel. "How about outside? Need to clear my head. Don't want it to affect my play, if and when we start up again."

"Don't think that's going to happen," said Sara. "Everyone looks pretty upset. Maybe Brenda will call it and use the scores so far. Glad I don't have to make that decision."

While they were leaving, Desiree was wheeled past them, strapped to the gurney, an oxygen mask on her face. Her friend Carolyn walked alongside carrying her purse.

"She doesn't look good at all," said Sara.

"There but for the grace of God. Sure hope she gets better." Hearing the familiar tapping on a microphone, she stopped talking. "Looks like Brenda is ready to make an announcement."

"Ladies, I'm afraid we are going to have to suspend our tournament. There's no way we can continue. To our dear friends who are ill, we are here to help you in whatever way we can. To the rest of you, thank God you're okay. If you are a guest at the hotel and begin to feel ill, please call the front desk immediately, and someone will come to your room."

People were hammering Brenda with questions. She had few answers.

"Can you believe that woman asked about the prizes?" Sara huffed.

"She probably has a high score, feels okay, and wants her prize money," replied Rachel. "Tacky yes, but what can you expect? Some people have no class."

"Yes, I hear your question," said Brenda. "In all the years we've been running this tournament, we've never encountered anything like this before. Please be patient with us while we sort through the best and fairest way to proceed at this point. The detectives have asked you to leave the area after you have been interviewed and given them your statement. Please do all you can to cooperate so we can get to the bottom of this horrible tragedy as swiftly as possible. Thank you all for coming. Please have safe journeys home. And remember, if you don't feel well, contact your doctor immediately."

Sara and Rachel gave their statements and contact information to two detectives.

"I need a drink."

"Wine sounds good," said Sara.

Rachel sadly surveyed the scene as they headed for the elevators. "I know we're scheduled for massages at five, but I'm not sure even a relaxing massage can wash away these images."

A few minutes later they were sitting at the courtyard bar

at an umbrella table, each with a glass of Chardonnay in hand.

"Do we have anything to drink to? Maybe cheers we didn't get sick," offered Sara.

"I'll drink to that," said Rachel, tipping her glass toward Sara's. "Why would anyone want to hurt us? We're harmless. Competitive players, but take us away from a mah jongg table and we're pussycats. Mothers and daughters and grandmothers."

"I know," said Sara. "None of this makes any sense. Did you see the guy at the far end of the lobby with the ice pack?"

"Yeah. I watched where you went and saw him."

"He works here. A server. I overheard him tell the police someone hit him from behind."

"That's not good."

"He said the next thing he knew he came to in a storage closet. His vest and name tag were gone. Not sure what to make of that."

"While I was waiting for you, I overheard one of the detectives say the food was the focal point of the investigation since people got sick an hour or so after lunch. They're trying to zero in on what the people who got sick ate."

"Do they think it was done intentionally?" asked Sara.

"Beats me. But that may be why there are so many suits with alphabet IDs here." Rachel thought about Daniel and what his role might be in a similar situation.

"The detective I spoke to asked me what time my table broke for lunch. I told him we finished fast, four games in forty minutes, kind of like playing mah jongg on speed, so we were in the area where lunch was set up before almost everyone else."

"Did he like the speed comment?"

"Not so much," said Sara. "He didn't laugh. Asked me if I saw anyone or anything suspicious around the buffet table. Told him no. Did your guy ask you that?"

"No, but I had already told him that my table was one of the last ones finished before lunch," said Rachel. "I hate to think someone would tamper with the food. I hate buffets as it is. The way this is going, I may never eat at a buffet again."

"It would be a great way to terrorize a lot of people. All-you-can-eat buffets scream America. Someone could get a job at one of these places and spike the food, and lots of unsuspecting people could get very, very sick."

"Sara, don't go there."

"Why not? It's true. There are a lot of sick people in this world. Not to mention the crazies who hate our way of life, hate everything America stands for, and want to kill us all. What better way to scare us than poisoning a group of innocent, happy people at a tournament, or a wedding, or some other type of event."

"The hotel has to have surveillance."

"I'm sure it does. Cameras and everything, but this is still considered a soft target."

"The hotel must be scrambling," said Rachel. "They've got a big convention group coming in tomorrow. They need the ballroom back to get it cleaned."

"It's going to take a lot of cleaning to get that smell out."

"I'll say. I really want to know what happened to make all these women sick."

Carolyn met with a detective at the ER.

"Not sure what more I can tell you, Detective. We had breakfast in the lobby cafe. Desiree hates cold, rubbery eggs."

"Did you both eat the same thing?"

"She had a three cheese omelet and I had pancakes and bacon."

"And for lunch?"

"We both had the roast beef wraps. I didn't add anything to mine but some salt and mayo. Desiree asked for horseradish. She loves the stuff. Always asks for it. Puts it on almost everything she eats. One of the servers brought it to the table."

"Do you remember if anyone else used it?"

"I'm not sure. I wasn't really paying close attention. I think one of the women she knew from Florida may have used a little."

"Can you describe the server who brought it to the table?"

"Not really. White guy, dark curly hair, maybe about six feet, dressed like all the other servers in the room. That's all I remember. I saw Desiree give him a tip. She's like that. Really thoughtful and kind to servers and staff. Kind of her thing. I always figured she worked those types of jobs when she was young and knew how hard they were."

As Carolyn finished, the doctor came out of Desiree's room.

"Doctor, I'm Detective Cam Spencer. When can I talk to her?"

"Not for a while, I'm afraid. She's sedated. You may want to come back tomorrow."

"Not my first choice."

"Maybe not, but our priority is to get her system under control."

Turning to Carolyn, Detective Spencer said, "Here's my card. Call me if you remember anything else. And if she wakes up sooner and can talk."

"Will do."

CHAPTER 7

Impossible situation, any way you slice it.

It was early Sunday afternoon. TJ stood in the middle of Claire's room, scratching his head, searching for a clue that would give him some hint, a direction, a place to start searching for his daughter.

There were clothes and shoes strewn everywhere. Neat and tidy weren't Claire's strengths. Lotions and potions, mascaras, and eye shadows in a rainbow of colors covered her dresser top. Looked like she robbed a drug store makeup aisle. Fragrances with names like Euphoria, Guilty, Passion, Romance, Addiction all spelled trouble. Where she got the money for all this stuff, he didn't want to know. But he did know. Or at least he thought he knew, which added to his fears for his precious daughter.

Rosa's sister, Estella, frustrated TJ no end. Her life sucked. Bad taste in men. Crappy jobs. Constant battles with her own drug demons had landed her several stints in rehab. An alley cat had better mothering skills. The results? Four kids, each from a different father, none of whom had stayed around long enough to learn how to diaper a baby.

What was it they said? The sins of the parents are visited on their children. Estella's three boys desperately needed a strong, positive male figure in their lives. TJ filled the role as best he could, but he had his own family. Unfortunately, the streets ended up doing the job.

Then there was Claire. A five foot eleven, beautiful, walking nightmare. He might be her uncle, but he could easily imagine the thoughts lurking in the minds of any men who saw her. Her slender legs went on forever, breasts teetering on voluptuous, on an otherwise slim physique. When she flashed her green eyes at you, it was hard to say no to anything she asked. Her long, honey blond hair had enough curl to frame her face in a way that rendered men hopelessly lost in fantasies about what they'd like to do with that hair…and her. And she was only seventeen.

Trouble followed wherever she went. She'd experimented with drugs and boys long before his own daughter, Bella, even knew these things existed. And Claire's drug use had obviously gone well beyond the experimental stage. He knew the girl needed the type of help she could not get at home. When Estella tried to stop her, she threw up her mother's own escapades as justification for her actions. After all, if her mother acted like a tramp in heat, why couldn't she? And Estella's only comeback? Her claim to want Claire to have a better life, not surprisingly, fell on deaf ears.

Try as he might to block it out, shadowy nightmares of his childhood haunted him. Memories of finding a body in the woods, memories of his own sister Angela's road to ruin, were seared into his heart. She'd been using and abusing drugs for years before she died. What could he have done? He was fifteen when she and her unborn child departed this world in a haze of drugs.

Claire was turning out like his older sister. Not what TJ wanted for his daughter. He knew the signs. And he had vowed a long time ago that, if given the chance, he would not make the same mistakes with his life, with his family, that his parents had.

The Marines had provided his ticket out. A semi-trailer rolling down the highway with an image of Marines standing tall sealed his fate, and his old life stopped cold that very day. He had found a purpose, a direction. He worked out, improved his grades, got in shape, and joined up. The Marines became the family he never had. Once a Marine always a Marine. He learned structure, discipline—and, most important, the Marines taught TJ about honor, integrity, and loyalty. Hungry for more, when his tour was up, he joined the Navy, made it through BUD/S, and became a SEAL.

He met Rosa, his soul mate, when he was stationed at Virginia Beach. They both wanted the same things—family and children. Very simple things, very precious. When he retired, they moved to Florida to be near Rosa's sister. And TJ swore he'd won the job lottery when he was hired to work security for Marco at the compound.

Within that first year, he and Rosa started their family. Eddie arrived first, and then Isabella. Where Eddie was outgoing and athletic, Bella was shy and more of a thinker. Eddie planned to follow in his father's footsteps and become a Marine. He also planned to attend medical school. Bella wanted to be a lawyer. Her idol was Justice Sonia Sotomayor, though she was way more conservative. She was Daddy's little girl in every way. And right now it was up to Daddy to find her.

Yesterday afternoon they filed the missing person reports for both Bella and Claire. The police said they'd get right on it, and both girls were entered into the Florida Crime Information Center database and the national crime database. A BOLO was issued to all jurisdictions. An Amber Alert went out immediately. No luck so far.

❖

Scheduling massages after the tournament proved to be a wise move. The massage therapists spent extra time working out the knots both Rachel and Sara had acquired, not just from sitting at a mah jongg table for hours, but also from witnessing the mayhem that ended the tournament...and wondering if they were next.

Neither knew if she had won any money, but regardless, tomorrow they would be spending some. It was part of their ritual, a planned shopping day, and Sara was a world-class shopper.

Still thoroughly relaxed from their massages, they entered the tapas bar for a late dinner and ordered a round of sangria. They read through the menu and selected five different tapas dishes that sounded good.

"This looks good," said Sara as she forked a shrimp sitting in garlic aioli.

"Lunch looked good, too—until it didn't," Rachel groused.

"Don't go there. We don't know if it was the food at this point."

"Right. Innocent till proven guilty."

"Look, musicians. Guess the show is about to begin."

Within minutes Spanish guitar music filled the intimate space. A couple dancing Flamenco joined the musicians. The mostly tourist crowd snapped their fingers and clapped in time with the rousing, seductive music. The dancers, invigorated by the enthusiastic audience, performed two encores.

Walking to the car hours later, Sara said, "You were kind of quiet after dinner. Anything wrong?"

"I think we need to make a slight detour before heading back to the hotel. My heart's racing. Has been on and off for about an hour. Started after we ate. Figured it would stop after a while. Didn't. Where's the closest hospital?"

"Shit, Rachel!" Sara's shriek rang out in the empty parking lot.

Unlocking the car door and pulling out her phone, Sara said, "Sit down. I'm calling 911."

"She's doing better. Honest, Daniel. It was scary for a while. Her pulse was up to 180 bpm when the ambulance arrived, but the paramedics were great."

"Yeah. Those guys are amazing. I've watched them in action more times then I care to think about."

"They had her on oxygen, gave her aspirin, and even did an EKG on the way to the hospital."

"Thank God they were well prepared. Then again, with Florida's huge elderly population, heart attacks are probably common 911 calls. So having the equipment on board makes sense. Look, I'll be there in the morning. I'll take the first flight I can get on to Orlando."

"You really don't have to come all this way. They gave her a bolus of Cardizem. It worked. She converted, so they didn't have to do another one or take more extreme measures. I was with her the whole time. Watched the monitor as her heart rate slowly came down. She's resting comfortably. I'll stay with her and change my reservations so I can fly back to Williamsburg with her."

"I'm coming. End of discussion," Daniel said sharply. Silence filled the air. "Sorry, Sara. I didn't mean to sound so harsh. I need to be there."

"I know you do. No offense taken. We both love her. The doctor is in with her now. Let me call you back when I find out what's up."

"Okay. By then I'll know my flight info."

Sara hung up. Of course Daniel was on his way. That's what people did for people they loved. They showed up. Tears welled up. Rachel was her best friend. Thoughts about life and living flooded her consciousness. Sara knew they were all over the cusp. Fewer days left. So many people didn't make it this far. She felt lucky.

"You can go back in now," said the doctor as she exited the room. "She responded well to the bolus. It looks like the episode's passed. She's going to be fine. I want her to rest here for a few more hours. Then you can take her home."

"Thank God. And thank you so much." Sara threw her arms around the doctor before she could object.

"I suspect you guys have had a crazy day. We're here for the mah jongg tournament at the Mystique, and we were there when all those people got sick this afternoon. So much for a quiet few days of girl-style R&R. You know, shopping, spa sessions, a little mahj, good eating and drinking."

"Yes. She told me she wasn't local. And it did get a little crazy here this afternoon. Didn't lose anyone yet, which is always a good thing."

"We're planning to leave Tuesday. Can she fly?"

"Yes. She can fly. I told her she can resume her routine. I've given her a prescription for metoprolol. It's a beta blocker. Started her on the lowest dosage. And told her to see a cardiologist when she gets home."

"Thanks, Doctor."

"Just so you know, if you're with her and she does experience any symptoms again before she gets home, she should take another pill and get herself to the nearest hospital ASAP. Got it?"

"Yep. Got it. Thanks again."

Standing in the hall as the doctor headed off to see other

patients, Sara took a deep breath, closed her eyes and whispered, "Thank you, God."

Walking into the room, Sara stared at her best friend. Rachel's eyes were closed, her breathing deep and regular. Sara slumped into the visitor chair and dropped her head back. Her arms and legs felt like they were dragging one thousand-pound weights. She closed her eyes, hoping to block out the images scrambling through her brain.

Crazy day. All those people getting sick at the tournament, and now this.

The serenity she felt after their late afternoon massages and relaxing dinner had disappeared in a flash. She craved her own bed, her quilt. The safety of her nest.

"Hey, you," Rachel's soft voice reached out to her.

"Hey, yourself. How are you feeling?" Sara came to her side and held her hand.

"Better. I'm sorry I ruined our evening."

"Don't go there. What matters is you're okay. Why did you wait so long to say anything? So stupid."

"I know." Rachel looked around the room and took stock of her current position—the EKG leads still in place, the oxygen tubes in her nose, the IV in her arm.

"After the day we had, all those people getting sick at the tournament, we were enjoying ourselves, and I kept thinking it would stop. If I wait a little longer, it will stop." Tears clung to her long, dark lashes.

Sara leaned over the bed and put her arms around Rachel as best she could.

"I know. It's been a rough few hours. But you're okay. The doctor said you'll be fine."

"I know. She told me that too. And to see a cardiologist. Shit! We used to swap names of hairdressers, manicurists and massage therapists. Now we're asking for referrals for cardiologists and urologists. What's wrong with this picture?"

"Nothing. Our bodies need their sixty thousand mile checkup, that's all. And some parts need repair."

"Always the clever one," laughed Rachel. "But the worst news. She told me to cut out caffeine. Switching to decaf will be easy. But to watch my wine and my chocolate. Only a little of each. What's a little bit of wine?"

"Good question. Shit. Sounds like a prison sentence."

"I can go cold turkey on the wine. It's the chocolate. In my world, chocolate is a major food group. Kill me now! There go my favorite two ice creams flavors, coffee and chocolate chocolate chip."

"You don't have to go cold turkey. Use it as a reward. Buy the really good stuff and savor it."

"Yeah. Is a little bit a bite? A spoonful of chocolate pudding or ice cream?"

"Don't know. You know me. I don't do moderation. Whole hog or no hog."

"This is going to take some practice and tons of willpower. And I don't want to think about the consequences if I get it wrong."

"You know you can do this."

"I know." A soft determination filled Rachel's voice. "Anyway, she wants me to rest here for a bit longer. Then she'll be in to take one last EKG reading and sign me out. Does Daniel know? Did you call him?"

"Yep. Figured you would want me to. He would want me to. Be seriously pissed if I didn't. Got his number off your cell and called him. He'll be here tomorrow."

"He doesn't have to come down."

"Yeah, right. You try to stop him."

"Give me my phone. That's exactly what I intend to do."

CHAPTER 8

"Aaaaiiiieeeee!"

Estella's piercing scream brought the boys running. The sight of Claire sprawled out asleep on her bed shocked everyone. Only Claire didn't move when her mother screamed.

Estella rushed to the bed and shook her daughter. Nothing.

"Quick, Pedro. Call 911."

Pedro pulled his cell from his pocket, hit the numbers and handed it to his mother.

"911. What's your emergency?"

"My daughter. I can't wake her."

"What is your location ma'am?"

"2025 South 163rd Place, Sand Isle"

"We're sending help, ma'am. I can see you are using a cell phone. What is the number you are calling from, in case we get disconnected?"

"561-555-0134. Hurry."

"Are you in the room with her now?"

"Yes."

"I understand you're upset. Try to stay calm. The ambulance is on its way. I need to ask you a few more questions. Can you tell me any more about her condition?"

"I don't know. I tried to wake her. She won't wake up. Hurry."

"Do you know if she took anything? Any drugs?"

"I don't know. She hasn't been here for a few days. I didn't even know she was home. I came in her room to change the sheets and she was here."

"Yes, ma'am."

Sirens announced the ambulance's arrival. Paramedics rushed in, equipment in hand. They went to work immediately, no wasted motions. Blood pressure, pulse, pinpoint pupils, redness and flaring around her nose area, plus other visible evidence, confirmed initial suspicions. Drug overdose. Which drug was the question.

"Got a pulse, thready. Do you know what she took?" The paramedic's eyes bored into Estella.

"No. Can you help her? Please help her." Seeing her daughter lying there, not responding at all, Estella's heart crumbled, and her voice turned shrill, verging on hysteria. "I don't know what she does, or where she goes, or who she hangs out with."

"It's okay, ma'am. Try to stay calm. We'll take good care of her." Turning to the other paramedic, he said, "I'm going to get the gurney." A private look shot between them before he turned to walk out the door.

His partner connected to the ER, sending them the required information. Blood pressure ninety over forty, respiration shallow, sixty bpm. He busied himself following the instructions he was getting over the phone. He started an IV, set up an oxygen flow, and pulled some blood.

As he worked he shot an occasionally glaring stare at Estella. He'd seen too many young people in this condition. And too many parents unaware of what their children were up to. Spotting a small purse on the floor, he opened it and dumped its few contents to get a better look. Nothing. No pill bottle, no drugs. Just the usual wallet, lipstick, cell phone.

His partner returned with the gurney. They lifted Claire onto it and strapped her in lest she move, though both knew movement from her was doubtful, given her condition. The decision had been made to transport her to the hospital for further evaluation before administering any drugs to counteract the suspected drug overdose.

The emergency staff was ready for them when the ambulance pulled up.

A nurse escorted Estella into a nearby waiting area. In addition to providing a sympathetic ear, her job was clear. Find out everything you can in a gentler, kinder, female-to-female way. The nurse sat close and held Estella's hand, her methods and approach the direct opposite of the police. Her questions were peppered with understanding, tissues, and sympathy. What might Claire have taken? Do you know where she had been during the hours before you found her? Is there anything you can tell us that might help the doctors treat her more effectively?

With her head cradled in her hands, Estella moaned. "I did the best I could...tried to be there for her...help her. What else could I have done?"

Pleading eyes searched the face of the nurse sitting next to her. The nurse's sole thought was Estella's recriminations, hand-wringing, and tears were hindering rather than helping her daughter.

In the trauma room, the doctors were hard at work. All visible signs pointed to a drug overdose. The paramedics were able to collect a urine sample during transport. The tox screen showed a mix of drugs. The next step, administer naloxone. Then stand back.

Claire came to with a jolt. Her eyes darted around the room.

"What the fuck? Where am I?" Anger fueled her outburst. With her arms flailing wildly, she attempted to push herself off the bed. The nurse's assistant grabbed her arms and pushed her back down, then checked her left arm to make sure the IV line was still connected and functioning properly.

"You're in the hospital," said the doctor. "Your mother found you unconscious. Now calm down or we'll have to put you in restraints."

Claire glared at the doctor standing over her. He met her stare with one of his own.

"We're treating you for a drug overdose. Can you tell us what you took?"

"I didn't take anything." Deny, deny, deny—Claire's fallback response when confronted.

"We both know that's not true," said the doctor softly. "If you tell me what you took, I can make sure the care I arrange for you provides you with the best possible outcome."

"I had a few drinks with friends. That's all."

"And when was this? Your mother told us she hadn't seen you for a few days."

"Saturday." Confusion crossed Claire's face. Rubbing her forehead, she asked, "What day is it?"

"It's eleven o'clock Sunday night. So you had a few drinks with friends yesterday? On Saturday? Or was it Friday night, perhaps?" And, not waiting for a response he continued, "What else did you share with your friends?"

Claire's eyes signaled her next move. The nurse read it right and produced the bed pan with lightning speed. She supported Claire's back as she proceeded to vomit, although there was no food in her stomach to throw up. Claire struggled to control her stomach spasms. Yellow bile coated the bottom of the bed pan. Foamy spittle dripped from her mouth.

Claire lay back down and closed her eyes. This couldn't be happening. The room was spinning. Try as she might to recall any details, her mind was blank. She couldn't remember anything. She didn't have answers to the questions they kept asking her.

"Stop," cried Claire. "I don't know anything. I just want to sleep. Please let me sleep." She closed her eyes, willing oblivion to take her.

"You rest now," said the doctor, placing his hand gently on her shoulder. "We can talk more later. Your mother has agreed to have you admitted for a seventy-two hour observation, to make sure you're okay and the drugs get out of your system."

Denial engulfed Estella. Looking at her only daughter asleep in the hospital bed unnerved her. How could this be happening?

No matter what happened, acknowledging it—let alone taking responsibility for it—made it real, too real for Estella to handle. To her, Claire could do no wrong. She was young, had a lot of spirit like Estella did when she was young. And when something went wrong, some nameless, faceless person was always responsible. Not her precious Claire.

A fancy machine with a TV monitor loomed over Claire's bedside, beeping every few seconds. A thin line moved across the screen, intermittently peaking sharply and dropping back down. There were lots of numbers. A bag dripped fluid through a tube into Claire's arm. A small clamp-like device clipped to her index finger had a wire connecting it to the TV monitor. The nurse had told her what all the machines did and what the numbers meant. Estella couldn't remember a thing.

Confronting Claire's drug problem head-on was more than Estella could bear. But bear it she must. In her heart she knew Claire needed help, so Estella made her latest deal with God.

Make her well. Let her be well, and I promise to be a better mother. I'll stop running around. I'll stay home and take care of my children, all of my children. I'll get a good job. I promise. Let her live.

When the doctor suggested Claire be admitted for a seventy-two hour psych evaluation, Estella gave her consent. If only the doctors could find out what was behind the drug use. Maybe they could help her before it was too late. Hopefully, Claire would cooperate. There was no guarantee.

"Mama?" A feeble whisper reached Estella's heart.

"I'm here." Getting up from the chair, Estella came to the bedside. Taking Claire's hand, she repeated lovingly, "I'm here baby. Mama's here."

"What happened?"

"I found you at home. I couldn't wake you, so I called 911. They brought you here. You're in the hospital. The doctor says we got to you in time. You're going to be fine."

Tears welled in Claire's eyes, matching her mother's.

"I'm sorry, Mama. I'm so sorry."

"Shhhh. Everything is going to be fine. You rest. I'm right here."

Estella leaned in and kissed Claire's forehead. Gently, she stroked her cheek and brushed strands of hair away from her face. She took her daughter's hand and held it tightly, fearing Claire would somehow vanish if she let go. So they held hands and sat looking at each other, smiling, working hard to ease each other's pain.

After a few minutes Estella said, "When you feel able, Uncle TJ wants to talk to you. He and Aunt Rosa are in the waiting room with your brothers."

"What does he want to talk to me about?"

"It's Bella. She's missing. No one has seen her since late

Friday. She left her mother a message saying you two were going to the library. But your brothers told Uncle TJ you went out clubbing with a girlfriend Friday night. They didn't know who she was. Do you remember going to the library with Bella?"

"Oh," Claire gasped. Disjointed images flashed in her brain.

TJ remained behind when Rosa, Estella, and the boys left Claire's room. Their hour-long visit had been a roller coaster of tears and laughter.

TJ was quickly running out of patience. Dark visions of what might be happening to his baby girl filled his mind. For the past hour he'd been fighting back tears. He focused ahead, preferring to shed tears of joy when they found Bella rather than tears of fear and grief now when he needed to be clear-headed and ready for anything. He had questions that demanded answers. Claire was the only one who could provide them. Claire would provide them.

Kyle loomed in the doorway to Claire's room, standing over six feet tall, with mocha-tanned skin, a bald head, and a square jaw accented by a neatly trimmed goatee and intense hazel-green eyes.

He didn't know Claire well and did not want to intrude. But he wanted to be there for TJ. They'd been through a lot together. This was the next big thing in a long string of big things they had overcome together. TJ and his wife and kids were family, almost the only family Kyle had.

"Claire, what can you tell me about Bella?" asked TJ. "Do you know where she is?" His voice was soft. His tone warm and loving.

Claire's teeth raked her upper lip. She looked into her uncle's eyes, seeing hurt and pain and fear lurking there. Her own fears forced her to turn away.

"Uncle TJ, I'm really tired right now," she said as she faced the windows. "Can we talk later?" Guilt pressed heavily on her heart.

"No, sweetheart. Not really. I need to know about Bella. I'm worried about her. No one has seen her since she left to go to your house Friday afternoon. She hasn't been home. Aunt Rosa and I are very worried. Can you tell me anything?"

"I'm so tired. I…I can't remember."

She kept her head turned away from TJ, praying he couldn't see her face. She did remember—all of it. The club. The drugs. The deal. She had no idea where Bella was, or if she was hurt, or…or worse. It would take time to get rid of the guilt pressing on her heart and souring her stomach. That clock couldn't start ticking until Bella was home safe and sound. Any other outcome could prove fatal for Claire.

TJ and Kyle exchanged looks. Claire's refusal to make eye contact with TJ meant a great deal. She was hiding something, knew something she didn't want to tell them.

"Try to remember, honey." TJ reached for Claire's hand. "Even the smallest detail could help. What time did she leave your house? Did you two go out together? Where did you go? Anything that might help me find her."

"Bite me." Glowering eyes met his as a defiant Claire snatched her hand away and turned back from the window to face him. Her anger surprised both of them.

"What? What did you say?"

"Bite me."

Her vicious tone and menacing smile enraged him. He hadn't felt this level of fury since Iraq, when he witnessed unspeakable atrocities perpetrated on human beings by people claiming to be acting in God's name. TJ lost it. His arm went up. Kyle's swift move caught its downward swing before it made contact.

"Are we done?" hissed Claire.

TJ grabbed Claire's arms, lifting her off the bed, shaking her violently.

"Hey, man. Let her go." Kyle's firm grip on TJ's shoulder got his attention and stopped him.

He let go with a forceful push. She dropped back to the bed.

"We are a long way from done, little girl." Rage roughened TJ's voice, and he towered over her as she lay in bed.

Then his tone changed, low and slow, and he seethed, "Bella is missing, and I know you are up to your pretty little eyeballs in this. What happened? What did you do? What did you talk her into? You have a lot to tell me, little girl. And you better start talking now."

Claire cowered in the bed.

"Talk. What happened Friday night?"

"Oh God...oh God...oh God." A barely audible whisper followed. "I sold her."

"What? I'm sorry. I couldn't hear you. What did you say?"

"I...I...I didn't know what else to do. It's not my fault. I didn't have the money I owed them. I was scared. They said they wouldn't hurt her, just give her a moment of ecstasy, a night she would never forget."

TJ struggled to wrap his head around what he was hearing, what she was saying.

"You *sold* her?"

"I owed them money. Someone wanted a virgin. She is..." And then, after a long pause, "...was. They won't hurt her. They p-promised me they'd let her g-go after they w-were d-done." Mucus oozed from her nose, mixing with tears rolling down her cheeks. Her voice hitched and she stuttered as she fought for breaths in between her sobs.

"Keep going," demanded TJ.

"We were at this club. We were dancing, and then she wanted to go home. And I told her a little while longer... And she went to the bathroom, and then I started making out with Pete...and we fell out the door...and...and...I don't remember anything after that."

"You're both underage. How did you get in?" asked Kyle.

"I got us fake IDs. And we dressed up. I helped Bella get all dressed up. She looked great."

"What club?"

"I don't remember."

"What. Club." TJ's eyes bored into her shriveled little soul.

Her arms rose protectively around her head as she cowered in the face of her uncle's rage.

"Metamorphosis. It's called Metamorphosis. Out on Route 1, past the railroad tracks. I swear, Uncle TJ. That's all I remember."

TJ raced out of Claire's room with Kyle on his six. He passed Rosa, Estella and the boys without a word. Rosa's questioning eyes met Kyle's.

"You don't want to know." Kyle's words hung in the air as he hurried down the hall after TJ.

The two men started back to the compound without saying a word. What was there to say? Claire's admission hit them both hard. Kyle stared out the window as he went over what he had heard again.

TJ pounded the steering wheel.

"Damn it. Did you hear her? She sold my baby girl. What the fuck was she thinking?"

"She wasn't thinking."

"I really lost it back there. Almost hit her. Thanks for stopping me."

"That wasn't you. It was your old man."

TJ shot Kyle a knowing look. "What am I going to do? What am I supposed to do now?"

"We," Kyle said, with clear emphasis on the we, "are going to get the guys together and take care of business. Like we always do."

"Not a word of this to Rosa. Understood?"

"Definitely. I'll call in. Ask Marco to get everyone together."

It was midnight. Nine serious men had been huddled in the library at Marco's home since TJ and Kyle returned from the hospital, hard at work planning and calculating what to do next. A soft knock reached Marco's ears.

"Come in."

"May I replenish the table, sir?" Jesse surveyed the remains of an evening's food offerings. His philosophy, that people couldn't do anything well on an empty stomach, was borne out by the empty chafing dishes and mounds of dirty plates.

"Yes, please. And bring more coffee. The stronger the better," said Marco.

"Do you have any of those cinnamon sweet roll things?" asked Kyle. "I could use some sugar."

"I'll see what I can do, sir."

Some stood, some paced, some sat staring off into nothingness. All were strong men of action; none of them were any good at waiting. All eyes were on TJ. He stood just under six feet tall, with deep set brown eyes, a long, thin nose and jutting chin, with not an ounce of fat on his body. He was nimble on his feet, agile on any terrain, and a born leader. Marco loved him like the son he never had, always thinking that if he'd had a son he would have wanted him to be just like TJ.

TJ hadn't said much in the last hour. Claire's revelation, that she had sold her cousin, his precious baby girl, to pay for her drug habit, took over, shredding his brain like a patch of briars, decimating his self-control. TJ was normally optimistic about life, but pessimistic about people because, in his experience, most people were frail, designed to disappoint.

A father's worst nightmare was now his inescapable companion. Right now, all he wanted was to find and reclaim what was his. No point in doing the blame game. There would be more than enough time later to sort out who did what, and who was responsible. And to mete out punishment.

Kyle saw the fire in his friend's eyes. He'd seen that look and that side of him on the battlefield, where it belonged. He knew TJ could be ruthless when pushed. And right now, he was being pushed close to his limit.

"We've been at this for hours. What have we got?" asked Brett, the group's computer geek. For him the answers lived in cyberspace. Without his computer he was lost.

"Not much. We've got a club name: Metamorphosis. Two guys: Rick and Pete. Beyond that, nothing." Pushing himself out of the chair, TJ walked to the door. "Be right back. I need some air."

"Let him go," said Marco, grabbing Kyle's arm as he sprang to his feet. "This is personal, blood personal. He needs some space. He'll sort it out and be back ready to work."

Sensing the need for a calmer, fatherly figure, Marco took the lead. "According to its website, Metamorphosis is, and I quote, 'an exciting, hip dance club to meet and be seen, with famous DJs spinning the latest music through the best sound system, and dramatic lighting to energize your every move and keep you dancing all night.'"

"Makes me want to run right over," said Brett, feigning a smile. "All those hot chicks in slinky tops."

"Hell, man. You're too old and too married for this stuff. Now, I'm still single, a stud if I do say so myself, and ready to parrr-DEE," said Steve, adding some hip gyrations for emphasis and sliding his hand across his head. "You know what they say, bald is beautiful."

"Shit, we're all too old," said Russ. "Not sure our knees can take it anymore. Too beat up pounding out other moves."

"If I may continue," smirked Marco. "We know two names, Pete and Rick. We're assuming they're street hustlers into easy scores. Trying to make names for themselves. Gain some credibility with their peers. Sounds like Claire knew them before Friday night."

"The whole thing seems amateurish," said Casey, who had been quiet most of the night. "Not well thought out. Claire shows up at home. How did that happen? Did they let her go? Drive her home? Or was she passed out somewhere? Woke up and stumbled home. Something's not right."

"You should have seen her," said Kyle. "I was standing in the doorway. She went from drugged-out sleepy to major bitch lashing out like a rattlesnake striking its prey. It was scary how fast she turned. Real Jekyll and Hyde stuff. Glad I can still move. I saw TJ's arm go up to take a swing. If I'd been a step slower, he would have broken her jaw. I'm sure of it."

"Let's nail down specifics of the recon," said Brett. "We're still agreed that recon should be our first step, right?"

"Actionable intel's a must at this point. Need to get a look inside this Metamorphosis club," said Kyle.

"I can do some selective hacking to see if there are any floor plans out there," Brett said.

"I love it when you talk all geeky," kidded Casey.

Brett flipped Casey the finger and got one in return.

"Good place to start, Brett, I agree," said Dom. "None of us can go to the club. We'd stick out like a sore thumb. Don't fit the profile of club goers."

"Speak for yourself," chided Steve. "I could still pass."

"In your dreams, man. In your dreams," laughed Kyle. "Dom's right. We need someone younger. Knowing how to dance wouldn't hurt. Maybe a couple. Look less obvious."

"What about the new guy, Art? He's young. Looks like he may have a move or two left in him." said Casey. "He's on patrol now. Maybe hook him up with Tina."

"Brett, call them please," said Marco. "Ask them to stop up here on their next pass down the beach."

"You got it."

Darkness surrounded Bella. Her body was moving. No, not her body exactly. Everything was moving. And there was music. In a car? But it was so dark. And cramped. She reached out and felt around with trembling hands. A trunk. She was inside the trunk of a car. Panic seized her. Gulping for air helped her stifle her scream. *How long have I been here? Where's here?*

Her head was spinning. Her heart racing. Hours, minutes, seconds blurred together. Feeling around the trunk, she decided she was alone. Where was Claire? She struggled through her fear to focus on the last thing she remembered. Dancing at a club. Rick. Feeling sick. Dizziness in the bathroom. Claire and Pete falling into an alley. Running to help Claire. A sharp prick in her neck. Then nothing. Until now.

She'd let her guard down. How could she have been so stupid? She was sure she'd been drugged. With what? How?

Something in her drinks? The Margaritas. She rubbed her neck, thinking about the sudden sharp pinprick.

Her parents were going to kill her if her captors didn't do it first. Tears ran down her cheeks at the thought of her parents. Pulling her knees tightly to her chest and wrapping her arms around them, she sobbed softly for the only two people she wanted to see right now.

"Mommy. Daddy. Help me."

She longed for them desperately, aching to be home and safe in their arms. They would be furious with her. She was furious with herself. How could she have let Claire talk her into doing something so stupid? And lying to her parents?

Voices. Male voices. She smelled cigarettes. The music got louder. The car swerved one way, then the other. Nausea roiled through her with every turn and bump in the road, but throwing up was not an option in this small, cramped space.

The car was slowing down. Several bumps jarred her. Railroad tracks? The car made a few more turns. Tires crunching over gravel. Then everything stopped. No movement. Car doors slammed. Silence.

"What about her?" An unknown male voice.

"She'll be fine. Be out for hours." A different voice. Deeper, with an accent.

"Can't believe Julio's customer put off the drop. How long does he think we can drive around with her in the trunk?"

"Got me. As long as we keep her drugged she won't be a problem."

"Unless we get stopped by some nosy cop and he wants you to pop the trunk."

"Then I better make sure we don't get stopped. Gotta admit. She is one sweet thing. Wouldn't mind doing her myself."

"Don't even think it. The guy wants a virgin and that's what we better deliver if we want to live. Let's go. I'm starving."

What sounded like a fist hitting the trunk lid made Bella jump. She heard gravel crunching. Then nothing. Whoever they were, they were gone—at least for the moment.

Some man wants to rape me because I'm a virgin? Oh shit! No way! I've got to get out of here.

Think. Think!! I've got to get out. Have to escape. Have to get home.

But how? Focus. Concentrate.

Rubbing her eyes, she thought about her father. Though he didn't like to talk about it, every once in a while he did talk to her brother, Eddie, about his experiences during Desert Storm. Her father had been a SEAL. She used to eavesdrop so she could hear his stories. What would he do now?

And his words—his voice—broke through the drug haze, emerging slowly into her consciousness.

You're a smart girl, Bella. Stay calm. Don't panic. Assess your surroundings. Make a plan.

She repeated the words. If she was going to get out of this mess, it had to be through her own efforts. Wiping away useless tears, Bella took three deep, slow breaths. The voice she heard had claimed to be hungry. The footsteps had gone away from the car. If there was ever a time to escape, it was now.

First, get out of this trunk. The realization that she actually knew how to do that charged her with confidence. There's a latch. Her driver education teacher had talked about it during one of the classes. The students laughed when he said it even glowed. Not all cars had it. Only newer models. Maybe this one did. Uttering a little prayer, Bella thrust her hands out in front of her, groping in the darkness, twisting her body so she could look for the glow in the darkness that promised freedom.

There! Pull!

She heard a click, and the trunk popped up slightly. Dim light filtered through the narrow opening. She didn't know where the guys had gone, or if they were watching the car. If they were watching, they would see if the trunk flew open. Keep it low. Keep it close.

With one hand on the trunk lid, and the other underneath her to give her leverage, Bella slowly stuck her right leg out of the trunk and twisted her body forward so her foot could connect to the ground. Then she rolled her body over the lower trunk frame and slid out enough to get her left leg underneath her—

And fell flat on her face when her knees gave out and the world tipped and spun. She shook her head sharply, took two more breaths, very slowly, and when the spinning slowed, she closed the lid carefully, silently, and crouched behind the trunk.

Bella saw she was in the parking lot of an all-night diner. Fortunately, whoever had grabbed her had parked far away from any lights. Only two other cars were visible, and Bella could see inside the diner. A couple shared a booth overlooking the parking lot, and two guys were sitting at the counter, their backs to the lot, talking to the waitress. They must be her captors. No one else was in sight.

Turning around, Bella saw where the main road passed in front of the diner. That was her target. Get out to the road and then decide which way to go. A row of trees ran alongside the diner's driveway down to the road. The trees would give her cover. She'd head for them.

Shaking out her stiff, wobbly legs, Bella urged her body forward. Her knees buckled with her very first step and she went down again, dirt, stones and glass shards digging into her knees and the palms of her hands. Pushing herself up, Bella staggered forward, repeating her mantra—stay low, stay low, stay low. Her movements were tight and slow to the tree line, slow and careful in spite of the sharp rocks cutting into the soles of her bare feet. Shoes would have been helpful, but not the five inch stilettos she wore to the dance club.

Bella leaned against the first tree and removed a shard of glass from her big toe, then brushed off other small stones embedded in the soles of her feet. Her breaths came fast and furious. No time to rest. She hugged the tree line all the way to the road.

Deserted. Not a single person in sight. Nothing looked familiar. Buildings and storefronts lined the road to her left. To her right, a railroad crossing and open fields stretched endlessly. Easy choice. Head left. No reason to tempt fate and risk being seen from the diner.

Bella limped along. Staying in the shadows of shrubbery and buildings gave her some cover. More stores appeared. Buildings got larger and closer together. She could see laundry hanging when she looked down darkened alleys. Laundry meant apartments. Apartments meant people. People meant help. Signs in the store windows were in Spanish. But she saw no people. No cops. Nobody.

Overcome by dizziness, Bella labored with every step. Finally, waves of nausea forced her to stop. She leaned against a building while her stomach convulsed. Nothing came up. Her head pounded. Saliva dripped from the corners of her mouth. Wanting desperately to rest, Bella turned down an alley, searching for someplace to hide for an hour or two.

She finally found a rusty green dumpster piled so high with foul-smelling black garbage bags that its lid was propped almost all the way open. The stench started another wave of the dry heaves. Exhausted, she could go no farther.

Bella wedged herself between the dumpster and the cold brick wall of a building. Pushing herself as far back into the darkness as she could, Bella slumped into her repulsive sanctuary.

So far so good. I'll rest for a bit. Those guys will never find me here. Maybe a store will be open soon and I can get help.

Bella mouthed a silent prayer that daylight would bring a savior across her path, someone to help her get home.

CHAPTER 9

Monday

Daniel rolled over onto his back. Raindrops splashed against the window. Most mornings he loved the sound of rain, found its patter against the window soothing. He didn't love it when he had to be someplace. And today he had to be someplace.

Shit, why were the weathermen always right when he had an important meeting and no umbrella? Maybe it would stop before he had to leave the hotel.

Rubbing sleep from his eyes, he moved his arms above his head, pushed his hands against the headboard and stretched through to his toes.

God, that felt good.

Red digital numbers on the clock told him he had plenty of time to shower, shave and grab some coffee before his nine o'clock meeting. He could lie here a few more minutes.

His lower back screamed for Aleve. The drive to D.C. last night qualified as a trip from hell. Four hours turned into six. There had been a time when he could do the drive easily without any stops. Now, however, neither his bones nor his bladder cooperated.

To make matters worse, he'd left Brooklyn later than he wanted, which landed him in some version of rush hour traffic through much of New Jersey. And Mother Nature decided to make it rain all the way. It was close to midnight when he got to his room. He decided a quick swim to loosen up stiff muscles and some time in the steam room would help him sleep. The TV turned itself off at two a.m.

He was emotionally spent, Rachel front and center on his mind. Her sudden heart issue scared him. He replayed their conversation from last night. She was direct—more direct than he expected or wanted—emphatically told him not to make a rushed trip to Florida today. She swore she was fine. The heart palpitations episode had passed. She'd spent several hours under the watchful eyes of the doctors. Sara was playing the mother-hen role quite well. Besides, he had an appointment to discuss a new project that might ease his transition into retirement. That was important. They'd see each other Tuesday when he picked her up at the airport.

He thought about the case he caught late yesterday. Wife stabbed her husband with a kitchen knife after he admitted to cheating with his secretary. Then the secretary showed up at the guy's house. The two women leapt into a major cat fight, clawing at each other on the front steps. Neighbors whooped it up, enjoying the show. Two street cops could barely pull them apart. One cop sustained a huge gash above his eye when the wife swatted him and her diamond ring cut into his skin. Heavy bleeder. He'd surely need a few stitches.

What is it with people and their commitments? He thought of Anna, his beloved wife, whom he'd lost when the North Tower came down. All the years they were married, the idea of cheating on her never crossed his mind. But so many husbands and wives cheated.

What was that all about? What made husbands stray? Was it midlife crisis? So many men turned into couch potatoes, absorbed in sports and video games. Some went the workaholic route. Or they cheated, seeking the magic they once had with their wives. When they found it—if they found it—they got hooked.

And wives weren't innocent victims. Some embraced the mommy role to the point that their kids became all-consuming. They forgot about, or were too tired, for the wife and lover roles. They had no time for their husbands, who began to take them for granted. Resenting this, they indulged their fantasies and were easily seduced by the first man who paid attention to them. An innocent flirt led to coffee, then lunch, and then dessert, the kind that isn't fattening. It was enticing—mysterious, and naughty, like in romance novels. Was it worth it in the end? Rarely. Almost always ended in broken marriages, hurt children, destruction and sometimes death.

His relationship with Rachel was barely eight months old. He was smitten. The idea of being unfaithful, though they'd yet to make any firm commitments to each other, was the furthest thing from his mind. Hardly a day went by that he didn't thank God for bringing her into his life. Who would have guessed his investigation into a rash of elderly deaths— where the deceased had all been represented by the same lawyer—could have such a wonderful outcome? Okay, not so great for them. Fantastic for him.

This morning's meeting could prove interesting. Mac McCoy, an old Marine buddy, had called last week, inviting him to a breakfast meeting with the Deputy Director for Special Projects at FBI headquarters. The call's timing couldn't have been better.

He had been sitting behind his desk in his almost empty office thinking about his retirement. Soiled edges and nails showed where photos, citations and remembrances of over thirty years of service had hung on his office walls. His awards and commendations were now in a box on the credenza. The framed American flag that had flown over Bagram Air Base, given to him by a returning soldier, now had a new home above his bookcase in his apartment. An empty office surrounded him. Without this job—not being detective Daniel Berger—who was he? Who would he be?

Enough! Getting out of bed, he flipped on the TV, tuned in to Fox, and headed for the shower. Time to get his head screwed on straight for his meeting.

Thankfully, the rain had stopped. Daniel knew he looked good as he walked up to the first of several security checkpoints at the entrance into FBI headquarters. He had chosen to wear his lucky suit, a crisp charcoal gray with a hint of a white stripe. Whenever he wore it, things seemed to go his way. In Daniel's mind, a white shirt was de rigueur for a meeting at the FBI. He decided to show a little flair by selecting a purple, red and yellow paisley tie.

The officer checked his credentials and photo ID. Daniel handed him his firearm and went through the metal detector. Clearing security, he walked into the courtyard of the Hoover building at eight fifty a.m. More security. More screening. More protection. 9/11 had changed America. The naiveté, the "it couldn't happen here" bubble had burst. Now Americans were on guard. Unfortunately, not as on guard as they had been right after it happened. He could see ever-increasing signs that people were becoming lax and complacent. Had too many forgotten the lessons of 9/11?

"Hey, Detective Berger. Danny."

Turning toward the voice, Daniel came face to face with Mac McCoy. They had joined the NYPD together. Mac left after a few years to join the FBI.

And he recognized the man standing beside Mac, Jim Greene, a member of the FBI's Organized Crime Bureau. Their paths had crossed last October when they were both trying to get Ben Collins, the lawyer Daniel had been investigating about the elderly deaths in Brooklyn, to turn on a loan shark named Anthony D'Angeli—Big Al. Greene's deal with Collins to become a witness against D'Angeli had won out over anything Daniel could offer him. Collins was the loser in every respect. He never got to take advantage of the WITSEC deal. They found him dead of ricin poisoning in his apartment several days later.

"Hey, Mac. Great to see you. How's Peg? Your boys?" A man hug followed.

"Everyone's fine. Both boys are Marines now. Serving their country like we did."

Daniel turned to Jim Greene.

"Well, this is a surprise. Or is it?" asked Daniel. "Since I don't believe in coincidences, I take it this is not a chance meeting."

"Good thinking," replied Greene with a chuckle as they shook hands. "Let's all grab some breakfast at the coffee shop across the street."

"Sounds like a plan."

Most of the breakfast crowd had gone. A perky hostess led them to a booth at the back of the restaurant, and steaming mugs of coffee arrived before they could even open the menus. The server returned a few minutes later and took their orders.

"What's this all about? Is there really a meeting with a big FBI guy, or was that a ruse to get me down here?"

"I love a man who gets to the point, don't you Mac?" said Greene. "It's about you. We heard a rumor you were retiring, leaving Brooklyn. That true?"

"Yeah. That's the plan, anyway. Aiming for June at this point. Hard to set a firm date. Cases keep piling up. Don't want to leave them short-handed." Taking a sip of coffee, he laughed, "Murderers are completely unwilling to adjust their activities to accommodate my retirement plans."

"I know what you mean," said Mac. "Peg's been bugging me for years to pull the plug. But every time I think about retiring, I look at the pile of cases on my desk and think there's no way I can leave right now."

Breakfast arrived. Conversation ceased as plates laden with bacon and eggs were set in front of them, salt and pepper passed, toast buttered, coffee mugs refiled.

"So what's this all about?" Daniel spoke directly to Jim Greene. He had a suspicion Jim's prompting had triggered this meeting. "And what's your part in all this, Mac?"

"Jim, you want to take the lead here."

"Sure thing. I have a new assignment. I'm heading a special task force to try and slow down if not stop the sex trafficking that's become a booming business in this country. Low overhead, low costs. The young and the innocent. Easy victims."

"I know we've got a big problem in New York. Worked several of those cases over the years. Too many to count. Cut my detective teeth on one. Dead girl in the park. Gruesome. Linked her to a sex crime ring but never found the guy who did it. Always haunted me."

"How come? What made it stand out?" asked Jim.

"A seven-year-old kid playing hide and seek found the body. I always wondered what happened to him. Not something you get over without help. Didn't get the sense he'd get any. His father had a screw loose—a total jerk."

"It's gotten a lot worse. A lot of young girls," said Mac, waving a piece of bacon in the air. "Gullible. Stars in their eyes. They want to experience what they read about in magazines. Become famous. Get themselves involved with some scumbag, and before you know it they're strung out on drugs, prostitutes winding up dead along isolated stretches of roadway or hidden deep in wooded areas."

"New York, L.A., and Florida are hot spots. D.C., Chicago, Atlanta and Phoenix aren't far behind," said Jim.

The serious tone of the conversation sucked Daniel in. He stopped eating and started listening carefully. They all understood the problem. And he was being offered an opportunity to become part of the solution.

"Mac and I have been tasked with pulling together a group of law enforcement people who are aggressive, competitive, smart problem-solvers. We're recruiting them from a few different agencies across the country to focus one hundred percent on sex trafficking crimes. Mac thought of you—said you think outside the box."

"My partner, Cooper, calls it my detective gut."

"Then it's a good gut. He told me how you stopped that terrorist plot against the Lion King matinee, saving all those children. Impressive, Detective, very impressive."

"Thanks. I caught a lucky break."

"Lucky for a lot of children," added Mac.

"And when I heard you were retiring, well, I thought maybe I could entice you into giving this a shot," said Jim. "Can't see you sidelining yourself. And I'm willing to bet you'll need something you can sink your teeth into when you do make the move."

"You've got a point. I've always been afraid that I'll get old and fat and stupid once I retire. Kept me in the game way longer than I planned. Emptied out my office last week. Depressing. Felt like I was coming close to my expiration date."

"A little over the top, don't you think? You've a long way to go and lots to look forward to," said Mac. "I hear you're crazy about a woman named Rachel. You can't tell me being with her doesn't fire up your furnace."

"I see you've done your homework." Daniel's grin spread from ear to ear. "Yes, Rachel is one terrific lady. Got lucky. But I think I need more."

"Figured you might. Cold-turkey retirement doesn't seem like a good exit strategy," said Jim.

"There have been task forces for years," challenged Daniel. "Haven't amounted to much. What's going to be different now?"

"This task force, we're calling it Project Buyers Beware," said Mac. "The more traditional route of going after the prostitutes hasn't worked. We've convinced some higher-ups that going after the buyers and the suppliers—you know, follow the money—might be a better tack to take. Break the backs of the traffickers."

"We're bringing in key people from across the country, fresh eyes, people not steeped in FBI protocols and culture. People who color outside the lines. People who don't give a rip about playing nice and getting along," added Jim.

"And we want you," said Mac. "We see you as a valuable resource, too good to be put out to pasture."

"Thanks," said Daniel. He looked from Mac to Jim. "As soon as I joined the force, I knew I wanted to join homicide, earn my gold shield, put the bad guys away, make a difference."

"Right. And you did that. Here's your chance to keep doing it. Different bad guys, live victims, though sometimes, sad to say, we do get a body or two," said Jim.

"Is there anything else I can get you gentlemen?" asked the server as she cleared away empty plates.

"Just a refill on the coffee," said Jim, "and I'll take the check."

"Whoa. Thank you, Uncle Sam," laughed Daniel.

A million thoughts swirled in Daniel's mind. This might be the answer to his prayers. He thought about Rachel and the great times they'd had these past few months. Christmas in Williamsburg was magical. The whole town turned out for the Grand Illumination and First Night celebrations. He was looking forward to spending more time with her, making plans, making a new life with her.

But a deeper fear always haunted these images. Boredom with retirement life might taint and ruin what they had going if he didn't have enough to keep him busy. He'd get old, stale, stodgy.

These two guys were giving him an opportunity to stay in the game. He needed more information, to be sure, but still... What was the saying about God opening a window even as He closed a door. Had his window just opened?

Bella rubbed her eyes. It was light out. She must have been asleep for hours. Moving slowly she crept out from behind the dumpster and peeked down the alley. Cars were speeding down the main street. People hurried past the alley's entrance on their way to work. Several young kids ran through the alley with their backpacks heading for school. None looked her way.

Bella's only thought was to get home. Find a phone. Call her mother to come get her. She watched the people who used the alley as a short cut, hoping to see someone who could help her—someone who looked kind—someone she could trust. Voices drew her attention to the far end of the alley. A gray-haired woman with a young boy in tow approached her hiding place.

Remembering the windows she passed a few hours earlier

she spoke her plea in Spanish. "Abuela, abuela, ayúdame," whispered Bella, revealing herself to the elderly, gentle-looking woman.

"Madre de Dios! Nina, ¿Qué te pasó?" The startled woman's hand instinctively went to her mouth.

"¿Hablas inglés?"

"No inglés."

Damn, thought Bella. Dear God, I hope my high school Spanish is enough.

"¿Llamo a la policía?" asked the woman. The boy tucked in behind her leg, hiding himself in the folds of her turquoise flowered skirt, his brown, doe-like eyes wide with fear.

Easy one, she thought. I need a phone to call home.

"No policía, por favor. Mi madre. Necesito un teléfono, por favor. Tengo que llamar a mi madre," wept Bella as she grabbed for the woman's skirt. "Dame el teléfono. Quero llamar a mi madre." Tears streamed down Bella's cheeks.

The woman held out her phone. Bella grabbed it. Fingers shaking, she punched in her mother's cell number. Bella swallowed back her tears while she listened to endless ringing. Then finally, the only voice Bella longed to hear.

"Mama, help me," sobbed Bella.

"Bella, my God, Bella. We've been so worried. Where are you?"

"I don't know. Help me, Mama!"

"Tell me where you are and I'll come get you."

Turning once again to the woman, Bella asked, "¿Dónde estoy? ¿Que calle está esta calle? ¿Cuál es la dirección?"

"No sé. Espera aquí. Preguntaré en la gasolinera."

"Gracias. Por favor no digas nada de mí." Returning to her mother, she said, "The woman who gave me the phone is going to ask someone at the gas station where we are. Oh, Mama, I am so scared."

"Shhhh, baby. It's okay. Don't cry. I know you're scared.

As soon as you tell us where you are, we'll be there as fast as we can. Everything will be okay."

Minutes seemed like hours. *Where is she? Is she coming back?* The wait was agonizing. Then the woman appeared. Crossing the street, dragging the little boy, who struggled against her grip.

Bella relayed her location to her mother.

"Stay where you are. I'm going to grab Karli. We're on our way."

Handing the phone back to the woman, Bella said, "Muchas gracias, abuela."

"¿Qué más puedo hacer para ayudarte?" *Is there anything else I can do to help you?*

"Nada. Mi madre está en su coche ahora. No se lo digas a nadie de mí. Y muchas gracias. Muchas gracias." *No, nothing. Don't tell anyone you've seen me. And thank you. Thank you so much.*

Bella could see the woman did not want to leave her alone there, but knew if she remained she would draw attention. And her grandson was clearly scared.

"Aquí. Toma mi teléfono. Cuando venga tu madre, tú puedes devolvérmelo. Estaré en el minimercado." Bella had made a good choice. The woman handed Bella her phone.

Bella hugged the phone to her chest—her lifeline. Words of thanks poured from her lips. Insufficient, but they were all she had. Followed by a whispered thank you aimed toward heaven. Only He could have sent such a kind woman down such a dirty alley to save her. Could Bella now rescue Claire?

God had answered Rosa's prayers. She and Karli flew out of the compound in Karli's silver Acura MDX. TJ and Kyle followed in the Range Rover. The car's navigation system showed that Bella was somewhere west of the Florida turnpike, a forty minute drive if they didn't hit traffic. But it was Monday morning. People were going to work. Traffic was a given.

"She didn't want me to tell her dad," said Rosa. "She's going to be angry with me."

"No, she's not. Not telling TJ would have been wrong. We don't know where we're going. Having TJ and Kyle with us is the smart call, the right thing to do, Rosa. Who knows what we'll find."

"I know you're right. But...she sounded so scared."

"I'm sure she is scared...very scared. Everything will be okay. We'll get to her and bring her home." As Karli spoke, her hand gently stroked Rosa's arm.

The two cars crossed the inlet bridge and picked up A1A south. As expected, heavy traffic. TJ called Karli, telling her to let him take the lead and to stay close. She maneuvered into the right lane to let him pass her and then tucked in behind him. He turned off A1A onto West Indiantown Road. It would be stop and go for miles, but this was the most direct route to Bella. TJ weaved in and out of traffic—sped up—then was forced to slam on the brakes. Karli did her best to stay behind him and avoid plowing into him.

As they drove over the turnpike overpass, Rosa's nerves began to get the best of her.

"What if she's hurt?"

"Don't go there," said Karli. "Don't even think it. We'll know soon enough. And we'll take care of her. Whatever we have to do. We'll take care of her. You know we will."

"Yes, I know. I'm..." Rosa bit her lip and stared out the window at the stores that were opening for business on this bright, sunny Florida morning.

"TJ was so angry when he left the hospital yesterday. He

and Kyle were in Claire's room, and then he stormed out. So unlike him. I don't know what happened—what Claire said to make him so mad. And Kyle told me not to ask. Then they all went to Marco's. I haven't spoken to him since. I don't know what's happening."

"It will all be over soon. We'll pick her up, take care of what needs to be taken care of, and put this behind us."

"Thank you for coming. For being here with me. If you weren't driving right now I'd hug you."

"Hold that thought. I never pass up a hug."

TJ's car slowed and Karli followed suit. They were coming up to the intersection where Bella said she was hiding. They saw the gas station she mentioned to her mother. He turned into the alley across from the gas station and stopped the car. Four car doors slammed in unison.

"Let me, honey," said Rosa as she gently touched TJ's arm. "She didn't want me to tell you. She's ashamed."

Rosa walked down the alley with Karli a few steps behind her, their eyes darting in every direction, searching for any sign of Bella. TJ and Kyle waited by the cars and watched their progress.

"Bella. Bella. It's Mama, Bella. I'm here."

The wheels of the dumpster to Rosa's left squeaked as it moved out. Rosa and Karli stopped in their tracks. Bella darted from her hiding place into her mother's arms. TJ and Kyle ran down the alley.

"I'm here. We're all here. Your dad and I have got you. We won't let you go." Bella crumpled into her mother's arms and wept like a baby.

TJ drove while Rosa and Karli held Bella tightly between them in the back seat of Karli's SUV. He kept one eye on the road and the other in the rear view mirror. He could see his beautiful daughter clinging tightly to her mother, the glisten of tear tracks on her cheeks. She was safe. The men who did this, thought TJ, not so much.

The quick exam Karli conducted once they were home showed her to be in good shape. Karli cleaned her feet, gave her a tetanus shot and applied antibiotics to the cuts. Then she asked Bella for permission to do a pelvic exam. Bella wept but she consented. When she was finished, Karli assured her nothing had been stolen from her.

She was dehydrated and hungry, both problems quickly remedied by Rosa, who made her a grilled cheese sandwich, her favorite, which she quickly devoured. Clean after a long hot shower, fed, and given a sedative by Karli, Bella nestled into her own bed and promptly fell fast asleep. Karl said it would be several hours before she woke up. Rosa pulled her bedroom door to within an inch of closing. She wanted to be able to hear any movement, any indication Bella might need her.

"I can't thank you enough," said Rosa, hugging Karli tightly, "for all you've done. I don't know what I would have done if we lost her."

"You didn't, so get that thought out of your mind. She's going to be fine. Do you want me to give you something to help you unwind? A valium or two?"

"No. I'll be okay. I'm going to sit here." Rosa dropped into the kitchen chair. "TJ's back at Marco's. Lord only knows what they're planning."

"You don't want to know. Let them do their thing."

The back door burst opened. Marissa and Sophia rushed into the kitchen.

"Well, the gang's all here," laughed Karli.

"Where is she? How is she?" Marissa silently prayed for good news.

"She's sleeping," said Rosa.

"And, thank God, she is fine in all the physical senses of

that word," said Karli. "She will need to talk to someone about what happened, but it can wait a day or so. I'll make a few calls and get a good therapist lined up."

"Rosa, you know, whatever she needs, whatever you need. It's taken care of."

"Yes, Miss Marissa. I know and I am so grateful to all of you. How are you, Miss Sophia? Are you feeling better today?"

"A little tired still. But whatever I ate at the tournament is out of my system. Where's TJ?" asked Sophia.

"He went back up to Marco's once Karli gave us the good news that she had not been violated."

"Good. Not sure how a father actually works through all this," Sophia said while she busied herself opening drawers. Finally, she pulled out the corkscrew she had been searching for. "But I am sure the guys will help him get his head on straight. And I brought the wine to help us. Grab some glasses and let's go sit on the lanai."

"The men have been at Marco's for hours," said Karli as they settled themselves on the screened porch. "Anyone know what they're planning?"

"Better not to know." In the back of her mind, Marissa recognized that, in this instance, ignorance might be bliss. "Bella's back safe. That's what matters. Karli, you said she was not raped, so that's a really good thing. Claire is still in the hospital. Seventy-two hour hold for a psych eval. I suspect she's going to have some really difficult times ahead of her if she wants to kick the drugs."

"Claire's definitely going to need some help," said Karli. "During my residency I worked with a lot of young people trying to kick drugs. Some made it. Others didn't. There are so many variables. And let's face it, Claire doesn't exactly have a great home life. With all due respect, Rosa, your sister is no Mother Theresa."

"I know." Taking a sip of wine, Rosa leaned back into the sofa cushions. "She's got a lot of problems. And with four kids, way more than she can handle. I'm thinking of asking TJ to let Claire come live here for a while."

"Better check with Marco, too," said Sophia. "You know how he likes to have the final say about everything that happens on compound grounds."

"Not sure that's the best idea," said Karli. "Bella may not want her around once she finds out the truth."

"What truth?" Rosa put down her wine glass. Sitting up straight on the edge of the sofa, she looked directly at Karli, who suddenly realized she'd slipped. She knew something Rosa didn't yet know. TJ had not told her.

"Rosa, I love you dearly. You know that. I just made a huge mistake. I said something Dom told me in confidence when we talked a few minutes ago. He called to check on me, see how I was doing. I'm sorry. You need to talk to TJ."

"I will talk to TJ, but right now, I'm talking to you. What truth?" Rosa's voice didn't waver. Her riveting stare shackled Karli's eyes to her own. "You know something I need to know—have a right to know. Tell me." She pressed her lips tightly together, awaiting Karli's next words.

Karli looked from one woman to the next. Trapped. There was no way she could take back her words. She knew she had to break her husband's confidence and tell Rosa. She'd repair the damage with him later.

"Claire sold Bella to pay off her drug debt. At least that's what she told TJ at the hospital. That's why he went storming out. That's what she said to him."

Rosa's eyes widened. Her mouth fell open. Horrified, she slumped back into the sofa. Time stopped. No one spoke.

"Oh...my...God..." Marissa breathed.

"That can't be true." Rosa looked at Karli. "You must be mistaken. Claire's got her problems. But she wouldn't do that to Bella. We're family." Deep inside, Rosa knew what Karli said could easily be true.

Karli joined Rosa on the sofa. Hugging her tightly, she said, "I'm so sorry. I should never have said anything. I thought TJ told you."

"He wasn't here long enough to tell me anything. Once you told him—told us—she hadn't been violated, he kissed me and held me for a few minutes, then he went back up to Marco's. That was right when your cell rang."

Rosa broke away from Karli's hug. Her breaths came fast. She struggled to put the pieces together—to make sense of all that transpired since this nightmare began.

"I don't understand." Rosa sat back and looked into Karli's eyes. "How do you sell somebody? What does that mean?"

"Let's not get ahead of ourselves. Wanting to provide a safe place for Claire is very kind and very generous of you. Maybe Dom was wrong. Maybe I misunderstood. We only talked for a few minutes. Wait until you and TJ have a chance to talk, to really talk. Then you can decide what's best for Bella. And if what's best for Bella, and you all as a family, is to offer Claire a more stable place to heal, then I'm sure we can figure out a way to make it work."

Carolyn rested in the tan vinyl lounge chair in the corner of Desiree's hospital room, watching her sleep. She'd been at Desiree's side since the paramedics brought her to the hospital late yesterday afternoon. The doctors had pumped her stomach and given her Digibind to counteract the digoxin that showed up in her tox screen. She'd been asleep for hours.

The heart monitor made its rhythmic beeping sounds,

lulling Carolyn into her own private slumber. Things had gotten terribly out of hand after lunch yesterday at the tournament. She remembered Desiree saying she had a funny taste in her mouth, but chalked it up to indigestion. She'd popped an antacid and hadn't mentioned it again. Then all hell broke loose. So many women got sick. Desiree was one of the women transported to the hospital. Carolyn turned white when the nurse said they believed she had been poisoned. She flipped open the top of her silver ring and stared at the snowy white powder inside.

A soft murmur drew her attention to the bed. Snapping her ring closed, she went to Desiree's side and held her hand.

"Desiree. It's Carolyn. I'm here."

"Water." Her voice was so weak, Carolyn had trouble hearing her.

"Shhhh. It's okay. You've been through a lot. Let me get one of the nurses to make sure it's okay."

After returning with a nurse, who checked Desiree's vitals and assured her sipping water would be fine, Carolyn slowly lifted Desiree's head. She held the water container and straw for her.

"How are you feeling?"

"Tired." The word barely escaped her lips when she fell back into a semi-conscious sleep.

Carolyn brushed back a few strands of Desiree's hair and held her hand. What a strange twist of fate, she thought.

"Shhhh. You rest. I'm here to help with anything you need," whispered Carolyn, her voice consoling and gentle. "I've got your things. The doctor asked me to go through your purse to see if you had any medications he needed to know about before he treated you. I found Lanoxin. The doctor said he wants to keep you here for a few days to monitor your care. Is there anyone I should call?"

The question was never answered as Desiree's deep,

steady breaths told Carolyn she had fallen back into a deep sleep. Carolyn walked out of the room to the nurses' station.

"How is she?"

"As good as can be expected."

"Do you really think she was poisoned—that all those women were poisoned?"

"That's the working theory. We don't know what type of poison, but her digoxin level was off the charts, so it was clearly something in that family of drugs. She's one of only three people actually admitted to the hospital, so whatever it was hit her really hard, probably because of her heart condition."

"I didn't know she had a heart condition. She's very private." Carolyn absently twisted the silver ring on her finger.

"You look very tired, and you've been here all night. Why don't you go home and get some rest? We'll call you if there is any change."

"Sounds like a good idea. I could use a few hours of sleep and a shower. We were here for a tournament, staying at the Mystique. Here's my cell. I'll take Desiree's things with me for safekeeping."

Carolyn walked back into Desiree's room. The numbers showing on the monitors had not changed. She moved to the bedside and again held Desiree's hand.

"Desiree, I don't know if you can hear me. You rest. I have your things so they'll be safe. I'll be back in a few hours, and bring you a fresh nightie, some clean clothes, and your toothbrush."

Carolyn left the hospital with Desiree's jewelry, clothing and purse stuffed into the mah jongg tote that was given out as a door prize. Most important, she had Desiree's room key card and her phone.

As awful as it sounded, Carolyn knew she'd been given a

golden opportunity. She'd be able to learn a lot more about Desiree in a shorter period of time than her years of befriending the woman had accomplished so far. For starters, Desiree's cell phone contact list and call record could prove extremely useful. Who knew what a treasure trove of information might be waiting for her in Desiree's room? Desiree's misfortune could prove to be the gold mine of information that could help her find her daughter.

Rachel opened her eyes and put her arm over her head. Had yesterday been real? What a mess. The hospital didn't release her until close to two a.m. The last EKG looked good, and all of her vitals had been stable for more than an hour, so they said she could leave. She peered at the clock on the nightstand, ten thirty-five in bright red numbers. The room was bathed in sunlight. Another beautiful Florida morning. Looking over, she could only see the top of Sara's head; the rest of her was still buried under her covers.

Rachel had to pee. Pulling back the covers, she found her flip-flops on the floor. She didn't remember getting undressed. Walking into the bathroom, she took a quick look in the mirror. She still had her makeup on. It was rare for her to go to bed without washing her face, and her slight raccoon eyes made her grimace. Her body ached. Probably from all the sitting at the tournament and then lying around at the hospital. A warm shower would take care of that.

The tournament—what a mess! She wondered how all the people who got sick were doing. Had anyone died? She had a memory of Sara asking someone that question in the ER, but couldn't remember the answer.

Flushing the toilet, she turned on the shower to get the

water warm. Quietly, she opened the door and went to the closet to get her terry robe.

"Morning."

"Morning yourself. Sorry if I woke you. I know it was a long night for both of us. How'd you sleep?"

"Good. Took my pill when we got back. It finally kicked in about four thirty. That's the last time I remember noticing."

"I'm going to take a shower. You relax. But not too much. I'm starved."

"Okay. I'll shower when you're done. Then we can find some breakfast." Looking at the clock, Sara added, "Lunch may be more like it."

Fortunately, the cafe off the lobby served both a full breakfast menu and lunch until three o'clock, when it closed and the other restaurants in the hotel took over. Rachel ordered bacon and eggs while Sara opted for a hamburger and fries. Rachel hesitated when the server asked about the coffee.

"Decaf, please," said Rachel thinking about the new routine she would have to get used to. "The police are still here." Several police cars were visible from the restaurant's windows. "What do you think's going on?"

"Hard to say. The nurse I asked last night...ugh, make that this morning...while you were getting dressed said one woman had died."

"Oh." Rachel's heart squeezed. "That is so sad. I wonder if it was anyone we met or played with. This was supposed to be a fun weekend. No one expects to die at a mah jongg tournament. Lose maybe, be upset you can't make a mahj hand and are earning all your points from wall games, embarrassed if your score is so low you win the boo–hoo bear, maybe. But die? Nobody would expect that."

As they were finishing up, there was a commotion in the lobby. Side doors opened, and the police walked out with a young man between them. He looked to be in his early thirties, and was dressed in a royal blue golf shirt with the gold hotel logo on his chest and black Dockers. His hands were cuffed behind his back. He kept his head down, not making eye contact with anyone, as the police escorted him through the lobby to the waiting police cars.

"Do you think that's about what happened at the tournament?"

"Your guess is as good as mine, but probably," said Sara. "Can't be more than one incident here requiring a police presence. He looks really upset."

"Yeah. Wonder who he is and what he could have done." Rachel watched as a police officer put his hand on top of the guy's head and helped ease him into the back of the police car.

"He's one of the catering managers," said their server as she placed their checks on the table. "They locked down the catering kitchen yesterday after everyone started getting sick. There were investigators swarming all over it, dumping the garbage. Took away boxes of evidence and samples of food. I overheard one of them saying they suspected it was something from lunch. Something in the food."

"We ate the lunch and didn't get sick. Other people didn't get sick either," said Sara.

"That's all I heard," said the server. "Anyway, thank y'all for coming in. You have a nice day."

"Couldn't they have taken him out a side door? Something less obvious," said Rachel, forever the defender of the little guy.

"Makes more of a statement this way. You know the whole perp walk thing."

"Yeah. But he isn't some scuzzy politician," said Rachel. "He's a kid. Okay, well not exactly a kid. But still. What about innocent until proven guilty? His reputation is ruined."

"Not if he didn't do it," said Sara. "And the people standing around out there are mostly tourists. They never saw him before and won't ever see him again. And if this is all a big mistake, the hotel is going to ensure everyone who works here knows it. The last thing they want is for one of their own employees to have done something horrible enough to make so many hotel guests sick. And if someone did die, like the nurse said last night, it's murder."

Grateful for the line of taxicabs waiting at the entrance to the hospital, Carolyn told the driver to go to the Hotel Mystique and then settled in for a few minutes of peace. It had been a crazy twelve hours. Her body ached from sleeping in the lounge chair in Desiree's room. A hot shower and some food were clearly in order, but both would have to wait. By the time the cab pulled up to the hotel, Carolyn had decided her first stop would be Desiree's room.

The elevator pinged at the eighth floor, and Carolyn emerged holding Desiree's room key card in her hand. Anyone passing her in the hall would easily see it and realize she belonged on this private concierge level. Letting herself into Desiree's suite, she did a quick walk-through to get a feel for the space. The Mystique had spared no expense with the room's decor. The furnishings, bed coverings, and bathroom tiles and fixtures all screamed expensive.

She didn't know what she was actually looking for, only that she wanted an inside look at Desiree's world, and this was her opportunity to snoop. Starting in the bathroom, she went through Desiree's toiletries. High end brands, but nothing unusual. Carolyn moved back into the main room and went through the drawers. Nothing.

She saw clothes hung carefully by color in the closet. The one open suitcase also revealed nothing. There was no laptop or other technology. Searching the room proved to be a total waste of time. She took a plum-colored satin nightgown and matching robe from the closet, Desiree's hair brush, toothbrush, and fresh clothes to bring back to Desiree in the hospital as promised.

Returning to her room on the fifth floor, Carolyn took off her shoes and stripped out of her clothes, dumping them in a heap on the bathroom floor. She pulled the silver ring off of her finger and took it to the sink. Flipping open the secret compartment, she stared at the white powder and thought about how close she had come to using it. Quickly, she turned on the hot water and flushed the tiny compartment clean. A wave of relief washed over her. However Desiree had gotten sick, it had not been her doing, and for that she whispered a grateful prayer.

A good shower—such a blessing after the last twenty-four hours. She turned on the water full blast and had it coming out of dual massage heads and six body sprays. She slowly slipped under the warm water and breathed a sigh of relief. The lavender scented bath gel filled the small glass-enclosed shower with a relaxing fragrance.

Ordering a hamburger and sweet potato fries from room service took care of her second need, food. She poured herself a glass of white wine from the bottle she brought and fluffed up the pillows on the bed. Getting comfortable, she turned on the TV for some background noise while she examined the contents of Desiree's purse.

Carolyn pulled out her wallet first. She found the usual credit cards and a few hundred dollars in cash. The most interesting item was a piece of paper tucked behind

Desiree's driver's license. It had a series of numbers and words written in pencil. Guessing these were passwords to various devices and accounts, she took a close-up picture of the list with her cell phone and copied them into her journal.

Then she picked up the cell phone to see what treasures it held. Shit! Password protected. Unlocking it was her first challenge. Starting at the top of the penciled list, she methodically typed the numbers she saw into the cell phone, looking for the one sequence that would grant her access. Slowly, patiently, persistently, she worked her way through the list. Her tenth series of numbers hit pay dirt. She was in.

Carolyn installed 2Spy, a mobile tracking software she purchased on the internet, on Desiree's cell phone. It gave her immediate access to the phone's call and text history, contact list, and GPS history. It was like being in Desiree's skin—her shadow. Carolyn could now trace her past movements, see where she had been, read texts, emails, and see her internet usage.

The knock at her door told her dinner was served. Stopping for a few minutes to eat and watch some mindless TV couldn't hurt. She was starved. Other than some vending machine peanuts, her last meal had been the disastrous lunch the previous day. Besides, Desiree wasn't going to be released from the hospital for a few more days. Time was on her side.

The scent of bacon grabbed her full attention as the server carried the tray past her and placed it on the small round table in front of the windows. Her stomach gurgled and she smiled sheepishly at him.

"Sorry. It's been awhile since I've eaten."

"No problem. We're known for our bacon burgers, so I hope you enjoy it."

Salivating, she stole a sweet potato fry from the plate and then signed the bill. Locking the door behind him, she tore into the succulent hamburger, its juices rolling down her arm with her first bite, devouring it in record time.

Carolyn spent the next several hours immersed in Desiree's life. The picture file in her phone produced several dated shots of a rundown motel in different stages of renovation, with palm trees and the ocean clearly visible in several of the images. The last shot, taken from the street across from the motel while workers painted a small building at the entrance to the property, had a Route A1A sign in the lower right foreground. Florida. Bingo!

Scrolling through a text file filled with cryptic messages, Carolyn studied the texts, looking for a decipherable pattern of letters and numbers she could use to break the code. There were also several recent texts to someone named JV in Sand Isle about the movement of packages and the safe arrival of a new package. Could packages be of the human kind? Desiree's license had a Sand Isle address. Making this type of link could be the answer to her prayers.

Carolyn jolted awake at the sound of the ringing phone. Looking at the small clock on the nightstand, she saw she'd been asleep for about two hours.

"Yes?"

"Mrs. Conrad?"

"Yes."

"This is Debbie Sloan, the nurse you spoke with this morning at Orlando Doctors Hospital."

"Oh, no. Has something happened to Desiree?"

"I'm so sorry. Since you are the only contact we have, you may want to head back to the hospital. She has taken a turn for the worse."

"I'm on my way."

❖

"I'll be at the airport to pick you up. See you tomorrow. Love you."

"Love you too," said Rachel as she hung up.

Rachel left the room and headed for the hotel fitness center to find Sara. They'd spent the afternoon shopping and were planning an early dinner. They both had early flights in the morning.

Sara and exercise didn't exactly compute in Rachel's mind. Her best friend had been on a fitness binge for the last few months, her logic being that butt spread was a major problem when you got older. Rachel figured it had more to do with the handsome man who bought the townhouse next door to Sara's a few months back. He was a physical therapist, and had convinced Sara to do more regular exercise and weight training. He'd even talked Sara into doing the senior version of the Tough Mudder challenge in the fall.

The more Rachel thought about it, the more she realized she should also increase the amount of exercise she got. Walking a mile every few days probably didn't cut it. She'd wait to find out what her new cardiologist thought.

The elevators in this hotel had to be the slowest ever built, thought Rachel, all patience gone. Exasperated after endlessly hitting the down button, she pushed through the stairway door. The fitness center was on the second floor. She was on the fifth. It was only three floors, and using the stairs would do her good, considering she had decided to talk to Daniel rather than join Sara on the treadmill.

As Rachel headed down, muffled sobs echoing in the stairwell reached her ears. They were coming from above her. Stopping in her tracks, Rachel considered her options. Mind her own business and continue down to meet Sara.

Reverse course, head up, and see if she could help. As usual, her rescuer genes won the day. She turned around and trudged up the stairs. Three steps above the sixth floor landing a young girl was crying her eyes out.

"Are you okay?" asked Rachel as she sat down next to her. The girl had on a cobalt blue jacket with a gold name tag bearing the hotel's logo and the name Stella.

"It's nothing."

"It's not nothing. I've been here, done this myself. Well, not in a stairwell. But the crying part."

This brought a smile to the girl's face. Smeared mascara streaked under her eyes.

"Look, I'm a stranger. You can share what's got you so upset with me. I won't really know who you are talking about, so I can't go telling tales out of school."

"They arrested my best friend a little while ago. He's so scared. And I know he didn't do anything. He's the kindest, most gentle man I've ever met. Wouldn't hurt a fly. I know everyone says that, but in Jeff's case it's really true. I saw him catch one—a fly that is. Didn't try to slam it dead. Took it outside and freed it."

"Well now, that is an admirable quality. Can't say I've ever known anyone who did that for an annoying fly."

"It's awful. They walked him out like a common criminal. Said because he was the manager in charge of lunch yesterday, when all those people got sick, he must have done something wrong."

Rachel sat quietly. What could she say? She didn't know the man, but had witnessed the police escorting him out, and she had been one of the people eating the tournament lunch. One of the lucky ones, in her mind, who hadn't gotten sick.

"I was at the tournament."

"Oh. I'm so sorry. Did you…were you…"

"No. I didn't get sick, and my friend didn't either. But I

know a lot of the women were very sick. I'm sure the police are just doing their jobs."

"I work at the front desk. When they came in and were talking to the hotel's General Manager, I heard them say it was poison. They narrowed it down to people who used the horseradish."

"That was fast. Sure am glad I'm not a horseradish eater," laughed Rachel. Her comment brought a brief smile to Stella's face.

"We don't serve horseradish. I know because I used to be a server here, before I got promoted. We never had horseradish in the kitchen."

"Maybe they changed the menu since you changed jobs."

Stella blotted the corners of her eyes with a tissue. She rested her arms on her thighs pulling at the tissue, trying to straighten it out.

"I know who did it."

"Excuse me. What did you say?"

"I said I know who did it."

"That's a big accusation. What makes you say that?"

"At least I think I know who did it. I'm not really sure. But she's the type. Vindictive, mean, a real psycho bitch. Sorry for my language."

"Who are you talking about?"

"Someone who works here. She and Jeff were dating for a while, and I'm sure she had something to do with him being arrested at least."

"What makes you think that?"

"Because she's crazy. Last year, one of my friends got a promotion she wanted. Do you know what she did? That very night she followed her home and beat her up in her driveway. They could never prove it was her, of course. My friend had a bad concussion. Had to quit her job. And guess who got the promotion."

"Did you talk to the police?"

"No. I…I really don't have any proof. I know in my heart Jeff didn't do anything. He couldn't possibly do this. They were dating and he broke it off about a month ago. He told me she was too crazy for him. She was a looney. Used to call him all the time, badgering him about where he was, what he was doing. She kept following him. Stalking him."

Stella swallowed and sniffled. "I saw her in the parking lot screaming at him after work the other night. Said she was not going to take this crap from him…that she'd get even. He'd be sorry he dumped her. She went nuts all over him. And he just stood there. Even when she punched him, he didn't hit back. That's what I mean. He couldn't hurt anyone."

"The police will want to hear about this, you know."

"But I don't have proof. It's my word against hers. And she's a manager here. But Jeff, he's the sweetest man. We're not dating or anything. Just friends. Known him like forever. Wouldn't mind dating him. He thinks of me like his little sister. And you just don't date your sister."

"Let's go," said Rachel standing up and holding out her hand to help Stella up. "We need to find someone to talk to. Trust me. My boyfriend is a detective. The police will want to hear what you've told me, especially the fight in the parking lot. Your information will give them another lead to follow. Who knows? Maybe they'll find something."

"Will you come with me?"

"Honey, I'm sticking like glue. Won't leave your side until you tell me to."

CHAPTER 10

Tuesday

"God, I missed you," said Rachel, flinging herself into Daniel's waiting arms. She felt a tingle of excitement pulse through her. Neither one of them let go for several minutes. Finally, Rachel pulled back slightly, keeping her arms around his neck. "Thank you for not coming down. I know that was hard for you, and I really appreciate your understanding."

"It was very hard. I was so worried about you."

"I know. But it's all good. I'm okay. Sara watched over me like a hawk. We were able to do our shopping thing yesterday and relax."

"I'm glad you were able to finish your girls' weekend. You and Sara are so close, it's kind of like you're joined at the hip. Seeing her always peps you up."

"I'm pretty sure she talked to one of the flight attendants on my plane. The woman kept watching me, asked me if I was okay a few more times than normal. Brought me a bottle of water before the plane took off in case I needed it for anything. Knowing Sara, she probably paid her off."

"That's our Sara." Daniel kissed her forehead. "I'm even happier now that you're back safe and sound." He didn't make any move to let her go, fearing if he opened his arms, she'd vanish.

"Well, I don't know how sound. Let's get my suitcase and get out of here."

As they entered Route 64, Daniel said, "Tell me more about what happened at the tournament and the people who got sick."

"There were tons of suits roaming around with all sorts of initials on their name badges. Talked to a woman who works at the hotel's front desk. She said they ruled out terrorism. Narrowed it down to something from lunch—some type of poison stirred into the horseradish. Only people who used it got sick. No one is sure what the poison was yet."

"Labs are pretty good at tracing stuff given enough time. And they could get lucky and track down who did it, which might help narrow down the type of poison."

"Too crazy. Making ladies at a mah jongg tournament sick. I'm harmless."

"Yeah, right. Wait until we get home. Let's see how harmless you are or how I can entice you into being a little bad." His smile warmed her heart.

"What do you want to do for dinner?" She could tell by his smile food was not his most urgent thought. It wasn't hers, either. *Great minds think alike.*

"I've got dinner all ready to go. We're grilling filets, and I'm making another one of my super-duper wicked Caesar salads."

"Yum." Rachel sat quietly for a few miles, lost in her own thoughts.

"There was one thing that was strange at the tournament."

"Stranger than a bunch of people being poisoned?"

"There were these two women we kept running into. Had

a few meals with them. One of them had a cameo brooch that looked exactly like my Aunt Lil's. I mean identical. Sara pooh-poohed my concerns. Said cameos were popular in the fifties and sixties. Said there were probably thousands of them still around, especially in Florida, considering all the snowbirds and people from up north who have relocated there."

"Sounds about right." A glance at Rachel told him there was more. "But you think...what?"

"I don't know what I think." Rachel picked at invisible lint on her black crop pants. Finally she said, "I think it's my aunt's cameo brooch. That's what I think. What I don't understand is how that woman got it."

"That's a huge leap, Rachel. Don't most cameos look alike?"

"Not really. And this one. I've got this feeling. I can't explain it."

"Is that your gypsy blood talking?"

"Could be, and it's usually spot on."

"Let's let this mystery go for a bit and enjoy our evening. Okay?" he asked, as he pulled into the garage.

"Yes. I'm looking forward to a quiet evening with you. Only no wine for me. Doctor in the ER said to limit my wine. I can have a little bit. A little bit of wine. A little bit of chocolate. What does a little bit mean?"

"Don't know. A glass maybe? A small candy bar? A Hershey's kiss?"

"I can think of a different kind of kiss I'd find much sweeter and more enjoyable."

"Be happy to oblige." Daniel winked at her before opening his door. He came around and opened her door, grabbed her suitcase from the trunk and followed her into the house.

"My little heart episode was too scary. I don't want a

repeat performance."

"I agree. You're cut off. No wine."

"It's the chocolate. That's going to be much harder. I may have to cheat a bit there."

"Stick with me, kid. I'll help you cheat a little. Won't tell a soul."

Rachel smiled at this wonderful man. How did she get so lucky? The heart thing had gotten her attention more than she wanted to admit. She'd already called her doctor, gotten a referral to a cardiologist and actually had an appointment set for tomorrow. Tonight, she had other plans for her heart.

"We've had a tense few days around here," said Marissa slipping her hand into the crook of Marco's arm when they met on the beach midway between their two homes. Meeting like this for a quiet walk had become part of their new-normal routine since returning from Paris.

"Yes. Between Sophia getting sick at your tournament and the mess with Bella, what else could go wrong?" Marco stopped walking and gently guided her around to face him. Looking into her eyes, his fingertips softly stroked her cheek. He slowly leaned in and planted a warm kiss on her lips. "I missed you. Wanted to talk to you as soon as you got home yesterday morning, but there was so much going on. It was crazy."

"I know." The welcome home kiss they exchanged spoke volumes. What they had begun in Paris remained alive and well on this isolated stretch of Florida beach they called home. She lingered in his arms, enjoying the comfort of his embrace.

"I checked in on Sophia about an hour ago. She's feeling much better." Holding hands, they started walking down the beach. The tide was coming in. Walking through the low waves and kicking up the water gave a playful edge to their much heavier conversation. "We're going to go visit Bella again this afternoon. I know Rosa could use some moral support."

"TJ's coming around. He and some of the boys were up at my place using my gym to work off some of their pent-up anger and energy. Think he might have gone home by now. Bella's not solely TJ and Rosa's daughter. We all care about her."

"What do you think he'll do?"

"Don't know. He's eating himself up inside. TJ's a proud man. Happy Bella is home safe, and furious with Claire for putting her in so much danger. Angrier still at whoever did this. Did you hear Claire actually sold her to pay off her drug debt?"

"Yes," exclaimed Marissa. "What was she thinking?"

"She wasn't. She was frightened and too self-absorbed to think of anything but saving her own ass. She saw a way out and took it. Didn't think about Bella...about what being kidnapped and raped would do to her. All Claire thought about was Claire."

"What's going to happen to her now?"

"She's still in the hospital. Estella signed off on a seventy-two hour hold. I think they have a meeting with one of the doctors tomorrow afternoon. Then they'll decide what to do."

"I feel so bad for Bella. She must have been so scared. The poor thing. How is she ever going to recover from this?"

"I don't know. But she's strong. And I told Rosa and TJ not to worry about costs. Get her the best care available. The costs will be handled. Been thinking a lot about Claire, too— and other girls who find themselves in this kind of predicament."

"We were sort of there once. Ours was different, but we

all felt lost and alone."

"I remember all too well. I built this compound—high walls to keep trouble out and all of us safe. Seems trouble found its way in." Marco looked out across the ocean. "We'll take care of what needs to be taken care of first. Then maybe it's time for us to do a different kind of payback. Find a way to be helpful."

Marissa stopped walking. She pulled Marco around to face her.

"That's what I love about you. Underneath this hard exterior," she said, placing her hand on the warm skin of his chest and patting ever so gently, "is a heart of gold."

"For people I love. For people important to me. That's true." A long, intimate kiss affirmed his words. "But what I'd like to do to whoever is at the other end of the deal Claire made isn't pretty, or kind, or loving."

"We take care of our own. We always have."

"And we will now, too."

Marco pushed a wisp of hair away from Marissa's face. It was time. He loved her. Why wait any longer? He searched her violet blue eyes for signs of confirmation. He saw it there—knew it had always been there.

While they had been working their cons, it was important not to allow any romantic attachments to interfere with the jobs. But now they were done. They voted. Getting out of the business won. He planned to grab whatever years he had left, and make them happy years, shared with Marissa.

The security jeep rolled by. Casey and Tina waved but did not stop. Marissa watched the jeep head down the beach, leaving only tire treads as evidence of its passing.

"Alone," whispered Marissa. "No one will be by for hours. The guys are blowing off steam. Karli is at the clinic. Sophia is resting. We're alone on our own private beach. Whatever shall we do?"

Marco smiled as he sought her lips. His long, warm kiss was met with equal fervor. He pulled Marissa down onto the sand. Her schoolgirl laughter filled the air.

"We'll do whatever comes naturally." His strong arms were around her and his lips found hers.

"Sounds good to me," she said when they broke for air, "but let's do it at my house. I'm too old to deal with sand in places where sand should never be."

Bolting up, Bella looked around. Familiar things greeted her, and she melted back down into her bed. She was home. In her own room. Safe. Pressing her hands against her eyes, she angrily fought back tears.

Much of the last forty-eight hours remained fuzzy, but her nightmare was real, and of her own making. Images flashed in and out of her consciousness. All bad. How long would they last? She had walked straight into danger without a thought. Would she ever feel safe again? How could she have let Claire convince her to go clubbing?

Then again, she hadn't needed much convincing. Her jealousy of Claire's wild lifestyle overrode her own common sense. She'd wanted a taste of Claire's action. When her cousin dangled the carrot of a night out dancing with hot guys, Bella bit. Got way more than she bargained for. Stupid, stupid, stupid.

Her mouth felt like an army had marched through it. Slowly, Bella pulled back the sheets. She rolled over, turned onto her side, moved her legs over the edge of the bed and planted her feet on the floor. Every move deliberate. Every move making her more nauseous. Supporting herself with a hand on the wall, she made her way to the bathroom. After doing her business, she reached for her toothbrush.

Catching her reflection in the mirror, Bella gently touched the bruise under her left eye. Ouch! She couldn't remember how she got it. A few minutes later, with her face washed, teeth cleaned, and hair brushed out, she opened the bathroom door. She could hear muffled voices coming from down the hall. Her parents were in the living room talking. It was time to face the music.

They were owed an explanation and an apology. She had lied. Broken their trust. Total disappointment. Now she had to atone. They'd probably ground her for life.

Slowly, Bella made her way down the hall, past the gallery of photos highlighting her and her brother's youthful accomplishments. Her smiling face in her cheerleading uniform made her wonder if she would ever feel that innocent again. She stood still at the entrance to the living room, waiting for them to see her. It didn't take long.

"Hi," she said meekly when they finally looked at her.

"Honey. How are you feeling?" Rosa started to get up, but Bella held up her hand. Rosa sat back onto the sofa. Her father remained silent and still. She saw no judgment in his eyes, only tears welling up and a slight smile warming his face.

"I...I need to talk to you both."

"Come. Sit down," said Rosa as she moved over and patted the space on the sofa between them.

"No. I prefer to stand." Refusing to lean on or take advantage of her mother's kindness, Bella looked both of them squarely in the eyes. She didn't move, but knew she needed to close the distance separating them. Slowly, step by step, Bella moved forward. She stopped when she felt the coffee table brush her knees. There she stood, in front of her parents, ready to face their judgment, to accept whatever punishment they dished out.

"I want to apologize...to say how sorry I am. I lied to you

Mama—"

"Oh, baby. It's okay," interrupted Rosa.

Bella held up her hand "Let me finish." Taking a deep breath, she stood tall in front of them.

"No, it isn't okay I lied to you. Daddy, you've always taught me to face my problems. Well, this is all my fault. I need to face it and make it right."

Bella brushed the tears from her eyes. Standing silently for a few minutes to regroup, she blew her nose into the tissue clenched in her hand.

"I don't remember much, but I remember calling you and leaving a message that Claire and I were studying and I was staying at her house. I lied. And I suspect my lie caused you enormous pain and worry. And I am sincerely sorry. Then it all goes blank. I've been trying to remember, but all I see are faces and lights and darkness. I know you don't trust me now. And I plan to do everything I can think of to earn back your trust."

Big brown eyes filled with tears that clung to dark lashes met eyes of steel softened by love. TJ and Rosa got up and came to their daughter. Strong, loving arms encircled her. She collapsed into their safety. Swaying gently, they held one another tightly.

TJ flashed back to myriad other times he had held Bella. The times she placed her little pink-socked feet on his size twelves and they danced around the living room. He dreamed of the day he would walk her down the aisle, giving his baby girl to another man, to have and to hold. But in the end, she would always be his baby girl. He mouthed a silent thank you to God.

"I'm so sorry," Bella murmured.

"We know. We're so glad you're safe." There they stood. Three souls locked in love.

And then another thought hit home for TJ. That special

bond between fathers and daughters was one Claire had never experienced. Whoever her father had been, his only claim to Claire was as a sperm donor. Claire had never known what it meant to have a father's love. Perhaps that's what she was searching for, the inner hunger that fed her wild side.

He could have stepped up—probably should have stepped up. He knew what it was like to come from a broken home. And he'd promised God he would never put his own family, his own children through that. His tunnel vision for his own family had blinded him to dangers that had threatened to undo all he and Rosa had worked so hard to achieve.

And so, a new vow left his lips. Uncle TJ would step up, be there for Claire and her brothers. TJ closed his eyes while he continued to embrace his daughter and his wife. He prayed Bella and Claire would heal from their wounds and, in return, he promised God he would step up for both his own and his extended family.

CHAPTER 11

Carolyn stopped at the Army Navy store for supplies before leaving Orlando for her drive down the coast to Sand Isle. Desiree would not be released from the hospital for at least a week. The doctors thought she had a mild heart attack and moved her to the cardiac care unit. Carolyn appreciated the freedom of movement this turn of events presented to her. She wouldn't have to worry about accidentally running into Desiree while she roamed around Sand Isle looking for the motel property matching the photos she found on Desiree's cell phone.

It had been a long five years. Even as she harangued the Biloxi police yearly on the anniversary of Amelia's disappearance, and pursued every lead that came her way, nothing had brought Amelia home. Carolyn couldn't let go or even think of moving forward with her own life knowing she had not done everything in her power to find Amelia.

Befriending Desiree had been a long shot. Call it woman's intuition. Carolyn felt in her bones that Desiree was the key that would unlock the puzzle of Amelia's disappearance. She puts on a good show, thought Carolyn, but she's not who she seems to be. And now, with the information from Desiree's cell phone, I'm getting closer and closer to proving it.

Slowly a picture emerged of an outwardly flamboyant woman who was the silent operating partner for an exclusive private inn that rented rooms by the hour—not the night. And Desiree had lived in all the places where other girls had gone missing, and in the only two places where bodies had been found. And when an inconvenient body was discovered, the inn closed quickly and Desiree faded into the night, to be reincarnated as a new version of herself—with a different name—at a new inn, and in a new location. Coincidence, maybe, but Carolyn was betting her daughter's life on the fact there was no such thing as a coincidence. And she planned to prove it.

Leaving Route 95 at the Indiantown Road exit, Carolyn made her way east. Turning onto A1A as she approached Jupiter, Carolyn drove south, searching for the one landmark she had seen in the photos on Desiree's cell phone—a nondescript white building with the word Office in black letters centered above the door located maybe a hundred feet away from an A1A route sign, and surrounded by palm trees. Total long shot, but persistence had a way of paying off. Once she found it, she'd check into the nearest motel and put the next phase of her search and rescue operation into action.

The men gathered in Marco's conservatory breathed a sigh of relief now that Bella was home. Everyone still wanted to get the guys behind her kidnapping—teach them a lesson they would never forget. Justice must be served.

TJ's forceful baritone voice controlled the room. Direct and commanding, it belonged to a man who got everyone's attention when he spoke—a man others did not ignore.

"First, this isn't part of your job. Any of you want to walk away, now's the time. There'll be no hard feelings."

Silence fell over the group. The men exchanged glances, but no one moved. TJ knew he had the best team out there, and they had confidence in his leadership.

"Okay then, we're agreed," said TJ. "We go after these guys. Bella may be home safe, and for that, I thank God every minute. The local Leos may have closed this case, but this is not over—not by a long shot."

"What did the police say when you met with them?" asked Casey.

"Convincing them a kidnapping took place is proving to be a problem. The guy I talked to yesterday chalked Bella's disappearance up to a young girl wanting some adventure. Told me I should be happy she was home. And I am, but..." His voice trailed off.

"They seem to be circling the wagons," he added after a brief pause. "Not sure why." TJ pondered his words. His instincts were on high alert. Who were they protecting and why?

"This can't be the first time these guys, whoever they are, pulled this shit," said Brody, the newest member of the team.

"Through our efforts, we can make sure it's the last time. I don't want any other father, any other family, to go through what Rosa and I have had to deal with these last few days."

"Let's put the fear of God into them. Send them to live with the devil if need be." Brody's youthful enthusiasm powered his words.

"Lock it down, Brody," said Kyle. "You know the drill. Emotions make you sloppy. Emotions make you stupid. Emotions get you killed. This is a mission. Nothing more. Nothing less. We've been on hundreds of missions before. We'll get the job done. We always do."

Looking directly at Brody, TJ said, "That we will do,

Brody. We will put the fear of God into them. On our terms. We are who we are—warriors. And the bones of our warrior code are honor, integrity, and courage. We have time on our side. Let these shits get complacent, think they got away with their little adventure in kidnapping. What was it Khan said in that Star Trek movie, 'revenge is a dish best served cold.' They're going to feel cold, all right—cold and alone when justice is served." Wisdom acquired in combat strengthened TJ's words.

"And we start tonight." TJ made eye contact with each man in the room.

Art and Tina entered Metamorphosis shortly after ten p.m. Tuesday evening. They estimated there were about a hundred people partying. Slow night. Most were on the dance floor, but a few couples sat in the plush VIP booths, sipping cocktails and talking. Everyone was dressed to kill.

Tonight's job was simple—recon. They were there to watch. To observe. Blend in. Have some fun. Dance. Drink. Be merry. Be friendly. Focus on chatting with employees. Don't arouse suspicions by being too aggressive or too nosy, or by asking too many questions. Play the role of new people in town looking for some fun clubs.

And take pictures. From their observations and the photos they surreptitiously took with their little hidden cameras, a plan would emerge. It would be refined later. They were all committed to the ultimate goal: find the perps and bring them to justice. There would be no stopping the plan's flawless execution.

Their first stop, the bar. Two bartenders were working opposite ends. They found two empty stools in the middle of the bar. When one bartender approached them, name tag said Javier, they ordered Margaritas. Under his breath, Art said, "smile" as he fondled the intricately carved cross around his neck to snap a full face shot of the guy before he walked away to make their drinks.

Tina pulled her cell out and made a pre-planned call using the speaker feature. Holding the phone mouth high, she snapped a few shots around the room as she chatted with her friend. When their drinks arrived, Art handed Javier a credit card and told him to start a tab.

"I haven't seen you here before," said Javier when he returned Art's credit card.

"We're new in town. Heard about this place from a guy at the apartment complex where we're renting. Said it was the hottest spot in town."

"Sure is. Tonight's slow. You'll have to come back on Friday or Saturday. The place really rocks then."

"We'll be sure to do that. I'm Art and this is Tina."

"Javier. The head bartender and all around go-to guy. Since you're new in town, if you need anything, I'm your guy. Know everyone and everything."

"Thanks. I'll keep that in mind."

"Even when I'm not working, I come here for the action. A lot of great-looking ladies. But I see you already have yourself a great-looking lady." Javier smiled and winked at Tina.

"Thank you," said Tina, tilting her drink in his direction, matching his smile with one of her own.

"Just telling the truth. Saying what's so. You two enjoy yourselves, and if there is anything I can get you, let me know."

Hours of dancing followed. Metamorphosis lived up to its billing as a hot club. Perfect acoustics. The DJ kept the music flowing with flash-bang lighting that made the dance floor rock.

Heading back to their bar stools after a long dance set Tina excused herself, "Where is the ladies room?"

"Down that hall," said Javier pointing to the far end of the bar.

Art watched Tina walk the length of the bar and disappear down the hall.

"I think the guy at the end of the bar is trying to get your attention," said Art. Short and balding, the guy's appearance screamed accountant more than a patron of Metamorphosis.

"Yeah. I'm trying to ignore him." Javier looked away from the stubby-looking man.

"It's not working. Looks like he went through a meat grinder."

Art could see that his shirt collar was unbuttoned and his tie knot pulled away from his neck. Tufts of hair seemed to be growing out of all visible skin. He wiped perspiration from his forehead.

"Jeez, he's sweating like a pig. It's not that hot in here."

Javier set another drink in front of Art and signaled the man he was next. "Guy clearly needs a drink. Be right back."

"Looks like he needs way more than a drink. Better make it a double. Tell him it's on me."

Swiveling around on the bar stool, ostensibly to get a better look at the dance floor, Art strained to watch the interaction between the two men. Javier poured some Grey Goose over ice and placed it in front of the man, pointing in Art's direction. The guy raised his glass and shot Art an appreciative nod.

His body was a mass of movement as he spoke to Javier. Clearly worked up, his jabbing finger broadcast the tenor of the conversation. Art wished he could hear what was being said, but he was too far away, and the music was too loud.

Javier turned back to the counter behind the bar, picked up the phone and made a quick call. As if the gods were on their side, the DJ lowered the music's volume to make some announcement. Art overheard Javier tell the guy someone named Julio would be right out.

"What was that all about?" asked Art when Javier came back to his end of the bar.

"Unhappy customer. Julio will get it straightened out."

"Funny he doesn't look like he fits here. He come here often?"

"First time I've seen him. He's not a regular."

"Okay. Cut me off. I've had too much to drink. I thought you said he was an unhappy customer."

"At Julio's other place."

"He's got another club? Busy man, Julio. Running this place looks like a full time job."

"Different type of club. Very different," laughed Javier. "More exclusive, private party type activity, if you catch my drift."

"Oh, really?" Art sensed another guy approaching from behind.

"Hey, Rick, say hello to Art. He and his lady are new in town. Want him to feel right at home."

"Like Javier said, man, anything you need, we're your guys."

"This place is fine for my tastes."

"Good for you. But if you change your mind, let us know." Rick whirled the pretty brunette standing next to him around and led her out to the dance floor.

"One day you might want a different kind of entertainment," said Javier. "Knowing who to go to helps, you know what I'm saying? I mean, your lady is gorgeous, but stuff happens."

"I'll remember that."

Art kept one eye on the action taking place between the sweaty, disheveled guy at the end of the bar and a well-dressed tall man who approached from the hallway at the back. Must be Julio, thought Art, and he again fingered the cross around his neck to take Julio's picture. After a brief exchange, Art saw Julio pass a key to the sweaty guy, who mopped his brow again and finished off his drink. The conversation was done.

"Here comes my lady now," said Art as Tina emerged from the same back hall Julio had disappeared into. "Good timing. Sounds like the DJ is going to slow things down a bit."

Finishing off his drink, Art wrapped his arms around Tina and led her onto the dance floor. Leaning in close he whispered in her ear, "Short, bald guy, gray suit, coming out. Follow him. May lead us to the promised land."

"Copy that," came through his earwig.

When the music ended, they returned to the bar.

"I think we're done for the night."

Closing out their tab, Javier caught a glimpse of his tip, smiled, and said, "Now remember, anything you need, you come to me. Hope to see you again real soon."

"Think we'll try for Friday. What time do we need to get here to avoid a line?"

"No problem. Matt will be working the door Friday night. Big guy, handlebar mustache. More muscles than brains. Tell him you're my special friends. Hand him my card. He'll let you right in."

Art pocked the card Javier handed him. "Thanks. See you then."

They left. Round one done.

CHAPTER 12

Wednesday

The chimes from the Westminster clock sang out. Bong...Bong...Bong...Bong...Bong. Five o'clock. Rachel slowly slid her hand along the sheets, reaching for Daniel. Not there. She opened her eyes and stared at the empty space. Insomnia had robbed him of a good night's rest—again. Throwing back the sheets, she rubbed her eyes, rolled her legs over the edge and slipped her feet into her Crocs.

Walking slowly down the dark hall, Rachel could see the outline of Daniel's head above the sofa on the screened porch.

"You okay? I didn't feel you get up."

"Yeah. Couldn't sleep. Didn't want my tossing and turning to wake you."

"Want to talk about it?"

"There's nothing to talk about."

"Your current sleep situation, or lack thereof, tells me otherwise. Over the last few weeks I've found you out here more times then I care to count. And those are the nights we're together. I don't know how many sleepless nights you've had when you're alone."

"A lot going on. A lot of stuff on my mind."

"I'm sure. You're about to retire from a job you love, that's been your whole life. There's this new job you're considering. And then there's us. Your thinking plate is rather full, if you ask me."

"Let me make some coffee."

"You sit. I'll get the coffee."

Making her way to the kitchen she flipped the switch to start the coffee pot brewing. Daniel wasn't the only one with a lot to think about these days. Her hand moved to her chest, seeking out her beating heart.

How often had she ever thought about her heart beating? It was just there. Doing its thing. Until it went haywire and scared the shit out of her.

The memory of all those people in scrubs encircling her, jabbing her with needles, plastic tubes in her nose, hooking her up to machines, unnerved her. At one point she had lifted her head to look at the monitor and saw it blinking out one hundred and eighty in red. She knew enough about pulse and blood pressure to realize one hundred and eighty bpm was not a good number. The nurse at her side saw the horror in her eyes, smiled at her, gently touched her shoulder, whispered relax, and quickly turned the monitor so she couldn't see it. Good move.

Daniel's sleeplessness also concerned her. She could tell the idea of retiring weighed heavily on his mind though he didn't talk about it much. He'd been alone a long time and wasn't used to sharing. She knew his work was important to him, gave him a reason for being, a purpose to his life. He had never not worked. The stories he told her about friends who retired were not pretty, but their retirement stories didn't have to be his retirement story.

He needed to write this next chapter of his life differently.

"Bless you," said Rachel at the sound of his sneeze.

"Thank you. You need any help?"

"Nope. Be right there."

A smile crossed her face. Her old reliable, habit-forming, routine-driven, compulsively neat self was morphing into someone whose nipples got hard when a certain man walked into the room, someone excited about making love in the afternoon with a man who made her quiver and shiver and tingle in places she hadn't even known existed. And there was laughter.

Was this love? Yes. Rachel knew in her heart it was—finally. She'd done her time. Earned her merit badges. She deserved to be in love and to be loved. Biologically, the heart is a muscle, a hardworking pump. Emotionally, if the eyes are the windows to the soul, the heart is the soul's center. And after her heart issue, she didn't want to waste any more time. She longed for her soul to fly.

Rachel finished preparing the coffee tray, added warmed croissants, butter and jelly and carried it out to the porch. They had lots to talk about.

"Here we go." Rachel held a cup out to him.

"Thanks." He took a sip. "The meeting I had Monday...Mac, my old Marine buddy—I've told you about him—was there. So was an FBI guy I knew in Brooklyn. They really want me to join this sex trafficking task force they're putting together."

"Really?" Rachel shifted her position to face Daniel more fully. "That's interesting."

"The FBI guy, Jim Greene, heard I was making a change. Retiring. Said I'm too good to go off into the sunset and retire. He wants me to be on the team."

"That's impressive. I knew you were good. And clearly others know it, too."

"Yeah," said Daniel. He broke off a piece of croissant, holding it in his hand, lost in thought. "They're so damn young."

"Who?"

"The girls...they're so damn young. I'm usually pretty good at compartmentalizing stuff. You know, keeping work at work and home—you and me stuff—at home. But this sex trafficking stuff keeps bleeding through."

"It's horrible. You wouldn't be human, wouldn't be the man I love if it didn't affect you."

As she spoke, Rachel settled her hand over his heart. He covered it with his own, lifted it to his lips, kissed it softly and returned it to his heart, pressing it lovingly against his chest. She could see the wheels turning in his head—knew he was playing out how it might work, what would be involved if he took the job. Getting pulled into a new task force after he retired offered him an exciting possibility to do important work. The down side? It could have a major impact on the life they wanted to build together.

"Anyway, we need to talk about how it will impact our life together."

"You should take it. Sounds like it was tailor made for you. Plus, you love putting scum away."

"Yes, I do." Daniel looked at Rachel. "But we have other plans. You and me type plans."

"There is nothing to say our plans can't co-exist with this job. Would you have to be in D.C.?"

"No. The task force is working outside normal channels. There are satellite groups forming in several major cities around the country. They're planning to attack the problem on many fronts simultaneously. Makes it interesting. Good funding, too. Going to use the best technology has to offer. Looks like Jim Greene, Mac, and me, if I sign on, will be the lead guys. It's a tempting offer."

"I feel a but coming."

"But…what I just said. There's us. What we've been talking about. The lot. The house we're planning to build."

Rachel poked him. "You're an ass, you know that?"

"Hey, I'm a guy. Of course I'm an ass. Tell me something I don't know."

"We will be fine. To be honest, I never could see you stopping cold turkey," she said softly. "This will be good for you. A good transition into a different kind of life. And you get to help a lot of people—innocent, young people. Scared, innocent, young people."

"You make it sound so easy. So simple." Daniel wrapped his arms around her and pulled her close. "That's what I love about you."

"What I love about you is your desire to help others, to put their needs ahead of your own. Sex trafficking is horrible. I cringe when any of the TV cop shows do a story about it. What if that had happened to Jenny? You know how strong-willed she is now. David and I had our hands full with her when she was a teenager. So defiant. Rebelling against everything we said. What if, in her need to lash out at us, she'd gotten herself involved in something so dreadful. A mother's nightmare. Daniel, this job is a mitzvah, a good thing."

"I know." He poured himself another cup of coffee and refilled her cup. "Sex trafficking is at epidemic levels. It's a hidden crime. Goes on in the shadows, and no one really wants to talk about it. The job is to bring it out into the open. Shine a light into the darkness. Make it visible. And let the bad guys know we're after them. That they've no place to hide."

"Sounds perfect. Like it was written for you. When do you have to let Mac know?"

"I told him I'd give him an answer in a few days."

151

Daniel's cell phone buzzed.

"Wonder who that could be so early," said Rachel.

"Berger," he said.

"Do you know who this is?"

"I recognize the voice," said Daniel after a brief hesitation. He caught Rachel's eyes as he spoke. She mouthed a silent "who?"

"I need to call in that favor you offered me a few months ago. I need your help," said the voice on the other end of the phone.

"I'm listening."

"My friend's daughter went missing. Gone less then forty-eight hours. Found her. She's back now. She was grabbed, taken against her will. Police won't do anything. Said to be happy she's home. Chalking it up to her being a teenager."

"Okaaaaay." Drawing out the word, waiting for a hint of how to help, he asked, "What do you want me to do?"

"You're connected. Got the police thing going for you. We could use a liaison person between us and the local PD. Can't really get too involved myself. Have to stay on the fringe."

"I think I understand. Where'd all this go down?"

"A little town called Sand Isle, Florida. In between Jupiter and Ft. Lauderdale."

"Never heard of it. Sounds idyllic. How long was she gone?"

"Maybe forty-eight hours, give or take. Her parents did the missing person report on Saturday afternoon. Somehow she got to a phone and called them Monday morning. Cops put it down as a done deal—all's well that ends well. We can't let it go. Thought you could help here. I'm passing the phone to her father, TJ. He works security for me. He can fill you in. And thanks. Consider us even."

Daniel could hear some grumbling as the phone was passed.

"Hey. This is TJ."

"Daniel Berger. So what can you tell me?"

"We handle most things ourselves down here."

"I get that. Doesn't always work out best. Can you tell me anything about what happened?"

TJ took a deep breath. "Did you ever lose someone you loved?"

"Yes."

"These bastards took someone from me. Someone important. And yes, we got her back safe, and God willing, she will recover after some time and good therapy. Most people would let it go. But I'm not most people. They gotta pay. The police won't do anything. Say it's over. Be glad she's home. To them, it's another case of a teenager stepping out on her parents, experimenting with life. But I know, we know, it isn't true in this case...in a lot of cases. These guys are predators, and they need to be put down."

"I know a guy who retired down there. Said he preferred the ocean breeze to our shit cold winters and all the snow in New York. Heard he joined the force. Not sure where. Let me give him a call. See what I can find out."

"Sounds good."

"Where can I reach you?"

"This number works."

The line went dead.

Daniel stared at his cell. Strange call. Things appeared to be coming full circle. And wasn't that the crazy thing about life? The universe seemed to like closure—had a way of tying up loose ends. The mystery of who bugged Rachel's home, who called him that day to warn him Rachel was in trouble, was now almost solved.

"Who was that?" Rachel returned from having taken

153

away the coffee dishes while Daniel was on the phone, giving him privacy.

"Guy with a problem. Needs my help. Funny, my gut is telling me his problem may line up with the work Mac and Jim are talking to me about. Looks like the universe aligned to show me the way. Guess I've found my retirement job."

❖

"Okay, Art," said TJ. "What did you and Tina learn last night?"

"The Club is guarded like a fortress. Doesn't appear to be, but looks are deceiving. You gotta know what you're looking for. There are CCTV cameras everywhere, even when you go to take a piss."

"Makes sense. Probably have their own security in case something breaks out," said Brett. "These places are great, lots of fun, until they're not. Trouble can happen in an instant."

"Can you lay out the space for us?"

"Already done." Art reached down and grabbed the roll of brown craft paper he'd brought with him. "We mapped out the place last night when we got back to Tina's." Unrolling it on the hassock in the center of the room, he secured the four ends with whatever heavy object he could grab.

Tina taped the photos they took to the white board, saying, "We also printed out the photos so everyone can see what the inside of the club looks like—see the people we met."

"There were two bouncers at the door. Pure muscle, no brains. There's a narrow, dark hall right inside the front door. Goes about twenty feet," Art explained as he traced the entranceway with his index finger. "Opens up to the main floor of the club. You've got your VIP seating around the walls, with a huge dance floor taking most of the center space. There are two bars, one either side of the room. Only one was in use last night. The photo on the far right is the bartender Javier. He said it was a slow night."

"What's the lighting like?" asked Kyle.

"Like most clubs. Low lights around the edges. Flashy, bright colors on the dance floor. Strobe gets used when the music heats up. Another hall leads off the main floor to bathrooms and a door labeled private. I'm thinking this is where the security room is. Video monitors and maybe an office. Don't know if there is a door in there leading outside. We didn't walk around the outside of the place. Might have looked too suspicious."

"Would make sense to have one," said Brett.

"Right. Won't be hard to check out. Bathrooms are down here, and there's a fire door with a crash bar," said Tina.

"Alarms?" asked TJ.

"Maybe. Not sure. The sign on it says an alarm will sound when it gets opened. Tina and I started fooling around in the hall to see if it was alarmed. She hit the bar with her back when I pushed her into the corner. It opened, but no alarm sounded."

"At least nothing you heard," offered Kyle.

"Good point. Whether something sounded in the security room, I don't know. But no one showed up to check on it. And we stayed there about five minutes more."

"If I was fooling around with Tina, I'd have stayed longer than five minutes," laughed Jersey.

"Yeah. And I would have kicked your ass," grinned Tina.

"The guys watching any video feed would have seen us making out. Probably figured there was nothing happening even if an alarm did sound in the security room. So maybe they decided there was no need to check it out," said Art.

"Would sure like to get a peek inside the security room. Get a better sense of the systems in place," said TJ. Rubbing his chin, he worked to commit the roughly drawn blueprint to memory.

"Let me take a crack at it after we're done. I may be able to find something online," said Brett. "A lot of plans get scanned and filed digitally these days."

"What about the people?" asked Brody. "See anyone who looked like a person who could be behind what happened to Bella?"

"Now that's where it gets interesting." Art's cunning smile surprised everyone.

"Javier, the bartender," he said while Tina pointed to his picture, "got really talky when Tina went to the ladies' room. She took her slow, sweet time so I'd be alone for a while. Anyway, Javier comes over and asks if we're married. When I told him yes, ten long years, he asks if I ever got bored. I catch a head nod, and this other guy comes over. Rick. No last name." Tina moved in front of Rick's photo and gave her best Vanna White impression.

"Anyway, one thing leads to another, and I get the feeling if I want to get hooked up with someone else, for a few hundred or so, this Rick kid could make it happen."

"Ah, a player," grinned Kyle. "You hooked yourself a player."

"Looks that way. Or an asshole who wants to be a player. Either way, the kid has shit for brains if you ask me. Talking to me like he was. A total stranger. He didn't know me from jack shit and he was offering to set me up."

"How'd you leave it with him?" asked TJ.

"That I might be interested. See where it goes. He could be our ticket in."

"Yes, he could," said TJ. "Rick was the name Bella remembered. He was the guy she was dancing with."

"What about the guy I told you to follow?" asked Art. "The guy who got the key passed to him. Where did he go?"

"Glad you asked. It gets more interesting," said Casey. "He went a few miles down A1A to a small inn. The Sand Isle Inn to be precise."

"That dump," laughed Brody. "God, we used to go there when I was in high school. Rented rooms by the hour. Great place to party. Know a lot of girls lost their cherries there."

"I forgot you grew up here," said Casey. "Well, it isn't a dump anymore. Looks all new from what I could see in the dark. Place may be worth a closer look."

"Good job," said TJ. "Tonight we check out the Inn."

"You're looking good today," said the petite nurse in flowery pink scrubs as she opened the blinds of Claire's hospital room. "There. That's better. Let in some light. I'm Beverly, and I'll be taking care of you today." She went over to the dry erase board, erased the previous nurse's name and printed her own in bright red letters.

A low groan emanated from the bed.

"How are you feeling today? Are you in any pain?" Behind the cheery voice, Beverly already knew the answers from years of experience working in drug rehab units. Before that, Beverly had lived through her own personal torment. She knew precisely what and how Claire felt. And she knew today was the beginning of a very long, hard journey.

"I need to pee."

"Here let me help you."

Beverly stayed close, helping Claire back into bed when she finished.

"I'm going to check your vitals and help you freshen up a

bit. Dr. Brewster is doing rounds this morning and will be in to see you shortly. And then later, Dr. Oliver, one of our counselors, will stop by to talk with you."

Beverly proceeded to take Claire's blood pressure, check her pulse and refill her water container.

"I can stay while you wash up in the bathroom and brush your teeth, if you'd like. Cleaning up a bit will help you feel a whole lot better."

"Leave me alone."

"You sure?"

"Go away."

"Okay. You rest."

Beverly looked down at the child in the bed. In Beverly's mind, that's what Claire was, a child. She fought back images of another child, at another time, in another bed like this one.

Too many young people turning to too many drugs, fighting off too much pain. While she did not know the cause of Claire's distress, she knew the girl in the bed was at a critical juncture in her life. Could she make the right choice? The choice that led to happiness? Or was she, like so many before her, doomed before she even got started?

"I'll be back to check on you later. Here's the call button if you need anything. These buttons turn on the TV and adjust the channels and volume. See this big red button? It's for me. Press the big red button and I'll come right away."

Claire nodded like she was paying attention. Dr. Brewster's visit was thankfully quick and soon she was back flipping through TV channels. Lunch arrived shortly before noon. Claire only knew the time because she asked the guy wearing green scrubs as he set her lunch tray on the rolling table in front of her. The water container got refilled. Did they think she was a camel? She'd barely had any of the water already in there. Claire stared at the food. A hamburger, fries, green gelatin, and milk.

A soft knock at the door drew her attention.

"Hi Claire. I'm Dr. Oliver. I'll be taking care of you for a few days. Mind if I sit and talk with you while you finish your lunch?"

"Whatever." Claire slowly dredged a French fry through the ketchup, giving him a half-hearted shrug which spoke volumes.

"How are you feeling?"

"Pretty shitty. I was hungry until this crap showed up." Pushing the plate away, her eyes glanced off his and drifted away. "Green gelatin? Really? Who the fuck eats this green goop?"

Dr. Oliver smiled to himself. "Do you know why you're here?"

"Not exactly."

"What's the last thing you remember?"

"I...I...can't remember much of anything." Claire pushed the tray table down toward her feet. "I'm tired. I want to sleep."

"I understand. We found the remnants of eszopiclone, a powerful sleep medication, in your stomach. It doesn't interact well if a person has been taking other drugs and drinking. That's probably what landed you here."

Silence. Claire rolled her head toward the windows.

"Was that why you took all the sleeping pills? Because you wanted to sleep?"

"Duh? Ya think?"

Dr. Oliver said nothing. He sat quietly, smiling at her. Finally, she looked back at him and said in a low, conciliatory voice, "I really don't remember."

"Take some time now, Claire, and tell me, what is the last thing, the last place you do remember?"

"Dancing. We were at a club. And we were dancing."

"Who's we?"

Claire rubbed her eyes. Again, she sought the safety of staring out the window. Dr. Oliver waited patiently. It was a game, and he'd played it many times before.

"My cousin. I was there with my cousin, Bella."

"And where is Bella now?"

Dr. Oliver saw a look of confusion cross Claire's face.

"I don't know. She left. And I left. And then I was home in my bed. And then I woke up here."

Dr. Oliver watched Claire closely. His next question and her response would prove to be a seminal moment for her. Would she be able to handle the information he was about to share? Or would it send her over the edge?

"Do you know you're pregnant?"

An audible intake of breath, her green eyes doubled in size. Her nostrils flared as she rose to a sitting position.

Perhaps not his best bedside manner, he scolded himself. But he'd definitely gotten her attention. Which he knew he needed to do—fast. He had less than twenty-four hours to complete his evaluation and gain her trust—the crucial element in a doctor patient relationship. He might have been a bit harsh, but he needed to know where her head was, and he didn't have time to pussyfoot around.

"Claire, did you hear what I said?"

"What?"

"I asked if you heard what I said to you?"

"Yes," she whispered. For the very first time, Claire's eyes locked on his. "You said I'm pregnant. Can't be. I had my period."

"Do you remember when? A month ago, perhaps?"

Claire thought about it. She couldn't really remember when she had her last period. It could easily have been over a month ago.

"I don't remember," she mumbled.

"You are very early in your pregnancy. So we have time."

"Time?" The question hung in the air. "Time for what?"

"Time to help you. And time to help your baby. May I ask how long you have been using drugs?"

"It's just some pot. No big deal. I don't know. Not long. Maybe a few months."

"That's good." Dr. Oliver let the lie breathe. "You said pot. Marijuana. Is that it? Can you tell me what else you're using?"

"Do we have to do this now? I'm really tired."

"The longer we delay, the more harm may come to your unborn baby. You don't want that, do you?"

"No," she whispered on the verge of tears.

"Good. We're both on the same side here, Claire. We both want what's best for you…and for your baby."

"Stop saying that."

"Saying what? That you are pregnant and going to have a baby?"

"Yes. I can't be. I only did it once. To see what everyone was talking about. How it felt."

"And…how did it feel?"

"It hurt. It wasn't like in the movies. It hurt."

"Do you know who the father is?"

Claire shook her head. A barely audible "no" escaped through an exhaled breath.

"Okay. We can talk about that later. What we need to do right now, today, is decide about your treatment."

"Why do we need to do this right now?"

"Because you are being discharged from the hospital tomorrow. And I'd like to offer you a place in our CARE program so we can begin to work together to help you."

"Whatever."

Dr. Oliver hated the teenage, "I'm not responsible, do what you want" response. He'd heard it so many times. It was their defense mechanism kicking in. Their "I don't care. You can't hurt me" protection. False bravado. They did care. What they didn't know was who cared about them, and who they could trust.

"Dare I state the obvious, Claire? You have a drug problem. Or truthfully, you have a personal problem, and you are choosing drugs as your way to block it out instead of dealing with it. What I'd like to do is offer you a different option. One that can change your life."

"And what's that?"

"Join the CARE program. We can talk about what is bothering you. Then I can help you learn how to handle whatever is bothering you, whatever is causing you to retreat into drugs, in more productive, less harmful ways."

"Just like that, huh?"

"No. I would be lying if I told you this is going to be easy. And I promise, I will never lie to you."

"Right."

He could hear her disbelief. *How many people have lied, repeatedly lied, to this child?*

"This isn't going to be easy. It will probably be the hardest thing you ever do. But your rewards far outweigh the challenge before you. Drugs can't solve your problems. Drugs can dull your pain, push reality away for a few hours. But eventually you come down, and whatever was there before is still there. Nothing's changed. Except you have gone farther down the rabbit hole. And each time you go down there, it is harder to get out. Soon you'll find yourself so far down you can't reach the edge to lift yourself out. Is that what you want?"

Distrust was like an arrow shot from her eyes. "Let me think about it."

"Okay. But what is there to think about, really? If you don't stop using, your baby can, probably will, be born addicted to drugs. Your baby is innocent. He or she won't have any choice. She or he will be addicted. Without having any idea what is happening, he or she will have to go through the agony of withdrawal. You've had a rough few days. What you have been experiencing...the shakes...the nausea and vomiting with nothing to throw up...the sweating, runny nose, ache all over your body that won't quit. Do you want your innocent baby to feel that? Do you want to cause your baby so much pain?"

Shaking her head, small tears sliding down her cheeks, Claire mouthed, "No."

"Good. That's really good. That's the mother in you coming out. You care about your unborn child, and I am really proud of you, Claire. You may not believe me right now, but you do have options and choices, and no one can take them away from you. The only person stopping you is you. A man named Mordecai Kaplan once said, 'your past has a vote, not a veto.' You're only seventeen. You have your whole life ahead of you. Why be so quick to throw it away?"

Big green eyes filled with tears and dawning hope stared at him.

CHAPTER 13

"You okay? You seem distracted," said Daniel as the server took away their empty salad plates.

"Thinking about how crazy the tournament turned out. And then the whole heart thing. I never thought I'd have a heart thing. I know it doesn't make sense, but in my mind, heart conditions are for old people. And I'm not old. I realize how stupid that is. Heart episodes happen all the time, and sometimes to very young people."

"But the doctor said you'd be fine. That's what you told me when you came home this afternoon after seeing the cardiologist. She said you'd be fine."

"That's what she said. Called it atrial flutter. No surgery necessary at this point."

"You had flutters? You never mentioned any flutters."

"I didn't want to worry you. They didn't last long. I figured they'd go away like they started."

"And that line of thinking got you a rushed visit to the ER. What if you hadn't been able to get to a hospital? What if next time you are alone and can't get to your phone?"

Rachel could see anger behind Daniel's words. Not anger really. More fear...fear for her...fear of losing her.

"I hear you. I'm sorry. I didn't mean to upset you. Please don't be angry with me."

"I'm not angry." Daniel reached across the table and took her hand in his. "I don't want to lose you. Until a few months ago, my work was my entire world. I think of it as BRT— before Rachel time."

"Cute."

"I love you," said Daniel softly. "It's been a very long time since I said those words. Never expected to say them again. And now, I am. Here, with you."

"And I love you too. More than you can imagine." Rachel saw the opening for a long-overdue conversation. "But these days I don't need a knight in shining armor on a white horse to slay dragons and protect me. I can take care of myself."

Rachel stopped. She smiled at him. "Okay, I still get scared, but I'm learning how to take care of myself, and I love the feeling. What I want is a partner. Someone to love and cherish and share my life with. Someone I can take care of as much as he takes care of me."

"Then we both want the same thing."

"Speaking about what we want, tell me more about this new job thing."

"Ah. Changing the subject, are we?"

"Yes," smiled Rachel. "And no. It's the same subject— us—only a different branch. How dangerous is this new job going to be?"

"Not as dangerous as walking a beat on the streets of Bed-Sty when I was a rookie and didn't know what I was doing."

There was nothing she could say. No way to respond. She watched him tense, could see his fingers tighten on the stem of his wine glass. A little more pressure and the delicate stem would surely break.

"Rachel, these guys are predators, pure and simple. Sex

crimes are a cancer. They live below the surface, ignored. Whatever their motivations, they are preying on others, innocents, to get their jollies. They don't give a rat's ass about the person they're screwing as long as they're getting their needs met."

"But you care."

"These Johns, they're average guys—your neighbors. Most of the time they are married, with children. But something is missing for them. Maybe it's the excitement, the thrill of sneaking around, doing something naughty, illicit. Of course, most of them aren't thinking about the possibility of being infected with an STD."

Daniel noticed her somber expression and knew it was time to lighten the mood. "Did you know STDs are becoming the number one health problem for senior citizens?"

Rachel snickered. "No, I didn't know that. Guess they're having way more fun during retirement than in the olden days. Something to look forward to."

The server showed up with dinner, and it was time to relax and enjoy themselves.

"Sorry," he said. "Didn't mean to ramble on. It's important work. I'll be doing something that matters, to those young kids and to me.

"Don't be sorry." The conversation she had been putting off for too long had come full circle. "This is what I want. Both of us doing things we believe in, that are important to us. I've got the Raphael Fund, and you—now you have this. And being there for each other at the end of the day."

"So my invitation to move in still stands?"

"Most definitely."

"Well then, I accept. What I need to know are the rules. If we're going to live together, I need to know the ground rules.

I'm a guy. I need to know the rules so I don't screw up."

❖

"Time to put up our eyes in the sky and see what we can see," said Brett. "Steve and Brody are in position on the beach a couple of miles away from the Inn that Casey followed that guy from the club to. They're ready to launch. This shit is so cool."

"Launch it," said TJ.

Brett acted like a kid in a candy store as he manipulated the images coming into his monitor. The thermal imaging camera on the high-flying drone Marco got for them was top-of-the-line equipment—featuring cryogenically cooled technology that produced great resolution. The man spared no expense.

"Shit, if we get lucky, we can probably see a guy holding his friggin' dick from a thousand feet up with this stuff."

"Focus, Brett. Focus," said Kyle squeezing Brett's shoulder.

"Thermal imaging, high-flying drones. This is not your run of the mill, buy it on Amazon or eBay equipment. How the hell does Marco get this shit?" asked Gabe.

"Don't ask. Don't tell," smiled Art. "We really don't want to know how he gets any of this stuff. Think of it as gifts from Santa. You never questioned where those came from did you?"

"I'm Jewish man," laughed Gabe. "Santa wasn't involved. We had candles and eight days of presents. The closer Chanukah came to Christmas, the bigger the presents got. Ya gotta love screwed-up parents competing for the love and affection of their equally screwed-up children."

"I've been at this all day. City definitely needs to get some better security software. Breaking into their system was a piece of cake. Here are permit requests to remodel the Inn."

"Forget a simple reno," said Art as he read through the permit requests. "I used to work construction. From these permits, it looks like they leveled the place."

"Yep. Tore down the old forty room strip motel like you see all over America, and built these quad-type units," said Brett. "Found some artist sketches. Impressive."

Brett pulled up image after image showing sixteen elegant and spacious cottages, arranged in quads. A porticoed entrance, designed to appeal to a discriminating and discretion-seeking clientele, ensured privacy once a car came onto the property.

"They were definitely shooting for privacy with all this latticework and fencing separating the rooms," said Kyle. "You can't see who is going into any room."

"The website says the place offers a romantic interlude— 'an intoxicating, sensuous, sexual experience for all guests,'" said Brett. "Champagne, caviar, fireplace, and the latest in audio and video technology. Not exactly a description of a place one would expect to house a brothel."

"Look at this room layout. They may change the sheets by the hour, but this place gives a whole new meaning to a little afternoon delight. Hot tub, Roman steam spa shower— sign me up," said Gabe.

"Okay, guys. Can we switch back to the drone feed, please?" asked TJ. "Brett, how many rooms are occupied?"

"Looks like we have heat signatures in ten rooms. Blueprints show it has sixteen."

"Business must be slow," said Art.

"Ten rooms show at least one heat signature. Most rooms have two right now. By their movements, I'd say the rooms with two are going at it hot and heavy," smiled Brett.

"But we are sure there are at least ten people we assume are being held against their will at this point?" asked TJ.

"Yep. That's the best count we have right now. I'll track it for the next few hours and see how the numbers change."

"Held against their will is a mighty big assumption. You know what assume means," said Kyle.

"Ass of you and me. I know," chuckled TJ. "Been there. Done that. Got the T-shirt."

"Wish we could get real eyes on. Someone inside. Like a customer," said Art. "The bartender did tell me if I wanted another type of activity to let him know. I could go back. Tell him Tina and I had a major fight. Act all down and depressed and see where it leads."

"Too dangerous in my book. You don't look like the type who needs to pay for it," said Kyle.

"That's part of the problem," said TJ. "None of us really look like guys who can't score our own action."

"Don't really have anyone else to send in," said Kyle. "No one we trust looks like that fat, sweaty loser Casey followed the other night when he left Metamorphosis. And following him is what led us to the Inn."

"And we can't put too many strangers into the Club without raising suspicions. These guys aren't stupid," added TJ.

Brett rubbed his eyes. He'd been staring at his monitors for hours. "Hey, guys. Check this out," he said, pointing to a moving heat image in the wooded area behind the Inn.

"Probably an animal," said Casey as he turned around to look at the screen.

"That movement isn't animal. That's human. What he's doing there is the more interesting question."

"Anyone want to go find out?" asked Kyle.

"Sure. I'm game," said Casey.

"Suit up. Be ready in ten. Brett, keep him in your sights."

"Will do."

Kyle pulled the black SUV into the shrubbery at the rear of the public parking lot, adjacent to the beach access ramp about a mile from the Inn. Dressed in black from head to toe, balaclavas in place, he and Casey retrieved the rest of their gear from the trunk. Not knowing what to expect, they suited up for the worst possible scenario: NVGs, bulletproof vests, Sig Sauer 9 mils locked and loaded, extra clips, KA-BARs. After they embedded their earwigs, Kyle performed a comm check.

"Testing. Geek, can you hear me?" asked Kyle, using Brett's military call sign.

"Copy"

"Jones?"

"Copy that," said Casey, whose Jones moniker referred to the mythical railroader, Casey Jones. "Geek, any movement from the target?"

"Negative. About two klicks straight north from your current position."

Casey followed Kyle into the dense underbrush heading for the Inn. The target was more than a mile in front of them.

Stealthily moving through the brush, maintaining position on either side of their target, Kyle considered their next moves. Not knowing who was out there or why gave him an adrenalin rush he hadn't experienced since Iraq. Patrol at the compound was a walk in the park. He craved danger. He craved action. His enlistment in the Navy and ultimately earning his Trident had fed both needs. This little escapade had adrenalin rushing through his veins.

"Scratch?"

"Copy." A case of the crabs during boot camp had earned Kyle a call sign that stuck like glue.

"Target in sight," said Jones. "Alone. Binoculars aimed at the Inn."

"Night vision?"

"Can't tell. Probably. No use if they're not. What's the plan?"

TJ's voice came into their ears. "Grab him. I'm leaving now. Got one stop. Will meet you at the toolshed."

"Got it," said Casey. "I'll make a sound to draw his attention in this direction. Scratch, you do the takedown."

"Copy that."

Kyle crawled as close as he dared. He heard the twig snap. The target heard something too, and turned in the direction of the sound.

Kyle was on him. Pushed him down hard. Had his face planted in the dirt within seconds. He jammed his right knee between the target's shoulder blades, his left hand gripping the guy's neck, securing against any movement. He pressed his Sig firmly against the back of the guy's head.

"Don't move. No sound or you're dead. Nod that you understand," he hissed into the target's ear.

The target flinched slightly. Kyle could tell the thought of extracting himself from his current situation crossed his mind. Kyle pressed the Sig harder. The nod came. The target didn't move. Casey applied flex-cuffs to his ankles to minimize any kicking. He pulled the target's hands behind his back to flex-cuff them, but stopped abruptly. Casey caught Kyle's eyes and directed his attention to the target's hands. Polished fingernails.

"What the—?"

Casey yanked the watch cap from the target's head. Shoulder-length blond hair tumbled out, surprising them both. He was a she.

"Here's what we're gonna do," said Kyle softly into her ear. "I'm gonna take my knee off your back and roll you over. My hand is gonna be around your throat. And you're not gonna make a sound, or I'm gonna squeeze so hard your eyeballs will pop out of your head. Nod that you understand."

Another nod.

Kyle moved slightly to allow the target to roll onto her back—his Sig now pressing between her eyes, his left hand positioned around her throat. Determined steel blue eyes met his. She wasn't at all what he'd expected to capture in the underbrush.

"Now, my friend here is gonna apply some duct tape across your mouth, and then we're all gonna take a little ride. You've got some explaining to do. And I can't wait to hear it."

Duct tape in place, Kyle pulled her up and hoisted her over his shoulder like a side of beef. Slowly, the threesome made their way back to the SUV with Casey in the lead. At the SUV, Kyle carefully laid her down in the cargo area and then took the wheel. Casey rode in the back, keeping a watchful eye on their prize. Not that she was going anywhere. Hog-tied and gagged didn't leave her many options.

Driving along deserted, darkened streets, Kyle made sure to stay at or under the speed limit. The last thing he needed was to get stopped by a curious local Leo. Their cargo would be hard to explain. He could hear her soft grunts when he hit a bump in the road.

Won't TJ be surprised to see what they caught?

CHAPTER 14

The toolshed—a cinder block, hurricane-resistant, four-room structure housing the motor vehicles, tractors, lawn equipment and tools used to maintain and protect the compound—was quickly repurposed after Casey radioed they were bringing someone in for questioning. A table and two metal chairs were placed in the center of the smaller cement block equipment room. A cot and blanket filled one corner, and Brett set up a simple CCTV system so everyone could watch while TJ questioned their incoming guest.

After Kyle steered the SUV through the narrow gates at the south end of the compound, Gabe secured them and followed the SUV down the dirt driveway. When the SUV came to a stop in front of the shed, Casey opened the back and dragged the woman to the edge, lifted her over his shoulder, and carried her into the shed.

"I'm going to untie you now," said Kyle after Casey unloaded her onto the cot and walked out of the room. "If you cooperate, this will all be over soon."

Taking out his KA-BAR, Kyle cut through the flex-cuffs, freeing her hands and feet. She immediately ripped the duct tape from her mouth and began rubbing her wrists.

Hostile blue eyes stared up at him from a determined oval face.

"Be back shortly. There's water on the table. Help yourself."

Kyle left the room and ripped off the balaclava hiding his face. He walked over to the table to watch her on the monitor. She didn't move.

"What now?" asked Casey.

"We wait for TJ."

The words barely left his mouth when TJ strode into the room.

"What have we got?"

"Take a look," said Kyle, pointing to the monitor and stepping back to give TJ a full, front-on view.

"A woman?"

"Yep. Surprise. Surprise." Casey's Gomer Pyle imitation fell flat.

"Shit. What the fuck was she doing out there?"

"Don't know. But I bet you're gonna try and find out," said Kyle.

"Damn right."

A determined TJ strode into the room. The woman remained on the cot. He threw the bottle of water at her. She caught it one-handed like a pro.

Impressive.

"Who the hell are you and what the fuck were you doing out there?"

"Ah, the direct approach. I like that." Her voice did not waver or quiver.

"Well good," said TJ. "I aim to please." *She's not scared. Most curious.* "Now suppose you answer me."

The woman unscrewed the cap from the water bottle and slowly took a sip. Her eyes never left TJ. She pushed herself off the cot. Standing up straight, she stretched and shook her arms and legs to get circulation going. TJ could see muscled strength beneath her clothing—strength in her eyes.

She's trained. This isn't some housewife out for a romp in the woods at night. This is a woman who's been trained. Maybe even seen combat.

"You haven't answered my question. Who are you and what were you doing out there?"

"No colorful metaphor? You left out the fuck."

TJ watched her repeat the water routine, her eyes locked onto his. The slightest of smiles crossed TJ's face. *She's sizing me up.*

"How long we gonna dance?" asked the woman.

TJ studied her closely. "As long as it takes for you to tell me what I want to know. Dance steps could get more dicey in a while."

"Oooh. A threat. I like that, too. You know, I've got some questions of my own. Like who the hell are you and what the fuck were you doing out there?"

"Now who's using colorful metaphors? Ladies first. I suspect your answers will be way more interesting than mine." TJ's sixth sense kicked in as he and the woman bantered back and forth. He was sparring with an intelligent adversary. He took a gamble. "Considering we were in the same place, surveilling the same location, it may be we have some common interests. Maybe we can help each other?"

"Now that would be interesting." Her lips curved upward granting TJ a slight grin which twisted into her sarcastic tone. "And since we could end up dancing around each other all night, and I have more pressing things to do with my time, I'll start. I'm Carolyn Conrad. Research Librarian. Divorced. Mother of Amelia Conrad. From Bangor, Maine." Her words staccato, all fired at him in one breath. "Your turn."

"On it," said Brett's in TJ's ear. TJ heard another voice in his ear say "librarian, no way." He was sure it was Kyle.

And he agreed. Damn. A librarian? She didn't fit the image. Not what one would expect from a librarian sitting behind a desk staring at a computer screen most of the day. No bun at the nape of her long, enticing neck restraining the blond hair framing her strong, oval face. No buttoned-up blouse hiding the mounding breasts that looked ready to burst free from her tight black T-shirt. No dark-rimmed eyeglasses hanging from a chain around her neck, concealing crisp blue eyes that now sparkled like ice in sunshine.

"Maine? You're a long way from home."

"Yes I am. Have business to attend to. And you are?"

"What sort of business?"

"That's my business. And you are?"

"Not ready to say yet."

"A man who doesn't play fair. Tsk, tsk. Not nice. Didn't they teach you anything in kindergarten?"

"Never went." Ooooh, he loved her sass.

"Too bad. You missed out. Kindergarten was fun."

"Maybe. And as for fair, whoever promised you fair? I took fair out of my vocabulary a long time ago. Nothing is fair. What do they say? The only guarantees are death and taxes."

Flashing a wicked sparkle from icy blue eyes, she finished off her water, crushed the empty plastic bottle and tossed it on the table. "What are you? FBI? Special Ops? What?"

"What makes you think that?"

"The haircut's a dead giveaway," she said pointing at his head. "The way you carry yourself—ramrod-straight like you've got a stick up your ass." Walking around the table as she spoke, she had TJ circling it too. "You were clearly watching the Inn. That's the only way you saw me. But why you were watching the Inn is more interesting to me. Can only think you've got some business down there." She stopped moving. "It's an interesting place, the Inn, don't you agree?"

"It has its moments" In his ear, he heard Brett's voice confirming Carolyn's identity. "So what's your interest in the Inn?"

"What's yours?"

"You ask a lot of questions."

"And you don't answer any."

"My prerogative, considering we just met and all."

"So, we're not friends yet? How sad."

"If you keep this up, we could be here all night. And as you said, you've got pressing things to attend to."

"You were listening. How rare for your species. My questions go with the territory. I'm a researcher, remember? Years of training. Ask, then listen to what is said…and what is not said."

"Interesting. And, at the risk of repeating myself, which I hate to do, why were you watching the Inn?"

"Come on. We could go round and round, play this bullshit game, but honestly, I don't have the time or the temperament right now for that. I answered your questions. It's only fair you give me something."

"You're the prisoner here, remember?"

"If I was really a prisoner as you say, we wouldn't be doing this…what did we call it?…dance. Kind of reminds me of the Texas two-step. You'd be much more hard core. Come in all fists and tough, go Jack Bauer on me. But you didn't. Why is that? By the way, did you get confirmation on me yet?"

"Excuse me?"

"The earwig. Did whoever's on the other end confirm me yet?"

TJ smiled. *Smart, observant, well-informed woman.*

In the other room, Kyle was clearly enjoying his role as voyeur, witnessing the repartee unfolding on the video monitor. The hint of a smile played along the corners of his mouth while a warm glow spread through his loins. The entire encounter had been laced with gaps, half-truths, and long silences—TJ and Carolyn each angling to learn as much as he or she could without revealing too much.

"You're good." TJ appreciated and admired Carolyn's commitment to whatever was behind her midnight foray into the woods.

"Yes, I am. Been trained by the best. So, time to speak up. I'll ask again: what's your interest in the Inn?"

"Let's say my interest is personal. A family matter," said TJ. "Resolved itself. Thank God. But in my mind, it's not over by a long shot."

"Ah, revenge. The cruelest master of them all. Got you by the short hairs," smiled Carolyn. "We do have something in common. My interest is personal, too. And involves family."

She stared into TJ's eyes. He could see her pupils darting slightly from side to side. *She's reading me.*

"Okay. I'll go first. My daughter. I think she's inside the Inn. Being held there. I'm here to get her out."

A rap on the door got TJ's attention.

"Excuse me," he said.

"Of course. Got any coffee? Think we're going to be getting up close and personal, and I could sure use a cup." She turned toward the red light on the camera in the upper corner of the room. "Black, one sugar please."

"Who is this woman?" demanded TJ as he emerged from the interrogation room. "She is remarkably unfazed by her situation. Does she have any idea what she's up against?"

"Don't know," said Kyle while quietly considering the sassy blonde he had just watched go toe-to-toe with TJ, verbally wrestling him into a stalemate. Not too many men dared breach TJ's manly fortress, but this woman took him on, and seemed to be enjoying it.

And he was enjoying watching her. "I like her." He could feel his smile turn into a grin.

"Excuse me? Anything going on here I should know about?" TJ met Kyle's eyes and then looked down, noting a slight bulge between Kyle's legs, evoking a cheeky smile from TJ.

"No. Appreciating an intelligent woman. She knows we're watching her. And I don't think she gives a damn about what she may be up against. She mentioned her daughter. Pure lioness, mother-protector instincts raging inside her. Strong heart. Protect your young at all costs."

"Interesting analysis. Keep watching in case I miss something. And you may want to take that shit-eating grin off your face."

"Will do."

TJ reappeared with two cups of steaming coffee.

"Thank you," called out Carolyn as she took a sip and raised her cup toward the camera in a mock salute.

Kyle smiled at the video feed. All her bravado could not mask the pain and suffering evident on her face. But he saw something else there, too. An eagerness to face down whatever evil resided at the Inn. *What a woman!*

"What makes you think your daughter is in there?"

TJ put down his coffee cup, pulled out one of the chairs and sat down. Carolyn followed his lead.

"Hours of research—hundreds...no, thousands of hours of research—and it all leads to that Inn. Got the last piece of the puzzle Monday. She's in there. I can feel it."

"Research?"

179

"Yep. Good old-fashioned research. That's what I do...did. I'm a librarian. Was a librarian. Quit my job when Amelia went missing. So when the case went cold and the police stopped looking, I did the only thing I knew how to do. I hit the books. Well, the internet really. Started researching cases of missing girls. Do you have any idea how many missing girls, missing children, there are?"

"Not really. Probably way more than there should be."

"There are thousands. Runaways mostly. They pretend they have no family, that they won't be missed, that no one would come looking for them, which makes them very easy, and very tempting, prey. And most cases go unsolved."

"I can believe that."

"I researched cold cases of missing girls. One case led to the next, and the next, and, unfortunately, the next."

"That's too many nexts."

"I agree. What I think I know is the culmination of all my hard work, conjecture, wild guesswork and many sleepless nights. The only thing I am one hundred percent sure of is my daughter is down there, in that Inn. It's where all my research leads me. And with or without your help, I'm going down there to get her back."

"And how do you plan to do that?"

Carolyn looked away, her voice faltered for the first time. "Haven't gotten that far yet." Turning back to look at TJ, her voice stronger now, "but I'll figure it out."

Decision time. TJ quietly studied her. Her research angle aroused his curiosity. How did she connect enough dots to get from Bangor, Maine to Sand Isle, Florida? If she found some link, some bit of information that could help end whatever was really going on at the Inn, then maybe doing some sharing now could play out well for all concerned.

He cleared his throat.

"Daughter, too. Went missing Friday night. By the grace

of God, she got herself out of danger. Is home now. Physically safe and getting the care she needs to be mentally sound. Though I suspect that is going to be a long, hard road."

"Glad to hear things worked out for you."

"Thanks."

"I failed my daughter. I'm her mother, and I failed her. I didn't do my job. I didn't protect her."

"Don't be so hard on yourself. Kids these days…let's say things are very different from when we were young. They put themselves out there—expose themselves—like they believe only their friends can see the stuff they post. Scares the hell out of me most times. Want to lock them up to keep them safe."

"She hated me when I threw her father out. But I had to. It was the only thing I could do. I didn't want a replay of my own childhood. The drunken, cheating father, beating my mother when he didn't get his way or when she questioned where he was going. I swore I wouldn't live like that."

"Know the feeling."

"And then I was." Her hands moved from her sides for emphasis. "Snuck up on me before I even realized I was repeating my mother's life, and I hated myself for it. Then one night when he came home drunk, I caught him in Amelia's room. He was standing at the foot of her bed, staring at her sleeping in a way a father should never stare at his daughter."

Tears pooled in her eyes. Her hands wrapped around her coffee mug, clutching it tightly, her fingers white, bloodless. She took a deep breath.

"That was it. I threw him out. Threatened to tell everyone if he didn't leave right away. The schmuck valued his precious career more than us—more than her. Piece of shit. When he left, he never looked back. Left her cold. Never called her. Never wanted anything to do with her. It wasn't my fault, but she blamed me. And I couldn't...I couldn't take it anymore."

"And you shouldn't have to." TJ's instant flashback to the ugly fights he witnessed between his own parents gave power to his words. His father cheated and brutalized his mother. Then one Christmas he was gone. Maybe Santa was real. He'd granted TJ his Christmas wish that year.

"Thank you for saying that. My memories of my parents' marriage aren't pretty. I swore mine would be different. But it wasn't. The pattern...the screaming, the fighting, the lying. It was all there in spades. Then came the cheating and the drinking. But that night, when I caught him standing over her bed and saw the look in his eyes—he had to go."

"Maybe we can be of some help to each other. How the hell did you get here? Bangor, Maine is a long way from south Florida."

"Think I found a pattern—actually a common thread."

"Oh?"

"Found it while reading a newspaper report of a teenage girl who went missing outside of Memphis about ten years ago. Town boomed when riverboat gambling took hold. Brought in all sorts of lowlife scum. Police found a body along the river. Never did identify her. Still a cold case. But the girl had the tattoo of a green dragon on her lower back. You know, a tramp stamp."

"Lots of girls get tramp stamps. And a green dragon seems as good as any other design. A bit more unique than a rose or a butterfly."

"That's what I thought. The local paper ran a photo of the tat, probably trying to see if anyone recognized it. I enlarged it and taped it to my wall. Stared at it every night. Don't ask me why."

"Did you find anything?"

"I think I did. One God-awful day, when I was really down, I started Googling dragon tats. Shit, I Googled dragon images any way and every way I could think of. There were so many images. Nothing that matched the tat. But I came across this photo of a woman wearing a jade necklace. Blew it up. Same dragon shape as the tat. Caption said it had been taken at the opening ceremony for a new riverboat casino in Memphis."

"Okay, they make a lot of things out of jade. Jewelry seems logical."

"Yeah. I know. But the design of the tat and the necklace were exactly the same. Trust me. I had looked at so many dragons I was seeing them in my dreams. This one stood out to me. They were identical, the tat and the necklace."

"You may be making more of this than is really there."

"Thought that, too…at first. So I started Googling jade jewelry and pendants in the shape of a dragon. And another woman came up wearing the same pendant at a mah jongg tournament. Seems she won it."

"The pendant?"

"No, the tournament. Blew up the photo and hung it next to the first. The pendants matched."

"Where was that one taken?"

"Vegas, three years ago. Call me crazy, but even though their names and the places were different, the more I looked at the photos, the more I became convinced the two women were really the same woman."

"Just because you want it to be so doesn't make it so."

"I know. But I found another case of a dead girl in Biloxi who had the same tramp stamp. My daughter went missing in Biloxi. Worked at the same casino as the dead girl. I remember her telling me about a friend who went missing, and how upset she was when they found the girl's body. And then she shows up again. In New Orleans."

"Who shows up in New Orleans?"

"The woman with the pendant. Photo of her at some charity auction. And I got to thinking maybe she was the link between all these cases. That woman and her dragon pendant were the linchpin. They connected everything and everyone."

"A little far-fetched for me. Sounds like you've been watching too much crime TV."

"Maybe."

"Do you have the photos?"

"Back in my room. I'm convinced there's a connection between the women in the photos, the dragon pendant, and the dead girls with green dragon tats."

"But how does that get you here?"

"I found the woman."

"You're kidding." TJ stopped pacing, his hands moved to his hips, and he stared at Carolyn. "How did you manage that?"

"Became friends with her. One thing led to another, and here I am."

"You are good."

"Damn right I am."

"How are you paying for all of this? You independently wealthy—got a trust fund or a sugar daddy?"

"No such luck. I'm a researcher—a damn good one, if I say so myself. I do online research for a few private clients. Easy stuff like background and reference checks, and some of the higher-end industrial snooping type stuff. Nothing illegal, of course."

"Of course."

"The work pays well, and I can do it anywhere. Only need a WI-FI connection."

"I've got a geek on my team. Magic fingers on a keyboard. He may be able to find a stronger connection, or I'm sorry to say, burst your bubble. You game?"

"Totally."

"Good. Sit tight. I'll be back."

CHAPTER 15

Thursday

"There's a new wrinkle," TJ announced while the security team cooled down after its morning run. "Marco's bringing in someone he thinks can help."

"How come?" asked Casey.

"Not sure. He has his reasons, and that's good enough for me."

"What's his background?" asked Kyle.

"Detective with the NYPD. I talked to him yesterday. Seems the guy owes Marco a favor. I didn't ask for details."

"How much does he know?" asked Kyle.

"I gave him a SitRep. Says he knows some people down here at local PDs. We'll take it slow with him. See how it plays out."

"If he has contacts down here, he may be able to get us more info on the guys behind this," said Art. "Doesn't feel like the work of street punks looking for a quick thrill."

"I agree with Art," said Casey. "Easier ways to get laid than grabbing girls at a club. Bad press for the club. Bad for business."

"Ah, capitalism. Ya gotta love it," said Gabe.

"This guy Marco wants us to use," Brody began, and then paused to nail down his thought. "You know, he could help narrow down who we're looking for. It could go deeper than the Inn or the club. I've heard stories about some really shitty stuff going down around here lately. Thought it was talk, but now, maybe not."

"We'll see what he comes up with before we expose ourselves too much," said TJ. "What's that saying, 'Trust in Allah, but tie up your camel.' And if he has the ties Marco thinks he has, he could clean up any collateral damage our little excursion into revenge may create once we take care of business."

Brody snapped his towel at Casey as they all headed off toward the showers.

"Want a beer?" asked Marco when he caught up with TJ outside the security team's locker room.

"Always. Thanks."

Marco pulled two bottles from the refrigerator in the kitchen area, popped the caps, and handed one to TJ.

Their "Cheers," said in unison, was followed by bottle necks clinking. TJ took a long swig.

"How's it going?" asked Marco.

Marco considered the man standing in front of him. TJ was one of the most driven men Marco had ever met. Failure was not an option, not a word in his vocabulary. He wouldn't stop until his mission was accomplished. And this job was personal.

"As good as can be expected. Still a lot of holes. A lot of moving parts. Too many unknowns need to be fleshed out before we move. And we caught an interesting fish last night."

"So I heard. Think she'll be helpful?"

"Has been already. She's got an interesting theory about this woman she thinks is connected to the Inn. Think Kyle's got the hots for her."

"Good for him." Marco took a sip of his beer and grabbed an Oreo from the cookie jar. "Love these. Not sure they go with beer."

"Everything goes with beer."

"Right. Let's take a walk," Marco suggested, pointing toward the beach. "You've had a rough few days. A change of scene will do us both some good. The ocean has magical healing powers."

"You believe that shit?" asked TJ.

"Don't know what I believe at this point. Things are changing quickly around here. Got a feeling there's more change on the horizon."

"That what's keeping you up at night?"

"Yes. That, and the whole Bella affair. I am so sorry this has happened to you and Rosa and Bella. You know whatever you need—she needs—is taken care of right?"

"Yes, and we really can't thank you enough. Rosa is worried sick."

"Mothers—good mothers, and Rosa is the best—never stop worrying about their kids."

They stopped at the water's edge. Cooling spray glistened on their faces. Froth and foam tickled their toes.

"So tell me what's keeping you awake at night."

TJ let the question hang in the air for a few minutes. Swallowing another swig of beer, he pointed to a small crab making its way across the sand.

"The little things. The things we don't know, can't see. We think we've got everything figured out. It's the scenario we can't imagine that worries me, keeps me up at night."

"What are you going to do about it?"

"Simple. Focus on what we know, what we have, and

move heaven and earth to get these guys." TJ smiled as he tilted his beer bottle in Marco's direction for another clink. "Payback's a bitch."

"It's probably not that simple," said Marco. "Feels like there's a piece missing. Something we're not seeing. Someone we don't know about. Higher up and very in charge."

"That would change things. Any idea who?"

"Not yet. Want to wait and see the photos the woman claims to have. We may have caught a break there."

"How does a woman do this to other women, to girls...to *young* girls?"

"You'd be surprised what people are capable of doing to each other. In the name of God or money, success, greed, jealousy, you name the sin, somewhere, someone is perpetrating something horrible on someone else. It's an ugly world out there."

"Tell me about it." TJ's calm demeanor masked the anger burning inside him.

Marco thought about how his own activities and escapades over the years had been carefully planned down to the last detail, and yet always got screwed up because something unexpected happened.

"We live in a world of complications. Kind of makes it more fun, don't you think?" chuckled Marco.

"Oh, yeah. Way more fun." TJ kicked at the water. "We're planning a little more surveillance. Got Casey shadowing that Julio guy. See who he meets with. Where he goes."

"And Daniel? How's he working out?"

"Time will tell." TJ paused in his assessment. He didn't want to offend Marco with his own feelings of mistrust. He had nothing to base them on. Marco trusted this guy. "He'll be here tomorrow."

"His idea or yours?"

"His. He offered."

"Good."

"Didn't realize his PD contact was actually in our little corner of the world. How's that for a coincidence? Thought it would be Lauderdale or Jupiter or Palm Beach. You know hobnobbing with the rich and powerful, not slumming down here."

Waving his beer bottle, Marco laughed, "If you can call this slumming. You know I can't get too involved in the details, right? Gotta keep my image up. Plausible deniability. I'm an upstanding pillar of the local community."

"Gotcha. Not a problem. The equipment alone is priceless. And you're doing way more than I can thank you for to help Bella. Don't know how I'll ever repay you."

"Not necessary. Glad to do it."

The two stood in silence for a time. Waves crashed to shore as the tide came in.

"Daniel can be useful. He knows the law, and you know what needs to be done. You can cross lines he can't. He can keep you from crossing lines you shouldn't cross."

"Works for me." Long pause. "Until it doesn't."

"Keep me in the loop."

"Absolutely."

"Good luck."

"Thanks."

Estella sat alone in Dr. Oliver's third floor waiting room. She smoothed an invisible wrinkle from her floral print skirt, and she'd already made sure her crisp white cotton blouse was buttoned all the way to her collarbone. She'd pulled her hair back into a low pony tail and wore simple hoop earrings. Flat black sandals completed her look. It was all very conservative—constrictive—reminiscent of the outfits her teachers wore when she went to Catholic school. Appearances were important. She wanted the doctor to know she was a caring mother. How her clothes would do that, she wasn't quite sure, but Rosa assured her they would.

Claire was due to be released from the hospital today. Dr. Oliver wanted to meet with Estella before signing Claire's release papers, because she was a minor and there were important, life-changing decisions to be made.

The appointment was for two o'clock. She and Rosa arrived five minutes before two. It was now two fifteen. Rosa had stepped out to go to the bathroom after bringing Estella coffee. Her hands trembled as she held the Styrofoam cup.

The door to the doctor's office opened. A tall, thin man with gray hair, a mustache and round, wire-framed glasses magnifying soft, blue-gray eyes smiled at her.

"Mrs. Calderone?" As she was the only one in the waiting room, he approached with his hand out.

"Yes." Estella rose and went toward him. They met in the middle. When they shook hands, she cursed herself for not wiping her clammy hands off first.

"I'm Dr. Oliver. It's so nice to meet you. Sorry for my delay. I had a minor patient crisis to deal with. Come in. Let's sit and talk for a while."

"My sister, Rosa, is here with me. Could we wait a second for her to return from the bathroom?"

But there was no need to wait, because Rosa had just turned the corner and joined them. Pleasantries were exchanged while Dr. Oliver ushered them into his office. It was small, and decorated in warm earth tones, giving it a cozy, homey feel. In addition to the usual desk and credenza, there were two tapestry-upholstered club chairs and a sage green sofa nestled into the corner, making a nice seating area in front of large windows which looked out onto the park across from the hospital. Pictures of cool mountain streams and soft ocean vistas adorned the walls.

Dr. Oliver herded them toward the sofa and club chairs. "We'll be more comfortable here. Please sit down. We have a lot to talk about."

Rosa took one of the club chairs. Her role here was to comfort her sister, not be part of the conversation. Dr. Oliver seated himself in the other club chair facing Estella, who positioned herself in the center of the sofa.

"Thank you. How is Claire doing, Doctor?"

"She's resting comfortably. We'll go see her when we are done here."

"That would be great. I've been so worried. We both have." Looking at Rosa for support, Estella's fidgeting telegraphed high stress. She couldn't figure out what to do with her hands. They were in her lap, at her sides, picking at a thread on the sofa, and back in her lap.

"Claire and I met briefly yesterday, though she was still quite out of it and really didn't remember me. I went to visit her again today at lunch time, and we had a good conversation. She's very angry. And very confused."

Estella bit her lip. Every ounce of her being braced herself for what she was sure was bad news.

"I don't know what to say. I don't understand. What happened?"

"Well, the lab tests on her stomach contents… You know they had to pump her stomach?"

"Yes. The doctor told us Sunday night."

"Good. She is a minor, so it is important you know everything that is going on. They found traces of both stimulants and depressants in her system. That's a lethal combination."

Dr. Oliver spoke slowly and chose his words carefully. He didn't want to use medical terminology that would frighten Estella. He needed to enlist her support to treat Claire, not scare her so much she would continue denying Claire's drug problem.

"Think of it as an elevator ride. The laws of nature must apply. What goes up must also come down. The stimulants, amphetamines, bring you up, give you a euphoric sensation, like you can fly. The barbiturates bring you down."

Looking from one woman to the other, Dr. Oliver paused to allow his descriptions of the drugs' effects to register. Estella stared at the carpet, avoiding eye contact. To him, this spoke volumes about the possibility of drug use by more than one member of this family.

"Mrs. Calderone, do you have any questions?"

"No. My Claire, she's a good girl. She helps me with her brothers, watches them when I go to work."

"Has she been upset about anything lately?"

"She's a teenager. They're always upset about something. It passes in a day or so, you know. One day it's this boy, the next day it's some other boy. I know she's been studying hard for the state tests next week. She needs to pass them to graduate."

"I see." He made a quick note on a small pad. "Worrying about passing the exams can be stressful." The emotional distress Dr. Oliver witnessed from Claire's mother concerned him. There was more here to learn. He decided to push the envelope to see where it took him.

"I am wondering, Mrs. Calderone, about what drugs might be in your home. Do you take any types of medications? For sleep perhaps? Or stress? Are there any drugs like I've described in your home?"

"No doctor." The words she spoke did not match the look

on her face. "The only thing I have in the house is aspirin. You know, for when I have a headache. And I keep it locked up like I'm supposed to. You know, so none of the children can get to it."

"Well, that's good to know." Like mother, like daughter, thought Dr. Oliver. She's lying. Drugs have played, and may still be playing, a larger role in her life than she cares to admit.

"I do have one other bit of information. Kind of complicates Claire's treatment. Since Claire is only seventeen and considered a minor, I need to inform you that she's pregnant."

Estella gasped, her hand flew to her throat. Rosa blanched and turned to stare at her sister.

"No. That can't be. Like you said, she's only seventeen. She's a good girl. She doesn't go with boys."

"The tests don't lie. We repeated it twice to be sure. She's about one month pregnant."

"Does Claire know?" Rosa had been a passive observer until the pregnancy news. Pregnancy changed everything.

"Yes. She knows. I told her earlier today when we talked. Whether she knew before…well, she said she didn't know when I told her. She seemed genuinely surprised. She might not have missed a period yet. Or if she did miss, she could have chalked it up to nerves and not bought a home pregnancy test."

"Dr. Oliver," said Rosa. "Pardon my bluntness, but do you think Claire might have done this on purpose? Mixed the drugs, I mean. Do you think she did this on purpose?"

"I don't know yet. And our job now is to support her with love, not judgments. Make sure she receives the best care possible so she doesn't try it again. I'm sorry to say, but teenage suicides are rampant.

"But that's a sin," said Estella. "We're Catholic. Claire wouldn't do that. She's a good girl. She knows it's against the church's teaching. It's a sin."

"That may be, Mrs. Calderone." Dr. Oliver felt for this woman. His eyes remained on her as he moved from his chair to sit beside her on the sofa. He took her hands into his own. They were ice. He nestled them between his own hands so he could share his warmth with her.

"But we need to face what we have in front of us and deal with it head-on. Find out if this was a terrible accident or something more. Very often, when someone takes an overdose on purpose, they may fail at the attempt the first time, but the second time they're usually not so lucky."

Estella pulled her hands out of Dr. Oliver's and wrapped her arms tight around her body. Her eyes were darting all over the room, seeking a safe place to focus. She dared not look at Rosa, fearing the harsh judgment she might see in her sister's eyes.

"What I'd like to do is enroll Claire in our CARE program. We conduct it here at the hospital. It's a residential program, and since Claire is due to leave today, if you agree, we can simply move her to our facility. It's a small, intimate space across the courtyard. If you are willing, we can all take a tour of the space and get Claire settled in."

Estella abruptly stood and spun toward the windows. Rosa went to her side, arms outstretched, offering a hug. Estella moved away from her sister's embrace, her defensive barricades overtaking her working brain. Rosa could tell Estella had mentally left the room. The pregnancy. The drugs. All of this was too much for her. Claire was not the only member of this family needing care, support, and love right now.

"Come," said Dr. Oliver, standing and holding out his

hand to Mrs. Calderone. "Let's all go see Claire. She's down the hall."

❖

Carolyn's claustrophobia flared up. The walls of the small toolshed closed in on her. She'd lost track of time. She knew she had slept some, and hours earlier someone had brought her some food, more water and escorted her to the bathroom. She needed to get out of here. She had important things to do.

Trying the door, she found it unlocked. *That was stupid. Why didn't I try to open it hours ago?* Once she stepped outside, the scent of salt water greeted her. The cool night air was a welcome relief. Stars twinkled in the sky as darkness began to give way to dawn. Shit, she thought, hours wasted.

"How are you doing?" asked Kyle.

Carolyn jumped at the sound of his voice. She turned to see a tall handsome man standing behind a pickup truck. She felt a stirring, a tightening of muscles long ignored. She blushed. And hoped it was too dark for him to notice.

"I didn't think anyone was here."

"Just straightening some things up in my truck before I drive you back to wherever you left your car."

"Boys and their toys. Don't let me stop you." *I wouldn't mind you doing a bit of straightening up with me. Shit, I'm so horny. And you look sooo good.*

"I'm done. Can I get you anything? You look cold."

"Feels good. Refreshing. The walls were closing in on me in there. Not big on small spaces. Couldn't believe the door wasn't locked. And it's nice to hear you're letting me leave. Whose idea was that?"

"TJ."

"So he's human after all. How about that? Mind if I take a walk down to the beach before we go?"

"Be my guest."

"Want to come?" *Shit! Nothing like inviting trouble.*

"Sounds good to me."

They walked over the dunes and onto the sand, heading for the water. Carolyn stopped, leaned on Kyle as she pulled off her sneakers and socks. Cool sand tingled between her toes.

"So, what do you do besides grabbing unsuspecting women who are minding their own business?"

"Excuse me, but you were in the woods at night using night vision binoculars to spy on a private business. Doesn't sound like minding your own business to me," laughed Kyle.

"You could see it that way," smiled Carolyn. "So what do you do?"

"I work security at a private estate."

"Wow. A private estate. Like for a rich celebrity?"

"No. No one famous. A man who relishes his privacy."

"Interesting. Is that how you know TJ?"

"No."

"A man of few words. How mysterious."

"I relish my privacy too."

"I can see that. What else do you relish?"

"Hot dogs, potato chips, and beer."

"Good answer for a man who relishes his privacy. Any chance of learning anything from you about TJ? Sure could use a read on him, in case he decides to go all badass on me."

"Sorry to disappoint you," said Kyle, "but that's not going to happen."

"Seriously?"

"Yeah. The fact that the door wasn't locked and you're out here roaming free should tell you that."

"Only tells me he's cutting me some slack for now. And that could change."

"Not likely. Not his style. I've known him longer than dirt."

"Brothers from another mother?" Carolyn kicked at the water as it encircled her feet.

"Something like that. We've been through a lot together. TJ doesn't have a vindictive streak. Acts like he does. Maybe even sometimes, like now, he might wish he did, but it isn't in him. No revenge bones. More like integrity bones, with a huge heap of honor on top, and a strong moral compass to guide his actions."

"Nice to know."

"Rest easy, Carolyn. TJ's one of the good guys, the really good guys." Kyle watched for any reaction to his words. Seeing none, he added, "Hope that doesn't disappoint you."

"I'm not disappointed at all. I want him to be one of the good guys, someone who can help me find my daughter."

"How long has she been missing?"

"Five years. Went to Biloxi for a job when the casinos opened. Wanted to be someplace exciting. Not boring, freezing-cold Bangor. Had dreams of being famous. Stars in her eyes. And then she was gone."

The haunting tone of her voice touched Kyle. Having no kids of his own, he could only imagine the power of the parental bond, and he longed to experience it. His own parents had too often been indifferent about his antics when he was growing up. They had been too deep into their own careers to notice.

"Must have been hard all these years." Kyle stopped walking. The mysterious woman next to him intrigued him. Impressive tenacity, a lioness in a graceful, lithe body. He found himself wanting to know her better—wanting her.

"Yes, it has been." Carolyn stared out to sea, into the

darkness. Her voice resonated against the melancholy wail of a passing gull. "The police—they told me to be patient. That was five years ago. Five years. I think I've been very patient. They weren't doing anything, so I did what any mother would do. I quit my day job and started looking for her myself. I knew in my heart she wasn't dead. And I had faith that if I was diligent I could do what the police couldn't. I could find her. Once I started searching, I couldn't stop."

"And you think you've found her?"

"Yes. I'd stake my life on it."

"That's rather melodramatic."

"Maybe so. But it is what it is." Carolyn turned and faced Kyle, pulsing with a power beyond a mother's love for her child. "I can't find peace until I find her, until I know, one way or the other. I need to know. Not knowing is unbearable. I can't move on. Grieve. I'm stuck. Trapped. In limbo."

Their eyes locked. Carolyn's breath caught in her throat. All motion slowed. He was so close to her. Too close. She could feel his breath on her face, the scent of him bringing her body to life. She reached out and touched the cleft in his chin.

Kyle caught her hand, gently kissed her palm, leaned in for another kiss. After the kiss, he brushed away a strand of her windswept hair. His fingertips continued down her cheek and traced the outline of her lips.

She shivered.

He pulled her close, enfolding her in his warmth.

She made no move to free herself, wanting to stay in the safety of his strong embrace forever. Tension from her quest to find her daughter melted away in the warmth of his protective arms—the kind of arms she'd longed to have hold her all of her life. She nestled into him, wrapping her own arms around his firm, heated body, never wanting to let go.

"This is probably not a good idea," she whispered.

"Probably not."

"We barely know each other. What will people think?"

"I'm not the kiss and tell type." Kyle brushed her lips with his. "Mmmm, salty."

"We are at the beach."

"Aren't we, though? Alone at the beach. No one around for miles."

She slipped her hands under his shirt relishing the way his muscles rippled when she danced her fingers on his chest. Her longing intensified.

He covered her mouth with his, his tongue inviting hers to play, then searching deeper into heated, secret places.

Pulling away slightly, he looked directly into her eyes and he murmured, "Sweet, like sugar. You are one amazing woman." His lips brushed hers, then found their way across her cheek and down her neck, under her chin and back up.

"Make love to me," she whispered. "I want to feel you inside me."

"With pleasure."

Strong hands cupped her face. Warm lips met hers. Easy, gentle, tentative at first. After pecking the tip of her nose, his lips glided across her cheeks before his mouth covered hers again, more demanding this time. Her breath tasted of the sea. Kyle could feel her heart beating faster and faster against his chest, matching his own beat for beat.

Kyle pulled back a bit and searched her face. He kissed her forehead and nuzzled into her hair. Ever so gently their bodies found the sand, legs intertwined, exploring one another with each kiss, with each touch.

Erratic breaths escaped into the night along with soft moans and guttural grunts. Muscles tightened. Carolyn's back arched. Tentative thrusts until their rhythm meshed and ignited their fire. An ecstatic gasp escaped her. Dual explosions rocked them—wave upon wave of heat rippled through their bodies—and they fell back, spent.

The intensity of their lovemaking caught Carolyn off guard. "Oh, that felt so good. It's been a long time. I've been so focused on finding Amelia. I forgot how wonderful making love can be."

"Sweet. I knew it would be."

She lay in his arms, his shoulder her pillow, staring up at the stars.

"This isn't how I normally behave," she said, flustered and a bit embarrassed now that she'd come back to earth. "I don't want you to think I do it willy-nilly."

"Don't give it another thought. I don't think any less of you. I like you. Your straightforward style, the way you sassed TJ, your commitment to finding your daughter. It all suits you. And just so you know, I don't do this with everyone I meet either. So we're even." Rolling onto his side, he brushed her hair away from her face. "I better get you back to your room. You need some rest. And so do I. We've got important work to do."

"You're right. We should go."

Neither one moved. Finally, Kyle stood and pulled her up into his arms. His mouth engulfed hers, hot and hungry for more of her.

Feeling him harden she said, "You start this again, and I promise you we won't get any sleep."

"I'm a guy. I've got a pulse. As for the rest," he chuckled with a huge grin, "it doesn't take much."

"Good to know. Wouldn't want to think I caused that."

"Don't be too sure you didn't. How about a rain check?"

"Absolutely."

Heading back to his truck, he kept one arm snugged firmly around her shoulders. Carolyn remained tucked into the side of a man she found incredibly appealing in ways too numerous to count. Suddenly a knot squeezed her stomach, reminding her it had been a long time between meals.

"How about some breakfast? Know any all-night diners?" Blurting out the invitation surprised her; the reason did not. There was something about this man. She didn't want their time together to end yet.

"There's a good one not too far from here."

"Take me back to my car, and I'll follow you there. That way we can go our separate ways after we eat."

She told him where she parked. He pulled up next to her car. Reaching for the door handle, Carolyn started to say something and stopped.

"Yes? You were going to say something?"

"No. Nothing important. I'll be right behind you."

As Kyle watch her get settled behind the wheel, he couldn't help but wonder whether a whole new chapter of his life was about to begin. Carolyn was definitely a woman deserving of some serious time and his undivided attention. He was ready to put his past behind him.

The Dear John letter he received while in Iraq had torn a hole through his heart, and he had retreated into a restricted world free of romantic emotional attachments. He learned how to be alone. Ashes to ashes, dust to dust—his was a one body to a casket theory. He'd put it into action while he was still very much alive and kicking. Did he dare climb out of his box and put his heart out there? Invest in loving?

Alone behind the wheel, Carolyn crossed her arms, hugging herself, pretending to be in his strong embrace. Unplanned sex. She could smell Kyle's manly scent on her T-shirt. And she had no intention of taking it off anytime soon. Such a sexy man. Square jawed, with that small cleft in his chin that she wanted to lick every time. And warm, hazel-green eyes, the color of a forest in spring, in that rugged, tanned face. An outdoors man. All he needed was a checked flannel shirt.

She'd been wired tight for the past few years, all her resources devoted to finding her daughter. Relentless. Never giving up hope. And that hope had fueled her. Now a different kind of hope stole into her thoughts. The kiss had been perfect. Like a first kiss should be. His touch was tantalizing, the encounter on the beach pure fantasy. Dare she wonder what promise a second encounter might hold?

CHAPTER 16

Friday

Rachel stood still, letting warm shower water glide down her body, marking its own path from the top of her head to the tile shower floor. The scent of lavender surrounded her. She chuckled at the extravagance of converting her simple shower to an aromatherapy steam experience. It was good to be home.

She'd always lived simply. Nothing extravagant. How things had changed because of her aunt's inheritance! Now she had more money than she could ever have imagined, even in her wildest dreams. Most was in a trust for the Raphael Fund. Even after setting it up and investing to ensure its ongoing viability to help wounded warriors, there was still plenty left. Her children, Jenny and Scott, and her grandchildren would never want for anything. Neither would she. At least monetarily.

The weekend at the tournament with Sara had been more than she bargained for. The trip to the ER conjured images of David's sudden death and reignited old fears. None of us really know how long we have, she thought. Life is tenuous.

It can be gone in the blink of an eye, the snap of your fingers, in a heartbeat.

The heartbeat metaphor hit home. She wanted her heart to keep beating in a normal rhythm. Closing her eyes, she again replayed Sunday evening in the hospital. When an orderly walked in, looked at the monitor, and said "whoa," Rachel had known she was in trouble.

Serious choices lay ahead about what she wanted to happen next. A big part of next involved Daniel. These last few months, they'd been like two ships passing in the night. She stopped at his apartment when she was in New York on Fund business, and he came down for a quick interlude before going back out to sea—or, in Daniel's case, back to work.

That's what just happened. He'd picked her up at the airport on Tuesday when she got back from the tournament, but left to go back to New York early Thursday. They barely had time for a nice dinner. He was on his way back today and planned to stay for a week. She planned to entice him into retiring sooner rather than later.

What then? Williamsburg would be a far cry from Brooklyn. Like another planet, without a decent bagel and no belly lox in sight. His whole life centered on Brooklyn. How could he pick up and move? Then again, wasn't that exactly what she had done?

The immediate plan called for him to move into this home. They were both in love with a two-acre lot in her gated community that backed the James River. It would be truly perfect, with plenty of room for the dream home design she'd seen in an issue of Better Homes and Gardens years ago. Although she never cut out the blueprints, she could describe it to any architect they might hire.

His new job opportunity sounded perfect. Building furniture, target shooting, and biking were his major hobbies, but they weren't going to be enough for a guy used to a life of adrenalin rushes. He kept saying he'd be fine, that police work was mostly paperwork. Bullshit. She watched enough Law and Order and Criminal Minds episodes to know police work was about catching bad guys and running down criminals.

Emerging from the shower, Rachel checked her timing. Daniel would be here soon. A little afternoon delight followed by dinner and then maybe some evening delight. Giggling to herself, Rachel felt the heat flushing her cheeks…and then the rest of her…with anticipation.

While she was drying her hair, she rehearsed her plans. She had two bags of rose petals, which she planned to trail from the front door to the bedroom. Her new rose pink teddy lay on her bed, waiting for her to slip into it. She had soft music set to go in the stereo. The champagne was in the refrigerator chilling. She didn't want to go against her doctor's orders about only having a small bit of wine, so she planned to allow herself only a sip or two of the champagne. However, she had nixed the chocolate-covered strawberries in favor of larger, plain strawberries dipped in sour cream and rolled in brown sugar. She had a moment's pause. *Stimulants aren't good for my heart. Wonder if sex is? Hell, if making love with Daniel kills me, at least I'll go out with a smile on my face.*

Hearing the phone, she put on her robe and went to answer it.

"Hello"

"Hey, honey. How are you?"

"Good. Where are you? When do you think you'll get here."

"Slight change of plans, hon. I'm sorry. Remember that call I got the other morning? Need to do a favor for someone who once did a big favor for me—for us. He called in his chit and I'm happy to oblige. Looks like that favor requires me to be someplace else."

"Oh." Her disappointment was hard to hide.

"I'm at LaGuardia heading to Florida. My plane leaves in thirty minutes. I tried to call you before, but there was no answer."

"I was out running errands and I've been in the shower."

"Shower, huh? Sounds like fun."

It would have been if you were here, she thought. "How long do you think you'll be down there?"

"A few days. But when this one is over, I'm thinking maybe I should tell Mac and Jim I don't want to be on the task force."

"Then what would you do? Sit around the house twiddling your thumbs?"

"Not a pretty picture for the next thirty years, give or take."

"Exactly. So go. Do your detective thing. We'll be fine."

"They're boarding my flight. I'll call you later to tell you where I'm staying. I love you."

"Love you too."

Rachel hung up and fell back on the bed, an arm flung to either side. *Shit! There goes the afternoon. Can you freeze rose petals?*

The afternoon sun baked the cement. You could have fried an egg in seconds. TJ chose the only table with its umbrella fully extended. Floridians weren't stupid. They knew better than to sit outside at the hottest time of day. Even under the umbrella's shade, beads of sweat rolled down his face. He sat down with his back to the building and scanned the street. He could see Kyle sitting in the shade on a bench outside the barber shop across the street.

Within minutes he spotted their mark. TJ watched the man cross the street. A pale blue golf shirt tucked into khaki Dockers, sandals and no socks. Thank God for no socks. TJ felt his grin come alive. Tourists in sandals and socks drove him crazy.

"Detective Berger?" said TJ, standing up. The detective had him height-wise, by about six inches.

"Yep. TJ? Nice to meet you." Each held out his hand to the other. Handshakes combined with dueling once-overs.

"Can I get you something to drink? I'm sorry, I know it's hotter than hell out here. But it's private. Inside's crowded."

"Something icy cold sounds good. Lemonade if they've got it."

"Be right back."

Daniel watched him enter the Starbucks. Definitely former military. Special Forces maybe. You could usually tell. There was something about how they carried themselves. All confidence. No bullshit.

TJ returned with two bottles of Snapple, one lemonade flavor, one iced tea. He also carried two large Styrofoam cups filled to the brim with ice. Each man got down to business with his drink of choice. The silence stretched. Thirty seconds. One minute. Who would break first? Let the foreplay begin.

"So, where you from?" asked TJ.

"Brooklyn. Can't ya tell by my accent?"

"Haven't heard you talk enough yet. Me, too."

"Me too what?"

"From Brooklyn. Long time ago."

They sipped their drinks in silence, looking up and down the street, stealing sideways glances at each other.

"What's does TJ stand for?"

"Getting personal, are we? Thaddeus Jamison. Too much name. TJ fits me better."

Daniel's memory flashed at hearing the name. "This may sound crazy, but I think we've met before. There was a kid in the park a long time ago, He found a body."

Shocked, TJ said, "Shit. You were there?"

"Yes. My first case as a detective. I've often wondered what happened to that kid. Didn't get the sense he was going to get much help from his parents. Father seemed like a real jerk."

"That kid—that was me. And my dad was worse than a jerk. That day changed my life. Went down a rough road for a while. You know, usual adolescent rebellion stuff. Then something snapped. Joined the Marines."

"Looks like you turned out okay. I'm glad. I worried about you."

"How do you know Mr. Rogers?" asked TJ, using Marco's alias. When he leaned back, the white plastic seat burned, but he didn't dare flinch.

"Mr. Rogers? As in Mark Rogers?" asked Daniel. The last dot finally confirmed. It had been Mark Rogers bugging Rachel's home. Then again, there really was no Mark Rogers. A made-up name for a made-up man.

TJ nodded silently.

"I don't know him. I know his voice on the phone. He helped a friend of mine out of a tight spot. Though I'm sure you already know this."

"I may have heard a bit about a guy with a gun. Other than that, Mr. Rogers likes to keep his business private."

Yes, Daniel thought. He likes his privacy, but has no trouble invading the privacy of others.

"And he said you work for him. What type of work do you do?"

"Security management."

209

This guy's not exactly big on conversation, thought Daniel. "Think we need to get down to business so we can both get the hell out of the sun. Why don't you fill me in on what's going on?"

"My daughter. As I said on the phone, we got her back. She's home safe."

"That's good. A blessing she wasn't harmed. I assume you'll get her whatever help she'll need to cope with her experience."

"Already on it."

"You want the guy who hurt your daughter punished. I get that. What I don't get is why you need me."

"Your connections, to be precise. You can go places we can't. My gut tells me this isn't the first time these guys, whoever they are, have done something like this. Maybe the cops have some information that can help us take these guys down."

"So judge, jury, and executioner all in one?"

"Not my first choice, Detective. Doing all three jobs fits more in your line of work. But these guys gotta pay. And if the system won't do it, I will."

"Can I make a suggestion?"

"Shoot."

"Let's find out who they are first, and the extent of their crimes second. And if we do these two things diligently and thoroughly, cross our t's and dot our i's, then I'll make sure the system does its job."

"Must be a cop thing," laughed TJ. "You know you can't promise that. You don't have any control over the system. And it's screwed up more cases, and let some really bad people continue to prey on the innocent, more times than I can count."

"Consider me the ultimate optimist, then."

TJ smiled. "We could use your help with the local PD.

See if they've had any cases that fit a similar MO. Any suspects. Stuff like that."

"This I can do. I've got friends in several local PDs. Guys who wimped out on the snow and cold, but how they take this heat is beyond me. After we set up our meet, I called one of them to let him know I was coming down. Winds up he isn't on one of the big forces. Said he worked in a small municipality called Sand Isle. How's that for a coincidence? We made dinner plans. We're also going golfing tomorrow morning. Between dinner and a round of golf, I should be able to find out something useful."

"Sounds like a plan."

Daniel finished his lemonade and stood. He dumped the cup and bottle in the garbage, took one last look at TJ, nodded, and headed back to his car.

TJ's barely perceptible nod had Kyle on his feet. He ditched his drink and headed for his own car. Kyle pulled out of the parking lot behind Daniel. TJ slowly walked to his car, which was conveniently parked on the street in front of the Starbucks. He got in line behind Daniel and Kyle, and all three headed south on A1A.

CHAPTER 17

Saturday

An early morning run along the beach always helped clear her head. Bella splashed in and out of the water with long, powerful strides. Her feet pounded into the cool sand. Running along the ocean had started out as a dad/daughter affair, quickly becoming their special thing. Slowly, it became special to her for itself, as a way to clear her mind and focus her attention on her dreams and her goals.

Low tide matched her mood. How close she had come to losing everything. Disappointment in herself, and guilt for lying to her parents, dogged her steps. Curiosity had won over her common sense. It wasn't supposed to happen this way. She had just wanted a taste of Claire's life, to try it out, experience how it felt to be Claire—go out and party like the popular girls. If only for one night.

When she saw Miss Marissa, all decked out in white and coming toward her, she slowed her pace. They both stopped when they came face-to-face.

"Good morning, Bella. What a beautiful morning it is. It's great to see you out here. How are you feeling?"

"Good. I'm good." Bella rinsed sand away from her taut calves, redid her ponytail and adjusted her T-shirt and shorts.

"I'm so glad. All of us were so worried about you."

"I know. I am so sorry."

Marissa sensed there was more she wanted to say. If given the time, she'd spit it out.

"I love coming out here to look for sea glass." Marissa bent down and started to pick through the broken shells and seaweed that had washed up onto the beach. "You've seen the jars all around my home with my sea glass collection, haven't you?"

"Yes. It's been a while. I'm sure you have more now."

"It is getting a bit out of hand. But the glass is so pretty. And aimlessly looking for it allows my mind to wander. I can think about things more deeply out here in the fresh air and sunshine. Kind of cleanses the soul."

Marissa straightened up and looked into Bella's eyes. She was now part of an elite club, a sisterhood few girls wanted to join, the walking wounded. They connected instantaneously, knew one another by sight, even though their victim stories differed.

Marissa put her arm through Bella's. "Let's walk."

Sunshine glistened off the wave caps. Cooling water refreshed their toes. Salt spray kissed their faces. The wind untamed their ponytails.

"Do you think they will ever trust me again?"

"That depends on you. You've got to make amends for the lie, of course, but none of the rest of it."

"What do you mean?"

"What happened as a result of the lie you told your mother was beyond your control. Bad things happen to good people all the time. If you had not lied, it might not have happened the way it did."

"But it did happen."

"True. But something bad could have happened if you had gone to the library like you said you were doing. Or the mall. Or the movies. We'll never know."

Marissa could see Bella thinking through what she had said.

"Bad things don't happen at libraries, except maybe a headache from studying too hard," Bella chuckled.

"What you need to remember is your parents love you very much. They were out of their minds with worry. Their emotions are raw. They're angry and relieved and disappointed and happy all at the same time."

"I do know that...that they love me. And I know how lucky I am to live here. I wanted a little freedom, that's all."

"Freedom isn't free. There is always a cost, a price. Your desire for freedom cost you some of your integrity. It cost you some of the trust your parents had placed in you. Thank God it didn't cost you more."

"I know." Bella stopped walking. Tears rolled down her cheeks. The sadness in Bella's voice had tears welling up Marissa's eyes.

"Look at this ocean. The power of wind and water is tremendous. We see it in the hurricanes. Sometimes I think that's why hurricanes are given human names, because of their power to destroy and to create. They destroy homes, uproot people's lives. And then, after the destruction, people stand tall. They dig down deep, rally, and rebuild."

She looked over at Bella, who was staring out to sea. Not sure if Bella was following her analogy, Marissa continued.

"For me, the ocean restores my soul. It strengthens me, especially after I've been away on a business trip. The price you paid...your integrity, the trust...what was broken can be healed. They are not gone forever. These can be restored.

You can earn them back. It will take some work on your part. The important thing here is to learn from your experience."

"Got that part. I learned big time. It's funny. I have friends who lie to their parents all the time, and nothing ever happens to them when they get caught. I go and lie this one time and wham."

"How do you know nothing ever happens to your friends?"

"Because they say they didn't get punished.

"Then the price they paid, the cost of their lies, is much greater than yours in this instance. Their parents are showing a lack of caring when they don't hold them accountable for their actions. Being accountable for our actions is, in many ways, all we have."

Bella turned to face Marissa and embraced her tightly. Marissa returned the hug.

"Thank you."

"You're welcome."

"We didn't meet by accident, you know. I knew you'd be out here. You're out here every day."

"I know, baby. I know," whispered Marissa in Bella's ear. She knew Bella's experience would leave scars, invisible scars. In time, most would heal. Others, perhaps not.

Carolyn moved to the front of the room and clipped four photos onto the white board.

"I think this person may be who we're looking for. The person in charge of the entire operation."

"That's four people," said Casey.

"Maybe." She paused long enough to let seeds of

possibility form in the minds of those present. "I think she is one person, the same person."

"What makes you think they're the same person?" asked TJ.

"Something about the eyes. In each photo they strike me the same way. I can't explain it better than that. And, of course, the dragon pendant around her neck. It's the same intricate, unique design. Look closer."

TJ silently examined the photos hanging side by side. Four different women photographed in different places at different times, with different names mentioned in each caption. One blonde, two brunettes, one redhead. One dancing on a riverboat with a dashing older man. One posing at a groundbreaking ceremony in Biloxi for a new casino after Katrina destroyed much of the waterfront. One holding a trophy from a mah jongg tournament in Vegas in 2009, and one on stage at a charity auction in New Orleans.

"I don't see it," said Gabe.

"Look around the eyes," said Carolyn. "Get closer. Got a magnifying glass?"

"On it," said Brett. "Be right back."

"I think of her as an opportunistic predator. She slips out of one character and into another as easily as we change our underwear. Doesn't care who she hurts, or who she destroys, as long as she gets what she wants."

"And what do you think that is exactly? What she wants, I mean?" asked Kyle.

"If I had to play amateur psychiatrist, I'd guess acceptance as one of the beautiful people. Rich. Famous. Invited to the best parties. Accepted, not shunned. I'm guessing crappy childhood, white trash, dirt."

"And you think these women are all this woman— Desiree De Maurier?" asked Daniel.

"Yes." Facing Marco, she asked, "That is Desiree in the tournament photo, isn't it?"

"Looks like her," said Marco. He slowly moved from photo to photo, examining each one with the magnifying glass.

"In each photo she has a different name," said Gabe.

"Yes. She changes her name, but always uses the same initials. Coincidence?"

"No such thing," said Kyle.

"I agree. Here she's Diana Delacroix," said Carolyn pointing to the riverboat photo, "and Delilah Du Bois, Daphne Driscoll, and Desiree De Maurier. Must be something about those initials in her past."

"A sociopath with a sweet as honey southern drawl," said Gabe. "Dangerous combination."

Turning to Marco, Casey asked, "What if she's right? What if all the women in the photos are the same woman, and Desiree De Maurier is behind this? What do you think?"

"The Desiree connection surprises me. And I'm not easily surprised. Always wondered about her." Marco put down the magnifying glass. "Sharp eyes there, Carolyn. You've made a good case. Convinced me."

"She's a big deal around here, isn't she?" asked Carolyn.

"In her mind, maybe," said Marco. "Acts like the sheer force of her personality can open doors. Kind of like the parting of the Red Sea."

"Heartless bitch," growled Casey, "beguiling others with her flamboyance and false charms while doing the unspeakable under the cloak of a legitimate business."

"If all of these are the same person, Desiree De Maurier, then we know a lot about her," said TJ. Now he had the magnifying glass and was moving from photo to photo to photo.

"We do? Like what?" asked Steve, confusion written all over his face.

"She's a fighter, highly adaptable, resilient, dangerous when cornered, and hard to kill. She thinks she's invincible—and invisible—so she flaunts herself. She lives here in Sand Isle, within a couple of miles of both the sex trafficking business and the club. Knows how to work men. You should have seen her in action at Marco's party last Friday night. Sucked all the air out of the room."

"She's dug in deep. I suspect she also has people around her who have a lot to lose if she goes down," said Kyle. "Bet she's a bookkeeper."

"Wouldn't surprise me," said TJ.

"What do you mean by that? What's a bookkeeper?" asked Carolyn.

"Someone who keeps records, good records, cryptic records, hidden records. The kind of records politicians and people with a lot to lose fear," said Kyle. "We need to find out who all the players are, their connections and ties to one another, and, most important, who is at the center pulling the strings. People like this don't exactly play by the Marquis of Queensbury rules."

"Eureka! They can run, but they can't hide from me, Brett, hacker extraordinaire." Rubbing his hands together and cracking his knuckles, he continued, "I cracked it. I'm in."

"In what?" asked TJ, startled by Brett's sudden outburst. The man had been silently hammering on his laptop keys for over an hour.

"Layers of companies within companies held by corporations with initials for names owned by other companies. I love it! A spider's web of shell companies buried behind and under other shell companies to obfuscate ownership."

"Like playing hide and seek with yourself," said Gabe.

"Look here," said Brett pointing to his screen. "These same two names—Julio Vargas and Dawn DeSoto—pop up connected to the club or the Inn, or both."

"Julio's the guy Javier said owned the club," said Art. "Who is Dawn DeSoto?"

"If the pattern holds, it's Desiree," said Carolyn.

"Then other business names appear, adding a dash of complexity mingled throughout legitimate businesses. A company called Shale Enterprises purchased the Inn about two years ago. It also owns Metamorphosis and another club, called Kaleidoscope, in South Beach."

"Well done, Brett." Marco gave Brett's shoulder a firm squeeze.

"Companies that only exist on paper make paying crooked cops and politicians to look the other way a whole lot easier. Skim a little here, bribe a little there, and soon everyone is beholden to you, and no one wants to shut down the gravy train," added Kyle.

"Forever the cynic. That's what I love about you." TJ slapped Kyle on the back.

"Thanks, bro. I think."

"Does give you leverage, should any of these people decide they want to blab. You've got records of transactions you promise won't ever see the light of day as long as everyone keeps doing what they've been doing," said TJ.

"Wonder if there's film," said Kyle. "Brett, can you do some digging and see if their security includes video inside the cottages?"

"On it."

"If Dawn is Desiree—" TJ stopped mid-sentence and turned to Carolyn. "Know anything else about her?"

"Yes. I know exactly where she is right this very moment." A demure flash of icy blue eyes and a Cheshire cat smile crossed her face. "Planned to put her there myself, you might say. To keep her still, someplace where I could get to her if the need arose. But then fate took over. Someone else intervened."

Totally confused, TJ asked, "What are you talking about?"

"Brett, remember yesterday when I was in here, you mentioned something about finding a cell call from the club to Orlando Doctor's Hospital?"

"Yep. Still trying to track down who was on each end."

"That lady, Desiree De Maurier," said Carolyn pointing to the photos, "was the intended receiver. But she couldn't receive." Carolyn's voice reeked of sarcasm. "She's in the cardiac intensive care unit. Not taking calls. Been there since last Sunday."

"How do you know this?" asked Daniel.

"Because I was with her when the paramedics took her there. Figured the easiest way to get close to her without arousing suspicions was at the mah jongg tournaments. The woman is addicted to the game. I learned how to play, practiced to get good enough, and started going to tournaments. Connected with her in Vegas in 2011. Played the mousey friend to her flamboyant personality. Okay, I sucked up big time. I've been following her around for over two years now. Surprised she went for it."

"My girlfriend was at a mah jongg tournament in Orlando," said Daniel. "She said a lot of people got very sick. Is that how Desiree wound up in the CCU?"

"Yes. She was one of the people who got sick."

"Really? Small world, huh?"

"So did Sophia," added Marco.

"I'm extremely sorry so many people got sick, but I didn't have anything to do with it. I knew she was going to the Orlando tournament a few weeks ago, so we made plans to meet there. Remember, she knows me as this mousy nobody from Maine. To make a long story short, I had planned to arrange it so she would be incapacitated, out of the picture for a while, so I could do my snooping. But then the stars aligned. Something, or someone, took her out before I could. And here I am."

"Took her out?" questioned Daniel in his police detective voice. "I think you left out some important details there."

"Yes, sir, officer, sir." Carolyn gave Daniel a slight salute.

"Detective. That's Detective, sir, if you please."

"I know what you're all thinking. I'm not a monster. Just a mother. Please understand, this is the home stretch for me. I'm sure she has something to do with Amelia's disappearance. She had ties to so many of the places where girls went missing and a few showed up dead—Memphis, New Orleans, Biloxi.

"So I pushed it last year when we were in Vegas. Sneaked a touch of ecstasy in her champagne. She only drinks champagne. It did the trick. Got her loopy fast. Had to help her back to her room and put her to bed. And for one moment she let her guard down. I remember her words clearly. She must have thought I was someone else when she said, 'This can't come back on me. Do you understand?'"

"'Yes ma'am,' I answered, figuring that was what she would expect to hear.

"Then she said, 'Do what you have to do to clean up your mess at the Inn, but keep me out of it.'

"Bingo! There was a mess at some inn. Now I had to find out where. So I followed her. Bought some wigs. Changed my look. She's so damn into herself I doubt she ever noticed me. For most of the last eight months, I have been her constant companion, a shadow on her ass. Never got the Sand Isle connection. I thought she still lived in New Orleans because she spent so much time there."

"How'd you get here? Make the connection to this Inn?"

"When they took her to the hospital, they gave me her purse for safekeeping. I went through her stuff. Found her passwords in her wallet."

"She wrote them down?" Brett's incredulous outburst made her grin.

"Yep. Too stupid for words. Hid them behind her license. Her cell phone was a gold mine. Found photos of an inn under renovation. It was clearly Florida, palm trees in the shot. And then—dumb luck. In one of the photos there was a sign for A1A. Her driver's license showed she lived here. I put two and two together, drove down here and went up and down A1A looking for anything that matched what was in the photos. Found it—Sand Isle Inn. Jackpot!"

"Big jackpot!" said Kyle.

"Maybe that was why all those people got sick?" said Daniel. "Because someone wanted her out of the picture, and it didn't matter who else got in the way. Wouldn't be the first time that's been done."

"That's something on your list, Daniel," said Marco. "Check it out with your connections"

"Definitely."

"And remember the tat?" asked Carolyn.

"What tat?" asked Gabe, looking around the room to see if others were as confused as he was.

"Two bodies of girls were found. One in Memphis, one in Biloxi. Years apart," said TJ. "Unifying fact: they both had small green dragon tats—tramp stamps—on their lower backs. Carolyn thinks the tat and the pendant match, and confirm Desiree's involvement."

"So where does this leave us?" asked Kyle, hoping to connect the dots, make sense of all the information they'd gathered.

"Thanks to Brett's magic fingers hacking into the security

company's files, we've learned the Inn is fully wired to alert when anyone crosses onto the property; plus it has a CCTV hookup," said TJ.

"We've been surveilling the place for a few days now. How come no one came out to talk to me when I went walking along the beach the other night?" asked Casey.

"Not totally sure. Could be they saw you on the camera and didn't see you as a threat. Could be the beach is the one break in the invisible fence system. Not sure," said TJ.

"We need to cut the feed before we go in," said Kyle.

"And how are we going to do that? asked Brett, taking a break from his hacking to listen to the conversation. "It's a closed system. They don't use the company that installed it to do any monitoring,"

"I may have a solution," said Carolyn.

"Pray tell, what might that be?" asked Kyle.

"I've kind of befriended one of the maids. Tuesday after I found the Inn, I went to the office to try and get a room. She was there, crying her eyes out, arguing with the guy behind the desk. Not sure what was going on, so I followed her when she left. Caught up with her at a Starbucks. We had coffee. She talked about someone she knew who was in trouble. Didn't get more. Planned to accidentally on purpose run into her again, but you grabbed me."

"Guess we need to get the two of you back in touch fast," smiled TJ.

CHAPTER 18

Rachel thanked the bellman as he held the front door open for her. Wheeling her suitcase up to the registration counter of the Hyatt, she brushed back her hair, pulling it into a scrunchie. It had been a long flight. Horrendous weather delays. The humidity hit full force when she walked out of the Ft. Lauderdale airport, and sweat soaked her to the bone. The thought of Aunt Lil's favorite line, that ladies glow, men perspire and pigs sweat, brought a smile to her face. After the chilly blast from the air conditioned limo ride, all Rachel wanted now was to get to her room, take a shower, and get something to eat, not necessarily in that order.

"I have a reservation. Resnick." Rachel smiled at the pretty young girl as she handed over her license and credit card.

"Yes, ma'am. King bed. Non-smoking. Ocean view."

Slipping her card and license back in her wallet, Rachel took the room key card.

"Is there someplace where I can get a sandwich?"

"Yes ma'am. The cafe is around the corner to the left. We do have twenty-four hour room service."

"Thank you. It will be easier to get something and bring it

with me. That way I can put the do not disturb sign out and relax."

"Totally understand, ma'am. Traveling is hard these days, and with that weather front that came through a few hours ago... Well, I'm sure it upset everyone's timing."

Turning to the bellman, she handed him five dollars and asked him to take her suitcase to her room.

"With pleasure, ma'am."

Rachel walked around the corner to the cafe. If the heat and humidity hadn't told her she was in South Florida, the cafe's decor surely did. Turquoise, coral, and yellow gave the restaurant a bright, cheery, tropical air. Floor-to-ceiling windows let in tons of sunlight, which bounced off the mirrored wall that ran the full length behind the old-fashioned soda fountain-style eating counter. Vinyl booths hugging the windows and linoleum floor tiles in alternating colors gave the restaurant a '50s feel. A row of stainless steel swivel stools with seat pads in alternating colors of coral, yellow, and turquoise ran the length of the counter, providing seating for guests who didn't want table service. A tabletop jukebox system completed the nostalgia look the designer clearly had in mind for the restaurant.

"Can I get a tuna sandwich on whole wheat, tomatoes, no onions, and decaf iced tea to go please."

"With pleasure, ma'am."

Rachel slid onto the turquoise stool at the end of the speckled white and gold Formica counter to wait for her food. Her spur of the moment trip to Florida had all the earmarks of a wild goose chase, so she hadn't mentioned it to anyone.

She felt bad about lying to the mah jongg tournament director, Brenda, to get Marissa's address. Lying wasn't her thing. But the forces driving her behavior lately seemed beyond her control. In the end, Brenda had been a true friend and told her what she needed to know. They talked about how badly the mah jongg tournament had ended. Brenda had to give refunds to several players who were over-the-top furious. And it had been poison: oleander. One elderly woman died due to complications from her heart condition and the poison she ingested. There was still one woman being closely monitored in the CCU at the hospital.

Through the mirror Rachel watched the traffic on the street behind her. A wailing ambulance sped by. Rachel followed its progress in the mirror. Her eyes came to rest on one of the two men occupying the last booth at the far corner of the empty cafe.

She knew him.

"Is something wrong?" asked the waitress as she placed Rachel's order on the counter.

"Huh?"

"Are you okay? You look lost."

"No...yes. Give me a minute."

Rachel stood up and started to walk silently toward the last booth.

The man facing her stopped talking. His eyes met hers. She froze in her tracks. The name Mark Rogers escaped her lips. Heat rose in her body. Her jaw hurt as her teeth clenched tighter and tighter.

"I think we've got a problem," said Mark Rogers to his booth companion.

The other man turned slowly to see what he was talking about.

"Daniel." His name caught in Rachel's throat. Questions and wild suppositions bombarded her travel-weary mind. They coalesced into two. What was Daniel doing with Mark Rogers? And what were they both doing here? Daniel was supposed to be on a case. Mark Rogers had something to do with her Aunt's death. Why were they here, together, acting so chummy?

"Rachel. Oh, shit," said Daniel.

Rachel backtracked to the counter. Looking at the waitress who had been watching her, Rachel said, "I'm fine, just fine, thank you."

She placed a twenty dollar bill on the counter, picked up her food and walked stoically out of the cafe. She quickened her pace as she headed for the elevator, wanting only to escape into its confines.

"Rachel. Rachel! Wait for me, Rachel." She heard Daniel behind her, calling her name.

Pushing the button, she pleaded with God to have the doors open before Daniel arrived to confront her.

He darted across the lobby after her and caught her arm just as the elevator doors opened.

"Don't touch me." Rachel ripped her arm from his grip.

"What are you doing here?"

Rachel stepped inside the elevator with her hand on the door frame so it would not close until she had her say. Gathering as much strength as she could muster, she straightened her shoulders and glared at Daniel.

"Right now what I'm doing is going to my room. I've had a very long day. I'm going to eat, take a shower and relax." Her words were clipped—her tone biting. "You can go back to your male bonding, or whatever it was you and Mark Rogers were doing back there, all chummy."

"Rachel it's not what you think."

"Don't handle me. You don't know what I think."

"Excuse me," said Mark Rogers as he approached.

Rachel shot daggers in his direction.

"Stop right there. You are not excused. Given our history, I strongly urge you to stay away from me. In fact, get out of my sight. Now!"

The coldness in her voice stopped Marco in his tracks. He looked to Daniel for some sign. The elevator alarm caught them all by surprise.

"We're done," said Rachel as she stepped back to allow the doors to close and pressed the button for her floor. Struggling to catch her breath, she watched the red digital readout of each passing floor. Three, four, five, praying to reach eight without any stops, without anyone intruding into the cramped, stuffy car—her temporary sanctuary.

Marco and Daniel stared blankly at the closed doors. Rachel's coldness startled them both. Neither had seen this side of her before.

"I'd better go. We'll catch up later," said Marco as he turned and left.

Daniel stood alone. He knew Rachel needed some space to process what she had seen—he and Marco, aka Mark Rogers, enjoying lunch like they were old buddies. *What must she be thinking?*

He hadn't been specific the last time they spoke about where he was going, only saying Florida for a new case. She hadn't said anything about coming to Florida. Simple things left unspoken. *What is she doing here?*

Part of him wanted to race to her room to explain. Another part thought restraint might be a better option, to give her some time to work through what she had seen. How much time was hard to gauge. Enough to calm down, but not enough time to allow an overactive imagination to create a story his truth could not overcome.

Rachel slammed the door and leaned her back against it, as if her added weight would ensure it stayed shut, keeping the outside world at bay. A deep, mournful sigh escaped her lips. Her head ached, and her body was stiff from sitting in uncomfortable airport chairs and crammed in a hot first class cabin. What should have been an easy flight had turned into the flight from hell, where every mishap that could happen short of crashing did happen.

And now this. Daniel, all chummy, with Mark Rogers, a man who wasn't real.

Tight shoulders hugged her ears. Her heart thumped inside her chest. She took a few long, deep, cleansing breaths, working to calm herself down, afraid her distress could bring on another heart episode, or a migraine, or both. The last thing she wanted was to get carried out of the hotel on a gurney and wind up in the ER. She quickly brushed away a tear.

"No," she said defiantly. "I'm not going to cry. I'm done crying."

Kicking off her sandals, Rachel unwrapped her food and dove into her sandwich like a ravenous dog that hadn't eaten in days. It was gone in two bites. The knot in Rachel's belly began to ease when food filled it.

This whole trip was a wild goose chase, a stupid, sentimental longing disguised as a cameo brooch, a yearning to know the unknowable. *Why did Aunt Lil have to die?* Okay, stupid question. She was over ninety. Ninety-year-old-people died. Rachel's obsession with the cameo unnerved her. Sara told her to let it go. Move on. If only she could.

What was she planning to do? Knock on Marissa's door and demand the cameo back? Demand she tell her where she got it? Demand…what? Clueless, she had no plan. So not like her. Then again, she had changed so much in the past six months, sometimes she didn't recognize herself. *Why is Aunt Lil's death still haunting me so much?*

Putting her suitcase onto the luggage stand, she pulled out her bathrobe and flip-flops, and headed into the bathroom. *How can the man I love and trust be so friendly with a guy who isn't real?* Daniel had done the investigation. He told her that Mark Rogers was fake.

No tub. Shit! So much for a good, hot soak. A shower would have to do. Surprised by the glass-enclosed, double-headed, pulsating shower, she cranked up both faucets to the max. While steam filled the bathroom, she stripped off her clothes, letting them fall in a heap on the floor before she slid under the warmth of the cascading water. The pulsating thump of water on her neck and upper back eased the tension in her shoulders. She rolled them backwards three times then forwards three times. Leaning over, she placed her hands on the wall between the faucets, allowing the water pulses to move down her lower back.

What was Daniel doing with that man, with Mark Rogers? Calm down, she whispered to herself. We've had our first fight. We can survive this. There is an explanation for what I saw. He's a good man. He wouldn't throw away what we're building.

Fifteen minutes later Rachel emerged from the shower. Wrapping a towel around her body and one around her wet hair, she went into the bedroom area of the suite and turned on the TV. Mindless diversion. Getting lost in other people's problems might put her own on her mental back burner for a few hours. Returning to the bathroom, she dried her hair. Applying serum, she pulled out her trusty Instyler, hoping to delay the onslaught of the frizzes for at least a few hours. Slipping into a powder blue negligee, Rachel propped up the pillows and climbed into bed. She settled in for a solitary evening with her iPad, the TV remote, and her phone. She punched in Sara's number.

"We had a fight."

"Oh, dear."

"It wasn't really a *fight,* fight. I saw him with Mark Rogers. You remember. Beemer guy."

"Wow, didn't expect to hear that name ever again."

"They were sitting having lunch at my hotel, being all chummy, and I lost it. Ran out of the cafe like an idiot."

"Did Daniel follow? Never mind. Stupid question. Of course he followed you. He loves you."

"Got me at the elevator. Told him to leave me alone. Mark Rogers followed, too. Tried to say something. Told him to shut up."

"You said shut up?"

"Well, no. I told him I didn't want to hear anything he had to say."

"Then what?"

"Saved when the stupid elevator alarm starting squawking. I'd been holding the door open. I got in and left them standing there."

"So now what?"

"I don't know."

"Wait a second. Hotel? Elevator? Cafe? Beemer guy? Where are you?"

"Florida."

"We just left there. What are you doing back in Florida?"

"Oh." Rachel's tone went flat. Seconds of silence filled the air. "You're going to kill me. I called Brenda. She told me where that woman, Marissa, lives. You know the woman from the tournament who had my aunt's pin?"

"You didn't! We talked about this. You don't know it's your aunt's pin."

"I know. But…"

"But what? You gave it to that Millie woman as a thank you for spending time with your aunt. Let it go."

"And I appreciated that she took the time to have tea with my aunt. She seemed to care about her. It's just that…whenever I wear something that belonged to Aunt Lil, I feel connected to her all day long. When something happens, I find myself thinking about what she might have done in a similar situation. Crazy, huh?"

"Not so crazy. Things given to us by people who love us are what connect us to them, and to who we were, who we are and who we could become. Whether we like it or not, we are all part of the people who came before us. Shit, every time I hear my mother's words coming out of my mouth, I bet she's laughing in heaven. Did Daniel know you were coming down there?"

"No. I hadn't told him. It was last minute. I got on the plane."

"Why didn't you call me? I would have come with you."

"No. You would have told me I was being stupid and tried to talk me out of it."

"You're damn right. What are you going to say to her? Have you thought about that?"

"Not really. Hang on. I think I hear someone knocking at my door."

"It's probably Daniel."

She hit the mute button on the TV and waited. It came again. She got off the bed and walked to the door. Peering through the peep hole, Rachel laid eyes on a very sad man holding a single red rose looking straight into the peep hole.

"It's Daniel. I gotta go. I'll call you tomorrow."

"Love you."

"Love you, too."

Hanging up, Rachel opened the door.

"I screwed up, I know. I'm sorry." Holding out the rose to her, he asked, "Can we please talk? I need to explain. I don't want you thinking whatever it is you're thinking."

She stepped back from the threshold, allowing him to enter. He stepped far enough inside so she could close the door.

"Rachel, I'm sorry. I didn't mean to hurt you in any way. I was trying to protect you. It's what I do."

"I don't need protecting."

"I know you don't."

Rachel walked back into her suite. Daniel followed tentatively, prepared to react to any sign she might give as to what his next move should be. Placing the rose on the coffee table, she sat stiffly on the sofa and fixed a hard-nosed stare at him as he stood in front of her.

"May I sit?" Daniel asked cautiously, knowing he was on thin ice.

Rachel gave an indifferent nod and shifted her position slightly. Interpreting it as tacit permission, he sat down next to her on the sofa and reached for her hand. She pulled it away swiftly. Daniel cleared his throat.

"I didn't know you were coming down here. I was as surprised to see you as you were to see me."

"Seeing you with Mark Rogers, having lunch like you're old buddies, caught me totally by surprise. It was a gut punch. You said it yourself. He might have had something to do with my aunt's death. Knowing what he tried to pull, what were you doing with him?"

"I totally get how seeing me with him would upset you. I'm feeling like a real asshole at the moment for not being more up front with you about him being connected to my trip down here."

"Good. At the moment asshole suits you fine." Her exaggerated sarcasm forced Daniel to continue his explanation.

"You're right. Mark Rogers was someone I was suspicious of when I investigated your aunt's death. There was never any solid evidence to connect him to your aunt. My guess is that he was working a con to get the diamonds with the neighbor punk, Jimmy. And he probably still has some explaining to do. He's actually the reason I'm down here working on this case."

"Really?"

"Yes. Remember, you told me you were praying I would come back early when Ben showed up at your home with a gun."

"I remember."

"Well, I came back early because a guy called me and told me you were in trouble. Turns out that guy was Mark Rogers—Marco. His real name is Marco. And I also know he sent your mysterious neighbor Mel, whose real name is Dom by the way, to slow Ben down so I could get there in time."

"How did he know?"

"He's the one who bugged your place. I'm sure he'll apologize for that on his own. Probably something he wants to talk to you about—to clear the air. Remember the call I got the other morning when we were talking on your porch after you got home from the tournament?"

"Yes. It was so early."

"That was from him. He needed my help. And I owed him big time for helping you that afternoon. So that's what I'm doing here. I'm helping—paying back a debt."

"Nothing illegal I hope." Rachel's shoulders softened.

"No. He's shown himself to be different than my first impressions. The daughter of his head of security was missing for a few days. Her cousin, too."

"I thought you were with Mac and Jim working on a case."

"They're here too. I called them. The help Marco needs turns out to be connected to the new task force we're setting up. A sex trafficking ring operating right here in Sand Isle is kidnapping young, unsuspecting girls. The head of his security team's daughter got caught up in it along with her cousin."

"Are the girls okay?"

"They're home with their parents. I don't ask too much about them beyond the general stuff. They'll need a lot of good counseling, that's for sure. And I did overhear TJ, the girl's father, say that the cousin is pregnant. Not sure how that's going to play out. I know Marco is helping on that end."

"Oh? What's he doing?" she asked, not bothering to hide the bitterness in her voice.

"Not totally sure. I know he's paying some bills that need paying so the girls get the best care without a lot of questions or paperwork."

"That's admirable of him."

"Yes, it is. And that's what I mean when I say I changed my impression. You may find you two have some things in common in that department. What you did for Beth when Adam was so severely hurt by that IED. He's doing that for TJ and his family. He's not a bad guy when you get below the surface stuff."

"Really?"

"Yes, really." Daniel's voice carried with it an authoritarian conviction. He believed what he was saying and wanted her to believe it too.

"Anyway, that's what I'm doing here. Helping bring down a sex trafficking operation. As I said, Mac and Jim are here with me too. I'm the liaison with the local Leos, going through proper channels, while Marco's guys are doing their thing. I'm also trying to make sure they don't do anything they can't step back from. These are honorable men trying to do the right thing."

"Sounds important."

"It is. But you are more important." Daniel leaned in closer, gingerly laying his arm against the back of the sofa, unsure if touching her would be welcome or scorned. So far, so good. Rachel leaned back against the sofa and Daniel slowly moved his hand to her shoulder. She accepted his advances. Emboldened, he reached for her hand.

"I am so terribly sorry. I should have told you when I figured out it was Mark Rogers who helped you that day. With all that was going on, it slipped my mind. And then I forgot about it."

"It makes a little more sense now. I don't know what's gotten into me."

Daniel lowered his head clasping his hands behind his neck. Drawing them slowly forward, he rubbed his eyes and exhaled a deep sighing sound. Returning his eyes to hers. "You could have told me you were coming down here."

"I didn't know. It was last minute. And I didn't have a clue you would be here. You said you were off to Florida. You didn't say where in Florida. It's a big state. And I didn't think I needed your permission to do my own thing."

"You don't, and you know that's not what I mean. What are you doing down here?"

"I'm—." Rachel stopped, dreading his reaction. "Okay, I know this sounds crazy, but I'm trying to find the woman I met at the tournament...the one I think has my aunt's cameo pin."

"You're kidding." As soon as the words left Daniel's lips he knew it was the wrong thing to say. He could have remained silent and nodded supportively. But no. His protector genes were sabotaging his every move.

"No, I'm not." Rachel's sharp tone smacked him harder than if she had actually hit him across the face.

"Sorry. I didn't mean it that way. Of course, you're not kidding. You're here. How did you know where to go?"

"Brenda gave me her address."

"Brenda shouldn't have done that."

"I know. She did it for me. Because we're friends. And I

fibbed a bit. Told her I had to return a scarf I borrowed. Laid a full guilt trip on her. Guilt may be a wasted emotion, but in this case it worked. After how the tournament ended, with all those ladies getting sick, I figured she'd feel terrible and tell me. And she did. The woman I'm looking for lives down here, in Sand Isle, so I came down to find her."

"And then what? What are you going to do when you find her, if you find her?"

"I don't know. Haven't figured that part out yet. I know she has my aunt's pin, and I want to know how she got it. I need to know how she got it."

"This thing with your aunt's cameo. What is it about this pin that you can't let go of? What's got you so hooked?"

"My aunt. I can't let her go. Seeing the cameo again, on a stranger, made me feel like I lost her all over again. Like I severed our relationship, cut it. Not like she died. I gave the pin to someone I thought cared about my aunt. Maybe not as much as I do...did...but cared enough to have tea with her at night and listen to her stories. Whoever wears that cameo is carrying a bit of Aunt Lil with her."

"A bit of guilt rearing its ugly head here?"

"Yes. I'm feeling guilty, very guilty, that I left her. Moved away. I could have waited." Then more forcefully, "I should have waited."

"I didn't know your Aunt Lil. But from everything you've told me, it sounds like she would have been angry if she thought you were putting your own life on hold to wait around for her to die. Didn't you say she was happy you decided to move and start a new life for yourself?"

"Yes. She was totally supportive. Excited for me. But still, I was all she had, and she was more of a mother to me than my own. She loved me. Never played the stupid games my mother did when I didn't do what she wanted me to do."

"From the stories you've told me, your mother was a real piece of work. You deserved better."

"Aunt Lil loved me like every person should be loved. Unconditionally. No reservations. No games. I'd never felt that before from anyone. Not even David, I'm sorry to say."

"You are the most loving person I know. Loving to a fault. Trusting of everyone. It's your turn to be on the receiving end of that love. I want you to feel that from me. I love you for the person you are. And I want us to get past this."

"I'm finding that out, Daniel. Really I am. I know you love me. And I love you. It's…hell, I don't know what it is anymore. And I'm sorry I lost it downstairs. Seeing you with Mark flipped a switch."

"I get that. Maybe we can un-flip it. I think if you sit down with Marco and give him a chance to explain, even to make amends, you might find the two of you have some things in common."

"What could we possibly have in common?"

"Helping people. That's what we were talking about. He was telling me how he and his lady friend have a piece of property with an old hotel on it. They're converting it into a sanctuary for young girls who find themselves in awful situations, so they can get the help they need, regardless of whether they can afford it. Kind of sounds like your Raphael Fund.

"Interesting."

"Yes. The guy I've gotten to know is not some cheap con artist."

"How do you know he isn't really good at what he does, that he isn't conning you right now?"

"Because it's about family. One of his family is hurting. And for him, that changes everything."

Softness replaced her previous curtness. "Look. I'm tired. It's been a long day. Could we finish this tomorrow?"

"Over breakfast? I know a place that makes great waffles."

"Waffles, huh? With strawberries on top?"

"Strawberries, whipped cream, maple syrup, anything you want. Will make-up waffles end this misunderstanding so we can move on?"

"I can think of something we could do right now that would make my waffles icing on the cake."

"Your wish is my command."

Carolyn opened her motel room door to a smiling Kyle.

"What a nice surprise."

"Want to get some dinner?"

"Sounds good. I was planning a stop at Desiree's home for a look-see. Want to go?"

"I'm not into B&E."

"Who said anything about breaking and entering? I've got her keys and her codes, remember?"

"Can we eat first? I know a great seafood place."

"Sounds good. She's not going to show up for a few days yet."

They quickly settled in at a dockside seafood spot overlooking the Intercostal Waterway. The sun was low in the western sky, casting a soft pink glow that tickled the glistening water.

"What is it they say? 'Red sky at night, sailor's delight. Red sky in morning, sailors take warning.'"

"Sounds right. Being on the water is why I joined the Navy. Love the water. Sailing. Have a 24-foot Beneteau over there at the marina. She's a beauty."

"I don't know much about sailing. Been landlocked all my life. Why do they call boats she?"

"Because early sailors from the Mediterranean area referred to their ships as she and it stuck."

"What's her name?"

"Victoria B"

"Pretty. Named after anyone special?"

"My mom, of course. Maybe one day, depending on how everything turns out, before you leave I could take you sailing."

"That sounds like fun." She swallowed hard. Fun wasn't on her agenda. Emotions she locked down tight came flooding to the surface. Tears stung her eyes.

"It must be hard. I don't know how you've managed to hold it together for so long."

"Sometimes I don't. Not knowing one way or the other is the hardest part. Drives me crazy. Crazy drives me on. It's empowering, believe it or not. I won't give up until I know."

"I wish I'd been around to help you when all of this started."

"You're here now, trying to help me. Besides, it was my fault she left. I was too heavy-handed, too controlling."

"Don't beat yourself up. Not speaking from experience here, but I hear raising a teenager is hard work."

"I'll say. We fought a lot, both using words so harsh they were hard to take back. No matter what I said to justify throwing her dad out, she always had a mean comeback. There was no way to reason with her. Her desire for him to be a storybook, loving father tangled her reasoning till her excuses were asinine. Then she ran off."

"Must have been tough. As kids we don't understand the grown-up side of our parents' lives. We see them as Mommy and Daddy, not as partners and lovers."

"It was never about winning a fight with her. It was about trying to keep her safe, protect her from the cruel reality that was her bastard of a father. She must have wised up some. Maybe had a serious relationship of her own that fell apart. Prompted an apology phone call. We started weekly calls to check in. We were slowly repairing the damage, or so I thought—and hoped. Then nothing. The calls stopped, and my nightmare began."

"Let's go after we eat."

"Go where?"

"Sailing. Believe me when I say the ocean can soothe your soul and take your mind off your troubles like nothing else I know. My boat is right over there. It's going to be a beautiful night."

Out on the ocean, the waves and a gentle breeze pushed the Victoria B out to sea. Kyle's skill aligned with Mother Nature to ease the sails in and out, catching exactly the right amount of wind. The Victoria B rode the waves' crests while water lapped at her hull and the rigging clanked musically against the mast.

"It's beautiful out here. So peaceful."

"Sounds like the sailing genie may be casting her bewitching spell over you."

"I don't know about that, but I could get used to this."

Kyle opened his arm and motioned for her to join him behind the wheel. She nestled into his side, the wind blowing her hair in all directions.

"Here. Take the wheel."

"Me? You've got to be kidding. I don't know anything about sailing."

"Feel it—feel the wind. I won't let you get into trouble."

"Maybe next time. For now, let me sit here and enjoy this."

"Yes, ma'am. Consider yourself a deck bunny for your first sail."

"My God, look at that sunset." Carolyn's lips brushed his. Their salty taste and warmth begged for more. "Thank you for this."

Their sail turned into a night of a thousand kisses, alternating from soft to hard, gentle to crushing. Tying up at the dock as darkness stole the day, Kyle took Carolyn's hand and led her down the stairs to the boat's cabin. Its gentle rocking motion eased her into his arms quickly.

"Maybe we shouldn't do this again. With all that's going on, what will the others think—TJ and Marco and the guys?"

"You must have confused me with someone else."

"Who's that?"

"Someone who gives a shit about what people think. Besides, they're my friends, and they'll be happy we found each other, even if only for the briefest of times. Which I kind of hope this isn't."

"Isn't what?"

"The briefest of times. I'm enjoying getting to know you."

Tracing the line of her lips, brushing his fingers along her cheek, Kyle kissed the tip of her nose. Moving up to her eyes, he gently pecked and kissed, licked and tickled. She drew in a long breath.

Cupping her face in his hands, and looking into her eyes, Kyle whispered, "You are beautiful." He lifted her in his arms and placed her gently on the cushioned bed where he sampled her willing mouth, his tongue probing, sweeping.

She felt hard muscles rippling beneath his black T-shirt when she stroked his back. Her two new best friends—hot and bothered—were making a return appearance. Making love on the beach had reintroduced these joyful feelings into her life and here they were again. With heat bursting from every pore, Carolyn pulled at his shirt, lifting it over his head, running her palms down his solid, muscled chest. She ached for him, wanting him to push between her legs and thrust deep inside her. She was wet, hot and ready.

He nimbly unbuttoned her shirt, reaching behind her to unclasp her bra and free her full breasts. Hungry lips moved across her face, down her throat, between her breasts as he held them and played with her nipples. He gently suckled there, first one, then the other.

He seemed to be in no rush to enter her, and he seemed to be able to sense by how her body responded to his touch that her pleasure was off the charts. He knew it had been a long time between lovers for her—too long.

Finally she couldn't take it any longer. Rolling on top, she straddled him and felt him enter her. Breath caught in her throat as she cried out.

"Aren't we in a bit of a hurry?"

"No, not a hurry. I want to feel you inside me. This minute!"

"With pleasure, ma'am."

With a swift roll he was on top, pinning her wrists above her head. Encircling him with her long legs she eased fully under him and arched her back. United at last. He released her wrists and slid his hands under her. The heat of his skin matched her own and she wrapped her arms around his neck while her senses spun out of control.

Her moans and shudders urged him on. Together, they moved as one. He pushed himself deep inside her. She received all of him. They rolled together. She rode him now, arching her back, moving faster as he filled her again and again. Resting her arms on his chest, she used her tongue to play with his nipples. He cupped her full breasts, his mouth tugging and suckling and he caught her rhythm and moved with her while she rode him.

Holding her steady, he rolled them again, so he was on top position. Her legs tightened around him. His thrusts were faster now, moans deeper, his pleasure off-the-charts intense. This woman aroused him in ways few had done before, and he worked hard to return the pleasure.

Then they were spent. Stillness. Silence but for breaths. She could still feel him inside her, and she stroked his back while he lay on top of her, then traced and kissed the rim of his ear.

Kyle trailed his index finger along the scar at the end of her lip. "A laugh line seems a funny place for a scar. Hides it well. Tell me about it."

"A parting gift from my ex."

"And what did you give him in return."

"A fast shot to his balls with my knee. Doubled him over in pain. I'm sure he saw stars."

"That's what I like to hear."

TJ and Daniel took the midnight to five a.m. watch. They kept the car windows down to enjoy the cool night air and help them stay alert. TJ pulled a Mountain Dew out of their cooler and passed a Coke to Daniel, along with a Milky Way. Sugary snacks and caffeine-loaded drinks would fuel them and keep them awake through the night.

They were hunkered down in a parking lot a block west of the Sand Isle Inn's entrance. Their job was easy. Wait, watch, and photograph cars as they entered and exited. Now all they had to do was be patient. Not exactly a virtue in either man's skill set.

Expensive-looking cars rolled into the parking lot at regular intervals, each one photographed using a top-notch telephoto lens. The most important information was the license plate, which had to be captured quickly, because once it passed the entrance, the car and its occupants were totally out of sight. Car tags were recorded and texted to Brett, who had successfully hacked into and was manning the DMV database.

"Here comes another one," said TJ. The two men straightened up and grabbed their equipment.

Daniel peered through his binoculars at the car, which had entered the parking lot. "That explains it."

"Explains what?" asked TJ while snapping as many shots as he could.

"What I saw when I was at the police station."

"Huh?"

"The black Lincoln Town car that just pulled into the lot."

"Yeah," said TJ, lowering the camera and reviewing the images of the car. "I see it. No shot of the driver. What about it?"

"I've seen it before," said Daniel, "at the police station in the spot reserved for the Deputy Mayor."

"You sure?"

"Very." Daniel reached for the camera. "See. There. Attached to the license plate. There's a small gold star."

"Interesting."

"Yep. Very interesting. It all fits."

"What fits?"

"When I was there talking to the detectives who handle sex crimes, asking about incidents in this area, most of their replies were non-committal, like they didn't have any problem at all in this area. Which surprised me, considering Florida is huge for sex trafficking."

"Shit, man. It's a fact of everyday life in some parts. Big business at every Super Bowl. Did you know Florida has had more Super Bowls than any other state?"

"We're playing trivia now? No, I didn't know that."

"Well, now you know." TJ's smile broadcast his deepening respect for Daniel. "So tell me, what fits now that you've seen that car."

"The look."

"A look?"

"Yeah. You know, when you and another person know something no one else knows, but the topic comes up, and the two of you make eye contact, and 'the look' flashes between you."

"Oh, that look," chided TJ.

"The FBI and CIA guys call them micro-expressions. Their guys are trained to notice them during interrogations."

"We got some of that training."

"Bet you did. Well, I'm trained too. And I saw it, but tried to talk myself out of it. Couldn't be. I saw it, but chalked it up to something other than what we were talking about...so I let it go."

"And now?"

"Now, I know I wasn't imagining it, that my first impression was right. These guys are up to their asses in this shit."

"And we're just the guys to do a little ass-wiping."

"Amen to that, brother."

CHAPTER 19

Sunday

Rachel went shopping. Daniel asked her to stay for a few more days so they could enjoy some time in the sun after he finished up his business. Grateful for the time alone, she planned to explore Palm Beach and stroll through the shops on Worth Avenue and in Palm Beach Gardens Mall.

"Excuse me." A familiar voice said next to her ear. "Rachel?"

Startled, Rachel turned and looked into the warm, golden brown eyes of Mark Rogers, Marco, his smile as radiant as the day they first met—accidentally on purpose.

"Are you stalking me?"

"No. I need to talk to you."

"Really. What about?"

"I have some explaining to do."

"Look. I don't know what your game is, but I don't want any part of it, or you," said Rachel, believing her accusatory tone totally justified.

"There is no game. If you'll give me a moment, I know I can explain."

"You're not real. Daniel checked you out. You aren't who you claim to be."

"That's true. My name is Marco, Marco Alesi. If you will permit me to buy you a cup of coffee, perhaps we can walk on the beach while I explain."

A battle raged inside her—two voices locked in combat inside her head. Which way to go? Which action to choose? Should she listen to him? There was a part of her that wanted to know the truth—needed to know the truth—and part of her that wanted him to forever be charming Mark Rogers, aka Beemer Guy, the mysterious, handsome stranger she met on the road on her way to her aunt's funeral.

"It's too hot for coffee. Make it a water and I'll give you fifteen minutes."

"Thank you."

They headed down to the ocean, drinks and sandals in hand.

"Pretty beach," said Rachel. Bitterness fueled two simple words. Anger fed her nerves.

"Yes. A good place to talk, to have important conversations with people who matter, people you care about. And believe me when I say I care about you. Since we met that day at McDonalds, I've cared more about you than I can remember caring about any other person I was targeting."

"Targeting?"

"Yes, when we met, it was not an accident. I was deep into a con. That's what I do—did. It's the reason we met, and you're the reason I'm no longer in the game."

"I don't understand."

"We were after the diamonds, pure and simple. Then something went wrong and your aunt died. That was never supposed to happen. When I met you on the road...let's just say I wasn't expecting you."

"I'm sorry, I still don't understand."

"You were not what I was expecting. That day at the Cheese Shop I could see the sadness in your eyes and I can't explain why, but you touched me in a way that was very different from the other people we went after."

"Who's we?"

"There are four of us...two men, two women. We came up through the streets. Knew one another's stories before we really knew each other."

"And it was all a con to get the diamonds?"

"Yes." He blew out a heavy sigh and stopped walking. "No one was supposed to get hurt, let alone die. But that kid, Jimmy, was out of control. And then that lawyer got involved, and things went downhill from there. I pulled the plug on the con the day the lawyer pulled the gun on you."

"You called Daniel and told him I was in trouble." She knew, phrasing it more as a statement than a question.

"Yes. And I sent my guy in to slow things down until Daniel could get there."

"Ah, Mel, my mysterious neighbor." The answers she had been craving for so long were coming together neatly. "What stopped you?"

"You did. When I heard you talk about the fund you were setting up. I was in 'Nam. Saw a lot of ugly stuff, both there and when we all came home. What you're doing with the diamonds is amazing. Unselfish, caring, loving beyond words. So I ended it."

A long slow exhale punctuated the finality of his words.

She censored her words, suppressed her real thoughts. *Who does he think he is? He wants me to believe this line of garbage about caring about me? What a pile of BS. Does he really think I'm that naive or that stupid?*

"I'm done with the cons, and with the lying."

"Sometimes lies are safer."

"Not really. You've got to remember them. The truth and nothing but the truth is my promise to you, to Marissa, to everyone."

"Marissa?" Rachel's mind shifted to a woman named Marissa she had met at the mah jongg tournament—the woman she had come here to find and confront. Not a common name. *Couldn't be. Could it?*

"Yes. The love of my life, a love I denied for years to preserve the status quo. Figured it would wreck everything if I told her the truth, how much I love her. All it did was give us both lonely lives."

They walked a bit in silence. The surf pounded, the gulls wailed, children played in the sand.

"The other morning on the phone, that was you calling Daniel?" Again, an answer she already knew. Her mind drifted to that infamous line lawyers always say, never ask a question you don't already know the answer to.

"Yes. I knew he could help TJ when his daughter went missing. TJ's family...he's the son I never had. I didn't want him going off half-cocked and angry and doing something he'd regret, not that I really think he would. Daniel's my ace in the hole, someone to help TJ and make sure he doesn't cross any uncrossable lines."

"What now?" She gritted her teeth prepared for lies, half-truths and falsehoods.

"Now? They're finishing what some dirtbags started. I'm staying in the background, doing what I can do to help them acquire what they need to complete their mission. And doing what I can to help TJ's daughter Bella, and her cousin, Claire."

"Their mission I get. How are you helping Bella and Claire?"

"I bought a piece of property about five miles down the beach, an old hotel. Bought it a few years ago as an investment." He pointed south and her eyes followed his finger. "We're renovating it now and repurposing it. Turning the rooms into small studio suites, a private residential type facility. Thinking maybe some girls who find themselves between a rock and a hard place could use a safe place to heal."

"That sounds so noble."

"Hell. There is nothing noble about me. I'm not proud of what I've done. I knew it was wrong. Life isn't always pretty. Can turn on a dime. Mine did. Sometimes you have to do what you have to do to survive. I'm trying to make amends any way I can for a life I wouldn't wish on my worst enemy."

Marco searched her face intently. Had he made his case?

Rachel took a deep steadying breath. Her mouth flattened and she grimaced a bit as she gently rolled her shoulders to release some tension. "Interesting story. And I need to know all this because...why?"

"Because Daniel is up to his eyeballs helping us, and he needs your full support." He drew in a breath, turned to her and said, "And I could use your help. The Raphael Fund you set up—what you've done for the wounded warriors—I'm hoping you might be willing to help us do the same thing for these girls. I even followed your lead in choosing the name. Plan to call it Lazarus House, like Lazarus rising from the dead."

"How biblical of you."

"Seriously, Rachel. These girls need a place where they can rise up again. They have a long road ahead of them to find their way back from the hell they were in and on to living purpose-filled lives. They can't do it alone, and I want to help. I can move faster with your help. You've done it already. You know how to set up a fund. Know a lawyer or two who do this type of work. Will you help me?"

Too many emotions were bombarding her all at once. "I need time to think, to process everything you've told me."

"Take all the time you need. I'm not going anywhere. I'm done running. Maybe when all of this is over, you can stop by and meet Bella and Claire and get a sense of who these young women are, and how important it is to help them overcome what was done to them."

The planned late-night snatch and grab went smoothly. Even though the club was packed, Art and Tina were able to finger the target, Pete, based on their previous conversations with Javier. When he left the club, everyone was ready. They followed him to a mini-mart and flawlessly executed the grab when he returned to his car. Broken bottles from the six pack of Corona remained where he dropped them.

Pete sat in the dark, trying desperately to calm himself down. Rivulets of sweat trickled down his back. The last thing he remembered was coming out of the mini-mart with beer. Someone came up behind him, grabbed him, slammed a hood over his head. And then the menacing voice in his ear.

"Stop struggling. I know what you're thinking. You're thinking you can get away from me."

"No. I wasn't thinking nothing."

"Sure you were. I'm a mind reader," said the unidentified voice. "There isn't a thought going through that pea-sized brain of yours that we haven't planned for. So unless you think you can outrun a bullet I suggest you rethink your options."

Pete had stopped struggling momentarily, hoping they would loosen their grip. He slowly counted to twenty and then made one last desperate attempt to get away. He heard bone crunch as a fist contacted his jaw. The blow knocked him out. Next thing he knew, he woke up tied to a chair with a hood over his head.

TJ, Kyle, and Casey watched him struggle with his bindings on the video feed.

"Time to start the show," said TJ. "Let's go teach this little pissant that he needs to mind his manners around women."

Pete heard a door squeak open. The hood was pulled off his head. His eyes darted around the room and what he saw unnerved him. Three hard-eyed, muscular guys, dressed in black, surrounded him. Balaclavas hid their features. Except for their eyes. Angry eyes pierced his consciousness. He looked from one to the next, barely pausing a moment on any one of his tormentors. His left cheek throbbed where he'd been cold-cocked.

One grabbed a metal folding chair, setting it down in front of him. The other two retreated to the shadows behind Pete. The man who was clearly in charge swung a leg over the chair and straddled it, leaning his crossed arms against the backrest.

The man sat there, opposite Pete, staring at him. He snapped his fingers, and one of the men behind him produced a mirror and held it up so Pete could see his face.

"You're not looking too pretty," said the man sitting in front of him.

Pete could see a yellowish-purple bruise forming on his swollen left cheek. Blood congealed at the edges of both nostrils. He wiggled a loose tooth with his tongue.

The man in the chair snapped his fingers and the mirror disappeared. He pulled out a knife and played with the blade.

"You know what this is? KA-BAR. Very effective instrument."

With the most delicate touch, the man in the chair brushed the pad of his thumb over the blade. His menacing tone and swift movements with the knife promised pain. Turning it around, he used the tip to remove a speck of dirt from underneath his fingernail.

"Mine's sharper," said a voice from the shadows behind Pete. Footsteps approached. "Don't move," whispered the man into Pete's ear. A hand holding a different-looking knife came into Pete's view. The man slowly glided the blade up Pete's forearm. Small hairs appeared on its blade.

"Now that's what I like to see. A clean, close shave." Looking up, he spoke to the man sitting in front of Pete. "Told you mine was sharper. Bet your piece of shit KA-BAR can't do that."

"Who the fuck are you guys?"

Silence.

"What do you want?"

Silence.

"You've got the wrong guy. I didn't do nothing."

Silence.

Behind him, the third man in the room clapped his hands once. The sharp crack echoed off the cement walls.

Pete jerked in the chair, his bindings restricting his movement, his eyes bulging in terror.

TJ kept his eyes on Pete. This kid was low-hanging fruit. Had been easy to grab off the street. Probably didn't know much, but he might have a name that could help them connect the dots that needed to be connected in order to make a case even the Pope couldn't ignore.

"What do you want?" Pete cried. "I ain't done nothing."

The man in the chair opposite him finally spoke. "I

haven't asked you anything yet, so how do you know, as you so eloquently put it, you ain't done nothing?"

"You can't prove shit. I don't know nothing. I didn't do nothing."

"That's what we're here to find out. If, as you claim, you didn't do anything, then this will be over quickly, and we'll all go on our merry way. On the other hand if, as we suspect, you did a great deal of something—to someone important to me, important to all of us—then this could turn out badly for you. It all depends on you."

"Go fuck yourself."

"An overused phrase if ever there was one. Not very original."

The two men came out of the shadows walked across the room, opened the door and left.

The man sitting in front of Pete moved last. "We'll be back shortly. Take some time now to carefully consider your next actions."

And they were gone.

He was fucked no matter how he looked at it. These guys could definitely hurt him, might even kill him. His wrists ached. He could only guess at what this was about—who these guys were, who they worked for. He'd pissed off more than one person.

Maybe Dimitri found out he'd done a little skimming on a few of his last protection money pickups. Nothing major, a few thousand bucks all told. He had planned to blame the store owners for any shortfall if asked. Figured Dimitri would send his goons to the store owners to teach them a lesson for all to see.

Could be Javier. He'd helped himself to a few pills from Javier's stash. There was this hot chick and Pete had known for sure that doing her would bring him a night of pleasure she'd never remember. He had to get her in the right mood, and Javier had the right stuff to do the necessary attitude adjustment.

Then there was that dumb broad Claire. She traded her cousin to Julio, Metamorphosis' owner and her drug supplier, to pay off her drug debt. Unbelievable. How could anyone do that? To family, no less. Didn't matter. Like most people he knew, Claire was protecting herself. That's what people were hardwired to do. Look out for number one. She would have sold her own kid for a fix. Selling her cousin didn't even make her pause for thought.

And then her damn cousin got away when he and Rick stopped to get something to eat. Drugs they gave her wore off faster than they expected. Claire, the dumb bitch would pay for this. When Julio confronted him, he lied—said Claire had changed her mind and backed out on the deal. Small lie. Maybe Julio found out?

Suddenly, the door squeaked open.

"We're baaaaack."

Three men strode into the room, still dressed in black, faces still covered, and assumed their previous positions.

"So, Pete," said the one who again took the chair opposite him.

"You know my name?"

"Yes, Pete, we know your name. We know a lot more than your name. Here's the thing. We need to get your attention. Make an impression on you that stirs your deepest self-preservation instincts."

"I gotta piss."

"Interesting. It can be arranged, but you've got to give us something in return. You've got to earn the right to piss like a human being and not in your pants."

"What do you want to know?"

"Let's start with an easy question." The man in the chair

snapped his fingers, and one of the men behind Pete placed a color photo of Claire on the table. "How do you know this girl?"

"Never seen her before."

"Now, Pete. When you lie to us, and that was clearly a lie, we're going to hurt you. Tell you what I'm going to do. Since I'm such a nice guy, I'm going to give you one more chance. Same question. How do you know this girl?"

The man slowly tapped his index finger on the upper corner of the photo.

"Yeah. I think I've seen her at the club. Maybe danced with her once or twice."

"That's better. See, that wasn't so hard. Good boy." Another finger snap and Bella's photo was placed on the table. "Recognize this picture? Name Bella ring any bells?"

"Never seen her before."

The violent whack to the side of his head brought tears to his eyes and reverberated down to his toes. Pain shot through his jaw, and an agonized scream escaped through his clenched teeth. Pete felt something give. Blood dripped from his lip as his tongue found the loosened tooth dangling from its root in his mouth.

"If that was true—that you've never seen her before—then the crime scene techs wouldn't have found her DNA in the trunk of your car. But they did find her DNA there. So...want to try again?"

"You're cops. I knew it. I want a lawyer."

"A lawyer. You've got to be kidding me," said the man, the metal chair slamming against the floor as he shot to his feet. "Do we really look like cops to you? Does this shithole look like a police interrogation room to you? I'm sure you've been in one of those once or twice already."

"No," he said meekly as he pressed his back into the chair, bracing for the strike he feared was coming.

"No, Pete," said the man, righting his chair and sitting back down, "we're not cops."

"Who are you guys? And what the fuck do you want?"

"We're the good guys, Pete. The real good guys. Police, FBI, they come in with their badges and guns cocked ready to fire. But they rarely fire. They arrest you and you do the whole court thing. Sometimes you win. Sometimes you lose. We're the other kind of good guys. We don't arrest. We take no prisoners. But we do clean up scum like you, which makes us the real good guys." TJ leaned closer to Pete. They were nose to nose. "See the difference?"

Pointing to the photo of Bella, he said "Let's try this again. How do you know this girl, and what was she doing in the trunk of your car? These are simple questions, really. Tell us what we want to know."

"It was some harmless fun. A game, you know. Nothing more. Some spoofing. We were gonna let her go. Then she got out on her own. I don't know where she is now. Ya gotta believe me."

TJ's gloved hand was around Pete's throat in a flash, squeezing ever so lightly, but applying enough pressure on his carotid artery to cause pain and make him feel faint. Not enough to leave any marks. Pete trembled. Panic filled his eyes.

"And that's what we're doing here. Harmless fun. Consider it the same kind of game you were playing with this girl."

"But I don't know where she is."

TJ let him go with a push and sat back down.

"Let's change the subject. Tell us about the club, Metamorphosis, and the dirty little secret deals that go on behind the scenes."

"I don't know what you're talking about."

Standing up, TJ said, "Clearly we don't have your attention yet. But we'll get there, won't we guys?"

"You got that right."

"See you in a few hours."

Kyle crashed onto his bed. Tired went deep into his bones. He rubbed his head, letting his hand come to rest on the pillow. The past week had taken a toll on him; wanting to be there for TJ, holding down the fort for the compound's security, planning the op and this evening's escapade, grabbing and scaring the shit out of the kid, Pete. Letting his friends down was not in his DNA.

The surprise—Carolyn. He loved watching her spar with TJ. Feisty, aggressive, someone who didn't back away from a fight, even when she was clearly the underdog. A lot of terrier in her.

He hadn't had a serious relationship in years. One night stands were more his style. No strings. No one gets hurt. As the years went by, as he watched TJ's family grow, and he spent too many Thanksgivings and Christmases at their table, he wondered if he would ever meet someone he wanted to do the family thing with.

Had he met his match? So far she met his criteria. Physically fit, intelligent, resilient, resourceful. And she was beautiful to boot, icing on the cake. And her kisses sent him to the moon and beyond. He sensed an unfulfilled passion in her waiting for the right person to unlock it. She was perfect. And he wanted to know her.

Dangerous, he thought. Wanting what might be out of reach. Making love on the beach and again on his boat had been impulsive. Maybe even reckless.

The moonlight, the sea lapping the hull of his boat, the salt air tickling his nose. Kissing Carolyn had been even better than he imagined. Her soft, full lips tasted salty sweet, like the salt water taffy he used to buy down at the shore every summer. Her skin, silky soft to his touch, and then she shivered, inviting him to hold her tighter. His hormones got the best of him. He felt himself harden again as he relived the moments with her. Blissfully happy, he drifted off to sleep.

CHAPTER 20

Monday

Claire walked into Dr. Oliver's office at precisely nine-fifty. Their appointment was for ten o'clock. He smiled when his receptionist buzzed him to let him know she'd arrived.

Early was an excellent sign, especially considering she was only four days into the CARE program. She'd been late for the previous days' appointments, typical adolescent defiance. But yesterday's conversation had been different. He broke through. He saw her demeanor change, her defenses lowering a hair. He'd take anything he could get. Now she was early. He was thankful for this small sign that he might be starting to reach her. But he wasn't about to kid himself; there was a long and rocky road ahead.

Opening his office door, he greeted Claire warmly, noting her neater appearance. The sweats were gone, replaced by clean jeans and a nice yellow T-shirt with a floral design studded with sequins. She'd brushed her hair and added some eye makeup.

"Claire, how nice to see you. What a pretty T-shirt." To

leverage her early arrival and what he saw as a small win, he decided getting out of the formality of his office might help her be more open. "I thought we might take a walk outside today. It's such a beautiful morning. What do you think?"

"Whatever." Ugh, that word again. Okay, he thought, one step forward. Two steps back.

While he escorted her through the corridor to the elevator, her eyes remained glued to the floor in front of her as she walked beside him. Total silence. Pushing the down button, he asked about her evening and whether she enjoyed the movie night program he knew had been scheduled for the residents.

"It was okay. I've seen Independence Day a couple times already. Good pizza."

"Ah, pizza. A major food group. Could eat it every day."

Fresh air and sunshine replaced the more sterile hospital scents as he opened the door to the courtyard. It was mid-morning, and patients and visitors were beginning to make their way into the gardens. He was grateful for the benefactor who had funded the courtyard project. The beautiful flowers, terraces, fountains and cobblestone pathways always seemed to help his patients open up.

"I saw Beverly this morning in the parking garage. She told me she visited with you yesterday."

"Yeah. She stopped by to say hi. See how I was doing. She's really nice."

"Yes. I'd be lost without her. Works with many of my patients. One day, maybe she'll tell you her story. I think you might find it interesting."

They walked down the path heading toward the food trucks that were beginning to gather along the service road beside the hospital.

"I think you might find this fun fact interesting. My sister is having a baby. We were talking last night about the list of names she and her husband had drawn up. They found this online site where you can look up names and learn their origin and meaning. So I looked up your name online this morning."

Silence.

"Do you know what Claire means?"

"It's a name. Didn't know names meant anything."

"Well, they do. And yours has a French origin, Claire. Means bright, famous, clear. Kind of like the shirt you're wearing today. Bright. Or the weather today, clear. Not a cloud in the sky. And the famous part...well, time alone will tell."

"What does your name mean?"

"That's a good question. I don't know. Maybe you can look that up for me."

"Maybe I will. Your first name is Ted, right? I heard some of the nurses talking."

"Yes." Walking by one of the food carts Dr. Oliver asked, "Can I get you something to eat or drink? I'm ready for another decaf myself."

"Sure. A Coke please."

Dr. Oliver handed the vendor a five dollar bill, handed her the Coke and took his coffee. They continued their walk. One topic led to another as they meandered along the path.

"Mind if we play something I call the what if game?"

"What's that?"

"It's a game where you get to imagine anything you want. No holds barred. Everything and anything is possible for you. Want to give it a try?"

"Sure." A descending note of defeat permeated the one-syllable word.

"Okay, good. What if you could have any future you wanted? What would you imagine yourself doing?"

Claire sat down on a bench at the edge of the courtyard.

She took a sip of her Coke and looked around. Dr. Oliver sat down next to her, but not too close. In front of them children were playing on the swings, nurses' aides pushing them ever faster and higher until their giggles and laughter filled the air. Other patients and their families strolled in the gardens like she and Dr. Oliver had been doing. A group of doctors and nurses were enjoying an early lunch at one of the picnic tables. She turned to face him.

"I want to be like them."

"Like who?"

"Like them," she said, pointing to the group of nurses and doctors. "I want to be like Beverly. She's been so kind and...well, I haven't been very nice to her."

"So you want to be a nurse. Can you tell me a little more about your choice?"

"Nurses help people. People count on them. They're smart. They take care of people when they need help the most. When my brother Pedro was little, he had a really bad flu. My mother wasn't home. Out partying. He was really scared, I could see it in his eyes. I took care of him."

"Nursing is an admirable profession. I don't know what I'd do without people like Beverly. You could do that. Be a nurse."

"That's not going to happen." Failure resonated in her words.

"Why not?"

"Like I even have a choice."

"What makes you believe you don't?"

Claire didn't answer right away. She picked at her cuticles, chewed on the straw in her Coke, enlisted all sorts of stalling tactics.

"Claire, I asked you a question," Dr. Oliver said softly. "A pretty important question. What makes you believe that you don't have choices?"

"I'm not Bella. She has all sorts of choices. She's smart." Claire looked at him, her eyes narrowing. "What have I got? A mother strung out on drugs. And when she's not using, she's out partying. I'm her free babysitter, housekeeper, and maid. Will probably wind up cleaning motel toilets like her." Her voice sizzled with anger.

"Ah. I see." Taking a sip of his coffee, he let the silent pause play out. He picked at the lid of his coffee cup, his eyes glued to the cup.

"You know, you really can't control what other people do. They do what they're going to do. Your mother makes her choices. But, and this is the important piece, Claire, your mother's path doesn't have to be yours. There is no preordained destiny. We each get to choose."

"Yeah, right." Defeat was leaden in Claire's voice.

"You always have a choice, Claire. Sometimes it's between good and bad options. Sometimes it's between bad, really crappy, and downright horrendous options. But the choice is always there."

"Easy for you to say."

"Ah. The words of disbelief. Giving up before you even begin. Why is that?"

"Why's what?"

"What is making you give up before you even start?"

Silence.

"There's a poet I rather admire. Maya Angelou. Ever heard of her?"

"No."

"She passed away a short time ago, but she once said that 'You may not control all the events that happen to you, but you can decide not to be reduced by them.'"

"So?"

"So…when you say you don't have any choices, your heart hears the words coming out of your mouth. And your heart believes you. If you want to change what you think is possible for yourself, you must first change your words, so the new words can touch your heart, allowing new beliefs to take root." He took a sip of his coffee to allow some time to pass, time for his words to sink in. "What do you think about what I said? Make sense?"

"It's words. Fancy words."

"You can control what you do. The choices you make. The actions you take. You can react, stomp your feet, get angry, give up, do drugs."

As he spoke the last two words, he turned, repositioning his right arm along the bench's backrest. It appeared to embrace Claire without actually touching her. He made direct eye contact.

"Or you can set a goal for yourself. A worthwhile goal that will fill your life with purpose. And stay the course. Make your decisions in line with your goals and your dreams for yourself."

Another pause.

"What do you think about what I am saying to you?"

Silence.

"We can't change the past, but we can create a different future for ourselves. What if I could help you learn some new skills—new ways to confront whatever is troubling you, and new ways to take action to create the type of life you really want to be living? What would that be worth to you?"

Slowly she turned toward him. Big green eyes searched his face.

Success. His arrow had hit its intended target.

Wiping the steam from the bathroom mirror, Amelia clutched the pink bath towel to her breasts and stared at her reflection. Self-pity was not her style. Each girl here had her own version of the fairy-tale story that brought her to this place. Talking about it was taboo.

Biloxi had been the beginning for Amelia. From casino croupier to whore in a New York minute. He'd been so suave, so convincing. Told her he was a producer. Had an A-list of clients including some of the biggest stars. He couldn't tell her who exactly, because that would breach confidentiality, but they were names she'd recognize. He was sure she had what it took to join his pedigreed list. He asked to see her portfolio. And when she said she didn't have one, well, he had a friend who could handle that for her.

Her dreams were about to explode onto the silver screen. She was going to be a star. She had the look. The photographer she met said so. She could still hear his lavish words of praise, the stars in her eyes overriding her rational mind. Had she really been so naive? So stupid?

"Oh, yeah, baby. That's the look I want. Work it. Work it."

Sitting on a small pink tufted stool, smiling and pouting for the camera, Amelia moved her shoulder a bit and repositioned her head like she had seen models do in photo shoots on TV.

"Drop the neckline a bit, would you? Expose your shoulder."

"Like this?"

"Yes, that's the idea. Now turn toward me a bit more. Too much chin."

"Better?"

"Oh yeah. Think sexy. Think of the most gorgeous man entering the room. You want him to notice you…to want you. You're going to be famous. Just wait and see."

And they had wanted her. They broke her in, passed her around, drugged her, beat her, ripped away any vestige of self-esteem and pride she might have once had. Men who hated themselves for their own inadequacies, destroying and defiling helpless innocents so they could feel manly, if only for a moment. Cowards one and all, ego-driven, impotent losers who must prove their virility to themselves. What was done to her and the other girls like her was intimate—very, very personal, and very, very wrong.

Many of the girls were from families who didn't care about them, or cared too much, smothering them, forcing them to run. Her story was no different. Over-protective mother, using her for love and companionship because she made a bad choice in the husband lottery.

One of the other experienced girls, Miss Cynthia, told her she reminded her of someone she once knew. Amelia figured it was herself. She took Amelia under her wing, taught her the ropes, talked to her about her possibilities if only she cooperated. Amelia was nothing if not a quick learner.

And now? She had an exclusive clientele, a following. Doctors, lawyers, accountants. Even a few city officials. They were clean, smelled good, took care of themselves. And she made sure they got it up with her. Repeatedly.

Amelia dropped the towel and pushed up her breasts. Soft mounds of milky white flesh filled her hands. She swiveled her body right, then left, admiring herself in the mirror. Her tummy taut, not an ounce of fat anywhere. Staying in shape was critical. The men could get fat and sloppy at home. Pulling the towel from her wet hair, she bent over and ran her fingers through her golden mane. When she straightened up, damp tendrils of highlighted blonde curls fell across her face. Sad eyes belied her smile.

Cynthia had been a good teacher. Following her advice earned Amelia a promotion to New Orleans, where her revenue tripled in her first three months on the job. Talk about French flash. All red velvet and oooh-la-la chic.

"Now, don't that prove Mama didn't know what the hell she was talking about when she said I wouldn't amount to nothing." Amelia laughed out loud as the words left her lips. Tears welled up in her eyes at the thought of her mother. In a more sullen voice, a prayerful wish, "Oh, Mama. Help me."

Turning tricks in an expensive whorehouse wasn't a career choice many girls would make, but she wanted for nothing. Every need was taken care of. Every whim indulged. Great medical care, designer clothes to wear with no place to go, spa services galore, all meals provided, rooms cleaned, and dirty dishes whisked away. Nothing to do but please her clients.

Another promotion last year earned her a spot at the newest inn here in Sand Isle. And she had worked hard to be considered for the opportunity to come here. How crazy was that? The job description read like a dream come true. Her own suite, a garden, pool, beach privileges. The very detailed and demanding application process had lasted for weeks. She was the envy of so many others when she was chosen.

Yep, she fell for the fairy tale. Heaven turned into hell, a hell she had learned how to tolerate. Now five years in, Amelia knew there was no way out. Every once in a while someone tried to leave. The photos of their remains were passed around as a warning to the rest of them. This life, any life, was better than becoming worm fodder in a shallow, unmarked grave. The only thing missing was freedom.

CHAPTER 21

Tuesday

Another beautiful sunrise lifted Bella's spirits while she raced, feet pounding along the sand. Her morning run had become ritual, a way of cleansing herself at the dawn of each new day.

In the distance, a lone woman stood at the shoreline. Marissa was usually out at this hour. They often crossed paths, shared a few words and a hug, and then moved on, each off in her own world of thoughts and dreams. Something was different today. It doesn't look like Marissa, thought Bella. Where is her signature wide-brimmed white hat? She never goes out without it.

As Bella got closer, she slowed. Recognition. Claire. She stopped running.

Claire began to walk toward her slowly. She stopped in front of Bella. Within hugging distance. Bella's arms remained at her sides, as did Claire's.

Face to face with Claire for the first time since her kidnapping, Bella froze. What could she say? Her father and mother had told her what she needed to know: that her cousin had sold her to pay off the money she owed to her drug dealer. Some guy wanted a virgin, and Bella fit the bill.

Bella had dreaded this moment. She and her psychologist, Dr. Keegan, had role-played the possible conversation and how to handle it...what to say, how to act. Now the moment was upon her, her mind went blank.

For Claire, it was part of her healing. Step nine: make amends directly to the people you have harmed. And her actions had definitely harmed Bella.

And she had to do it face-to-face. She and Dr. Oliver had talked about this meeting for hours. Together they decided that meeting on the beach, at the ocean's door, would be a cleansing place. Claire called Marco and requested access to the compound, explaining what she wanted to do.

Recognizing the importance of what she was asking, Marco agreed. He met her at the gate himself, escorted her to a spot he knew would intersect with Bella's morning run. Then he retreated to his patio. And kept watch from a distance, a centurion guarding a precious jewel.

And here she was, face-to-face with the cousin she had hurt. As ready as she would ever be.

"Bella."

Bella refused to make eye contact. She watched a seagull pick at the sand, searching for food.

"Oh, Bella. I'm so sorry. So very, very sorry. I was scared. So scared. And they promised me... They promised me... You've got to believe me, Bella. I didn't mean for any of this to happen. I owed them so much money, and when I didn't have it, they said they would kill me."

Bella said nothing.

Claire watched Bella swoosh the water with her feet, first one, then the other, kicking through the froth and tiny waves that lapped the shore. She pushed her hair away from her face when the wind blew it around. The only thing she didn't do was make eye contact with Claire.

Claire's eyes, however, were glued to Bella's face on the off chance that they might connect, even for a moment. Claire wanted Bella to see her soul laid bare.

"And then he got a call. And I heard him say something about a virgin...needing a virgin. And I told him I knew someone who was a virgin, and maybe I could help him, if he would help me. And we made a deal. And...And..."

Claire heard herself losing control. She stopped talking. She looked out at the sea. The waves rolling into shore matched her tumbling stomach. She took a few deep breaths like Dr. Oliver had taught her to do when her nerves got the best of her. Doing it steadied her like he promised it would.

Turning back to Bella, Claire pushed back her shoulders, allowing her to stand a little taller, feel a little stronger. Calm returned to her voice. Filled with both remorse for her actions, and hope for a new future with Bella, she continued.

"I was willing to sacrifice your virginity, to sacrifice you, to get out from under my own problems rather than take responsibility for them. I know that now. And I know that my actions were wrong—very, very wrong. I'm asking you to forgive me. Please Bella, I'm begging you. Please forgive me."

That was all she had. She'd said her piece. Bella's silence was like a thousand knives cutting into her soul. She needed Bella's forgiveness. She needed to hear words that would help her healing, something only Bella could give her. She prayed Bella would say something.

Only silence.

"Say something, please."

"I don't know what to say to you. How can you be so morally paralyzed by your own pitiful little life that you don't understand that selling another human being is wrong on so many levels. Not just wrong. Sick." Fury shot from Bella's eyes. "I'm so angry...so hurt that you think I'm something you can sell, not a person, not your cousin. What were you thinking? How could you do this to me?"

"I wasn't thinking. Druggies don't think. We just want to feel good, make the pain go away."

"What pain?"

"What pain? How about the pain of no father? How about the pain of a slut for a mother? I've been taking care of my three brothers since I was ten. My own ready-made family without any marital benefits. I hate her. And I hate myself for hating her. Haven't you heard, you're not supposed to hate your mother."

"Is that why you do drugs? Because you hate your mother?"

"Who the fuck knows." Claire screeched. Her body shook. Eyes wide. "My life sucks." Her voice shrill. Her cheeks burned. Her lips quivering. She covered her mouth. "There are days I want to crawl in a hole and die. Then I smoke a joint or pop a pill and the world is beautiful, sunny, brilliant pink and I'm on top."

Bella's looked off toward the horizon. Nothing but ocean as far as she could see. She kicked at the water surging gently around her feet, stared at fluffy white clouds which ran like a ribbon low across the sky.

"All I hear is you feeling sorry for yourself and blaming your mother. Poor you. Poor little you. You didn't really mean to get me kidnapped and raped. You were just having a bad day. Poor you."

"But you got away before anything bad happened to you."

"And that makes it okay? That's bullshit! You're my cousin. We're family. You betrayed me—*sold* me. I would have never done something like that to you."

"How do you know what you'd do? You don't do drugs. If you did, and I don't recommend it, but if you did, you don't know what the hell you'd be willing to do for a hit."

"Don't you get it? The only reason I'm not dead or a sex slave is because I got lucky. The drugs they gave me wore off and the guys who were holding me got hungry. If they hadn't stopped God only knows what would have happened to me. But, yeah, I know, you're sorry. Big whoop!"

Claire was trembling. In the heat of the late morning Florida sun, Claire was trembling. Her practice sessions had not gone like this. She believed Bella would be kind, sweet, Bella. What she was experiencing here was rage. Bella was letting her have it, verbal guns blazing and Claire hadn't been prepared for it.

Bella's eyes bored into her.

"Maybe you should get online and see what happens to girls who are victims of sex traffickers. I did. And trust me, it isn't pretty. What you were willing to do to me and my family...for a fix...because your mommy isn't perfect. Please spare me your feeble apology. I'm sorry doesn't cut it."

"I know I need to do more than just apologize. I want to...need to make amends. I'm not sure what that looks like or how to do it exactly and I'm hoping...praying we can talk about that."

Bella didn't move. Her steel-hard stare did not waver.

"And another thing," Bella continued when Claire remained silent. "I don't appreciate being ambushed like this. You could have called me, but no, only thinking of yourself, you had to go and ruin my run. You want to talk to me again about this, call me and make an appointment."

"Okay. I can do that. I will do that. And when we meet again I'll be prepared with a plan for how I am going to make amends, to show you that I've changed, that I'm starting new and not going back."

"Until you do."

"No, I won't. Crashing is not fun. Smoke another joint. Pop another pill. Makes it all go away. I'm on top of the world again...flying. But the thing is, I always come down. I have to come down. And coming down is painful...very, very painful."

"I don't believe you. Don't trust you. I do think you've been selling yourself short. Giving up before you even get started...taking the easy way out. Drugs. You can do anything you want to do."

Claire lost it.

"Bullshit. What do you know about it...about me? No one fights for me like your parents fight for you. Your dad would have gone to the ends of the earth to find you. I don't know who my dad was."

Her voice died. Swallowing hard, Claire brushed away a tear with the back of her hand. "You're smart. You're going to have a bright future. Be somebody important. I've got cleaning toilets in my future. Your life didn't suck. Mine did."

"Did?"

"Yes. Did. I'm done. Dr. Oliver... He's helping me...helping me get clean. I've got to get clean." Claire took a deep breath. "I'm pregnant."

"I know. My mom told me. Another life you can ruin."

"No. I'm not going to ruin the life of an innocent baby. I'm going to change. Maybe that is the beginning of how I make amends."

"Maybe. But for now, we're done. Remember, call first next time."

Bella turned around and started to run, retracing her steps down the beach. She stifled the urge to look back.

❖

"We go tonight. There is nothing sanctioned about this operation. You in?" TJ stood in front of Daniel in his usual ramrod, bulldog stance, looking him squarely in the eyes. The rest of the team remained silent, watching their exchange.

"In for a dime, in for a dollar. Whatever you need, I'm here to help."

"That's all I need to hear. Everyone, gather around. Let's go over what we know."

Taped to the walls in the room were Google maps and surveillance photos the drone had taken of the property at different times of day. Neon green post-it notes pointed to security guards, blue to the housekeeping shed, red dots showed the location of girls in cottages, black dots meant they had company.

"Let's talk security first. Brett, tell us what you found."

"Couldn't find anything connected to the Inn itself, but when I hacked into the nightclub's computer system I found all sorts of interesting stuff. In addition to invoices for the standard CCTV systems for both properties, I found an invoice for more sophisticated detection equipment, the kind with a cable you hide underground to detect any uninvited guests on your property. Think invisible fencing. All top-of-the-line, high class stuff. Very cool."

"Thanks Brett. Good job, as usual," said TJ. "As for people. We know the Inn is secured by a three-man team. We've tracked and timed their movements over several days, and their routine hasn't varied much."

"Probably because they have an underground system," said Casey. "The guys add visible muscle in case anyone might be looking. But they're counting on the system to detect any perimeter intrusion."

"Brett, how far out from the buildings is the cable set?" asked Kyle.

"Can't tell for sure. But based on the amount of cable shown on the invoice, it looks like they've kept it pretty close to the edge of the main area."

"And they didn't seem to notice when Carolyn was there, hiding in the woods watching them," added Gabe. "She must not have tripped the system, or they'd have come after her like we did."

"Good point," said TJ. "Okay, two guys regularly sweep the grounds on foot in forty-five minute cycles."

"That's a lot of ground to cover. Must have six, seven acres altogether," said Kyle. "You figure you've got the beach access down here, and these dense, wooded lots on the other two sides. The survey Brett got from the city showed the wooded lots as Inn property."

"When I went walking along the beach the other day to test their security, no one stopped me. What we don't know is whether they saw me and figured I was harmless, or their system doesn't fully cover the beach side," said Art. "Did see two of the girls sunning."

"Interesting," said Daniel. "The girls were sunning? Not looking around like they wanted to leave?"

"You got it."

"These guys must have them scared shitless," said Casey.

TJ continued using a laser pointer on the map. "One guy stays in the office, which is up here at the street. It's about a half mile down this lane to the main part of the Inn. We figure they're armed, but haven't been able to get a good look at what they're carrying."

"Best guess would be an H&K MP5," offered Kyle. "That's what I'd use."

"Agreed," said TJ. "On the good news side, these guys are probably well trained, but because of the lax way they move, we don't think they anticipate trouble. Ever."

"Too bad, because trouble is about to pay them a visit," laughed Art.

"Kyle and I did a close-up recon the other night," said TJ. "We watched a customer leave, and a woman roll up a double-sided housekeeping cart. One side had linens and towels, but the other side looked more like a food cart."

"She knocked at the cottage's door, went in when it opened. Came out with dirty dishes and garbage and re-entered the room with arms full of fresh linens. Figure she was making the bed. When she came out her arms were full of dirty linens and towels. The entire process took about fifteen minutes. Then she pushed her cart totally out of sight into this shed," said TJ aiming the laser pointer at a building at the far end of the complex. "Ten minutes later, when another customer left from this cottage, the woman re-appeared and went through the same routine."

"More good news," said Kyle. "The line of sight from the office to the cottages sucks. The driveway curves downhill, and there are lots of trees and flowering bougainvillea obscuring any view from the office."

"Meaning," said TJ, "we may be able to pull this entire incursion off while the guy in the office is practically clueless."

"You're shitting me," said Casey.

"Nope. We've been watching the guys who man the office for several days," said TJ. "There's this one guy who mostly works nights. We're going on his shift because he pretty much watches TV or plays video games to pass the time. Gets an occasional phone call, but nothing more.

Doesn't have his eyes trained on the monitors like he should. Either very lazy or not expecting company."

"These guys change positions every three hours give or take," said Kyle, "so they all get a chance to go inside and take a load off their feet. And they each put in a standard eight-hour shift. So we're thinking of hitting them toward the end of a night stretch."

"Sounds like a cakewalk to me," said Steve. "Wonder if they get time and a half for overtime?"

"You thinking of applying for a job?" Kyle whacked the back of Steve's head as he passed him on his way to the front of the room to take over the briefing. "The stuff we don't know is the problem. We want to get the big guys, the people at the top. Shut down this operation for good. Put them away."

"It's been hard to pinpoint who's really in charge," said Daniel. "We've had our tech guys on this nonstop. It's an amorphous group. Like trying to nail gelatin to the wall. Every time we think we're close, something happens that changes the players. I'm convinced there is an invisible someone at the top who wants to remain that way. Invisible."

"Don't remember who said it," added Brett, "but dare I quote, 'Oh what a tangled web we weave when first we practice to deceive.'"

"Think that was Sir Walter Scott," said Casey.

"Aren't we well read?" chided Kyle.

"Hey, I liked *Ivanhoe*, so I read more of his stuff. The quote is from his poem, *Marmion*."

"Whoever owns Metamorphosis and the Inn is good," said Brett. "I've been at this for days. Gone down at least four layers of ownership, and still can't find a name I can actually trace very far. Looks like they started with an aged shelf company out of Wyoming."

"What's that?" asked Casey.

"Like a turn-key operation," said Daniel. "Companies get set up purely for the purpose of being ready to go when someone buys it. Gives you immediate status. You get everything: incorporation documents, seal, stock certificates. All real. All ready to go."

"Reuters and the Huff Post did stories about these a few years ago," said Carolyn. "I came across some of them when I was doing my research."

"Fascinating," said Casey. "And you can Google this stuff?"

"Yep. And it's all legal here in the good ol' US of A," said Daniel. "Gave us grief in New York whenever we went after mob operations. They had more layers for laundering money than you could believe. We'd get so lost in the maze, it was hard to make cases stick."

"So, they've set up a dummy corporation inside a shell company, using an aged shelf company, with straw people, starting in the great state of Wyoming and running them through both Belize and the Caymans?" asked TJ.

"Yep. That's what it looks like so far," said Brett. "Someone went to a lot of trouble. Doing a good job of hiding his or her identity."

"Whoever this is, he or she, does not want to be found. That's for sure," said Kyle.

"But find him…or her," said TJ added a nod toward Carolyn, "we must. That's one sure way to get your friends the Feds involved, isn't it, Daniel?"

"Not sure that's a given," said Brett. "Looks like there are some tax records for some of these companies. So it appears they pay their taxes, or at least some of their taxes, if you can believe that."

"Interesting. So it's more about identity evasion than tax evasion," said TJ.

"Looks that way. I'll keep digging and let you know if I find anything more."

"Thanks Brett. If anyone can find anything, it's you."

"Appreciate it, boss."

"Now, all of you. Go home, get some rest, and be back by six for a dinner and a final briefing before we go. Conner and Brody are taking care of security here for the next twenty-four hours."

They filed out. TJ remained, pacing the room, staring at the maps and the pictures. Like a caged panther. Arms at his sides. Body taut. Four steps and turn. Four steps back. Turn. Brows furrowed, deep in thought, he ran over options and possibilities. Approaches and risk scenarios. It had been a long time since any of them were deployed. Were they out of practice? Could they pull off a clean op, without anyone getting hurt?

Half an hour later found TJ sitting on a sand chair, fishing pole flung out to sea, his boonie hat sat square on his head. Oakley sunglasses shielded his eyes from the glare of the sun off the sand. He was bare-chested, with navy blue swim trunks completing the look—a ruggedly handsome man taking the afternoon off. With his tan legs stretched full length in front of him, he contemplated the vastness of the ocean before him.

He loved the ocean, considered it his most direct connection to God. Alone here, he could solve the world's problems. He took off his sunglasses and pinched the bridge of his nose when the glare off the water triggered spots in front of his eyes. He closed them for a moment and listened to the ocean's thunder. Gulls shrieked and called above.

This week he almost lost his daughter. If she hadn't

gotten away, might the memory of finding a dead girl seared into his soul years earlier have repeated itself? He'd been seven years old when he found the body in the park while playing hide and seek with his cousins. Ended his innocence—his childhood. Who could do such a thing to another human being?

Trust died that day for TJ. It was reborn in the cold Pacific Ocean during Hell Week. Arm in arm with his brothers, TJ endured the final tests of SEAL training. So many in his class had rung the bell, washed out, given up. But not him. He survived. The warrior spirit lived strong.

"Got your head on straight?" asked Marco, tapping TJ's shoulder with a cold bottle of beer. "You need to be fully engaged tonight. No wandering thoughts—no what ifs. Sense you've got a bug up your ass. Want to talk about it?"

The ice cold beer cooled his parched throat, but did little to erase Marco's sharp words.

"Thanks for the beer. Now go away. You're in my sun."

Marco ignored him. "Refills," he said as he plopped the small yellow and white Playmate cooler down between them. Planting his butt in the sand next to TJ, he took a long swig of his beer.

"No can do. Only this one. Tonight's a go."

And there they sat.

Waves crashed against the beach, an early spring hurricane giving surfers along Florida's eastern shore an unexpected and very welcome surprise.

"So, what's it gonna be?" asked Marco.

"What do you mean?"

"TJ, I've known you for—what?—twenty years now?"

"Yeah, something like that, but who's counting?"

"When you came back from Iraq you were all piss and spit. Remember the nights we'd sit out here and talk? You were some idealistic piece of shit back then."

"Hey. I did my time. I was pissed."

"Angry at the world."

"No, not the world, the people in a certain part of the world. What they did to their own. How they treated women and children, and people who didn't believe the way they did. Couldn't understand what we were doing there. Lost all those brothers and sisters. And some came home so messed up they may never get straight."

"And I gave you a job here. I saw something in you I wanted to know better."

"Yeah. When I came back, I knew I wanted something different for myself. After meeting Rosa, I knew what that something was—a family of my own. To take care of, keep safe, always be there for them. No one was going to mess with that. And then this shit happens and I almost lost it all—again."

"But you didn't. Your family is still intact. And you aren't your father. Gotta be who you are in this world. And one thing I know to be true about you is you are an honorable, decent man. Not a killer. A warrior, yes. A cold-blooded killer, no. So whatever happens out there tonight, remember that."

"You got that right."

"So what's got your knickers in a knot?"

"It's something Daniel said, and that you've alluded to. That there is something we're missing. Someone has gone to a lot of trouble here. What connects the dots?"

"Been bothering me, too. More and more. Something isn't sitting right. Nothing is as it seems. The photos Carolyn showed us were intriguing and convincing. The devil hides in many forms, some so seductive and alluring they're hard to resist. Whoever is behind this operation is a new kind of devil. Someone overly comfortable working in the shadows, deeper than I've ever come across before. A behind-the-

283

scenes type of guy, likes to pull strings, the ultimate puppeteer. And he or she used Desiree—flamboyant, over-the-top Desiree—as the perfect willing partner."

"More like dumb patsy, if you ask me."

"There is nothing dumb about Desiree. But this guy is smarter, more cunning, more evil. Profit is his...or her...only Holy Grail. And damn anyone who gets in the way. Not a good sign."

CHAPTER 22

Will this nightmare ever end? wondered Amelia, turning her face away from the sweating pig plastered on top of her. His fetid breath was proof of his most recent garlic-laced meal and his failure to even use mouthwash before his appointment. Considering the weight crushing her rib cage, the ass could use to skip a few meals. A soulful voice filed the space. Porky, her nickname for the guy, couldn't get it up without blues music to set the mood.

Ironic, she thought. If his friends could only see him now. This high-priced lawyer, a pillar of the community, passed out on top of a whore. A lonely tear slipped down her cheek as Amelia felt the beginnings of a mental enema coming on. Barely flowered and already dead, she'd lost these last five years in a bottomless pit of despair, loneliness, and guilt at having screwed up so royally before her eighteenth birthday.

And what about her friends? What if they could see her now? Her life in this hellhole was not what she'd planned. Not the glamour, not the fame, not the celebrity. How had it come to this? Miss most-likely-to-make-it-big-in-Hollywood-or-on-the-New-York-stage reduced to turning tricks. Yes, it was an exclusive setting, but rip back the splendid oriental rugs, the crystal chandeliers, the lavender satin sheets, imported French wine, and other elegant accoutrements, and it's still a whorehouse.

Amelia thought about her regulars. They were an eclectic bunch. Each guest's tastes and sexual proclivities directed their time together, and no two customers were alike.

Guttural grunts echoed in her ear. He stirred. At least he wasn't hairy. Wooly, her nickname for her previous client, was a bearlike man who wore a permanent sweater. He was a passionate yet gentle lover, but when they finished, tiny, curly, dark hairs stuck to her everywhere. Not to worry. There were thousands more.

Charger, her hard-riding cowboy, would arrive next, just before five, and saunter in like he'd just stepped off a horse. They'd playact some version of a damsel in distress rape scene. In his head, he knew how he wanted the scene to unfold. She'd follow his initial lead, and then improvise her lines. When she strayed from his fantasy, she'd feel the sharp crack of his hand across her jaw; hard enough to make her head spin, but never hard enough to leave marks. And they'd redo the scene until she got it perfect, or until his time was up.

Her costume had been delivered by private messenger this morning. Looked like he wanted to ravage the schoolmarm. Considering how many times Charger had "raped" her, she found the prospect of playing a bespectacled virgin for him very amusing.

She would greet him at the door wearing the long, hickory-colored skirt and buttermilk blouse with buttons that went to her chin. Lace trim at the top edge of the blouse would frame her face. He sent a photo showing how he wanted her hair piled on top of her head, secured by one long, ebony hair pin. The box contained an alabaster petticoat, stockings, and black shoes with square silver buckles. The final item of attire was an ivory lace bustier with a tiny pink bow where her ample breasts came together, forming deep, enticing cleavage. Charger loved to nestle his face here, cup her breasts and suckle her nipples. Clearly, this boy did not have a mother who breast fed him. Or perhaps she did for way too long.

Ah, well. Indulging in her client's fantasies did break the monotony, and made for interesting visits.

Somber chimes tolled four o'clock. Amelia glanced at the walnut grandfather clock standing watch in the corner. Time to rouse Porky and send him on his merry way. Back to his respectable life, and his boring wife, who didn't want anything more to do with him now she had her big house in an exclusive gated community.

Poor Porky, stuck in the reality of a loveless marriage, two screwed-up kids with mounting problems of their own, and a stress-filled, ambulance-chasing law practice defending vermin. His life totally overpowered his coping skills. No wonder he'd become her Tuesday and Friday afternoon regular.

Amelia gently nudged him.

"Time to rise and shine, Mr. Edwin."

"That was wonderful. You are the best," he said, groggily nuzzling her neck.

"Enough of that, now. Time to go."

"Okay, okay. Don't rush me. I know my time is up, but I don't want to leave. I don't want to go back. I want to stay here with you. All safe and warm."

"Now, you know you can't do that," said Amelia, her sultry smile belying her real thoughts. The voice between her ears screamed at the top of its lungs. *As if I'm safe, you asshole. There is nothing safe here. I'm a prisoner of my circumstances like you. Only you can change yours. You can leave. You can walk away. I can't go anywhere. Or I'll wind up dead.*

"Come on. Rise and shine." Amelia coaxed him more forcefully. Sliding out from under him, she pushed herself off the bed and reached for her cerulean satin kimono. She loved its silkiness against her skin, how the soft touch of snowy white lace at the elbow length sleeves made the cerulean pop. Tying the sash, she turned to look at Porky.

"Mr. Edwin, dear. I really must insist."

"I know. I'm sorry."

Reluctant to leave, but knowing he must, Mr. Edwin put his feet on the floor and reached for his boxers. He rubbed his eyes and did a full backwards stretch.

"Come here," he murmured softly.

Amelia complied. Standing between his spread legs, she endured his after-play routine. Untying the sash from her kimono, he put one hand on each cheek of her backside, pulled her into him and caressed her firm derriere while his tongue flicked in and out, tickling her belly button. He nestled his face into her breasts and kissed her.

"I don't know which I like more, your boobs or your butt."

"Don't be silly, Mr. Edwin," giggled Amelia. "You like all of me. That's why you come to visit so often. And I love that you do. But now it's time for you to be on your way."

He heaved a disquieted sigh.

"One of these days, I'm going to take you away from all this. Just you and me. We'll slip away to some remote island in the Caribbean. I'm making plans as we speak. You'll see. I'm a man of my word. Then I won't have to leave and you won't have to…well, do what you do."

"And what would your wife and little Aimee and Bradley have to say about that?" Amelia wiggled back out of his embrace and retied the sash of her kimono.

"Nothing," said Mr. Edwin as he stood to put on his shirt. "They'll be well taken care of. Probably won't even notice I'm gone, as long as the bills get paid."

He finished dressing. Amelia hooked her arm playfully through his and walked him to her door. A little more kissing and nuzzling completed their session. She sent Mr. Edwin off with a smile on his face and a bounce in his step.

Amelia returned to her bedroom to shower and get ready for Charger. After him, she had a special rendezvous planned with her last client of the day. On the nightstand beside the bed Amelia saw her payment. Ten one hundred dollar bills neatly arranged in a fan shape.

One thousand dollars. Not bad for two hours of work—and it was her tip. Her actual fee for services rendered was collected elsewhere. She quickly scooped up the money and stashed it away.

TJ looked around the room at the assembled group. Nine men and two women dressed in black for the evening's adventure.

"New moon. Dark night. The best time to go hunting." Kyle and the guys stood around a table loaded with guns, ammo, extra clips, flex cuffs, knives, and other assorted hardware they might need.

"Amen to that, bro," said Casey, pressing bullets into a clip.

"How's all this gonna go down?" asked Gabe.

"One team. One fight," said TJ, his commanding voice calling everyone to order. "Zero hour is two a.m., after closing at the nightclub. Remember, we're not some douchebag guys out for revenge. We're warriors. We're different from the street punks who took Bella, the assholes behind all this. You know it and I know it."

"Our goal is to end what is happening here with non-lethal finality. Close down this operation. Put these people away with overwhelming, incontrovertible evidence. What we don't want is a clusterfuck. Don't want a pile of dead bodies to have to explain. Don't want to give a smooth, shit-talking lawyer any way to get these douchebags off, so mind your manners."

"Hooyah!"

"Daniel will lead the team that hits the club, including Jersey, Brett and our two Fed friends, Mac and Jim, the guys with the real badges." Nodding to Mac and Jim, he asked, "Anything you want to say at this point?"

"Not really. Planning to go in full force with badges in plain sight, shouting orders about an official investigation probing the club's illegal activities," said Jim. He held up a search warrant. "Got a friendly judge to help us out. And we've got federal backup waiting in the wings. We plan to seize and tag whatever we find."

"My team will hit the Inn at the same time," said TJ. "The element of surprise is on our side. Brett's given us the latest update on which cottages are occupied. Two-man teams will take down the two security guards who roam the property. Kyle and Art will get the guy that crosses the beach path. Russ and Gabe will take out the other guy at the lower end of the driveway. Steve and Dom will head up the driveway and handle the guy in the office. Casey and I will enter each cottage and subdue the customer. Carolyn and Tina are going to be the feminine faces of the operation. They'll come in behind us to calm down any situation that looks like it's going to get out of hand."

"The plan is to chloroform then flex-cuff the guests, get

them ready for the Feds. No guns blazing unless the situation warrants it."

"And then we'll go in and see to the girls," said Tina, looking to Carolyn for a confirming nod.

"Listen up, guys," said TJ to quiet down the cross talk. "A critical assumption we're making here is these girls want to be rescued. When Art strolled onto the beach a few days ago, he saw two of the girls sunning. Concerns me that they were out there and made no attempt to make a run for it down the beach."

"Could be Stockholm syndrome," said Steve.

"Maybe. We don't know at this point," said Kyle. "So be prepared in case you find yourself an unwelcome guest at a private party they're enjoying."

"Any questions?" TJ's eyes locked onto each man and woman in turn, moving around the room, searching out questions.

"Okay. Gear up. We go in two."

TJ strode to the back of the room where Carolyn stood leaning against the wall, her arms crossed over her chest. A chill raced up her spine as he approached. Powerful emotions battled inside her, releasing a few tears even as she fought to stifle them.

He tentatively broached the subject that had to be on both of their minds. "You know, you could stay here. Let us do our thing. In case the outcome is not what you are hoping for. No one would fault you."

"Gee whiz, and miss all the fun?"

"What if she's not there? What if we don't find Amelia tonight?"

Carolyn shuddered, dreading the thought even as she had to accept the possibility. Searching for Amelia had been her normal life for a long time. What would her new normal be, especially if they didn't find her tonight?

"Not my style. I can't. I won't accept that Amelia is gone. I'd know. I'd feel it. But I don't. She's alive in some hellhole—that hell hole down there. It's my job to do everything I can to find her and get her back. And there is nothing you and your band of merry men can to do to stop me, short of killing me, and I don't get the sense you're in the killing business."

TJ could see determination written all over her face. Carolyn had turned her pain and grief into a fury that fueled her search. Each new discovery of a missing girl resembling Amelia ignited her passion, reinforced her actions. She was a formidable adversary in this game of hide and seek.

"TJ, are you listening to me?"

"Sorry. What did you say? I wasn't listening." A flashback to another game of hide and seek years earlier momentarily stole TJ's attention.

"I was saying you don't have to worry about me. I did my time in Iraq, know how to handle myself. Can shoot straight if I need to, and duck when I have to. I don't get hysterical like some girly-girl."

Kyle smiled, witnessing the exchange between his best friend and this woman who stirred a raw, intense curiosity. The itch he felt in other parts of his anatomy also made him smile. His cheeks warmed with the thought.

How tonight's game of hide and seek would play out was anyone's guess.

TJ looked at his watch. It was one thirty-five. Each team had twenty minutes to get into position. Once ready, they would call in to confirm. No one moved until everyone was set. Steve and Dom's target went first.

"Let's go. Stay close."

Casey led the way with TJ on his six. Carolyn followed in

TJ's wake. As she crawled through the underbrush, the unthinkable reared its ugly head. What if Amelia is not in one of these cottages? Carolyn pushed the thought out of her mind. It wasn't possible. She'd done her homework, conducted a thorough search. She was sure. Well, as sure as anyone could be about these types of things. Amelia had to be here. If she wasn't here, she was lost. There were no more clues to follow.

She reached out and tapped TJ's shoulder.

"Whatever happens tonight, thank you."

"My pleasure."

Russ, Gabe, Kyle, and Art split off from TJ's team. TJ watched as one by one the men disappeared into the night.

At the edge of the woody brush, Kyle and Art went low and crept along the sand with ten minutes to spare. Without their night vision goggles, they could barely see their hands in front of their faces. Adjusting their NVGs, they watched the path, waiting for the security guard to emerge. Hopefully Russ and Gabe had made their way through the woods and were ready to take down the security guy at their end. They had the more difficult route.

"Team 2 in position." Good, thought Kyle. He responded in kind.

"Team 1 in position."

"Are your targets in sight?"

"No," said Kyle for Team 1.

"Yes, rounding the bend now," said Russ. "He stopped to light up."

"Affirmative. See him now. He'll be on us in two," said Kyle.

"Team 3 in position," whispered Steve.

"Go Team 3."

Everyone heard the whispered signal in their earwigs.

Now they only had to wait for Steve's signal that the guy who watched the monitors was down.

Steve walked into the office of the Inn and stood at the counter. Dom remained in the shadows outside. A sleepy-looking guy stepped out of the back office. He rubbed his eyes as he approached the counter.

"No vacancies. Can't you read the sign?"

"I have an appointment."

"Excuse me? What appointment?" A look of confusion crossed the guy's face.

"For you to meet my Taser," laughed Steve. Two barbs of the Taser lashed out from Steve's hand and hit the guy squarely in the chest. Dom came through the doorway.

"Video guy down," whispered Steve, who was already in midair, vaulting over the counter. He and Dom carried the guy's body through the doorway into the back office and tied him up. Then Dom stood watch in the office while Steve headed down the driveway toward the main action.

Gabe held his breath as he removed a black cloth soaked in chloroform from the baggie. Positioned behind the security guard, Russ leaped up, tackling him as he finished taking a drag from his cigarette. Took him down in one swift motion. Gabe clamped the rag over his mouth. His squirming ceased quickly.

"Team 2, mission accomplished."

Kyle's takedown did not go as smoothly as he and Art wanted. Kyle's foot slipped a bit as he pounced on the security guy, so the takedown wasn't pretty. While Kyle rolled around in the sand wrestling the security guy, Art readied the chloroform soaked rag. The brief scuffle ended with a right chop to the jaw. Knocked the wind out of the security guy, whose gasps for air were met with Art's hand holding the rag over his mouth.

Kyle opened and closed his right hand, flexed his fingers and shook it. "Hope that hurt him more than it's hurting me. I'm getting too old for this shit." Followed by a murmured, "Team 1, mission accomplished."

"Gift wrap them. Then come join us. We're off." TJ signaled for his team to move out. The plan was to enter each cottage, one by one, subdue the customer, and assist the girl.

TJ had been watching videos and practicing picking locks for days. He used both old credit cards and a pick and wrench set he'd purchased online, and he'd gotten pretty good. Now it was time to see if his practice paid off when it really counted.

Approaching the first cottage, TJ gently touched the doorknob. Locked. Holding his breath, he slid the credit card in between the door and the doorjamb. With a barely audible slow exhale, he wiggled the card until he could feel the bolt slide back. The lock released. The door popped open. TJ grinned as he felt Casey's hand on his back in recognition of a good job. Slowly he pushed the door open.

Two men in black silently stole into the room in the glow of soft amber lighting. Feral grunting sounds mixed with feminine squeals. Quietly, they crept to the bed. Unaware of their presence, the John kept doing his thing. Terror filled the girl's eyes. The long black barrel of a gun touching the back of the John's head got his attention.

"Get off her," Casey growled through clenched teeth while he pressed the gun closer to the John's ear.

Panicked, the man stopped his violent thrusting, rolled backwards and fell off the bed. He grabbed the sheet to cover his now shriveled, rosy red penis.

"Don't hurt me. Please, don't hurt me," whimpered the naked little man, standing huddled between the bed and night table. "I was having some fun. Didn't mean any harm."

Carolyn, the third person dressed in black, rushed the man. All of her anger, frustration, and rage propelled the swift uppercut to his jaw. His head snapped back and he slumped to the floor.

"That was me having some fun," she snarled.

Stunned, the John fought to regain his feet, only to topple over when Casey landed a right cross squarely on the center of his face. Bone crunched. Blood splattered from his nose. His hands went to his face as he landed hard on his knees and shrieked in agony.

The girl screamed, "What are you doing?"

"Saving you," said Carolyn.

"Do I look like I need saving?" The girl stood naked with her hands on her hips. Her face was as red as her hair. "Hey, they take care of me. Know what I mean? I hadn't ever seen a doctor until I came here. And I see him every week. He's real nice. Talks to me like I'm a person. Takes my blood to check to make sure I don't get sick. And there's a pool, and we can go to the beach every day. And our meals are really good. And I don't have to cook, or clean, or do anything like that. Do you see my clothes? We can buy anything we want from these really fancy catalogues. And my home. It's gorgeous. Where I come from, only the rich have satin sheets and an indoor whirlpool and get massages. Do you hear what I'm saying?"

TJ and Carolyn stood in shock, dumbfounded by her attitude. Stark, staring naked, this girl was defending her situation, bragging about it with no attempt on her part to cover her nakedness.

Insolent bitch, thought TJ. Unsure what to do, but sensing trouble, TJ swiftly moved behind the girl. He looked at Casey, grabbed the girl's arms, pulling them tightly behind her back as he brought her down on the bed and simply said, "Rag her."

Casey opened another baggie carrying a chloroform-soaked rag and held it over her mouth. Within seconds, she was out.

"Now that was a surprise. Let's hope we find a few girls who are actually grateful we've shown up tonight. Casey, secure them both and catch up to us."

TJ, Carolyn, and Tina strode to the next cottage and repeated the entrance routine. This time they surprised the customer and girl in the hot tub. The John jumped out of the water and charged at TJ. TJ's fist caught the guy's chin. He stumbled backwards, slipping on the wet floor and landing hard on the travertine tiles encircling the tub. Adrenalin-fueled anger had him on his feet as TJ reached him. A knee to the guy's groin ended the altercation. The guy was down, holding his balls. He wasn't going anywhere fast.

"Let me help you out of there, honey." Carolyn's mothering tone drew the girl's doe-brown eyes away from the men. As Carolyn held a pink terry bath towel out, she slowly rose from the water. Carolyn wrapped the towel around her and held her in her arms. Unlike the girl in the first cottage, this one was passive, timid, and young, couldn't have been more than fifteen. She simply did as she was told.

"How did you get through the minefield?" she whimpered.

"What minefield?" asked a surprised TJ.

He and Casey exchanged glances. Had they been lucky and missed setting off a planted mine, or was it a huge lie concocted to keep the girls from attempting to escape?

"In the woods. On both sides, they planted mines so we wouldn't even think of trying to run away. And on the beach, past the property markers, there are mines in the sand, and the patrol boat keeps throwing chum into the water so the sharks will come feed here."

Carolyn flashed a knowing look at TJ. "Don't you worry

about any of that anymore. You're safe now. We're going to take you someplace safe and get you help."

"Thank you. Can I call my mother?" Sad eyes sought answers in Carolyn's face.

"Yes. Once we get away from here, it will be the first thing we help you do. I'm sure she'll be thrilled." Carolyn held back her own fears that one mother's peace of mind might not be restored tonight.

The journey continued. The small group went from cottage to cottage, surprising the customers and reassuring the girls. They caught most of the Johns with their literal pants down. Hard to profess your innocence with your pants around your ankles or hanging on the back of a chair. Before any of them could fully react to the interruption, a rag soaked in chloroform was shoved over their mouth and nose, rendering them physically helpless. Each John was then hog-tied and left for the local Leos to charge. Or not.

"Do you think these girls get a decorating allowance? Look at this pussy pen," said Kyle. Luminous globes rotated slowly, casting iridescent splashes of light throughout the room. Colors danced off the walls.

"This is one high-class brothel. Not that it really matters. What is happening here is wrong on too damn many levels."

"We've not found anyone resembling the photo of Amelia yet," said Casey to Steve as they approached the last cottage.

"Not good," said Steve.

"There is only one cottage after this one. That one over there only had one heat signature," said TJ. "And the maid Carolyn befriended identified that girl as her neighbor's daughter, so we know it isn't Amelia. She was so distraught seeing the girl here, she agreed to help us. That's how we got more information about the security routine."

"What do you think she'll do if we don't find her?" whispered Tina.

"Let's cross that bridge when we come to it. Maybe we'll get lucky." Nodding in Carolyn's direction, Casey added, "Maybe she'll get lucky."

Carolyn knew what they were whispering about. Butterflies slammed around like elephants in her stomach. What would this first meeting after five long years be like? What would she say? What would Amelia say to her? Their last fight had been vicious. Would she race into her mother's arms? Would she cast Carolyn aside in silence?

When they opened the last cottage's door, all they heard was loud snoring resounding through the room. Silently the team entered. Candles burned throughout the love nest. A sweet mélange of lavender, jasmine, rose and vanilla invaded TJ's senses. Shaking his head, TJ focused on the couple in the bed. He signaled for Kyle to move to the left side. Slowly, the two of them approached the unsuspecting John.

There was no movement from the bed. They were asleep, the man on his stomach with his face buried in the pillows. Beads of sweat on his back glistened in the candlelight. The girl lay on her side, her arms outstretched, her faced covered with shining strands of brown curly hair—her skin the color of ebony.

Competing emotions flashed, crowded Carolyn's heart and mind as all hope left her. This was the end of the road. Tears burned her eyes and throat, and she fled the room.

Kyle heard TJ say go and he followed her out. "I'm so sorry," he said as she crumpled into his arms. Her muffled sobs cut like a knife to his core while he held her tightly.

"I was so sure. Everything pointed here."

"I know. And you did all you could, more than many would, or could, have done."

"What am I going to do now?"

TJ came up beside them while she was asking this last question. "We're going to continue looking. Go back through everything. See where we might have missed something."

"Why would you do that? Bella's safe. Between here and the club, I'm sure you've got the guys who hurt her. And I'm sure Daniel and the Feds have collected more than enough evidence to close down both locations."

"But you don't have Amelia. The mission isn't over until it's over for all of us. That's the way we roll."

"Thanks, but I don't have any more leads. I don't know where else to look."

Dom's voice came through their earwigs. "Car just turned in. Heading down the driveway. Big town car. Looks important. You may want to make yourselves invisible."

"That's interesting," said Kyle. "You thinking what I'm thinking?"

"Not sure," said TJ. "All teams, let's make our latest guest feel welcome. Carolyn and Tina, stay back until we clear the area."

Stealthily, everyone moved into position on either side of the long driveway, waiting for the car to stop. It pulled up alongside a cottage that had been empty before the mission started.

"Hold your positions," whispered TJ. "Wait until the John steps out."

"Copy that."

The driver got out and opened the back door. A tuxedoed man got out and offered his hand to assist a fellow passenger. A long leg with a silver high-heeled sandal appeared first. A woman dressed in a long red gown glistening with sequins slowly stepped out of the limo.

"Amelia," gasped Carolyn. Fighting the urge to run to

her, Carolyn grabbed Tina's arm. "It's her. It's Amelia."

"Go." TJ's signal reached all ears and six men in black converged on the car, surprising the driver and his passengers.

"What's all this about?" demanded the man. "Is this a car-jacking? A robbery? You can't be serious. Do you know who I am?"

"Don't know and don't care," said TJ. He thought he recognized the car as one he and Daniel had photographed the other evening. He walked around to the back of the car to verify his suspicion. "Interesting license plate, Mr. Deputy Mayor." Turning to Casey he said, "Rag him."

Carolyn ran out of the shadows. She raced to her daughter stopping in front of her, arms outstretched. She swallowed a sob and took a deep breath, blurting out, "Amelia, honey. It's Mom."

CHAPTER 23

Everyone got back to the toolshed safely. Karli and her staff were giving eight of the girls brief physical examinations and collecting rape evidence at the compound's clinic. Cars were waiting to escort the girls to one of the area hotels where they could shower, change into clean clothes and get some much-needed rest under the watchful eyes of the FBI. There would be plenty of time later for questions.

The lone girl found in the very last cottage TJ's team entered was on her way to the hospital. They found her lying in her own feces, heavily drugged and severely dehydrated. Tina's corpsman training kicked in. She pulled an IV from her bag and got it started before the paramedics arrived. TJ called Daniel, who, along with Mac and Jim, hightailed it over to the Inn. Mac volunteered to ride in the ambulance, his badge clearly hanging around his neck to help them avoid any inconvenient questions the ER staff might ask. The answer was clear—FBI business.

The roundup at the club netted eight guys in custody. The Inn yielded eight Johns, a redhead with attitude, and the best prize of all, the Deputy Mayor. All were on their way to the police station. Flash drives, hard drives, and boxes and boxes of files found at the club were being loaded into an unmarked black van soon to be on its way to D.C.

As Marco watched the guys grab coffee and breakfast, one piece of the puzzle stood out like a sore thumb. The convoluted web of shell companies, ghost companies, layered one upon the next to hide whoever owned the Inn and Metamorphosis, still didn't make sense.

"What's up boss?" asked TJ, approaching with a smile, beer in hand. "You don't look happy."

"Everything's fine. You all did a great job tonight."

"Had a great team. None better. No better group of men and women to go into battle with, to have my back."

"I agree. It's over now. Bella's safe. She and Claire are getting the help they both need. Carolyn has her daughter back. All because of you. Get some food. You earned it."

Daniel walked up as TJ walked away.

"What's gnawing at you?"

Marco looked at him. "Not sure you guys are really finished yet. Something doesn't fit. Someone has gone to a lot of trouble to hide his identity. Kind of tickles me, really. Reminds me of old times."

"Professional envy?" asked Daniel.

Marco gave Daniel a knowing smile. "Usually you use shell corporations to avoid taxes. But Brett's talents uncovered evidence that taxes had been paid for both the Inn and the club."

"Mac and I were curious about that too. We were talking about it the other night, but decided to let it go until after tonight. One problem at a time."

"Good plan. The club and the Inn, both very public enterprises, out there for all to see. The nightclub catering to young, up-and-coming professionals. And even though the No Vacancy sign was always lit, the Inn wasn't hiding down some dark alley. It's right on A1A."

"Arrogance?"

"Could be. Don't know."

"And not knowing clearly has you hooked," smiled Daniel.

"It's the why. A dangerous question, if ever there was one. Like waving a red cape at a bull. You're asking for trouble when you ask why. Why go to all that trouble to hide ownership of a brothel that for all intents and purposes is so out in the open? You said so yourself, Daniel. The local Leos knew what was going on down that long, tree-lined driveway."

"They even joked that it was the driveway to paradise."

"So why hire common street punks like Javier, Rick and Pete to work at the club, and not trained professionals who know how to keep their mouths shut? Heard Javier paid the ultimate price for his wagging tongue."

"He sure did. Will probably never find the guys who killed him and cut his tongue out. By the way, we picked up Pete, the little prize your guys grabbed the other night."

"Good. Why dangle it all so openly and brazenly? People who want to stay below the radar aren't this brazen."

"Or this stupid. And with all due respect, my friend, you should know, having dabbled a bit under the radar."

Marco smiled. No response required. He understood the con, the path not taken, the way not totally revealed. "There's something more here than meets the eye." Like an itch he couldn't reach to scratch, Marco needed answers. And he understood the direction: follow the money.

Daniel shrugged. "At this point, I can't answer your question. And it's a really good question. Let me look into it."

"You do that. And get some rest."

Marco made his way over to Carolyn. She beamed.

Finding Amelia bathed her formerly brooding countenance with a clear light and a sparkle in her eyes.

"Got a second?"

"Of course." Carolyn followed Marco away from the crowd. "Amelia was sound asleep when I left her hotel room. There are FBI agents guarding the floor where all the girls are, so I thought I'd come by for an hour to thank everyone. Things went well tonight. Thank you so much for all you've done."

"Yes, they did. And a lot of that is because of you. Your fine research skills. Befriending that maid was a stroke of genius. Made all the difference tonight."

"My thing. Love it. Like putting a thousand-piece puzzle together."

"Glad you enjoy it. Got a job for you if you're interested."

"What sort of job?" asked Carolyn. "I'm going to be pretty busy getting to know my daughter again after five years, and seeing to it she has everything she needs right now."

"I'm working on that as we speak. But this is something else. Research. Something that might be right up your alley and keep your head in the game while Amelia is getting well."

"Then I'd like to hear about it."

"Good. Let's keep this conversation between us. Come for lunch tomorrow. I'll have a car pick you up."

CHAPTER 24

Wednesday

Dawn found the guys unwinding around a huge bonfire on the beach, ten warriors strong. Tina begged off to stay near the girls resting at the hotel.

TJ nudged Kyle, handed him another beer, and motioned for him to follow. "So, looks like you have something you want to say. What's up?"

"That shit-eating grin on your face doesn't work for you. What's with you and Carolyn?"

"Not sure."

"Spoken like a true schmuck. Something's going on there."

"Yeah. Can't stop thinking about her. She's in my head."

"Sure that's the only place?"

"Isn't that enough?"

"Heard you went for a late night sail with her. Looks like you've been bitten by the love bug."

"Shut the fuck up."

"No way, Mr. I'll-never-fall-in-love-again sworn bachelor. This is too good."

"What can I say? She makes me crazy. And I like it. Don't want her to stop. Don't want it to end. Now that Amelia is safe, I know they're going to leave soon. And I don't know what I'm going to do about it."

"You have nothing to prove here. My only advice? Don't be stupid. Alone is no way to go through life."

"That actually makes sense to me now."

"Here comes Marco. We better get back. Looks like he's getting ready to say a few words."

"Be right there," said Kyle as he stood staring out into the early morning sky, feeling the heat of the bonfire warming his back. He needed a moment.

He hadn't felt this way about a woman in years—decades. Back then, he'd been a kid trying to prove himself. And she broke his heart. He'd sworn never again. That oath starved every relationship that followed. One night stands, no problem. Of course, his no-relationships rule didn't include celibacy. But the intricacies and entanglements, give and take, of a full-fledged relationship meant making commitments he resisted.

What changed? He'd changed.

Now he was a combat-hardened vet with nothing to prove to anyone, especially himself. And Carolyn was not a needy, clingy teenager looking to get married and pregnant, not necessarily in that order. Sexy, smart and strong—three words that described her perfectly—a beautiful blond woman he couldn't get enough of. What was that about?

Sadness swept over him. Amelia was safe, and they would be leaving soon for Bangor. His life was here. Long distance romances rarely worked out well. The thought of not seeing her smile, the way her lips moved when she spoke, the twinkle in her eyes when she laughed depressed the hell out of him. He'd only known her a week, and yet not being able to be with her again was totally unacceptable.

Sparks from the bonfire exploded against the sky. Kyle followed them upward, watching them fizzle out. He walked back to the bonfire when he heard Marco clear his throat.

"It's been an interesting few days. All's well that ends well, and thanks to every one of you, this little excursion into truth, justice, and the American way has ended splendidly. Now go home and get some sleep."

"Hooyah."

The early morning tug on her leg told her Kyle had arrived. Pushing herself up from the bed, she melted into his arms.

Warm skin, soft, silky-smooth skin brushed his lips. Together, their heads found the pillows.

"You smell like fire."

"Bonfire on the beach. A guy thing."

"Is it time for breakfast?"

"It's early. Let me catch about an hour of sleep first."

Happy tears welled up in Carolyn's eyes while she lay snuggled in Kyle's arms. Outside a beautiful sunrise painted the sky in brilliant pink, gold and orange hues. Inside, the promise of a new life burst forth in her heart.

"Are you okay?" He brushed away a tear when it slipped down her cheek.

"Yes. Very okay. I've been so consumed with searching for Amelia for so long. And now it's over. She's safe and sound asleep right next door. I don't know how to feel...what to think."

"Think that if it wasn't for you, your research skills, your sharp eyes, seeing something that no one else saw, she'd still be in that hellhole. Along with nine other girls, all of whom except for one real bitch are now thanking their lucky stars that one of them, Amelia, has a mother who is part pit bull."

"These last few years have been a nightmare. And now that nightmare is over. Even has a happy ending of sorts, though I know Amelia is going to need a lot of care."

"And it is all because of you. You put the pieces together—found the Desiree connection."

"Now I get to pick up the pieces of my life, such as it is. I don't know what I'm going to do. A big chunk of what's been driving me is done...over. And now my life has to return to normal. Whatever that means."

"What about us? Where does that leave us?"

"You think there's an us?"

"After what we've been doing, there certainly is a possibility of an us."

"I've been alone a long time. With all the horror of what I've been dealing with, it's been easier to feel nothing."

"Easier maybe, but lonely. Very lonely. I should know. I'm the expert. Sworn bachelor. Funny, never bothered me until now."

"You and me...these last few days have been the one bright spot in an otherwise long, dark time."

Kyle saw the sorrow in Carolyn's eyes.

"We can make this whatever we want it to be."

"That's the question. What do we want it to be?"

"I say we take our slow, sweet time figuring that out." Kyle rose up on his elbow. "How does that sound to you?"

"On the surface it sounds great. I'm feeling something with you that I haven't felt in a very long time. But my primary focus is Amelia. I want to—need to—take care of Amelia. I want to get her the best care I can afford."

"Where will you go?"

"Not sure. It's up to Amelia. Wherever she can get the help she needs, that's where we're going."

"Maybe I can help with that."

"You printing money in your basement?"

"No. I know people who know people."

"It's been my experience that most people talk a good game, but when push comes to shove, they rarely show up with the money."

"Stay here with me. Let me prove your experience wrong. My people come through. They always have for me. And I suspect they will for you and for Amelia. There's help here for her. Marco's got something up his sleeve."

"Interesting. He wants to talk to me later today. Invited me over for a late afternoon lunch. Said something about using my research skills. He's even sending his car for me at one."

"TJ and I will be there too. Told us one thirty, so he probably wants to clear whatever he's thinking with you first."

"Probably should get up, check on Amelia and get showered."

Untangling herself from the sheets to get out of bed, Carolyn felt a strong grip on her arm pulling her back. His kisses took her breath away.

The limousine picked Carolyn up at precisely twelve forty-five for the short drive to Marco's home. Once through the wrought iron gates, Carolyn marveled at how opulent and lush and well cared for the landscape and gardens were. Four homes came into view, each one more beautiful than the next. Her destination had a curved driveway leading up to a Mediterranean-style brick and stucco home.

Carolyn already knew she was not the only guest Marco had invited to lunch. Since Kyle and TJ were not due for half an hour, she wondered what Marco wanted to discuss with her before their arrival. She didn't have long to wait.

Marco stood at the threshold, leaning on an oversized

wrought iron and beveled glass front door. Flashing his million dollar smile, he said, "Carolyn, welcome to Le Maschere."

"Your home has a name?"

"Yes. It's something people do down here."

"What does it mean?"

"It's the name for the dual masks of comedy and tragedy."

"How fitting."

"Come on in. Let's get you something to drink. Lunch will be served shortly."

Her choice of black capris with a floral top matched the casual style of his khaki shorts, sandals, and crimson golf shirt. Neither of their outfits fit the elegance of the entranceway. And straight ahead she feasted her eyes on the azure Atlantic Ocean.

"Wow. What a view."

"You like it? Wait, it gets better."

Leading the way through the house, he escorted her out to the screened lanai where a long walnut buffet table offered cold shrimp, stone crab claws, lobster salad, deli platters filled with fresh sliced roast beef and turkey, plus assorted breads and rolls.

"You expecting an army for lunch?"

"No, just some of the guys. TJ, Kyle, Brett and Daniel. I told them to come hungry."

"You could have invited the entire team and then some, considering the amount of food that's here." She picked up a cherry tomato.

"What can I get you to drink? Beer, wine, soft drink?"

"Chardonnay sounds good to me."

Carolyn looked from one amazing view to another as she surveyed her surroundings. She hadn't seen much of the inside of his home, but from her current position, it was obvious he hadn't spared any expense on his furnishings. Off to the right she could see the pool with a small cabana area. Beyond that lay sand and ocean.

"Here comes Daniel. Beer?"

"Sounds good."

"So, here we are," said Marco, handing her a glass of wine and Daniel his beer.

"It's been an interesting two weeks, don't you agree?"

"In many ways," said Daniel. "It will take some time to fully digest what we found at the club, but we're figuring we've got them for kidnapping, assault, and possibly murder. In a large part thanks to your solid research, Carolyn."

"Glad all that work paid off. It did for me. Amelia is back with me. Although I know she is going to need a lot of care."

"And we may be able to help her with that."

"In what way?"

"I've got another piece of property the next barrier island over, about five miles down the beach. It's an old hotel I bought several years ago as an investment. I'm turning it into a resort of sorts, more like a private sanctuary, for women like Amelia who need a safe place to recover from this kind of experience."

"Is that the type of research you want me to do? Research how to turn an old hotel into a rehab type facility?"

"Not by a long shot," laughed Marco. "There are interior designers for that. Already have them working on it 24/7. Should be done within two weeks. What I want from you—really, what Daniel and I are interested in—connects much more to the research you have already done."

"There's a piece missing, something we're not seeing," said Daniel as he took a swig of beer. "Someone bigger is at the bottom of all this, and to stop it—truly end it, at least this portion of it—we have to get the guy in charge."

"Hadn't really thought much about who was behind any of this. My focus was totally on finding Amelia."

"That's where it needed to be. And you accomplished that. We'd like to ask you to consider continuing your friendship with Desiree." Daniel picked up a slice of cheese waving it in his hand as he continued. "We think she may prove instrumental in finding out who is behind the sex trafficking ring your work exposed here."

"Really?"

"There were no files to speak of in the office at the Inn. And unfortunately, so far a cursory review of the documents we took from the club doesn't link Desiree to it or the Inn. We may eventually find something, but as you said, when trouble knocks, she has a tendency to disappear. If she's as connected as you think she is, that's her next move. To disappear. And the last thing we want. That's where you come in," said Daniel.

"What more can I do?"

"You can pay her a visit. She's home now. Came back Monday. I've had someone watching her house. You could get inside," said Daniel. "That's something we can't do."

"But you can. You're her friend," said Marco.

"Be all friendly and see if you can find her laptop. You said she didn't have one with her in Orlando. She must have one. Everyone has a laptop these days," said Daniel.

"You said her phone was full of good stuff. We suspect any laptop will be too," said Marco. "When she's not looking, we need you to clone it. Brett's got the software ready to go on a thumb drive. He'll give it to you when he gets here."

"Funny, I planned to search her house the other day, while she was still in the hospital in Orlando. Got sidetracked." A smile crossed Carolyn's face as she remembered exactly what had stolen her attention.

"Too bad. It would have been easier to do it with her out of the picture," said Daniel. "But all is not lost. Bring her a basket of bakery stuff, coffees and teas. Chat her up. Find out her plans. See what she's thinking now that she's home."

"You're not new in her life, so you showing up won't seem suspicious," said Marco. "After all, you were also at the tournament. You want to know how she's doing, if she needs anything. And you have her purse to return to her, right?"

She had played the role of meek friend for over two years, waiting patiently for the time to act. And when the time came, she acted with the help of the men here. She knew she couldn't have rescued Amelia without them. Now they were asking her to stay in the game.

"Yes! Okay! Stop tag-teaming me. Enough." She raised her hands in surrender. "You guys are good. I'll do it."

"That's the spirit," said Marco. "Knew you'd stick with us. Call her now and suggest coming over later today."

"Say you got hung up with family, and when you got back to the hospital you learned she had gone home. So you drove all the way down here to check on her. But that you'll only be here until Thursday, and you want to give her back her things and make sure she's okay before you head home."

"Sounds like a plan. Do I get to eat first?"

"Of course," said Marco. "Here comes everyone else. Just in time, guys. Let's eat."

After they all filled their plates, Daniel brought them up to speed on the latest information about the raid, the health of the women found, the Johns arrested and the documents seized.

When he was finished Carolyn asked, "You think there is a connection with what happened at the tournament, don't you?"

"Unless I misunderstood your slip of the tongue the other

day, isn't that kind of what you were planning to do?" The twinkle in Daniel's eye let her know he was teasing her.

"Planning and doing are two different things. I never actually did anything."

"But someone else did." The finality of Marco's statement brought everyone's attention back to the issue at hand.

"Why poison all those people? Doesn't make sense," said Carolyn.

"They were collateral damage, meant to obfuscate the intended target," said Daniel.

"Desiree." TJ steepled his fingers, splaying them and then pulling them tightly together. His chin came to rest on his fingertips as his mind played with the new facts he was hearing.

"Traces of oleander were found in the horseradish, something anyone who knows her knows she loves. You said so yourself—you've seen her ask for it," said Daniel. "By the way, Marco, please thank your chef, Jesse for not putting out horseradish today. Not sure I'll ever look at it the same way."

"Or use it," laughed Kyle. "Give me good, old-fashioned yellow mustard."

"What about the guy they arrested at the hotel?" asked Carolyn.

"They let him go. Alibi had him in another area of the hotel. Video surveillance shows a server putting two dishes of horseradish out. He put one on the buffet, and he brought the other one directly to Desiree." Daniel pulled some grapes off their stems.

Carolyn laughed. "I remember she even tipped him. Tipping the guy who's trying to kill you. Unreal."

"I'm guessing he didn't work at the hotel," said Kyle.

"Right. He wasn't an employee. No one at the hotel

recognized him. And whoever gave the order to our mystery poisoner knew Desiree had a heart condition, that the poison combined with the digitalis she already takes would kill her," said Daniel.

"They missed. She didn't die," said Kyle.

"She is one lucky lady. Orlando PD emailed me the police report this morning. Professional courtesy."

"I wouldn't get too comfortable, if I were her. She's on someone's shit list. We need to figure out whose before he tries again." Kyle stood and headed back to the buffet.

"Next time, he won't miss." Marco's matter-of-fact statement resonated around the table.

Carolyn's visit to Desiree was a short one. The flamboyant woman whose friendship she had courted so diligently seemed weak and frail. Her hair hung limp, gray roots clearly visible, her face plain and ghostly pale without makeup.

"I am so glad you stopped by. My stars, I must look a sight. I don't seem to have any energy."

"You look fine, Desiree. Here's your purse. Your jewelry and phone are in there. I didn't want to leave it at the hospital or in your hotel room. Didn't worry too much about your clothes and things like that. But you don't know about people these days."

"That's so true. I was wondering where my purse and phone got to." She rifled through her purse, appearing to search for something.

"There you are," she exclaimed as she pulled out her dragon necklace and clutched it to her heart. "My beautiful dragon. I was so worried when I didn't see it. It was a gift from a very special man."

"Then I'm glad I could keep it safe for you. When I went back to the hospital, the doctors said they had released you on Monday. So I came right down here to check on you."

"Thank you. And thank you for this basket of goodies. It has been a rather trying affair. Arnold, my driver, came to fetch me by car. The doctor didn't want me to fly. It is so good to be home."

"I'm sure it is. You have a lovely home, Desiree. With this ocean view, I'm sure you'll be back to your usual self in no time." Carolyn spotted a laptop on the hassock beside the sofa. Now to get Desiree out of the room for a few minutes.

"Might I get a glass of water?"

"Oh, look at me and my poor manners. Of course, honey. Harriet, my maid, left earlier today. I sent her home since I wasn't expecting any company. Let me fix us both some iced tea, and then we can break into this beautiful basket and eat one or two of these yummy-looking cinnamon buns."

"If it's not too much trouble, that sounds great."

"No trouble at all. You sit and enjoy my lovely view. They say the ocean does wonders to calm the soul."

"I've heard that before," said Carolyn, smiling at the thought of Kyle. "I'm sure it will help you recover more quickly."

"I certainly do hope so. A friend is taking me out on his boat on Saturday evening. He claims a sunset cruse is just the ticket. Says the sea breeze and a glorious sunset will do wonders for me. We can't go sooner because the nasty ol' weather is not cooperating."

"I heard on the news this morning that there were small craft warnings out for the next few days. Remnants of a hurricane moving up the coast farther out in the Atlantic."

"Well, hopefully it will stay out there. The last thing I need right now is some nasty hurricane barreling through here. What did they name this one?"

"Charles, I think. Named after my ex-husband, I bet."

Desiree laughed and headed off to the kitchen. Carolyn quickly connected the flash drive to the laptop and uploaded the program the way Brett showed her. It took barely a minute and she was done.

"Here we are, dear," said Desiree as she returned carrying a loaded tray. "Iced tea and cinnamon yummies."

"Here. Let me help you with that. Looks great." Considering the lunch she had eaten at Marco's, the last thing she wanted to do was eat. Picking at the cinnamon bun, she asked, "What did the doctors say about what happened to you?"

"Well, believe it or not, someone put poison in the horseradish. Isn't that the strangest thing?"

"Really?" Carolyn thought of the silver ring she had let slip into the Atlantic the night Kyle took her sailing. Its secret compartment, washed out in the sink at her hotel, had held its own stash of poison she planned to use on Desiree. Closing her eyes, she said a silent, grateful prayer that she had been spared the need to use it. Someone else had intervened.

"The doctor told me it was oleander pollen...pretty flowers, but very deadly. And because of my heart condition, it affected me and a few other women more than some of the other guests at the tournament. Who would do such a thing? I can't imagine anyone doing something like that on purpose." Even as she spoke the words, a cautious, knowing undertone crept into her voice.

"How awful," said Carolyn.

"Yes. Let's not think about it anymore. I'm fine. The doctors gave me a clean bill of health, told me to take it easy for a few days. Which is why my friend, Andre, suggested an evening cruise. He's an artist, you know. He did that beautiful watercolor of the green, fire-breathing dragon over there. Actually he has a thing for dragons, even designed my pendant." She gazed at the pendant sitting on the coffee table. "Anyway, he said nothing is as calming to the soul as watching the sun set from the deck of his boat."

Carolyn chuckled while Desiree kept talking and talking, barely stopping to take a breath.

"I went sailing for the first time a few days ago, and I totally agree with him."

"Want to come along? You'd love Andre."

"Sounds wonderful, but I already have my own sailing plans for Saturday night. A fellow I met recently is taking me out on his boat."

"Well, isn't that interesting. You'll have to call me Sunday and tell me all about it."

"Maybe our boats will pass in the night. I'll wave to you."

CHAPTER 25

Thursday

Morning's light streamed into Amelia's room. She'd been awake for a while, sitting on the balcony, coffee in hand, lost in the ocean's roar, wondering what was to come. A soft knock at her door drew her attention inside. She left the balcony and went to the door. Looking through the peep hole, seeing who was on the other side, brought a smile to her face. Slowly, she opened it.

Carolyn stood calmly at the threshold waiting to be invited in. She took nothing for granted. The memory of Amelia's cruel words the day she left hovered in her consciousness. They had been too long apart to make any assumptions about being welcome. Could they find a way to reconnect after all that had happened?

"Mom." Amelia rushed to her, wrapping her arms around Carolyn's neck. Carolyn's arms automatically returned her daughter's hug.

"I came to see how you're doing," said Carolyn, her voice faltering a moment as she thought of the lost years. "I've been sick with worry, fearing the worst."

"I'm all right. Just seeing you. You came. You found me. How did you ever find me?"

"I'm a researcher, remember?"

"Oh Mom, I'm so sorry. I really screwed up. I was so scared at first. Then…Then I gave in. I couldn't fight them off. The drugs, the beatings, treating me like trash…I tried to get away, but they found me. I thought it would never end, but I hoped, hoped beyond reason you would find me. After all those horrible things I said to you, I still prayed you'd come. How can you ever forgive me?"

"You were forgiven long ago. That's what mothers do. We forgive and forget. I thought maybe we could go get some breakfast and talk a bit."

"That sounds good. I have an appointment at ten with a Dr. Keegan. Karli, the doctor who has been taking care of me, recommended him. Said he's easy to talk to, and very easy on the eyes," laughed Amelia. "Not that I'm ever going to look at another man ever again."

"Let's hope that's not true. I've gotten to know Karli a little, and I respect her judgment. If she recommends Dr. Keegan, then I know he is a good doctor."

"Come with me?"

"Sure, honey. Anything you want."

"I want…" Amelia looked back to the ocean, seeming to gather strength from its power. Turning back to her mom, she said, "What I want is for us to start over. I was wrong about so many things. Blamed you for Dad's leaving. I've learned quite a bit these last few years. I know now…know he wasn't the man I made him out to be. That you were protecting me. I'm very sorry."

"I know. Men have a way of getting us to let our guard down. We see what we want to see, believe the fairy tales, want Prince Charming, when what we've really got standing before us is his evil twin."

"Are they all like that?"

"No." A smile warmed Carolyn's face. "I've met someone recently who might actually turn out to be a keeper."

"You deserve it, Mom. You deserve to be happy after all Dad put you through."

"Thank you. If you're up for it, you can meet him tonight at Marco's party. He's having everyone over who had a role in saving all you girls."

"He was one of the guys the other night?"

"Yes."

"I'd like that—to meet him—to thank him and the rest of them. I don't know how I can ever repay them for what they did for me."

"Going out there and living the rest of your life fully is all they want from you."

"With Dr. Keegan's help, I plan to do that. Have already been stupid enough for a thousand lifetimes. Plan to live smart from here on out."

Marco's home rocked with joy. Several of the girls they rescued from the brothel were there to meet their saviors and thank them personally. Claire found Bella waiting for her on the patio, dangling her feet in the pool.

"Thank you for agreeing to talk to me today." Claire felt her stomach clenching. She knew she was on borrowed time and needed to get through to Bella quickly.

"Thanks for calling first. I was planning to come today anyway, so sparing you a few minutes is easy."

"Marco has outdone himself."

"He's good that way."

"The party atmosphere, the food, everyone smiling. It's a

nice change from the way these girls have been living. I can't imagine what they've gone through."

"And yet you were willing to put me through it."

"I know." Claire's heart thumped, throat tightened with fear, but she forced herself to keep her eyes glued to Bella's face. "I've been doing a lot of thinking about what you said the other day; about how me saying I'm sorry and really showing it are two different things."

"And?"

"And...you're right. It isn't enough to say I'm sorry. I have to make amends. Dr. Oliver and I talked about what that might look like."

"What'd you figure out?"

"For starters that I want more than cleaning toilets in my future."

"My dad's always told me that I can be anything I want to be...do anything I want to do. I don't know what I'd do without my dad."

"You're lucky. I don't recommend it."

"I know." Bella kicked at the water in the pool.

"I know I always rode you hard about living here at the compound. I called it a prison. But the truth is, I envy you. Look at all you have. Parents who love you and support your goals. And give you enough structure so you can actually accomplish them."

"I know you've had a rough time. But you're pretty and smart. And I believe where and how you grew up doesn't set your boundaries unless you let it."

"You keep sounding like Dr. Oliver. He has been sort of saying the same thing to me. He helped me tap into the dreams I had, things I wanted to do but gave up on because I didn't believe I could do them...or didn't think I deserved them. He keeps saying my mom's history doesn't have to be my history unless I let it. I can't believe I was already following in her footsteps. It happened so fast. When I looked in the mirror all I saw was a big capital L for loser tattooed to my forehead. What I wanted for me didn't matter. Why even try? I wasn't going to get it."

"Why not?

"Not enough."

"Huh?"

"Me. In my mind I wasn't enough. Not pretty enough, not smart enough, popular enough, good enough. Dr. Oliver calls it the enough theory of life and I bought into it hook, line and sinker. So I started doing drugs. They made me feel good. And hanging with the crowd I was into covered the rest."

"There are other ways to feel good."

"I'm learning that. He helped me make a plan. Want to hear it?"

"Sure." Bella stood up and picked up a towel to dry off her feet. She slipped them back into her sandals and motioned to Claire to join her at one of the outside tables.

"First, I'm going to summer school to finish up and take my exams so I can graduate. Then I'm going to community college for nursing. I've also approached Marco about a part-time job at the Lazarus Center."

"What about the baby?"

"When I first heard I was pregnant...those first few hours...all I could think about was how to get rid of it. I wanted it out of me. But the more Dr. Oliver and I talked, the more I realized that my baby is innocent and has a right to life. So I decided to give it up for adoption. I know there are many loving couples out there who can't have children and helping one of them have a family is a small way to make amends."

"That's good, Claire, really good."

"Who knows? My kid could be the person who figures out how to cure cancer."

"Sounds like you've made a lot of progress."

"And if I ever get the chance to have a family of my own I'm going to do everything in my power to make sure I know who I'm marrying first." Claire dropped her eyes away from Bella's face for the first time since they started talking. Taking a deep breath she looked up at Bella again and asked, "What about us? How do I make amends to you?"

"I'm not sure there is a specific thing you can do. You've made some good decisions already. Maybe following through on them is a start."

The girls sat in silence for a few minutes. Claire slid her hand slowly across the table and touched Bella's arm. Bella looked up.

"How are you doing, Bella?"

"Working through it. Dr. Oliver and I talk every few days. And he's encouraged me to get back into my regular routine whether I feel like it or not. He says my morning run is critical."

Bella paused. Claire could see she was considering something.

"Want to join me tomorrow?"

"I'm not much of an athlete."

"Sure you are. We can start slow. And we can do it together. See how we can build a new relationship…together."

Rachel refilled her club soda with lime and walked out to the patio for a breath of sweet ocean air. Looking behind her, she marveled at the soaring two story, all glass back wall of Marco's home. Understated elegance.

The impromptu Thursday afternoon party was in

celebration of the success of the mission. Soon everyone would scatter back to their own lives. Before that happened, Marco had arranged for the saviors to meet the women whose lives they had risked everything for. Jesse, his chef, had laid out a feast fit for kings, queens, and princesses. And that's who showed up.

The kings—Daniel, Marco, TJ and his full team—who risked themselves unencumbered by laws and rights and legal shit that often prevents law enforcement from getting the job done. The queens—the women—Carolyn, Tina, Karli, who had joined the fight, determined to seek an end to this kind of abuse of women, to all sex trafficking. The princesses—Bella, Claire, and all the girls forced into a horrific life when they were too young to even realize what was happening, now freed from bondage.

"Looks like he's got a full house," said Daniel as he joined her.

"Yes. Consider it your first big win for the Project Buyer's Beware task force."

"Yes, Jim and Mac are very pleased. As are the big guys in D.C." He held up his wine glass to clink with her drink. "Have you met Bella, TJ's daughter?"

"Yes. She's really lovely. And smart. Wants to be a lawyer. Has her sights set on the Supreme Court, no less. How tenuous her dream. It teetered on the brink of disaster because of a thoughtless decision, made in haste."

"Kind of takes your breath away, knowing the thin thread that separates success from failure, life from death. Have you made a decision about Marco's proposal?"

"Now that I've met Bella and her cousin and all the other girls you saved, I think I'm going to help him. I'll tell him before we leave. Did you know her cousin Claire is pregnant?"

"No." The tone of his voice matched her own sadness for

Claire's predicament. "She's way too young to be pregnant. Babies having babies."

"She's decided to give the baby up for adoption."

"That's a good outcome for all concerned."

"She's had an awakening, a change of heart. Decided her life could be more, that she does have choices, like a ray of sunshine breaking through a cloud-filled sky."

"Nice way to put it."

"Mind if I steal your lady away for a walk on the beach?" Marissa asked Daniel as she joined them on the patio. Not waiting for an answer, she hooked her arm through Rachel's. "I'll bring her back soon. I promise."

Rachel did not protest. Without any effort on her part, the reason behind her impromptu trip to Florida was now walking by her side. How to bring up the cameo was front and center in Rachel's mind while they ambled down to the beach in silence. Music from Marco's party seemed to follow them.

"I'll bet I'm the last person you expected to find here."

"I was surprised to see you when I walked in," said Rachel.

"This is where I live. That's my home." Pointing to the Nantucket-style home next to Marco's, she said, "Sophia's home is beyond mine. Then Dom and Karli have the last home along this strip of beach."

"How is Sophia doing?"

"She's fine. Slept a lot when we first got home from the tournament. Doctor said she'll be fine."

"And you're friends with Mark Rogers." Rachel used his alias on purpose, wanting to elicit a reaction. "No, that's not right. What's his name now? Marco?"

"Yes. We've been together for ages. He's very special to me, like Daniel is to you."

Rachel stopped walking. She had things to say to this woman, things to ask her, but at this moment, the ball was in Marissa's court. "I'm sorry. I don't understand what we're doing out here."

"What do you mean?"

"Why you suggested this walk, dragged me away from the party. I'm here with Daniel who was a part of this operation, celebrating its success. What do you want?"

"Marco wants you to see him as he really is, and I'd like to help you understand why."

"He wants me to see him as what—a thief, a con man? He lied to me about who he was. He bugged my home and had me followed."

"I thought you two talked and he explained all that."

"Explaining it does not make it go away. He did all those things and probably more he still doesn't want me to know about."

"His head was in a different place then. He's a complicated man with a lonely past. I'm not making excuses for him. I only want you to understand where he was coming from—where we all were coming from—and then things changed."

"What changed?"

"He ran into you. Said you were the first person with a truly caring heart he'd ever run across during a con. Most of the marks were greedy, selfish bastards who deserved to be conned. But you...you were different."

Rachel's gypsy blood instincts went on high alert. She had questions to ask Marissa, but sensed what she wanted to know was about to be revealed without any effort on her part.

"Then why am I out here with you? You and me. Why this walk? What do you want? I get the sense there's more to it."

"Because I need to apologize too."

"For what? We just met at the mah jongg tournament." She watched Marissa look away. "What? What don't I know?"

Marissa held out her hand revealing a small gold pouch.

"I believe this is yours. And I want to return it to you and say how very sorry I am for everything."

"No!" Rachel stared at the pouch in Marissa's hand. She looked up at Marissa, searching her face, connecting to her eyes. She knew what was inside the pouch and felt no need to take it.

"Please. It's yours. You couldn't take your eyes off of it at the tournament. I knew you knew it was your aunt's cameo, and I've been determined to find a way to give it back to you. And then today presented itself."

"Dare I ask…do I want to know how you got it?"

"Long story short, you gave it to me, and now I am giving it back to you."

"I gave it to…Millie Raconti." Said in barely a breath, the name stuck in Rachel's throat. "I don't understand. You're—. You can't be. How? Why are you doing this? I don't understand."

"Because you did what I couldn't do. You helped us turn a corner, to see that we can be more than we were being, that it's not too late. You helped all of us let go of lives that no longer fit who we were as people."

"How did I do that?"

"You were so giving and genuine. That Fund you started was amazing. You could have kept all the diamonds for yourself, but you didn't. And because of you, Marco is becoming the man I always knew he could be. And I love him. He wants your help with his sanctuary project. It's important to him. And I love him too much to allow anything to stand in the way of you working with him.

Eventually our paths would cross and you'd wonder about me, about the cameo. Now everything is out in the open. And you can help Marco. Who knows? Maybe down the road we can become friends."

CHAPTER 26

Saturday

Rachel was very, very glad to be home. The Florida trip had challenged her relationship with Daniel in ways she was not ready to handle. When they flew in late last night, they each kept their own counsel. The takeout pizza dinner had been a strained affair, neither of them saying much about anything.

She left early this morning, before Daniel woke up, wanting time to herself. Stopping by the Starbucks for coffee and a muffin, she took her breakfast and went for a drive along Colonial Parkway. Now, standing at the shores of the James River she wiped away a tear. This was the lot she and Daniel were going to buy, but the sign on the marker said sold. Someone else bought it. Someone else would be building a home here.

She heard the soft rustle of the brush behind her.

"I thought I might find you here," said Daniel as he came to stand beside her.

"You following me?"

"Yes. I don't like how we've been these last few days. And I think we need to talk it out."

"Not sure that's such a good idea right now."

"I want to take care of you…make you happy."

"You can't on both counts."

"Of course I can."

"No. You can't. Only I can make me happy and take care of myself. You can be with me, share my experiences, color them with your smile and your charm. We can plan a life together, do things together. But you really can't make me happy. Only I can do that."

"How do we move forward? I'm an old dog. It's hard for me to let go of what I've been doing and learn new tricks. But I can."

"You have to understand, this is new to me, too. With you…with these feelings I never knew existed. I keep wondering if I am better off with you or without you. It plays like a never-ending loop. Sometimes my answer goes one way—with you. Every once in a while it goes the other way—and without you wins."

"I don't like the sound of that."

"I went crazy in Florida when I saw you with Marco. I didn't like who I was being at all."

"That was a bad time all the way around."

She threw her arms up, let them flop down and then ran her fingers through her hair. "David and I didn't…we… Our marriage was predictable, safe. When he died, I…oh, my God, this sounds terrible." She touched her lips and turned to him, sad eyes reached out to touch his heart. "When he died I felt free. Free for the first time in my life. And I loved that feeling. That I could come and go as I pleased, without having to ask permission. Don't get me wrong, David and I were good together. I loved him, and I know he loved me. But there was no magic. No spark."

Reaching out, Rachel touched Daniel's chest, covering his heart.

"You unlocked part of me that I thought only existed in fairy tales or movies. When you hold me, when you kiss me, I feel...oh, everything. I've waited my whole life to feel like this. And I don't want to lose it, but I also don't want to lose the me I'm becoming. Someone who can take care of herself, knows what she wants, doesn't do things to please everyone else, isn't afraid of every shadow. Am I making any sense?"

"Yes," he said. "Total sense." Daniel drew her to him, wrapped his arms around her ever so gently. With the lightest touch he raised her chin to look into her eyes.

"We both want the same things. If we keep that as our goal, reminding each other regularly in loving ways, we'll be fine."

"That sounds good, but—"

"I want you to be strong and in charge of your own life. I want to share your life with you. Be the sprinkles on top of your ice cream cone. And I'll admit it, I want to keep you safe. It's my job, because I love you. But I don't want to smother you. When you do that arched eyebrow thing you do, I know I've gone too far—that you're okay, and I try to back off. But, you have to know that I'm not going far. Just a side-step."

"That sounds good to me." Snuggling into his arms, Rachel murmured something under her breath.

"What did you say?"

"I love you." Rachel looked into his eyes, her own filled with love.

"And I love you. No ifs, ands, or buts about it. No hesitation. No qualms. The heart wants what the heart wants, and my heart wants you. You are the best thing to happen to me in a very, very long time. I'm crazy about you. I want to share my days and my nights with you. Corny? Trite? Maybe. But true, all true. I don't want to wait. Not to sound morbid, but none of us know when the grim reaper will call our name."

"Whoa. Not too morbid."

"Sorry, but it's true, and we both know it better than most. We both lost people we loved in an instant."

"You're right. I know you're right."

"So why wait? For what?"

Rachel pulled out of his arms, but leaned her head against his chest, quietly staring out across the James, the early morning sunlight glistening off the water's gentle flow. That was the ultimate question. Why wait to be happy and enjoy the love and companionship of this wonderful man? Why wait? For what?

"I want to enjoy every remaining moment with you, sharing my life with you. It's simple, really. My big regret right now is we didn't act sooner. This lot—our lot—it's sold."

"Say it ain't so."

"Didn't you see the big red SOLD plastered across the For Sale sign back there? Our plans to build a home here are kaput."

Daniel reached into his pocket and pulled out a folded piece of paper. "Yes. I did see it. And it is sold to me—to us, actually." Handing her the paper, he added, "No strings attached."

Daniel watched her unfold the paper and begin to read it. As she read, a smile spread across her face. It started at the corners of her mouth headed upward, lips parting to reveal gleaming white, straight teeth. Her eyes brightened, and the small lines at the outer corners sharpened as her eyes danced. Then her dimples appeared, two snuggly little places in her cheeks that added to her radiant glow.

"How did you do this?"

"Doesn't matter. It's ours, yours and mine. Both of our

current legal names are on the deed. I'm asking you—right here, right now—to marry me, but I don't want you to feel like there are strings attached."

"Yes, I'll marry you. Being your wife—there is nothing I want more. Having you in my life makes me happy. And I'm all about happy."

EPILOGUE

Saturday

He was not a man to be trifled with. He eschewed the trappings of power, preferring to live quietly, privately, outside any limelight. Googling his name produced no hits, no phone number, no addresses, no organizational affiliation. He was the ultimate ghost. And it suited him just fine.

He led a cabal of puppeteers who, through their more visible proxies, manipulated the strings of the world's economies for their own benefit—for his ultimate benefit. It was so easy to operate behind the scenes. Feed the masses drivel on the nightly news which they believed without question. Trap people into dependence. It was never going to change. It was his power.

The phone's insistent vibration in his pocket forced him to excuse himself from his dinner guests. Ten pairs of eyes watched him stand, holding his phone in his hand.

"Please excuse me. I have to take this call. Go on with your dinner. I won't be but a moment."

Leaving the dining room, he strode across the marbled

entryway of his penthouse suite and entered his library office. Standing at the floor to ceiling window, looking out over the bright lights of Palm Beach and into the darkness of the ocean beyond, he finally answered the call.

"Yes."

"Did you get the package?" The question was asked by a low baritone voice.

Looking at the plain brown paper-wrapped package sitting on his desk, he said, "It came today."

"Ready?"

Interesting question, he thought. The woman's transgression—flaunting herself, seeking attention—while not a full-fledged betrayal, still carried a price. He could wait, give her time to explain, to plead her case, promise to be more discreet, before he struck.

Or he could strike first, employ the element of surprise—a lesson others would surely understand and heed. There was no escaping his reach. Others had tried, only to face their untimely death squirreled away in some rathole, mouthing useless prayers that his wrath's tentacles could not reach so far. They lost.

Better to be safe now. She was replaceable.

"To quote Shakespeare, 'Ambition's debit must be paid.' Yes, I'm ready. Don't mess up like you did in Orlando."

"I won't. It will be perfect. The number is 291-555-0147. When she answers, press star. Hang up. Consider it done." The line went dead.

He walked to his desk, opened the package, pulled out the burn phone, and returned to stare out his windows. Slowly, he entered the phone number he was given. Three rings before a soft southern drawl answered.

"Hello."

And the night sky lit up as a fireball exploded on the

horizon. The only way to truly fire an employee, he mused. Dawn DeSoto was no more.

"Gotcha!"

He walked back to his dinner guests as flames danced on the water behind him.

BOOK DISCUSSION QUESTIONS

1. The most obvious question is the first. How far would you go to save your teenage child if he/she found himself/herself in a dangerous situation? Are you a sit around and wait for the authorities or a take action person? What circumstances might change your answer?

2. Where do you draw your revenge lines? When someone harms you, what are the situational differences that help you format your reactions and responses?

3. Addiction, in its many forms, has destroyed many lives. How has addiction touched your life? How might you suggest working with young people to foster stronger self-worth images so that fewer turn to drugs (or other addictions) as a way to solve their problems?

4. Sex trafficking is a huge problem around the world, often taking place in the shadows. What do you think are effective ways to combat this horrific crime?

5. Apologies and making amends are two different actions. What do you see as the difference between saying "I'm sorry" and really making amends to people you have hurt?

6. What aspects of Gotcha! hit home for you? Which story lines engaged you fully? Which story lines had the

strongest impact and/or the weakest impact? Which characters did you like / identify with the most?

7. If you and I could sit down for coffee, what questions would you ask me about Gotcha!?

Thank You...

I am so appreciative to everyone who has journeyed with me during the writing of *Gotcha!*

Thank you Carolyn Koppe. Your muse gifts challenge my plot twists and turns. Our walks and talks helped me flesh out my characters and plot lines. I truly appreciate your time and energy and your belief in the story that I wanted to tell. My editor, Faith Freewoman, at Demon for Details, totally rocks! What a pleasure and honor it has been to work with you on this story. Your generosity of spirit gently guided my writing efforts, helped me smooth out plot lines and add depth to my characters.

Thanks to all the people that helped me with the technical details: Jerry Limber, Dr. Adam Levine, Steve Foster, Bernie and Judi Newman, Mike Connolly, Chris Schwenker. My heartfelt thanks goes to my beta readers Lucy Oakleaf, and Mish Kara. Your insights and suggestions were so helpful. Thank you Dar Dixon for a fantastic cover. You are a talented graphic designer and a joy to partner with. Thank you to Amy Atwell and your team at Author EMS. Your formatting skills are priceless.

John, your love and support is what every woman wants from her husband and what I consider myself so lucky to have. You are a blessing in my life.

The story continues....

COMPLICITY

[k*uh*m-plis-i-tee]

Noun: the state of being an accomplice; partnership or involvement in wrongdoing. *Synonyms*: collusion, intrigue, implication, connivance. *Word Origin and History for complicity* – 1650s, from French *complicité*, from Old French *complice* "accomplice, comrade, companion' (14c.), from Late Latin *complicem*, accusative of *complex* "partner, confederate," from Latin *complicare* "to fold together" (see complicate; also cf. accomplice). Source: http://www.dictionary.com

See what happens to your favorite *Bamboozled* and *Gotcha!* characters as their adventures force them deeper into a world where nothing is what it seems to be and no one is safe.

Watch for COMPLICITY Fall 2016

MEET JANE...

It has been a whirlwind year, filled with exciting opportunities supporting my decision to become a mystery / romance novelist. Talk about change!

Developing interesting characters and placing them in situations where they are challenged by real world events adds the realism good stories need to become great stories. My stories continue to explore how adults navigate their life journeys which are always affected by the choices they make. Through story I want to offer my readers a new way to think about change, empowering them to make choices aligned with their innate talents and gifts, thus generating rich and rewarding lives.

Come visit me at www.janeflagello.com.